Betting
ON
GRACE

NE LTD

BECAUSE NAUGHTY CAN BE OH SO NICE.

By Nicole Edwards

The Alluring Indulgence Series
Kaleb
Zane
Travis
Holidays with the Walker Brothers
Ethan
Braydon
Sawyer
Brendon

The Austin Arrows Series
Rush
Kaufman

The Bad Boys of Sports Series
Bad Reputation
Bad Business

The Caine Cousins Series
Hard to Hold
Hard to Handle

The Club Destiny Series
Conviction
Temptation
Addicted
Seduction
Infatuation
Captivated
Devotion
Perception
Entrusted
Adored
Distraction

The Coyote Ridge Series
Curtis
Jared

The Dead Heat Ranch Series
Boots Optional
Betting on Grace
Overnight Love

By Nicole Edwards (cont.)

The Devil's Bend Series

Chasing Dreams
Vanishing Dreams

The Devil's Playground Series

Without Regret
Without Restraint

The Office Intrigue Series

Office Intrigue
Intrigued Out of the Office
Their Rebellious Submissive

The Pier 70 Series

Reckless
Fearless
Speechless
Harmless

The Sniper 1 Security Series

Wait for Morning
Never Say Never
Tomorrow's Too Late

The Southern Boy Mafia Series

Beautifully Brutal
Beautifully Loyal

Standalone Novels

A Million Tiny Pieces
Inked on Paper

Writing as Timberlyn Scott

Unhinged
Unraveling
Chaos

Naughty Holiday Editions

2015
2016

DEAD HEAT RANCH

Book One

NICOLE EDWARDS

Nicole Edwards Limited
PO Box 806
Hutto, Texas 78634
www.NicoleEdwardsLimited.com

BETTING ON GRACE – A Devil's Bend novel is a work of fiction. Names, characters, businesses, places, events and incidents either are the products of the author's imagination or used in a fictitious manner. Any resemblance to actual persons, living or dead, business establishments, events, or locales is entirely coincidental.

Cover Image: © Poulsons Photography | Fotolia

Cover Design: © Nicole Edwards Limited
Editing: Blue Otter Editing | www.BlueOtterEditing.com

ISBN (ebook): 978-1-939786-27-2
ISBN (print): 978-1-939786-28-9

Romance
Mature Audiences

NOTE FROM AUTHOR:

Boots Optional, book #0.5, is a prequel to this book. If you haven't read the novella, either in the anthology, *Some Like It Hot*, or in the *Boots Optional Novella* sold separately, I suggest that you do. The novella depicts how the three of them got together. Enjoy!

DEDICATION

To my brothers:

I'm not sure you'll ever truly understand what it means to me when you tell me that you're proud of my accomplishments. To know that you support me means everything. I love you both!

CHAPTER ONE

"GRACIE," GRANT GROWLED, UNABLE TO restrain the animalistic sound that began in his chest and quickly rumbled up past his throat. "Baby..."

He was attempting to warn her, to let her know that he wasn't going to last if she kept doing that ... *oh, fuck* ... that wicked, wonderful thing she was doing with her tongue. But heaven help him, her mouth felt so damned good wrapped around his dick, silky-smooth heat engulfing him, sending spikes of pleasure darting straight to his balls.

Holy... His sexy cowgirl was going to send him directly past the finish line with no other participants, namely Lane and Gracie, in sight if she didn't slow... *hell!*

"Ahh, damn." Lane's voice echoed in the small room, the welcome thunder of the man's guttural tone jarring Grant from his solo trip to completion.

Clamping his hand down on Lane's thick thigh, Grant struggled to ground himself, to focus on the warmth of Lane's skin against his palm, the flex of Lane's muscles beneath his fingertips as he, too, fought the inevitable. For Grant, it was the equivalent of counting backward from a million, just to keep from prematurely succumbing to the release that was so *damn* close...

"*Dayum*," Grant whimpered.

He and Lane were stretched out on Gracie's bed on their backs, where they'd been for the last few minutes, sprawled side by side, while Gracie was straddling their legs. Lane's thigh was pressed against Grant's, Lane's coarse leg hair rough and sensual against Grant's skin while the contrasting smoothness of Gracie's soft thighs pinned them in place. She'd been perched atop them as though they might be planning to get up and walk out of the room or something.

Like Grant was planning to go anywhere. Especially when she did *that*...

"Fuck," Grant cried out, his fingertips digging into Lane's leg. "Gracie... Oh, damn, darlin', slow down."

Oh, mother of all things holy!

Grant nearly came up off the bed when Lane decided to offer up his own brand of sensual torture: his big, firm hand gripping the base of Grant's cock. *Son of a...* Grant had to bite his lip to keep from exploding right in Gracie's lush mouth.

They were tag teaming him, something they'd done on more than one glorious occasion in recent months — and no, he wasn't complaining, but hell, he wasn't sure he was going to survive this. Not after the four-day dry spell he'd just been forced to endure thanks to their ridiculously stressful work schedule.

It'd been seven weeks to the day since the very first time they'd fallen into bed together, although "falling into bed" was hardly a fitting description for the life-changing events that had occurred during that first night they were together. Between then and now, they'd managed to sneak in a quickie at least three times a week — not *nearly* enough for Grant — but this was the first late-night encounter since that first mind-boggling weekend.

Although Grant was seriously tempted to let go, to give in to the carnality of the exquisite torment and allow Gracie's sweet mouth to suck him dry, he wasn't ready for this to end. Not yet.

With as much self-control as he could rally, Grant gripped Lane's wrist, holding the man's hand still. Of course, Lane being Lane, he simply squeezed, making all of the blood pool in the head of Grant's dick.

Daaayyuum! That was definitely not helping matters much.

At the same time, Grant slipped the fingers of his other hand into Gracie's long, silky blond hair, effectively subduing her, although she still had her mouth wrapped around the engorged head of his throbbing cock, flicking relentlessly.

"You two are gonna be the death of me," Grant said, his voice sounding as though he'd just gargled sand.

Gracie's answering smile was potent enough to light up the surface of the sun. She released him from the heaven of her mouth long enough to say, "That's the idea."

"Not yet, it's not," he informed her, shifting just enough to keep her from driving him stark raving mad once again.

Since he had their attention, Grant took the opportunity to turn the tables. Or more accurately, to turn *Gracie*. He moved, persuading her with a twist of his body to slide off his leg, and just as he'd anticipated, Lane wrapped his muscular arms around her, pulling Gracie back on top of him, her back to Lane's front.

"Oh, yeah," Grant crooned as he stared down at his two lovers. "Exactly where I want you."

"Which one of us?" Gracie goaded.

"Both of you," he replied, offering her a suggestive grin. Turnabout was fair play, after all. "Now don't move."

With Gracie now parallel to Lane, Grant eased himself between their spread legs while he slid his hands up the inside of Gracie's toned calves, past her knees, then over the supple skin of her inner thighs, stopping just short of her smooth, bare mound; all the while, Lane remained stone-still beneath her.

Yeah, Lane knew what was coming.

Him, if Grant had anything to say about it.

Using his forefinger and his thumb, Grant separated the swollen outer lips of Gracie's pussy, revealing the soft pink flesh beneath. Not wanting to give them an opportunity to take the reins from him, Grant leaned forward and skimmed his tongue through Gracie's slick folds, eliciting a soft, purring moan from her. Peering up the length of her slender body as he teased her sweet pussy, grazing her clit briefly, Grant noticed Lane was massaging her breasts. Grant was riveted, admiring the significant contrast of Lane's enormous, sun-bronzed hands against the full milky-white globes.

Gracie purred again as Lane kneaded her breasts gently while teasing her nipples by tweaking the dusky pink tips between his fingers. Her soft moans were louder than before, the lyrical hum of her satisfaction spurring him on. Grant focused his attention on lapping Gracie's pussy, rhythmically thrusting his tongue into her, pushing her closer and closer to the edge. If he had a choice, he'd feast on her for hours — no, make that days — just so he could hear her gratifying moans.

Not wanting to leave Lane out, Grant cupped Lane's heavy sac, using a similar motion on him that the other man was using on Gracie's breasts, squeezing each testicle gently yet firmly.

"Oh, yes," Lane groaned, fumbling with Gracie's breasts momentarily.

Grant pretty much lived for Lane's reactions, the way he writhed and lurched, trying to get closer to Grant's exploring fingers.

Lane clearly wasn't content with their current positions because the next thing Grant knew, Gracie's pussy was pulled away from his eager mouth as Lane drew her up his body, offering Grant better access to Lane's long, thick erection, seemingly reaching out for Grant's attention.

A quick adjustment and Grant was back in position, alternating between wrapping his lips around the head of Lane's dick, sucking slowly, and using his tongue to swipe the precum beading on the swollen head, purposely working Lane into a frenzy before sliding up to Gracie's pussy, offering her the same delicate attention.

"Grant," Gracie squealed. "I... Oh, God, that feels good. But I need more."

"What do you need, gorgeous?" Lane asked, the big man's voice raspy and rough, reflecting his own desire.

"I need one of you to fuck me."

"I think we can help you with that," Lane hissed, his hips thrusting forward when Grant sucked him into his mouth, sliding his lips down until Lane's pubic hair tickled his nose. "Oh, hell. Grant... Damn. Take all of me. Holy..."

Grant knew Lane was close; he could feel the gentle pulse of Lane's dick inside his mouth, the salty essence of Lane's precum coating his tongue. They were all hovering on the brink, something that was self-induced thanks to their absurdly demanding summer schedule. Even those fleeting interludes they'd had in recent weeks weren't enough to sate the lust that the three of them incited in one another. It was just enough to take the edge off, but even then, it was only short-lived.

"Grant, sonuvabitch, oh, God, yes," Lane cried out, his resonant Texas twang reverberating off the walls. "Don't... Not yet... Fuck."

Because he wanted to be deep inside Lane when the man detonated, Grant offered him a reprieve, letting Lane's cock slip from his mouth. As Grant sat up, he was hit square in the chest with a foil packet. Okay, no, make that *two* foil packets. When he looked in the direction that they had come from, he noticed Gracie grinning as she reclined on Lane's massive chest.

"Do the honors, cowboy," she said, her hands sliding up her flat belly, over her rib cage to join Lane's hands as they continued to squeeze her breasts.

Grant's cock throbbed, all but begging him to get on with it, but as he watched Lane and Gracie, he decided he had to do one thing first. Scooting forward, he leaned over them both, planting his arms on both sides of Lane's broad shoulders as he stared down at them. With his chest brushing against Gracie's beautiful tits, his erection gliding through her slick heat, Grant pressed his lips to hers. When she sucked his tongue into her mouth, his cock wept with anticipation.

Lane's head came forward, his hand sliding toward the back of Grant's scalp until his fingers were locked tightly in Grant's hair, pulling gently yet insistently. When Gracie released his tongue from between her lips, Grant leaned slightly to the left, his mouth meeting Lane's.

Lord, these two could probably make Grant come just from their kisses alone. And the difference between the two — the soft, soothing stroke of Gracie's tongue versus the demanding plunge of Lane's — was enough to make his head spin.

In-*fucking*-credible was what it was.

As usual, the way Lane's hand palmed Grant's head possessively had Grant surrendering to Lane's merciless tongue. But the kiss didn't last long because Gracie clearly had other plans... Her cool, nimble fingers wrapped around Grant's cock and stroked. He jerked back from Lane, fearful that Gracie was going to send him into hyperspace all by his lonesome.

"Condom," Gracie commanded, a sexy smile forming on her kiss-swollen lips when Grant seized her wrists and held her hands still.

You didn't have to tell him twice.

Well, technically in this case, he guessed she did.

Forcing himself to his knees, Grant sat on his heels, ripping open the packets with his teeth before easing one condom over his own oversensitive cock, then teasing Lane by doing the same, making sure to stoke the fire in Lane by jacking Lane's dick for an extra second or two first.

"Fuck. Me," Lane huffed. "You've got about two-point-five seconds to get that thing on me or it's gonna be pointless."

Grant grinned, finishing what he'd started and rolling the condom down Lane's long, wide cock.

"Lube?" Grant asked, leaning down and placing a kiss on Gracie's mound. Unable to resist the lure of her glistening sex, he slid his tongue through her slit again, stroking her clitoris until she was thrashing beneath him.

A firm hand gripped his hair, and he knew by the feel and the strength of the touch that it belonged to Lane. "Enough!"

Grant laughed, sitting up once more and grabbing the bottle of lube that Gracie was holding in one trembling hand. Without prolonging the agony any longer, Grant slicked his cock, meeting Gracie's bright blue-green eyes as he stroked himself. "Trade places," he instructed. "Gracie, on your back."

An easy smile tipped her lips, and then she was moving, making quick work of repositioning herself. Lane complied as well, rolling over and kneeling between Gracie's spread thighs. Without warning, while Grant was still coating his dick to ensure he could ease into Lane's ass without hurting him, Gracie pulled Lane to her, effectively impaling herself on him from the bottom.

Oh, hell. That was one beautiful sight.

Grant continued to kneel between Lane's strong thighs, his brain forgetting about the need for lubrication because he was now intently focused on the way Lane's substantial cock disappeared inside of Gracie.

"Oh, damn, baby," Lane moaned, his body tensing. "Aww, Gracie, baby, that feels so good. Hold up."

Lane's hand was gripping Gracie's leg while he held himself above her with the other, his fingertips white, and Grant knew that Lane was trying to pull himself back from the edge. A moment later, Lane's grip loosened, and he followed up with, "All good now."

Grant smiled even though neither of them could see him. Evidently, Gracie wasn't willing to wait. Her legs tightened around Lane's waist, and she pulled him to her, her hips beginning to rock in a slow, seductive rhythm from beneath Lane.

"Spread your legs," Grant ordered Lane, his growing anticipation sending fire along his nerve endings, making it damn near impossible to hold off any longer.

Lane managed to move without slowing his pace, continuing to thrust into Gracie as their mouths fused together, Gracie's arms banding around Lane's neck.

Not wanting to be left behind, Grant gripped his dick with one hand, Lane's hip with the other, and pushed his way inside Lane. Only when he had breached the tight ring of muscle did Lane stop moving altogether.

"Oh, fuck yes, Grant. Oh, yes, deeper. I want you balls-deep inside me."

Grant loved when Lane spoke during sex. He wasn't just motivated by the words that Lane said but how he *said* them. There was so much passion and longing in the man's tone, Grant felt it deep in his soul. Then again, everything about Lane had captivated Grant. There was something about Lane, something that had pulled Grant in and held him there. He wanted to say it was love that he felt for both of them, but he'd yet to accept that fully. There were countless reasons he was hesitant to acknowledge that this could possibly turn into something more than just casual sex.

Right. Like *anything* about this was casual.

But now was not the time to think about that.

Lane's tight ass gripped him, pulling him deeper, making him sweat. There was no way he was going to last long.

"Fuck me, Grant," Lane commanded. "Fuck me. Oh, damn, that's good. Grant, I... I need you..."

Grant aimed to please, so when Gracie began to move, rocking her hips forward, Grant withdrew before sliding back inside the scalding-hot recesses of Lane's body.

"You feel so good," Grant growled, gripping Lane's hips, the lean muscle flexing beneath his palms. "I'm not gonna last."

Lane grunted, but he didn't say a word, his body straining as Grant drove into him, lodging him deeper inside of Gracie.

When Lane shifted his legs wider, allowing Grant better access, Grant took advantage of the new position, driving his hips forward as he began to pound into Lane over and over while Lane used the momentum of Grant's thrusts to slam into Gracie's pussy.

Feeling the indicative tingle that signaled his inability to stem his release any longer, Grant knew it was time to fast track this or he was going to go solo.

Planting one hand on Lane's strong back, Grant slowed, tipping forward and sliding his other hand between Gracie and Lane, seeking her clit. When he found the little bundle of nerves, he used his thumb to massage it until she was crying out their names, begging them both to make her come. Lane, as usual, wasn't just a bystander, proving it when he shoved Grant's hand away and took over, leaving Grant with the ability to send them all careening into the abyss as he began to pound Lane's tight ass over and over.

When Gracie cried out her release, Lane followed not long after; then, and only then, did Grant let go, his cock pulsing deep inside of Lane's ass. He fought the urge to fall forward, not wanting to crush Gracie beneath them.

He remained just like that for several moments, his chest heaving, his head still spinning from the intensity of his climax.

"Time for a shower?" Gracie asked, her tone heavy with exhaustion.

"Not sure I can move," Lane answered.

"Not sure I *want* to move," Gracie admitted, making Grant smile again.

Yeah, he knew the feeling. If he had his way, he was pretty sure he'd spend the rest of his life just like this.

CHAPTER TWO

August, one month later
Monday morning

"WHERE'RE YOU HEADED?" LANE MILLER hollered from the south end of Dead Heat Ranch's main barn.

Lane had walked into the enormous steel building just in time to see, through a hazy dust-mote stream lit by the rays from the early-morning sun, Grant Kingsley high-tailing it across the marred concrete floor. Grant was moving like his ass was on fire, which was, quite frankly, a sight to see.

With the sound of Lane's heavy footsteps resounding off the metal walls, a few goats bleating their morning greeting, and the scent of manure and hay flooding his nostrils, Lane picked up his pace, attempting to keep up with Grant before he hit the wide-open double doors on the opposite end.

Lane was halfway across the barn when he noticed that, in his haste to ensnare the hunky cowboy trying to evade him, he had captured the attention of Budweiser, one of the three Labrador retrievers that lived on the ranch. The charming black dog ran toward him, tongue lolling, tail wagging, but Lane didn't pause to pet him as he normally would, fearful that Grant would disappear if he veered off course.

"Asking a question here!" Lane yelled, trying to get Grant to stop. "Where're you off to?" he repeated.

"Runnin' into town."

For a fraction of a second, Lane wondered if Grant meant *literally* because of the fast pace he was maintaining. Doubtful, but the mental image was quite amusing. And picturing Grant huffing it into town sure beat thinking about the way Grant had answered. Grant had drawled the response as though he didn't have a care in the world; however, he didn't bother to spare Lane a glance, which was Lane's first hint that something was up.

Hell, for as much attention as Grant was giving him, Lane could've been anyone, certainly not someone who was actually supposed to be important to Grant.

Drop it, Miller. Not gonna get you anywhere today. Chin up.

Doing his best to heed his own advice, Lane set off in a half jog, half run, in order to catch Grant before he got too far away. Budweiser, of course, thought it was a game and trotted alongside him, barking happily.

"Hey," Lane called to Grant again, trying to get him to slow his roll. It didn't seem to be working, so he glanced down at the animal scurrying along beside him. "Mornin', Budweiser," he muttered to the dog, earning another enthusiastic woof from the animal.

Well, at least someone was paying attention to Lane.

"What?" Grant exclaimed a little unexpectedly, and Lane hauled his gaze back up, where he saw that, yes, Grant had actually stopped walking.

Finally.

When Grant spun around to face him, Lane came to a jerky stop, surprised by the irritated expression on Grant's too-handsome face.

"You okay?" Lane asked, concerned, standing less than a foot away from the man who, in recent weeks, had sent Lane's entire world on its ear.

In a good way.

"Yeah. Fine. What do you need?"

Okay, so someone was lying, and since Lane wasn't the one spouting off that he was fine when he clearly wasn't, the award went to Grant.

"What's your problem?" Lane mouthed off, getting a little defensive.

It wasn't that he was surprised that Grant was in a foul mood; after all, this was Grant. He wasn't *always* chipper, but that hadn't been the case so much lately. In fact, Grant had been the picture of sunshine for the last few months, and Lane wanted to think that he played at least a small part in that. Rightfully so, Lane hadn't expected to be met with such animosity that early in the morning.

"I've got things to do, Lane, what the hell do you want?"

Lane glanced just past Grant's head, making sure they were alone, not wanting to risk someone stumbling upon them when he...

"Oomph."

Lane pushed Grant's lean body up against the inside wall of the barn, successfully slipping into the shadows before he crushed his mouth down on Grant's in a kiss that threatened to spark the dry hay stored there into an inferno. Again, Budweiser thought it was time to play, pawing at Lane's ass as Lane took control of the kiss, cupping Grant's stubble-covered jaw as he leaned into him.

Despite the attitude, Grant pretty much turned to putty in his arms, and Lane didn't let up, sliding his tongue into the hot cavern of Grant's mouth. He trailed his hands down Grant's neck, over the hard planes of Grant's chest, across his rippled abs, then lower until he was gripping Grant's narrow hips. Lane held him in place, rocking his erection against Grant's through the confining denim of their jeans, trying to get as close as physically possible because... Well, just fucking because.

Grant Kingsley was like rocket fuel, combustible and capable of intense heat. Even now, when it was clear Grant was inspired by something more than lust, if his sour mood was anything to go by, the man pretty much went up in flames right there in Lane's arms. Even with Grant's grumpy attitude, Lane found that he craved the man like a drug.

Grant's fingers knotted in the front of Lane's T-shirt as the other man pulled him closer, sending Lane's head whirling. Hot damn, it had been too long since they'd done this. *This* being sharing a kiss that made bright, colorful lights dance behind Lane's closed eyelids.

Another few heated moments passed while Lane tried to get his fix, plunging his tongue into Grant's mouth, tasting the coffee his lover must've had a short while ago, and desperately wishing they had just a little more privacy than the shadowed interior of the main barn.

No such luck, which was why Lane reluctantly drew back.

"Good mornin'," Lane said to Grant with a grin, still holding Grant's hip with one hand while absently patting Budweiser's big head as the insistent animal pushed his snout up against Lane's leg, begging for attention.

Grant rolled his eyes, but Lane was pretty sure that was a smile that curled the very corners of Grant's delicious mouth.

"What're you goin' into town for?" Lane asked curiously, forcing himself to take another step back, releasing Grant from his clutches despite his desire to slam his mouth on Grant's one more time for good measure.

"My dad called," Grant disclosed, a flicker of heat mixed with what Lane could only assume was aggravation — based on Grant's tone — glimmering in his ocean-blue eyes.

"Your dad's not *in* town, Grant," Lane offered helpfully, not telling Grant anything he didn't already know.

Lane wasn't up to speed on everything about Grant's parents, but he was aware that they lived nearly an hour *outside* of town, which meant that Grant's "in town" reference was supposed to deter Lane.

"No shit, Sherlock," Grant bit back.

"So what does he want?" Lane asked, pretending not to be bothered by Grant's snippy fucking attitude.

As with Grant's parents' whereabouts, Lane didn't know much about Grant's rapport with his folks, either, but from what Lane had gathered over the years, their relationship was strained at best.

"I need to stop by and talk to him."

Now Lane's Spidey senses were beginning to go off, and Grant wasn't helping with his elusive retort. "Need" was a pretty strong word, especially when Grant used it.

Grant wasn't much for running off to deal with personal business, nor was he usually quick to share the details of his life, but Lane figured it was safe to assume they had crossed a particular line in recent months. The one they no longer saw in their peripheral vision because they'd taken a few steps forward and zero steps back. And Lane wanted to believe that once they passed that line and it disappeared from view, it was only fair that they were expected to open up a little more than normal.

Someone probably needed to remind Grant of that because apparently he was regressing.

"What's up, man? Talk to me."

Grant met his gaze, and this time Lane saw defiance there. *Fucking hell.*

Scratch that. Grant wasn't *regressing*, he was running backward at lightning speed.

"Don't make me kiss it outta you," Lane threatened, doing his best to keep the happy-go-lucky tone he was known for.

"As much as I'd like that," Grant said hesitantly, his eyes darting across their immediate surroundings, passing over Budweiser, who was still watching them intently, before meeting Lane's once more, "I really do need to go."

"Fine." It was clear that Grant wasn't going to delve into the specifics about what was bothering him. At least not out there in the dusty barn.

Bearing in mind how much physical distance they had inserted between the three of them — him, Grant, *and* Gracie — in recent weeks, due to circumstances out of their control, Lane knew not to push his luck.

No, he would corner Grant later and kiss it out of him — just as he'd threatened — if he had to.

But for now, he opted to change the subject. "How 'bout dinner?"

Grant's eyes softened somewhat, but that was as far as Lane was going to let him go because he knew what was coming. Regressing had quickly turned to retreating, and now Grant was backsliding at a rapid pace. Lane had feared it was coming for the last couple of weeks.

Clamping his hand over Grant's mouth before the man could give him some sorry excuse, Lane said, "Don't do this. Don't come up with some bullshit reason to push me away. You hear me? We've come too damn far for this." Lane stared back at Grant for a long moment. "I'm going to work, and you're gonna be on your way. Whatever you think you want right now, you'd better give it some more thought. I'm not gonna drop this, so don't even ask me to."

Grant's eyes were wide by the time Lane released his mouth. And just like he said he would, Lane turned on his heel and walked away.

Right after he pressed his lips to Grant's for a quick, potent kiss.

■□■□■□■□

GRACE LAMBERT WAS COMING OUT of the six-thousand-square-foot main house, where pretty much all business-related activities associated with Dead Heat Ranch occurred, including the Monday morning meetings she had with her father and sisters, at about the same time Lane was going in. Where her head was at, she had no idea, but before she knew it, she was on a collision course with the delectable cowboy. The same cowboy who made her heart burst into a full gallop every time she saw him. The same one who, just a few months ago, she had tried to steer clear of.

Yeah, that ship had obviously sailed.

"Well, hello, gorgeous," Lane said huskily when she found herself flush against him, one hand clutching his huge bicep, the other crushed between them — the only thing saving her iPhone from a header on the wooden deck that wrapped around the house.

Their close proximity would likely appear an accidental collision to an onlooker, but based on the way Lane slid his hands along her hips, his chest pressed firmly against her breasts, what had started out innocent took a quick and abrupt turn to the lascivious.

Mmm... Lascivious. Some seriously delicious moments that they had shared over the last few months came to mind.

Grace didn't mind the close contact, although she prayed no one was paying any attention. Because if they were...

Stumbling back a step or two just in case someone did have them in their cross hairs, Grace shifted her attention from the phone in her hand to the devastatingly handsome cowboy in front of her. "Sorry," she muttered shyly, her face warming several degrees.

"Babe, feel free to knock me off my feet anytime you want. This certainly isn't the first time."

Unable to help herself, she smiled up at him. Way up.

Grace knew she wasn't even average when it came to her height of five feet four inches, although she was taller than her four sisters, but compared to Lane's six-foot-three-inch frame, she felt impossibly small.

"Someone's in a good mood this mornin'," she offered.

"Wish I could say the same."

"What's with you people today? You'd think it was Monday or somethin'."

"It *is* Monday, Lane," Grace informed Lane with a full-fledged smile.

"Oh. Well, hell. That explains it then. Where'd the weekend go?"

"No idea. I think I worked through it."

"Yep, I know the feelin'."

It had been an incredibly busy few weeks for all of them. With the official end of summer nearing as August came to a close, things seemed to be moving at warp speed. The days were tirelessly long and seemingly endless, with all of the guests who were cramming in a last-minute summer vacation before school was back in session.

Thanks to the steady influx of tourists visiting, they'd spent the last two months performing some much-needed updates on the ranch. They had worked continuously to get everything done in a short amount of time, including getting two of the extra cabins in tip-top shape so they could be occupied, providing the on-site store with a much-needed facelift, installing some new commercial appliances in the kitchen, and replacing a handful of the wobbly old tables scattered throughout the dining area. Not to mention all of the new things going on with the actual animals that were supposed to be the primary focus of their day-to-day chores.

They had recently purchased six new horses for the ranch, specifically to use for the tourist trail rides, and they'd all been pitching in with getting them acquainted with the ranch. Dixie, their beloved yellow Labrador, had inadvertently gotten herself knocked up by Budweiser a couple of months back, and they were all required to be on puppy duty as well.

It didn't help that Hope, Grace's older sister, was off on some crazy rampage about increasing the ranch's income potential. The spur in her sister's butt had caused a hiring trend during peak season, along with a shitload of new activities put in place for the guests.

"Gotta spend money to make money," Hope had spouted when they'd questioned her recent spending spree.

As far as Grace was concerned, they were doing just fine, thank you very much. Not that she was responsible for the books or anything. But Faith, the youngest of the five of them, was. And according to Faith, they were in the black, which was all Grace really cared to hear.

Possibly not for long if Hope had her way.

"Have you talked to Grant today?" Lane asked abruptly, pulling Grace from her thoughts.

"No." Shoving her phone in her back pocket, Grace gave Lane her full attention. Just the mention of Grant had piqued her curiosity.

It'd been at least three days since she'd spent any time with him, and even then, they hadn't been able to get much more than a stolen kiss or two on the go. It had been late every night when Grace finally managed to drag her ass home, desperate for a hot shower and a good eight hours of shut-eye. She'd managed the shower but not much on the sleep, because morning had come far too quickly every damned time.

Unfortunately, spending time with Lane and Grant in the last few weeks had been sporadic at best. Not because she didn't want to. Quite the contrary, actually.

Regrettably, life had kicked back in, insinuating itself right smack in the middle of the new relationship that she'd formed with the two men not long ago. Since they were all tiptoeing around in order to ensure her father didn't catch wind of what was going on with them, they'd had to perform a few evasive maneuvers recently just to throw him off their scent. Jerry Lambert was not an easy man to avoid, either.

Damn Mercy.

One of Grace's sisters had caught on to what was going on between the three of them probably before they'd even known it themselves, and now Grace feared Mercy was going to use it against her.

Not that she would let Mercy know that she actually cared who found out. She really didn't.

Well, no one except for her father. Jerry was a bear of a man, and he had growled his demands on more than one occasion for the cowboys at Dead Heat Ranch to keep their hands off his daughters. Any man caught touching one of them would risk his wrath.

Yeah, well…

If her father knew that there were *two* cowboys touching her specifically, he'd probably have a coronary.

"He mentioned that he had to go see his dad," Lane stated.

"Really? His dad?" she asked, shocked.

"Yeah. He wouldn't go into detail, but something was off."

"They don't get along," Grace said, figuring Lane already knew as much.

"I got that part. I know he doesn't go see them often, but this seemed like a demand, not a request."

Grace didn't know what to make of that. She didn't know much about Grant's parents, just that Grant's relationship with them was tense. Come to think of it, Grace didn't know much about Lane's parents, either.

Wow. For a woman who was sexually intimate with two men at one time, she'd just realized how little she actually knew about them. Then again, that was mostly her fault because she'd spent the last couple of years avoiding them at all costs.

What the hell did that say about her?

Oh, who really cared?

"Did he say when he was coming back?"

"Nope. And when I suggested dinner, he blew me off."

Grace could tell that Lane was holding something back, but she didn't get a chance to question him about it because — speak of the devil — her sister Mercy came walking up.

"Time to get to work, kiddos. No smoochin' on company time."

"Shut up," Grace bit out, sounding like a petulant, irritable child. Feeling like one, too.

Mercy brought out the best in her, clearly.

Grace was met with a shit-eating grin from her sister.

"Sorry, no can do. I'm comin' to let you know that we've got a family meetin' goin' on in just a few minutes."

"What? Another one?" Grace hadn't heard about another meeting. Hell, she'd just wasted the better part of an hour listening to Faith give them a stern talking-to about spending money.

"Yep, Hope's on a tangent. She wants to hire three more people. Time to talk it out."

"Where?"

"At the rec hall," Mercy said as she turned to face Lane. "And as much as we'd love to see your bright, shinin' face there, you're not invited. Not unless you've proposed to my sister and now I get to call you Bubba."

Lane smiled, which put Grace on high alert.

"Not yet, ma'am," Lane drawled. "But trust me, when it comes to that, I'll be sure to let you know."

Grace's head twisted around on her body hard enough to give herself whiplash. "Lane!" she yelled. "No more fuel for the fire, please!"

Just as he always did, Lane brushed off her warning. The guy didn't seem to have a care in the world. She had to wonder just what he'd say if her father were to confront him on some statement like that.

The sound of the screen door slamming behind Grace told her that Mercy had moved on.

Thank God.

"I've gotta run. We've got a group comin' in around noon, and I need to help out. How 'bout dinner?" Lane spoke to her directly, but he might as well have been talking to the whole damn ranch for as quiet as he was.

"We'll see," Grace said, tempted to search their surroundings, wanting to ensure some nosy-ass wrangler wasn't passing by.

"In my book, 'we'll see' is the equivalent of yes. I'll bring dinner to your place. How's that sound?"

Grace was just about to lay into him when he pulled her up against him, his mouth finding hers. "Your sister's gone, and there ain't another soul anywhere close."

Grace couldn't help it; she turned to liquid in his arms. As much as she wanted to punch him for freaking her out like that, she damn sure enjoyed when he put his mouth on hers. Or anywhere, for that matter.

"Gotta run, gorgeous," Lane said as he backed away slowly, his mocha-brown eyes peering into hers. Grace wanted to grab his arm and pull him into a dark corner somewhere for a few minutes of catching up, but she didn't.

She was restraining herself and all.

Something she found was getting more and more difficult as each day passed, especially the days when she didn't get to spend *any* time with Lane or Grant, or, which she preferred most, both of them at the same time.

"Dinner," Lane called out when he was several yards away. "Your place. I'll bring the food."

Grace nodded, praying like hell that no one was listening because...

Yeah, they were really going to have to do something about this sneaking around thing.

And soon.

CHAPTER THREE

"DAD, WHERE ARE YOU?" GRANT shouted when he walked into his parents' rundown trailer about two hours later.

If it hadn't been for the fact he'd had to chase down Jerry Lambert to let him know he needed a few personal hours, and then to make sure he had backup in the event something went awry while he was gone, Grant would've come and gone by now.

No such luck.

Oh, hell. What the fuck is that smell?

Grant's olfactory glands threatened to revolt against him, but he forced his feet to move farther into the house, closing the front door behind him.

No, wait, he was going to leave that bad boy open. *And* open the screen.

"Kitchen!" Darrell Kingsley bellowed back from somewhere in the house.

Grant raised the rickety glass on the cheap aluminum screen door, jamming it upward to keep it on the bent track, gulping in fresh air for as long as he could before turning back toward the offending smell.

His sinuses were assaulted by the stench of stale cigarette smoke, what he assumed was burnt food, and … holy fuck, was that cat urine he smelled? Whatever it was, it wasn't pleasant. Then again, the disgusting aroma of his parents' house — usually made up solely of cigarettes and cats — wasn't new to him, and, no, it wasn't something he'd ever gotten used to, either, though it had gotten significantly worse in recent years. Glancing around the small trailer that he had once called his home, Grant fought the urge to vomit.

How many fucking cats did they have now?

He caught sight of one, a fat gray-and-white tabby, as it snuck behind the worn couch, another, this one orange and black with a patch of white around one eye, that was sitting on a box near the window, and a solid black one that scampered down the hall. His mother had an obsession with cats, but unfortunately, she wasn't much for getting them spayed or neutered, so it seemed every time he came by, they'd multiplied in number. Which they probably had.

Trying not to breathe through his nose, he gave the room a quick once-over, cringing as he took in the ramshackle furniture and torn carpet. It wasn't that he was ashamed of where he'd grown up —that was a part of his life he couldn't very well change. No, it was more that he was a little embarrassed about the way the place was being kept these days. Or *not* kept, as was the case here. He would be the first to admit that their house wouldn't have won any sort of modern home award when he was young, but this... This was absurd.

The living room was practically trashed, with two overflowing ashtrays on the coffee table, as well as beer cans and empty plates lying on every other available surface. The pillows that belonged on the sofa were on the floor; one of them was puking up the stuffing that had once been inside of it. *Maybe the smell had gotten to it, too.*

Because of the mess, Grant didn't notice *what* was missing in the living room right away, but he knew something was.

Oh.

Shit.

It didn't take him long to realize that the *something missing* was the one thing his dad coveted probably more than his gun collection, or even Grant's mother, whom the man had been married to for going on thirty-five years.

How they'd lasted that long, Grant had no idea, but that was a story for another day. Or perhaps a month-long session with a shrink. Either way, Grant couldn't let his thoughts stray; he was too busy trying to ... breathe.

"Dad, where's the TV?" he asked as he stepped into the kitchen, having to sidestep the crap littering the torn linoleum floor that probably hadn't seen a mop in a decade. Looked like a tornado had hit and the only casualty had been the dishes. They were everywhere.

"Pawn shop," Darrell said curtly, concentrating raptly on the laptop in front of him.

"What the hell are you talking about?" Grant asked, his attention successfully focused on the old man sitting at the battered kitchen table. The same table where Grant remembered eating lukewarm TV dinners when he was a kid.

Not only had the table seen better days but his father had, too.

Darrell's once-dark hair was sprinkled with gray, his usually clean-shaven cheeks were salt-and-pepper dark with at least three days' worth of beard growth, and he had a cigarette dangling from his thin lips. If Grant wasn't mistaken, his father had lost more weight recently. Not that it was that obvious because his gut hadn't shrunk at all, which was probably thanks to the beer he chugged like water.

"You fuckin' heard me," Darrell spat. "I needed money."

"You needed... Wait. Back up. What do you mean you needed money? Why aren't you at work?"

"Laid off."

"You were *laid off*?" Grant couldn't quite believe his ears. His father worked at an auto parts store in town and had for the last eight or nine years.

"Well, technically, they said I was fired."

Okay, so Grant never quite knew what to expect from his parents. It wasn't a secret that they barely got by, both financially and otherwise. The two of them had what they considered an extremely passionate relationship, one that had, yes, included plenty of abuse over the years — on both their parts.

But even considering all that, something was off here.

W-a-a-ay off.

"So you pawned the TV?"

"All the TVs," his father corrected.

31

Grant dared to look around, trying to see what else might be missing. It was hard to tell because the house was a fucking pigsty. Not only was it cluttered with crap, the smell was unbearable.

"Why didn't you pawn the laptop?" Grant asked, fear of the obvious becoming an oppressive, stifling stench that competed with the rancid odor of cat urine. The culmination of it all nearly had him heading for the door.

"Why the hell would I do that? Then I couldn't find a way to get *more* money."

"So you're lookin' for a job?" Grant asked, hopeful that his father hadn't relapsed, but as he watched Darrell intently staring at the screen in front of him, a long string of ash about to land on his bulging belly, Grant already knew the answer.

"Nope. But this last bet I placed is a sure thing," Darrell answered confidently, his hazel eyes darting up to Grant only briefly.

God, that was not what he wanted to fucking hear. "Where's Mom?"

"Left."

"Where'd she go?" Grant's mother didn't work, and for as long as Grant could remember, Sandy Kingsley had spent her days camped out on the sofa watching her soap operas ... shit ... which she evidently couldn't do because there was no television.

"Don't know. Don't care," was the response he received.

Grant's frustration was kicking in, and he feared that he was going to lose the cool he worked so hard to maintain around his mother and father. It was hard enough to have parents with such volatile personalities, but through the years, Grant had somehow managed. That included remaining calm when his father would break out the belt, or a fly swatter, or whatever was close at hand, for absolutely no reason other than he felt like it.

In his father's defense, Darrell always had an excuse for the punishment. Sadly, it was just usually not Grant's fault — and Grant wasn't trying to duck any responsibility, either. He had been a fairly good kid, staying out of trouble, making good grades, going to school every day. None of it seemed to matter when Darrell flew off the handle, though. Luckily, for them all, that hadn't happened in nearly fifteen years. At least the physical aspect of the abuse, anyway.

"Why'd you call me, Dad?" Grant asked seriously, lassoing the last of his patience and yanking it close. He already knew the answer, but he desperately hoped he was wrong.

"I've got a favor to ask," Darrell stated, this time actually taking the opportunity to look at Grant.

"Which is?"

"I need to borrow some money."

Grant sighed. They'd had this conversation repeatedly over the years, and it generally ended up in a heated argument. That was the last thing Grant wanted, so he opted to deflect. "Have you talked to Morgan?" Grant asked, referring to his sister.

Morgan, older than him by three years, had packed up her shit and moved out as soon as she'd turned eighteen, foregoing her high school diploma to do so, which had been about four years before Grant had been given the same freedom. He'd finished high school, but college had been a pipe dream, which was why he'd settled for heading out on his own in hopes that he could come up with a plan that would allow him to end up a little better off than his parents.

Not Morgan.

She'd up and married some loser and moved to Arkansas but had since divorced that sorry bastard. Unfortunately, Morgan had merely traded one fuckup for another, and she was married again, this time living in Kansas with two kids in tow.

"Nope. She told me never to call her again. *Again.*"

Yep. That sounded like Morgan.

Great. And now Darrell had had another falling out with her, which explained the phone call Grant had received just that morning. If Morgan was in a tizzy, Grant's parents usually turned to him. *Again*, as his father had said. It seemed that every other week, Morgan and their father were going at it for one reason or another. Grant did his best to stay out of as many of their squabbles as he possibly could.

Grant pulled his hat off his head and thrust his fingers through the mess that was his hair. He'd crawled out of bed half an hour late that morning, and instead of running through the shower and then grabbing breakfast, he'd tugged on clean clothes and run out the door. Now he was starving and in desperate need of a shower. Not to mention, he was in a shitty fucking mood because of it all.

"So, you gonna loan me money or what?"

Had he not been so pissed, Grant would've found his father's use of the word "loan" slightly amusing. The man had never paid Grant back a dime in his life, and he suspected he never would. Which was why he replied, "Sorry, I don't have any money to loan."

Not that it was far from the truth. Grant had a little in his savings account, but not nearly as much as he had hoped to have at this point in his life. Considering his lack of bills thanks to living on the ranch, he would've expected to have significantly more. So not the case.

"I didn't fucking call you over here to listen to you bullshit me, Grant. I asked to borrow some goddamned money. You know I'm good for it."

Right.

Arguing with Darrell had never gotten him anywhere, and Grant wasn't going to give in to the taunting today. As it was, he was in a crap-tastic mood, and the last thing he needed was to have a run-in with the local police.

Figuring it was best to get while the gettin' was still good, Grant pressed his hat back on his head and turned toward the door. "Sorry, Dad. Ain't got money to loan. But I'll be more than happy to check around and see who's hirin'."

"Fuckin' worthless piece of shit," Darrell mumbled beneath his breath.

Yep, Grant had heard it all before.

Had people been required to get a license to have children, Darrell and Sandy Kingsley would've been shit out of luck. Unfortunately, there wasn't a law governing who could and couldn't procreate.

"I've gotta get back to work, Dad," Grant called as he moved toward the door.

From experience, he knew exactly where this was going, and he damn sure didn't have the wherewithal to put up with any of his father's abuse today, verbal or otherwise.

When Darrell began his rant, Grant double-timed it to his truck, never bothering to look back until he was safely inside. By the time he was backing out of his parents' driveway, Darrell was on the front porch, his fist flying as he tossed whatever verbal obscenities he felt were necessary to get his point across.

Grant could've saved the old man the energy. He'd already heard every damn one of them.

But the good thing was — if anything could be considered good in this fucked up situation — the fact that seeing Darrell served as an appropriate reminder of exactly why he had no intentions of having kids. After all, what the hell did Grant know about being a father? Look who his role model was, for fuck's sake.

■□■□■□■□

"HAVE YOU SEEN GRANT?" HOPE asked Lane as he made his way to the main house.

He had bypassed a shower in lieu of getting some grub before heading over to Gracie's as he had promised her he would. In fact, the possibility of seeing Gracie, having dinner with her, was what got him through the day, the one and only thing he was truly looking forward to besides seeing Grant.

"The technical answer to that is yes, I've seen him. If you mean now, then no," Lane retorted as he continued on his trek. He had spent the last two hours with Hope snapping at him for one reason or another, and if it was all the same to her, he just wanted to get the hell away from her.

It was after six, and Lane was desperately searching for food. And Grant. But he didn't bother to tell Hope that.

"Thanks, smartass, but you know what I meant."

Yes, he did. He knew exactly what she meant, but he wasn't in a talkative mood, and being stopped for a chat by the woman who'd made his day a living hell was not high on his priority list at the moment.

"He went into town this morning," Lane offered, keeping his hat low and his eyes focused on the big ranch house that was blessedly only a few yards away. So freaking close he could smell the food that wafted through the open screen door.

"I know that. But he was back before noon."

Really?

Now why should he be surprised by that?

"Have you checked his cabin?" Lane asked, trying his best to sound as though he didn't give a rat's ass that Grant hadn't bothered to let him know he was back. Instead, Lane devised the fastest route to Gracie's house in his head while he waited for an answer from Hope, praying she didn't want to draw out this conversation any longer than necessary.

"I did. He didn't answer the door. Damn it, Lane, stop!"

Shit.

Lane drew up short and turned to face Hope. His stomach grumbled an immediate rebuttal to stopping in his tracks. Knowing he would only prolong the suffering if he didn't talk to her, Lane gave up. "What'd you need him for?" he asked, growing more and more curious as to why Hope would've been searching for Grant after hours in the first place.

Not that they had a set work schedule. At Dead Heat Ranch, time was irrelevant. When things needed to be done, they did them. Sleep be damned.

But it wasn't like Hope to seek Grant out. Lane, sure. He was the closest thing to backup that Hope had. Being she was the head wrangler, he worked closely with Hope day in and day out. However, Grant was the ranch foreman, so it did make sense. Sort of.

"I needed to talk to him about something."

As much as Lane wanted to be nosy and question her further, he knew better. He was doing his best not to raise suspicions as it was when it came to his relationship with Grant. Everyone knew the two of them were friends, and that they hung out during their off time, but even he knew it would look a little questionable for him to get all up in someone's business for searching for Grant.

"If I see him, I'll let him know you're lookin' for him."

"Thanks," Hope mumbled and then walked off.

Well, hell. That had been too easy.

Lane stood staring after her for a heartbeat. He had half a mind to go to Grant's to see if the man was hiding out, but the smell of food coming from the kitchen was calling his name.

Turning back the way he'd been headed, he forced his feet to move.

God, he was tired. They'd had one hell of a day with the new horses they'd brought in, and it had gone from bad to worse when one of the summer wranglers had wound up getting stomped on because his idiot ass had done exactly the opposite of what he'd been instructed to do. That incident had required help from Zach, the ranch's medic, followed by the EMTs from the neighboring town paying them a visit. Thankfully, the kid was going to be fine, but he was going to have one hell of a bruise in the meantime. The dumbass.

Lane yanked open the screen door leading to the dining area just in time to nearly run into Gracie for the second time that day. Only this time, she looked up before he had a chance to feel her pressed up against him. The sparkle he saw in her eyes did wonders for his exhaustion but not much for his hunger. Although, now he was hungry for something else entirely.

"Hey," Gracie greeted.

"No, I haven't seen Grant," Lane declared a little forcefully, pulling his hat off his head as was customary when entering the dining room.

"Good to know," she said with a smile. "Actually, I just saw him. He was heading to his cabin."

"Hope's lookin' for him," Lane explained.

"Well, if she's smart, she won't seek him out tonight."

"Somethin' wrong?"

"He's in a piss-poor mood," she said bluntly.

"So nothing's changed since this morning?" Lane asked facetiously, forcing a smile. "You didn't eat yet, did you?" He tried to keep his eyes on her but found himself looking over her head to the plates of food that had been set out for supper.

The dining area was set up family style, with a buffet placed on two long tables against one wall, one wrangler making sure they never ran out of food while another assisted with cleaning the tables for the guests. The ranch personnel ate for free, and the kitchen staff generally made enough to feed a small army, but they all pitched in to ensure everything was kept clean. It looked like they were on their toes tonight, which was a good thing since Lane was prepared to scarf down enough for at least four people.

"Not yet. I don't think," Gracie said softly, turning to look around them before continuing, "that tonight's gonna be a good night. I've been avoidin' Faith for the last half hour, but I really do need to see what she wants."

"What about later?" he asked, realizing he sounded exceedingly hopeful.

"I really have to check with her first. God only knows what she wants. After that, I'm hopin' to head home and take a shower."

"Hmm…," he said, suddenly thinking about Gracie in the shower. Before he could tell her that he'd grab the food and meet her there, he caught sight of Faith, Gracie's youngest sister, coming at them as if wild dogs were nipping at her ass.

"Hey, Gracie!"

Yep, his dinner plans had just been thwarted. So much for eating dinner with Gracie. Or showering with her, for that matter. He knew by the look in Faith's turquoise gaze that the woman was on a mission and Gracie was her target.

Lane tried not to be bothered by the fact that their plans had once again been derailed. It seemed to be the case no matter the time or place these days.

Gracie turned away from him, but not before he noticed her rolling her eyes. Standing beside her, Lane watched as Faith came stomping across the room.

"Oh, shit," Gracie muttered.

"Problems?" Lane whispered.

"Always. And if the look on her face is anything to go by, I'm up shit creek without a paddle."

The lure of food was so powerful Lane decided that he'd leave Gracie and her sister to hash out whatever their issues were without his help. Just because he had a longing to touch her, he stepped behind Gracie and placed his hand gently on the small of her back, squeezing ever so slightly. "I'll catch you later."

When Gracie met his gaze over her shoulder, he was tempted to lean in and kiss her. That look spoke volumes, in a way that said, *I'd really like to find you naked in my bed later*, which was incredibly difficult to resist.

But he didn't have a chance to say or do anything before Faith was marching up to Gracie. "We need to talk."

"Good to see you too, Faith," Lane said with a grin. "Have a good night." And with that, Lane snuck off, not wanting to endure Faith's wrath. Whatever had that woman's panties in a bunch, he didn't want to have anything to do with it.

Lane had just grabbed a plate, piled it high with mashed potatoes, followed by two slices of Salisbury steak, another helping of potatoes, another piece of meat… Before he was finished, he had enough to sate his appetite for at least a week, although he'd probably be hungry again by midnight.

As he was grabbing two rolls, trying to hold on to his hat's brim with his fingers, balance his plate in one hand, a glass of tea in the crook of his arm and the bread in the other, for the second time in under an hour, someone asked him if he'd seen Grant.

"Do I look like his keeper?" he snapped.

"Whoa, dude," Cody Mercer snapped. "Who pissed in your Post Toasties?"

Lane blew off the statement, knowing better than to get into a pissing match at this point. He was his own worst enemy when it came to his emotions, and the fact that Grant was back and everyone seemed to know it but him didn't sit well, nor did knowing that his plans for spending just a few hours with Gracie were nothing more than wishful thinking.

"I just wanted to let him know that Hope was lookin' for him."

"I heard," Lane groused as he moved toward an empty table on the far side of the room. Without hesitation, he slid into the chair and put a death grip on his fork, ready to eat in peace.

Cody followed.

Well, so much for peace.

"Do you know what it's about?" Cody asked, dropping into the chair opposite Lane.

"Why don't you join me?" Lane murmured beneath his breath.

"Don't mind if I do."

That drew a smile out of Lane.

Okay, so his pissy attitude really didn't have a place here. Cody Mercer was a good guy, a little too cocky and self-assured for Lane's taste, but he meant well. Too bad the kid had a thing for Mercy Lambert, the wildest of all the Lambert sisters. That woman would chew him up and spit him out before he ever knew what hit him.

Not that Lane was going to bring it up. He'd actually been waiting for a couple of years to see it happen. Metaphorically speaking. Unfortunately, Lane had been the one to waltz right into the shop in time to see Mercy straddling Cody and...

"So?"

Lane looked up to see Cody was waiting for him to say something. Thank heavens for that. He did not want to remember that day, especially while he was eating. "So … *what?*"

"Do you know what Hope wanted?" Cody repeated slowly, as though he were talking to a child.

"Nope. Don't know. Don't care." That was only a partial lie. Right then, he really *didn't* care. Only because he was too fucking hungry to put forth the effort.

"Hope didn't seem happy," Cody mentioned, his hands resting on the table as he stared at Lane.

Lane didn't have a problem with an audience while he ate — or anytime, for that matter. But right now, he was hungry, so if Cody wanted to talk, he'd have to endure Lane having a mouthful of food.

"Does she ever?" Lane countered.

"Touché." Cody laughed.

It was true. Hope Lambert walked around with something stuck up her ass most of the time. Of all five of the Lambert sisters, she was the most serious. Lane had seen the woman in action. She didn't put up with a whole lot of shit, and being the oldest, she apparently took on a lot of the responsibility for Dead Heat Ranch, which left little room for fun. At least from what he could tell.

Unlike Gracie, Mercy, and Trinity, Hope wasn't the fun-loving sort. Not anymore, anyway … from what he'd heard. Then again, neither was Faith, the youngest of the bunch. Proof in the fact that it was closing in on seven o'clock and both sisters were still working. He wasn't sure the two of them ever stopped.

As for Hope, Lane knew she had taken on the task of managing the day-to-day operations of the ranch alongside their father, Jerry. Ever since their mother had died, when the girls were young, she'd been steadfast in her efforts to prove her worth to anyone who would pay attention. Not that she needed to. As far as Jerry Lambert was concerned, his daughters hung the moon and lit the damn thing every night, to boot.

But Hope had a one-track mind when it came to business.

Which was why Lane knew he didn't want to be around when Hope did eventually find Grant. Whatever she wanted to talk to him about was likely work related, which meant the man was in a shitload of trouble.

"Have you seen him? Grant?" Lane asked, probing as to what Grant had been up to when he'd returned to the ranch. Clearly, either Lane had been too busy or Grant was avoiding him altogether because Lane hadn't even been aware that the man had returned.

"Not since after lunch. He was pissy, so I hauled ass in the opposite direction."

"Can't blame you there," Lane said, shoveling food into his mouth.

"Have you seen Mercy?"

There it was. The real reason Cody had the sudden urge to chat it up. Lane forked more food into his mouth and shook his head. He hadn't seen her since earlier in the day. That woman was trouble with a capital T, and Lane tried to stay as far from her as possible.

It didn't help that Mercy seemed very aware of what was going on between Lane, Gracie, and Grant. She was acting like fucking Cupid, what with trying to force the three of them together.

Not that there was any force necessary.

Damn it. Now he was thinking about Grant again.

Maybe he should stop by, check on him.

Bring him food.

No.

Damn it.

"Well, if you do, let her know I'm lookin' for her."

Great. Now he was a fucking secretary. Another forkful of food went into his mouth as he nodded his head at Cody. There wasn't a chance in hell that he was going to mention Cody to Mercy, but the kid didn't need to know that.

"Night," Cody finally said as he pushed to his feet.

Lane wasn't trying to be an ass; he just wasn't in a talkative mood, so he sent Cody off with a curt nod.

In fact, he had something else entirely on his mind as he polished off what was left of the Salisbury steak and mashed potatoes that had been overflowing his plate moments earlier.

Shoveling the last bite in his mouth, he decided it was high time he addressed the issue.

Chapter Four

GRANT DIDN'T WANT TO DO anything except sit in front of the television. Hell, he didn't even want to get up and get another beer. Glancing down at the one in his hand, he realized that would be something he'd really need to come to terms with in, oh, say, less than three minutes.

Looking at the three empty bottles sitting on the table beside his recliner, he wasn't sure how good of an idea that really was. Especially since he had to work in the morning. But shit, he deserved it, and up to this point, he was still trying to achieve that ever-elusive buzz that was just out of reach.

After he had escaped his father's tirade that morning, he'd had to endure endless phone calls and texts from the man throughout the day. Grant never answered the phone and finally tossed the damn thing in his truck just to avoid it, but then he'd been met with forty-two texts and seventeen voice messages. They all said about the same thing, letting him know what a worthless piece of shit he was for turning his back on his father in his time of need. Yadda, yadda, yadda.

Nothing Grant hadn't heard before on numerous occasions.

It still irritated the fuck out of him to hear it. Irritation was all he would cop to, though, which was why he'd resorted to drinking from the second he'd stepped through his front door. He damn sure wasn't going to admit that the words actually hurt him.

Downing what was left of his beer, Grant tried to focus on the television. *See that, Dad, I've still got a television!*

Oh, for crying out loud.

For the better part of the last half hour, he'd been alternating between clicking the remote and replaying in his mind all of the hateful bullshit his father had left on his voice mail. As much as he had tried, clicking through channels, searching for something to watch wasn't enough to drown out the angry voice of his father still reverberating in his head.

Considering he didn't give a shit about watching television in the first place, it was no wonder he hadn't found anything that caught his attention. His thoughts were all over the map, so focusing on the screen was hard enough.

A sudden knock on the front door jolted Grant from his thoughts, but he didn't bother to get up.

"It's open!" he hollered, willing whomever it was to go away.

Not happening, apparently.

The door pushed inward, and in walked Lane in all of his handsome glory. Even after twelve hours of work, Lane looked good enough to eat. He was covered in a fine layer of dust, his straw hat crushed on one side, one of his pant legs tucked into his boot, the other covering his other boot. He looked like he'd tussled with the livestock for the better part of the day.

Yet he still looked so damn good.

"Hidin' out, are ya?" Lane asked, a hint of exasperation in his tone as he shut the front door behind him, effectively sealing them off from the rest of the world.

Grant knew he shouldn't be quite so happy about that, bearing in mind his current mood. No one had to tell him that he was acting like a hothead and had been for most of the day.

"Tryin'," Grant answered, meeting Lane's gaze. "What do you want?"

"You, but that's beside the point," Lane responded smoothly, his original weariness absent from his tone.

Why did that make him feel so damn good?

Grant tried to brush off the response, keeping in mind Lane's good-ol'-boy answer to everything. If he let him, Lane would strip Grant of all his frustration within seconds, and that would leave him … tired.

But he could think of something else Lane could strip off him.

That might make him feel a little better.

Speaking of stripping... Holy mother of God.

"*What* are you doing?" Grant asked as he sat fascinated by the sight of Lane standing in front of him, tossing his tattered hat on the table that currently held the empty beer bottles and then pulling his T-shirt over his head.

Oh, fuck.

Grant was spellbound from the first sight of the dark hair that disappeared into the waistband of Lane's jeans. He then let his eyes graze upward, following the dark blue cotton as it skimmed higher, admiring the sexy definition of Lane's abs, the smattering of dark hair that covered Lane's chest, the corded muscles of Lane's neck... And then the shirt was gone completely, and their eyes collided.

"Need a shower," Lane said easily, his attention on Grant.

Breaking the eye contact, Grant once again slid his gaze down the front of Lane.

"You know where it's at," Grant replied, yanking his eyes off the chiseled abs and hard planes of Lane's incredible physique.

"Sorry, I forgot where it was. Care to show me?"

Grant frowned at Lane. He was not going to play this game.

Right. Tell your dick that, too.

Grant ignored that little voice in his head at the same time he ignored his dick's reaction to the sexy cowboy now toeing off his boots in the middle of Grant's living room.

"Lane," Grant began, ready to offer the big man a warning.

"That's my name, don't wear it out," Lane shot back as he reached for Grant's hand and damn near launched him to his feet with one well-timed tug.

"Fucking hell," Grant grumbled when he found himself vertical, standing directly in front of Lane. "I don't have time for this shit."

Lane was unbuttoning his own jeans while Grant watched. He knew he should've stood his ground and pushed Lane away, but he just couldn't do it. This was exactly what he needed to take his mind off the shitty day he'd had.

"Show me the shower, Grant," Lane demanded, his rich brown eyes boring into Grant.

"Sonuvabitch," Grant complained half-heartedly, taking a single step forward but not getting anywhere.

The next thing he knew, Lane had wrapped his arms around him and pulled him close, their mouths meeting with a vigorous hunger that no amount of anger could dispel.

"Damn, you taste good," Lane mumbled against his lips. "My favorite combination ... Grant and beer."

Grant didn't get a word in edgewise because Lane fused their mouths together once again and proceeded to back Grant toward the bathroom. The next thing he knew, they were both naked, standing beneath the lukewarm spray in his small shower.

"You know what I need?" Lane asked, his lips trailing down Grant's neck, effectively eliminating all thought from Grant's mind.

Grant had to hold back a yelp when Lane ventured farther and then nipped his collarbone.

"I asked you a question," Lane declared firmly.

"What?" Grant asked, sliding his arms around Lane and gripping his ass, pulling Lane against him as their cocks rubbed together. Fucking shit, that felt good.

"Are you asking me to repeat the question? Or asking me what I need?" Lane asked.

Grant laughed. He couldn't help it. "Does it matter?"

"Maybe."

"What do you need?" Grant tried to keep his tone serious but failed thanks to the triple shot of desire that had been injected into his bloodstream. The only thing he could think about at that point was the sexy, naked cowboy in his arms.

Lane's lips and tongue traveled back up Grant's neck, making their way to his ear. Lane nipped his earlobe at the same time he said, "I need to feel your mouth on my cock."

Grant groaned. "Yeah?" he asked breathlessly as Lane wrapped his big, callused hand around Grant's dick.

Ahh, hell. Grant was pretty sure those were stars he saw behind his closed eyelids.

"Yeah. I want you on your knees with my dick in your mouth. I want to watch," Lane continued, nipping Grant's earlobe again, "my dick fucking your face."

At the moment, Grant wanted the same damn thing.

As though Lane just realized that Grant needed a little coaxing, Lane took a step back, placing one hand on Grant's shoulder and encouraging him to go to his knees. Which he did. Much to his cock's dismay, though, because as he lowered himself to the porcelain floor beneath them, Lane released the firm grip he'd had on Grant's dick, leaving him aching for his touch once again.

"Oh, fuck yeah," Lane moaned as he slipped his fingers into Grant's wet hair, pulling roughly, enough that Grant felt the tingle down his spine.

As the water sluiced over Lane's ripped body, Grant allowed the porcelain to bite into his knees as he positioned himself in front of Lane. He kept his gaze trained on Lane's chiseled face, their eyes locking together while Lane guided his cock into Grant's mouth.

"Damn, that looks nice," Lane growled softly. "I love watching my dick slide past your lips."

Grant groaned around Lane's cock, swiping his tongue over and around Lane's thick shaft, teasing the underside briefly, enjoying the fuck out of Lane's heated response and the salty taste of Lane's skin.

"Aww, hell, Grant," Lane muttered, his eyes rolling back in his head.

Grant cupped Lane's balls with his hand, kneading firmly as Lane rocked into him. When Lane's eyes were once again on him, he used his teeth to gently scrape along the length of him.

"I dream about this," Lane admitted, his voice little more than a throaty whisper. "I dream about fucking your mouth, watching you take me all the way."

Grant's eyes widened briefly, but he expanded his mouth, taking Lane deeper. Lane was a big man in every sense of the word. He was well beyond a mouthful, but Grant gave it his all. He loved watching the pure ecstasy on Lane's face. It got him every time.

"Just like that," Lane hissed, his fingers tightening in Grant's hair once again. The pleasure-pain sparked down Grant's spine, making his balls throb with excitement.

Grant relished hearing the deep cadence of Lane's voice as he continued to mumble incoherently, urging Grant to continue.

"Damn, baby, that's good."

Grant nearly fell over, planting his palms on Lane's thick thighs to keep himself up.

Baby?

Had Lane really called him that? The single word did incredible things to Grant's insides, his heart racing out of control. He'd never expected a term of endearment to mean so damn much to him, but seeing the reverence on Lane's face only solidified the meaning behind it.

Grant pulled back, gripping Lane's cock in his fist as he stared up at him. "Say it again."

It was Lane's turn to look bewildered, but then a sexy smirk tilted the corners of his lips. "You like when I call you that?"

Grant groaned in response, sucking Lane's dick back into his mouth, applying firm suction as he began to bob his head faster, stroking Lane at the same time.

"Fuck, that's good, baby. So damn good. That's it, take my dick all the way. Wrap your lips around me and suck. Suck me hard, Grant. Fuck yes."

Without hesitation, Grant put all of his efforts into making Lane explode. He would've succeeded, too, if Lane hadn't yanked his hair, pulling him back enough to keep him from sending Lane over the edge.

"Not yet," Lane said hoarsely. "Come here."

Grant got to his feet with Lane's help, finding himself banded in Lane's strong arms, their mouths melded together, their tongues dueling for control, as they both clawed at one another in an attempt to get closer.

49

Once again, Lane used his grip on Grant's hair to bring things to a halt, the two of them staring into one another's eyes as they fought for breath.

"I want to come in your ass," Lane whispered. "I want to be buried so deep inside of you that you forget your own name."

It was Grant's turn to say, "Fuck yes."

■□■□■□■□

LANE HAD COME OVER WITH every intention of calling Grant to the carpet, coercing him to talk about what his problems were, but then this happened.

And now he couldn't even remember what he wanted to talk about.

The only thing that mattered was sliding his dick into Grant's hot ass, making love to him until their eyes crossed and nothing else in the entire world mattered.

Thanks to one of their previous rendezvous in Grant's shower, there was a tube of lubricant tucked between the bottles of shampoo and body wash, along with a strip of condoms that were sitting in the narrow window near the top of the ceiling. Not that Lane had expected those few condoms still to be there a little over a month later, but time hadn't been kind to them in recent weeks.

But right now, time was all they had.

"Put the condom on me," Lane instructed as he reached for one and then handed the foil packet to Grant.

Grant's mouth opened slightly but then closed, a smile forming where the confused expression had been moments before.

Yeah, Lane knew that Grant liked to be dominated from time to time. Actually, more often than not, although he was quick to give his own demands, as well. Lane didn't give a fuck either way, but he damn sure enjoyed that disoriented expression on Grant's incredibly handsome face. And from the moment he'd stepped through Grant's front door, Lane had known that leaving anything up to Grant tonight would've gotten him nowhere fast. At least this way, Grant didn't have time to think about anything other than the two of them and the sweet impending release they would both find soon.

Lane knew that Grant purposely tortured him as he sheathed him with a condom, stroking him relentlessly, causing Lane to pant for breath, desperate to bury himself in the scorching recesses of Grant's incredible body. But he was holding off because he knew the moment he slid home, he'd be a goner.

"Don't forget the lube," Lane breathed roughly. He was having a hard time focusing with Grant jerking him off slowly … ever so fucking slowly.

And just as he had with the condom, Grant teased him beyond reason as he coated Lane's cock with lube, preparing him to take him. When Lane couldn't endure any more, he gripped Grant's thick wrist firmly, stilling his movements.

"Come here," Lane demanded, pulling Grant flush against him, their chests colliding as the water washed over them. Steam billowed around them, and Lane wasn't so sure it was solely from the water or if the mere touch of their bodies caused the influx of heat to intensify.

Finding Grant's mouth once more, Lane explored, keeping it leisurely as long as he could, desperate to rein in his control so that this didn't end before he was ready. While his tongue slipped into Grant's mouth, he glided his hands over Grant's smooth, warm skin, content just to touch him, hold him.

God, he loved this man.

Not that he dared mention that again because he knew Grant was still holding himself back, for whatever reason.

Not Lane. Lane knew that life was too short to hold out for something that he recognized was unavoidable. He would do anything for Grant and Gracie. Anything. Including giving his life for them. That's how he knew it was love.

So instead of saying so, he ensured that Grant felt the meaning behind the unspoken words in every movement, every touch, every kiss. He longed to pleasure this man until neither of them knew which way was up. Or what day of the week it was, for that matter.

"Oh, God, Grant," Lane said against his mouth. "I need to be inside you."

"Yes," Grant agreed with a groan. "God, yes."

Drawing back, Lane ran his hands over Grant's body again, down his sleek, muscled pecs, over the dips and valleys of his washboard abs, then between his legs, stroking him gently with one hand while he placed the other on Grant's hip, urging him to turn around.

Lane didn't release Grant's cock as he pressed his chest against Grant's back, kissing his neck, sucking on his skin. He wanted to mark this man, to let the world know exactly who he belonged to. But he didn't dare. That would only invite trouble, and as it was, they had enough of that with all of the watchful eyes around the ranch.

But right here, right now, in the small confines of Grant's shower, they were the only two people in the world. The only two people who mattered, and Lane was going to make love to this man.

He continued to stroke Grant's steel-hard length while he inserted two fingers into Grant's tight ass, prepping him. Knowing his restraint was slipping, Lane didn't play for long before he removed his fingers and brushed the head of his cock against Grant's puckered hole.

"I'm going to fuck you hard, baby. I'm going to take you right here, but I don't want you to come until I tell you to. Understand?"

Grant nodded, his hand coming around to latch on to Lane's thigh. Lane would never get tired of Grant touching him, always touching him. It was the greatest feeling in the entire world. "Baby," Lane said on a breathless moan as he pushed deep, his cock sliding into Grant's ass. "Oh, fuck, Grant. So damn tight." Lane leaned over Grant, forcing him forward. "Put your hands on the wall and don't move."

Lane released Grant's cock from his fist, needing both hands to grip Grant's hips. He couldn't take much more, and he wanted to bury his dick as far as possible, hear Grant beg him to send him over.

"Does it feel good?" Lane asked as he withdrew slowly before thrusting his hips forward and going deeper than before.

"So good," Grant groaned, rocking back against Lane. "Don't stop."

"I don't plan to," Lane said. Although they both knew it for the lie that it was. The scalding-hot depths of Grant's body pulled him, making him dizzy from the overwhelming pleasure. Lane tried to keep his pace slow, but that didn't last long.

Before he knew it, he was slamming into Grant, pulling Grant's hips back toward him with each forward thrust.

"Tell me," Lane insisted. "Tell me how good it is, baby."

Grant's ass clenched around Lane's cock, making sparks shoot off behind his closed eyelids. So fucking good.

"I never want it to end," Grant called out, his voice barely discernable over the sound of the water rushing down over them. "I want you to fuck me forever. Oh, God, Lane. Fuck me harder."

Lane did just that. He pounded into Grant over and over, his hands slipping and sliding over Grant's wet skin as he grappled to keep him within his grip.

"Harder, Lane. Fuck me harder!"

"Are you ready to come for me?" Lane asked as he pistoned his hips faster, burying his dick all the way into Grant as he kneaded Grant's ass cheeks with his thumbs, gripping his hips hard.

"Fuck yes," Grant groaned, his deep voice harsh with need. "Let me come, Lane."

Lane continued with his punishing thrusts, slamming into Grant until they were both moaning, their bodies tense from the release that was within reach. When the pleasure ignited every nerve ending in Lane's body, he knew he couldn't hold on any longer.

"Come for me, Grant. Stroke your dick and come for me."

One of Grant's hands disappeared from the wall, and Lane could feel the vibration as Grant stroked himself fast, incredibly fast.

"Fuck, Lane. Oh, fuck. I'm gonna come."

"That's it, baby. Come for me. And when you do, I'm gonna come in your ass."

Lane wasn't sure whether the words were what sent Grant over the edge or just the sheer ecstasy of it all, but Grant's body went rigid, his hand stilling as he groaned, the gruff sound echoing through the small bathroom.

"Ahh, fuck yeah," Lane said, digging his fingers into Grant's hips as the pleasure blinded him. "I'm coming, baby."

And while Lane was filling Grant's ass, Grant reached around and gripped Lane's thigh painfully hard, intensifying his orgasm tenfold.

It was so fucking good Lane was surprised that he didn't pass out.

CHAPTER FIVE

Tuesday morning

GRACE STEPPED OUT OF THE dining room and onto the porch in time to see a little girl clinging firmly to the hand of her father, both of them chatting away as they made their way up the steps. Upon seeing Grace, the little girl offered a cheeky grin, looking both timid and excited.

"Good morning," Grace greeted softly, admiring the little girl with her dark, curly pigtails and her wide smile.

It was still incredibly early, just after seven, but the ranch was already buzzing with activity. Breakfast began at five for the early risers and the wranglers and generally lasted until ten to ensure everyone was accounted for. From the looks of it, her two guests had already had breakfast. Or at least coffee, if the white foam cup in the man's hand was any sign.

From where Grace stood, she could hear the goats announcing their good mornings from the barn, the horses neighing in the stable one hundred or so yards away, the clank of dishes from the dining room behind her, and the chatter of people as they made their way to and from the main house.

She smiled, inhaling deeply. Living here, being a part of such an incredible place… It was a dream come true. A way of life she'd been born into, one that she could never imagine any other way. Grace loved this place, every little nuance, every incredible detail. And each morning when she awoke, she sent up a huge thank you for all that her family had been blessed with. Things hadn't always been that way, though. There had been a painful part of her life when she'd cursed God for taking her mother away from her. But as time had drifted forward, Grace had, too. Until eventually, now, she could be grateful for all she did have while still missing her mother. The grief had never gone away, but it had lessened somewhat over time.

Refusing to start the day off on a sour note, Grace shook off the errant thoughts. "How are you today?" she asked, directing her question at the little girl now hugging her father's arm while bouncing on the balls of her feet, shooting glances over her shoulder toward the main barn.

Grace followed her gaze, seeing that the barn had already been readied for the morning, two of its oversized doors open to greet the early-morning sun.

"Good," the little girl chirped, clearly enthused.

Grace looked up at the man to see that his dark brown eyes were shining brightly as he stared down at his daughter.

"What's your name?" Grace asked the little girl. She couldn't have been more than five or six, and she looked adorable in her overalls and her little pink boots, her dark hair, streaked with natural auburn highlights, pulled up into pigtails, long ringlets hanging down past her shoulders.

"Madison. Everyone calls me Maddie," she replied, her light brown eyes sparkling in the sunlight. The color surprising, not a standard shade of brown, more like gold.

"Well, my name's Grace, but everyone calls me Gracie," she told her.

"Are you a real cowgirl?" Maddie asked, looking up at Grace as though she were responsible for all of the exciting stuff at the ranch.

"I guess you could say that. What do you think a real cowgirl is?"

"One who wears boots and has a horse," Maddie said excitedly.

Grace laughed as she eyeballed her feet, hefting one booted foot up a little, then the other before lifting her gaze back up to meet the little girl's. "Well, I've definitely got boots." Leaning down close to the little girl's ear, Grace lowered her voice to a mock whisper and said, "And I've also got my own horse."

Maddie, bless her cute little heart, squealed with excitement.

Turning her attention to the little girl's father, holding her hand out for him to shake, Grace said, "And you must be Mr. Ruhl."

The man gripped Grace's hand gently but firmly. "Technically, Mr. Ruhl would be my father. You can call me Ben."

"Nice to meet you, Ben." Grace smiled at the handsome man, studying his face momentarily.

Although he looked content to be there, based on the sidelong glances he would give Maddie, Grace sensed that something was bothering him. As she spared him a full head-to-toe glance, purely to check out his clothes, she came to the conclusion that his outfit wasn't likely the culprit.

He wasn't quite as decked out in western gear as his daughter, but he was sporting jeans and a polo, which was a positive sign. Grace still found it baffling that there were men and women alike who would come to ride horses wearing less-than-appropriate apparel, namely shoes. Daring a look, Grace confirmed that the man was wearing sneakers. She smiled to herself as she looked back up at him. "My name's Grace Lambert. Welcome to Dead Heat Ranch. Hopefully someone already told you that I'd be your guide for the entire time you're here, which, if I remember correctly, is two full weeks?"

"Yes!" Maddie exclaimed. "I get to be a cowgirl for two whole weeks."

Ben chuckled at his daughter before meeting Grace's eyes, his smile strengthening with each passing second. "Yes, we're here for two weeks."

"Y'all are gonna have a great time. I promise. And we're gonna do a lot of fun stuff. Starting now. This mornin', I'm here to show Maddie the horses, maybe take y'all for a ride if you'd like."

Maddie jumped up and down, clapping her hands. "Yes! Yes! Yes!"

Ben chuckled, shoving his hands into his pockets and once again directing his focus on Maddie. "She loves horses. I've promised her we'd do this for a long time. So, here we are. Whatever you're willing to teach us, we're your eager students."

"Have you ever been on a horse, Maddie?" Grace questioned.

"Nope! But I wanna ride one."

Grace couldn't help but share the little girl's enthusiasm.

"So, I hear you wanted a tour of the barn?" Grace asked, once again speaking to the little girl.

"I wanna see the horses," Maddie corrected, her smile like a ray of sunshine.

"Well, the horses aren't actually *in* the barn. We keep them in stables. And on this ranch, we have many horses, which means we have a lot of stables. How about I show you the main barn first, then we'll head over there." Grace pointed toward the largest stable on the property, the one that they had recently relocated all of the family's horses to. "That's where I keep my horse. His name's Astro Boy."

They had previously housed several of their personal horses in the barn, but with the significant changes being made to the ranch in recent weeks, they had decided to allocate the barn fully to housing things other than the animals. Initially, Grace had refused to move Astro Boy, her beloved five-year-old paint, but when Grant had informed her that they were also upgrading the main stable, she'd relented to their demands.

"Are there any *real* cowboys here?" Maddie asked as Grace started to amble toward the barn, the pair falling into step beside her.

"*Real?* Like the guys who wear boots and have horses?" Grace teased, referring to Maddie's definition of "real."

Maddie nodded, bouncing as she walked.

"Last I checked, we have roughly forty, I think," Grace explained. "Everyone who works here also lives here."

"I wanna live here!" Maddie exclaimed, making her father chuckle. "We get to stay in a *real* cabin. It has walls and floors that are made of wood and everything. I get to sleep in a bunk bed. On the top. Oh, and I have a TV in my room! I don't have a TV in my room at home. That's why I like this place. I can hear the horses and cows when I'm sitting on my bed. Oh, but the stove is kinda weird."

Grace laughed as she tried to keep up with Maddie. The girl clearly wasn't shy, that was for sure.

Each of the cabins that they reserved for the guests was individually decorated to enhance the rustic appeal of the ranch. Somewhat drastically, in Grace's honest opinion. She knew there were working wood stoves placed in several, which was probably what Maddie was referring to.

As the three of them made their way into the shadowy interior of the barn, Grace explained what everything was, including the hay and the various equipment that they had stored there. Maddie was full of questions, continuing to pelt Grace with one after another, which she answered quickly and efficiently.

This type of tour was a regular occurrence at the ranch, although many of the guests came solely for riding horses, which, being in Texas, the weather allowed for almost year round. Dead Heat Ranch was known for the riding trails that had been forged into the beautiful Texas Hill Country, along with the giant lake they had on the premises. The fishing wasn't as good other lakes in the area, but Grace believed many of their guests came, a lot of them returning more than once, to enjoy the hospitality and the one-on-one attention they received.

Each week, on Monday morning, Hope led them through the guest list and any activities that had been planned or requested. Grace would assign each of her sisters, along with many of the wranglers, to each guest, ensuring that everyone who visited had someone who would show them around.

Maddie and her father had arrived on the ranch late yesterday evening and were staying for a full two weeks, which was about twice as long as the average length of stay for their guests. Not that she had a problem with that. The longer they stayed, the easier it was for her to get the activities lined up. After this tour this morning, she would give them a questionnaire so that she could learn what other interests they had so that, during their stay, she could ensure they had the best experience possible.

All part of her day-to-day.

"If you're up for the walk, I can show you the stables," Grace said, glancing down at Maddie. "I need to check on my horse, make sure he's been fed."

"You don't feed him?" Maddie asked, sounding somewhat disappointed in Grace, which, again, made Grace smile.

"Most days I do," she answered, heading toward the back doors of the barn that would lead them in the direction of the stable. "Sometimes, like today, when I get to hang out with cool people like you and your dad, I ask one of the wranglers to make sure he gets fed."

"What's a wrangler?" Maddie asked.

"That's what we call the cowboys who work here. They're responsible for taking care of the animals."

"Will I get to meet a cowboy?"

"I'm sure you will," Grace told her.

Approaching the stables just a few minutes later, Grace heard Astro Boy neighing softly, followed by a couple of snorts. Yes, she knew she was late. He wasn't going to be happy with her, but maybe if he was lucky, she'd take him to the arena later. Grace had a feeling Maddie would enjoy watching Astro Boy do what she'd trained him to do.

The question was whether or not she was up for it. It had been a long time since Grace had been in front of an audience.

■□■□■□■□

MERCY PRACTICALLY CRAWLED TOWARD THE main house. She had no idea what her deal was, but she hadn't slept much at all last night. Actually, for several nights now. Tossing and turning, she continued to have the most unwelcome dream. And, yes, damn it, she realized she was referring to the dream as *unwelcome*, not disturbing or inappropriate or… Yeah, *unwelcome* was the best she could come up with to describe it.

"Mornin'," she greeted her father as she stepped into the brightly lit kitchen, where they generally would meet up for coffee each morning.

"Good mornin'," Jerry replied, folding over the newspaper he had been reading and placing it neatly on the table in front of him.

She noticed immediately that his salutation contained the word "good," unlike hers. That was her first clue that he was far too perky for that time of day, which was exactly why she stood staring at him blankly. Was it her or was he in a strangely good mood?

"*What?*" he asked, his forehead wrinkled from the frown on his face. "What's the matter with you?"

Laughing, Mercy shook her head and made her way to the coffeepot. "Nothin'," she said, praying that the caffeine was going to help erase some of the cobwebs in her brain. That dream was making it damn near impossible for her to function. Unfortunately, there was only one person to blame for that and … tag, she was it.

"Did you sleep well?" Jerry asked, again his tone far more lively than she expected.

"Perfectly," she lied. "You?"

"Never better."

Okay, something was really off. Maybe she was still dreaming.

"Ouch," she muttered when she pinched her forearm just to make sure. Nope, not dreaming.

"Did Gracie assign you to a guest this week?" her father asked, his voice coming from behind her as she filled one of the nondescript white mugs with coffee.

"Yep," she told him. "Gracie had it in for me this week. She put me with a group of women coming here for a 'cowgirl' retreat," Mercy explained, lifting her hands in the air and crooking her fingers to signal the quotes.

Those were her favorite.

Cowgirls.

Riiiight.

If she had to guess, there would be at least three, possibly up to five; all of them were going to want to hang out by the pool in their skimpy little bikinis and wait for the wranglers to pass by. *'Cause that's what cowgirls do.* Which they would do. Every day throughout their stay. Then, when Mercy tried to convince them to go horseback riding, or something equally *cowgirl-ish*, they'd squeal and giggle and agree only if one of the men taught them what they were supposed to do.

Oh, joy, something to look forward to.

"They won't be here until Thursday, though," Mercy tacked on as she stirred sugar and cream into her mug.

"What'll you do till then?" Jerry questioned.

Mercy raised one eyebrow and glared at him over her shoulder. "Are you insinuating that I don't have anything to do around here?"

A huge smirk replaced the stern expression on Jerry Lambert's face. Her father loved to give her a hard time about not doing anything around the ranch. She, along with her four sisters, spent their days from sunup to sundown working, usually seven days a week. For Mercy, working at the ranch wasn't a job. It was a way of life, and she loved it.

"Nope. Not me," he answered, sipping his coffee and staring back at her over the rim of his cup.

"What about you? Did she stick you with someone this week?" Mercy asked.

Her father usually wasn't assigned to a guest, but for whatever reason, he had been getting more and more involved in the physical activities in recent weeks. In fact, Mercy was pretty sure he'd had a lobotomy because his entire demeanor had changed over the course of the last few months.

"Nope, but I offered to head up a couple of the trail rides."

"You sure your old butt can handle bein' in a saddle all day?" Mercy teased as she made her way to a small table, sliding a chair out with her foot before sliding into it.

"Girlie, I can still outride you any day of the week."

Mercy laughed, leaning her chair back on two legs. She was the fastest rider on the ranch, and with her horse, Shadow Mist, they were an unbeatable team. "Right. Believe that if you want to, Pops. If you ever want me to prove you wrong, just name the time and place. I'm ready."

Jerry snickered, placing his coffee cup on the table and relaxing in his chair, his work-roughened hands resting on his trim, flat stomach. Mercy didn't squirm as her father seemingly studied her. This was a recurring conversation, the two of them ribbing one another about who was faster. There was a time when her father had held that title at Dead Heat Ranch, but not since Mercy had been a teenager.

"You're on," Jerry finally said, his smile transforming his face from average to handsome instantly.

Mercy dropped her chair back to the floor with a resounding thud. "Shi— Er … crap," Mercy squealed when her coffee sloshed over the edge of her cup and onto her hand. Shaking her hand to knock off the liquid, Mercy stared at her father. "Are you serious?" she asked, unable to hold back her excitement. For years, she'd tried to goad her father into racing her. Not many people at the ranch would because they didn't like being left in the dust.

"Yep. Dead serious."

Mercy smiled, on both the outside and the inside, her stomach churning with exhilaration. "When? Where?" she asked, putting her coffee mug down on the table so that she didn't drop it.

"Sunday mornin'. Before it gets too hot."

"Scared of a little heat, Pops?" she teased, knowing that he was more concerned about the horses than anything else.

He merely replied with a tilt of one dark eyebrow up toward his hairline.

"Fine. Sunday mornin'." Mercy stood, nearly knocking her chair over. "I'm gonna let everyone know."

"Great," Jerry muttered, still smiling as he sipped from his cup again.

Mercy headed to the door, ready to run outside and announce to the ranch that she was going to leave her father in the dust, but she stopped instead. Turning to look at her father, she smiled at him. "Love you, Pops."

"Love you, too, girlie," he replied, his eyes softening. "This much."

Mercy grinned. Her father had started telling them that when they were little. It had been a game at first because he didn't use his arms or his hands to signal how much he was talking about. According to Jerry, he meant *this much* as all encompassing. It was still something he said to them, and every single time, Mercy felt just as giddy as she had when she was a little girl.

"You might wanna take some ridin' lessons this week," she informed him as she pushed the screen door open. "You're gonna need 'em."

With that, she went outside, the sound of her father's roaring laugh following her as she did.

Yep, it was safe to say that this week was looking up. And she could only hope that the anticipation of the race would help to keep that *unwelcome* dream from disrupting her sleep.

If not, she was going to have to do something about Cody Mercer because that damn mechanic was getting on her last nerve.

The worst part about it … he didn't even know.

Chapter Six

LANE'S AFTERNOON WAS ENDING ABOUT as well as his morning had started. From the instant that his eyes had peeled open, thanks to the annoying sound of his cell phone's alarm, it seemed as though he had been on his feet. And now, when he would've preferred to be heading back to the bunkhouse for a quick shower and then over to the dining hall for supper, he was being summoned to the arena.

For what, he had no idea.

The text had come from Mercy, which was a little surprising, but the message was clear.

Get to the arena now.

Yes, ma'am. It wasn't like he didn't have other things to do, thank you very much.

Fortunately, he hadn't been on the scheduled trail ride for the day, but that meant he'd been busting his ass working on fixing one of the back stables that had practically caved in on itself about a month ago. They had moved the existing horses from that stable several weeks before that, due to its condition, but now that they had acquired several more, they needed the thing desperately.

It felt as though they had been working more in the last couple of months than in the three years that he'd been there, combined. They were expanding, that was for sure. Not that he minded that the ranch seemed to be doing well. As far as he was concerned, Dead Heat Ranch's success was his success. And loving what he did made it all the sweeter.

But with work came exhaustion, something Lane was definitely feeling. He wanted to go jump headfirst into the swimming pool to cool off. Shit, it had been almost two months since he'd taken the time to do even that much. Then again, his priorities these days, other than work, were Gracie and Grant. He was more than willing to spend every spare second he had with the two of them. Even if it meant he had to forego sleep.

Lane looked up to see that he was only a few feet from his destination, a sigh of relief escaping him. Getting out of the blazing sun was his goal, and the arena was going to offer some much-needed shade, although it wouldn't do much for the one-hundred-plus-degree temps.

Dead Heat Ranch's event arena was rather impressive. The thing rivaled in size any state fair arena that Lane had ever seen, although the seating capacity was significantly less. The giant steel structure had to have cost a freaking fortune — not that Lane had any idea how much — but it was clearly worth the investment since it was always being used. Most of the time, Gracie, or one of her sisters, was teaching beginning riders what it meant to be on a horse within the steel building, and that was usually so they could avoid subjecting the horses to the direct sun.

From time to time, they would hold a miniature version of a rodeo for the guests, complete with a couple of bulls that the wranglers would try to outlast for that eight seconds of glory. Lane was proud to admit that he was a damn fine bull rider, even though it had been nearly a year since he'd been on the back of one. At thirty-two, he'd outgrown the need to be bucked off a seventeen-hundred-pound pissed-off animal.

But today, there weren't any kids running around chasing one another or any of the wranglers leading animals to and from. No, right now the place appeared to be a ghost town. Lane didn't even see Mercy when he stepped into the shade, making his way toward the bleachers on one side. The sound of clapping brought Lane's attention up to the staggered metal benches that rose up from the ground. There, on the bottom row, was a little girl and a man, sitting side by side. Lane was about to question what she was clapping about, but then he stopped dead in his tracks.

No questions needed.

Lane stood motionless, completely hypnotized by the sexy, petite cowgirl making her way out into the arena, Astro Boy proudly walking beside her. Gracie was dwarfed by the size of the horse, but even from as far away as Lane was, she was what drew his attention.

The woman was breathtaking. Long, golden-blond hair, those interesting blue-green eyes, her cute little nose, and those lips… Oh, damn. If he weren't careful, he'd be sporting wood just by thinking of how hot she looked in those sexy jeans, too.

Truth be told, Lane was quite partial to watching her with her horse. She loved that animal, and he was pretty sure she would've found a way to keep him at her cabin if it was at all feasible. She spent a significant amount of time with Astro Boy, refusing to allow anyone else to do more than feed him. And she was a sight to behold when she rode Astro Boy, which Lane suddenly figured out was her plan.

The sound of footsteps shuffling in the soft dirt behind him had Lane turning to see Grant walking his way. The scowl on his face told Lane that Grant's week wasn't getting any better than the last time he'd seen him.

"Mercy text you?" Lane asked as Grant approached.

"Yeah," Grant grumbled.

"Have you seen her?"

"Nope."

Well, it sucked to know that Grant still wasn't back to his normal chatty self. The guy really needed to get out of his funk. Lane wasn't at all fond of the mood, but more important, he wasn't happy with not knowing what had spawned it in the first place.

Turning away from Grant, Lane tilted his head in the direction of the arena floor, where Gracie was currently leading Astro Boy. "Look."

Lane made his way beneath the bleachers, trying to get a better view of Gracie and her horse. Reaching up, Lane clasped his fingers on one of the metal rungs of the benches that were standing tall and proud over his head. He was peering through the aluminum steps, hidden from view of the little girl and the man when Grant joined him.

"Okay," Gracie said, her voice echoing in the cavernous arena. "Maddie, I've got a job for you. Astro Boy really likes when you clap. So I expect to hear you loud and clear, all right?"

Lane realized that Gracie was talking to the little girl, Maddie, who was once again smacking her hands together gleefully while Gracie turned and said something to Astro Boy. The huge black-and-white paint knelt on one knee, bowing toward the little girl, which earned him a loud squeal in return.

"I haven't done this in a long time," Gracie continued, keeping her eye on Maddie as she started walking Astro Boy several feet one way and then turning him back, all while she rubbed her hand down his big nose, using the bridle to keep his head close to hers.

Lane glanced around the arena, noticing that there were barrels set up — one on each end. And that could only mean...

"Holy shit," Grant whispered, speaking Lane's thoughts aloud. "Is she...?"

"Looks like it."

And from that moment forward, Lane was rendered speechless, unable to do anything other than watch Gracie. And just like her name, the woman was pure grace as she led her horse around while still talking to the little girl.

"Are you ready?" Gracie asked.

"Hell yeah," Lane mumbled softly.

"Yes!" Maddie screamed.

Lane watched as Gracie walked Astro Boy several more feet, speaking to him tenderly as she did, readjusting the way she was holding his reins. When she began jogging, kicking up the dirt beneath her boots, Lane knew he wasn't going to be able to look away. And then she was running, Astro Boy trotting beside her, clearly doing just as she instructed.

Son of a…

Gracie mounted the horse while Astro Boy was at a full gallop, her much shorter legs keeping up until she propelled herself up and into the saddle. She directed Astro Boy with the ease of a cowgirl who knew her horse better than she knew herself. Lane was pretty sure his jaw was on the floor at that point.

Likely for the little girl's benefit, Gracie had Astro Boy perform a few basic stunts, a couple of high steps, a dizzying turn. Nothing significant, but clearly enough to impress Maddie. Then everything seemed to morph into slow motion as Gracie called out to Astro Boy, a signal for him to run.

And he did.

Riding full out, Gracie sprinted Astro Boy around the arena a couple of times, the little girl clapping louder and louder until the man was joining in as well. The energy in the place jumped several levels, and Lane realized he was holding his breath.

Then Gracie kicked it up another notch, running Astro Boy from one end to the other, circling the barrel, both horse and rider leaning into the turn perfectly timed. Lane observed in awe as Gracie raced that horse, Astro Boy doing exactly as Gracie wanted, until finally, they were coming to an abrupt stop directly in front of the little girl.

"That was awesome!" Maddie yelled.

"I'll say," Grant whispered, still standing beside Lane. "Have you ever seen her ride like that before?"

"No," Lane answered. He knew she was good with horses, but he'd never seen anything as spectacular as Gracie racing that beautiful horse at full speed, circling those barrels as if she'd done it a million times before. She was good enough to have gone pro.

Which made him wonder … why hadn't she?

BY THE TIME ASTRO BOY came to a stop, Gracie was breathing hard. Leaning forward, she talked to her horse while petting his face gently, telling him how proud she was.

"Very impressive, Gracie," Ben called, standing up and leading his daughter down to the rails that lined the front of the bleachers.

"Thank you," she replied, encouraging Astro Boy to move closer to the stands.

"Where did you learn to do that?" he asked as Maddie stood on the bottom rung and leaned over to pet Astro Boy's head, Ben's hand resting on Maddie's back, probably to keep her from leaning too far over.

"My mother," she told him, a sharp pang of loss echoing in her chest.

Her mother had taught her how to barrel race when Gracie was little. Being that her mother had been a champion barrel racer herself, Gracie had wanted to grow up to be just like her. She'd worked hard at a very young age, always adoring the time she had to spend with her mother, the two of them out in the arena — not the same one they were in now — working to perfect her form.

But then her mother had died, and Gracie had buried her dream of going pro right along with her. She continued to race, but only when no one knew she was out there. Ever since she'd gotten Astro Boy, Gracie had known that he was meant to run. She was pretty sure he loved it as much as she did, and they were quite the pair.

Not that she wanted anyone to know. It was difficult to keep her family and friends in the dark because they were a nosy bunch, but either she was successful or they were keeping their mouths shut where her extracurricular activity was concerned. She tended to believe it was the latter. What she didn't want was for people to start pushing her toward something she didn't want to do anymore. Sure, it was fun to race Astro Boy from time to time, but she didn't want to do it for a crowd. Grace was more than content with the way things were, spending her days working at the ranch. No rodeos for her. No thank you.

The sound of boots on the bleachers had Grace looking over her shoulder.

Oh, crap.

Coming toward her, with matching stunned expressions on their handsome faces, were Lane and Grant.

"Real cowboys, Dad," Maddie whispered, loud enough for everyone to hear.

"Hey, darlin'," Lane greeted Maddie, his signature crooked smirk falling into place.

Grace found the little girl was grinning ear to ear, likely falling head over heels in love with the man on sight. Rather than respond, Maddie giggled while grabbing on to her father's hand as if he were her lifeline.

"What's your name?" Lane asked, squatting down in front of Maddie.

Grace half listened to the conversation, her attention turning to Grant, who was staring back at her as though he'd never seen her before. Rubbing Astro Boy's head, Grace tried not to fidget under the scrutiny of his gaze.

They'd seen her race, if she had to guess. Which was exactly why she didn't want anyone to watch, having absolutely no desire to endure any of their questions or encouragement. And she could see in Grant's expressive blue eyes that he had loads of questions.

"Can we, Dad?" Maddie called out, drawing Grace's attention back to her.

"Sure, if that's okay with Gracie," Ben replied.

"Can we, Gracie? Can we have supper with you and the two cowboys? Pretty please?"

Grace laughed, enjoying the little girl's fervor. And yes, she did have to eat, but she shot Lane a look that promised retribution. He simply tipped the edge of his mouth into a sexy smile that made her body ignite immediately.

"Sure you can," Grace answered, pulling her eyes away from Lane. "What time is it, anyway?"

"Four-thirty," Ben said quickly.

"How 'bout we meet in the dining hall at five," Grace told Maddie.

The little girl clapped her hands giddily as she nodded.

"Come on, kiddo," Ben said to Maddie. "Let's go wash up so we can eat."

"See you in a little while, Gracie! Bye, cowboys!" Maddie called out as her father led her toward the exit.

Crap.

And now Grace was left alone with Grant and Lane. Clearly, she hadn't thought that one through all the way.

"Don't say a word," she told them, twisting in the saddle, preparing to lead Astro Boy back toward the stable.

She heard the creak of metal followed by the thud of boots on dirt, and she knew the two men had scaled the railing and were now following her outside.

"Why...?"

Grace quickly cut Lane off before he could get the question out. Turning to face them both, she glared down into their faces, daring them to argue with her. "I mean it. Don't. Don't ask me about anything you saw today. I don't want to talk about it."

Lane didn't say a word, but as she slid her gaze back and forth between the two of them, she knew they were preparing the questions they would likely bombard her with later. Maybe by then she'd be willing to tell them. But right now, with the memory of her mother weighing heavily on her heart, Grace just wanted a few minutes to herself.

Half an hour later, Grace was entering the dining hall, looking around to see if she was the first of her little group to arrive. She didn't see Ben or Maddie, but she did see Lane and Grant standing at the front of the food line, chatting with a wrangler who was adding additional plates to the buffet table.

The place was busy, with other guests arriving for the final meal of the day, along with her sisters, her father, and several of the wranglers. In a few minutes, she knew the place would be loud, which was what she was anticipating. With any luck, there would be too much going on for anyone to question what they had seen a short while ago.

"Hi, Gracie!" The excited voice chimed from behind Grace, so she turned to see Maddie standing there with an Oscar-worthy smile on her face.

"Hey, Maddie. Are you hungry?"

The excited little girl nodded her head emphatically, her pigtails bobbing.

"Well, we better get in line before the cowboys take all the food."

Grace, Maddie, and Ben all joined the line, waiting patiently to reach the tables that held the food. Ben's vivacious daughter was kind enough to provide comic relief, explaining in thorough detail all about their trip to the ranch. According to Maddie, she lived in Oklahoma with her dad but went to see her mother every other weekend when her mom wasn't out of town. Grace noticed that when the little girl mentioned her mother, there was a pained expression on Ben's face. She had to wonder whether their divorce — if they were actually divorced — was amicable. For some reason, she didn't think so, but she definitely wasn't going to pry into the details of his life.

After filling their plates with chicken-fried steak, corn on the cob, and ranch-style beans, the three of them wound through the tables until they reached the larger one in the back. Grant and Lane were already seated, and Grace wanted to laugh when she noticed they had reserved her a chair. Between them.

Rather than call attention to their clever move, she made her way over, sliding into the chair while Maddie did what Maddie did best — started asking questions.

Grant and Lane were both good sports, sharing stories and answering questions. Neither of them seemed at all put off by the fact they were having dinner with a six-year-old and her father. In fact, Grant seemed to have relaxed somewhat since she'd seen him earlier.

When they had finished their meal, Grant offered to escort Maddie to the dessert table, promising coffee upon his return for the adults. The conversation didn't stall with their departure, though. Ben was interested in the inner workings of the ranch, but he seemed more comfortable asking Lane questions. Grace wasn't sure whether that was because she was a girl — which she highly doubted — or because he figured she had enough to do just answering his daughter's endless questions. Either way, Grace hung on to Lane's every word, enjoying the easy way he interacted with Ben.

A short while later, Grace was sipping coffee and listening to Maddie chatter away about what she wanted to do tomorrow, when Hope walked up to their table.

"Hey," Grace greeted her sister with a smile. "Ben, Maddie, this is my sister Hope."

You could've heard a pin drop at that very moment. The moment when Ben met Hope's gaze from across the table, Grace was pretty certain she saw sparks fly.

"Very nice to meet you, Maddie. Ben," Hope said, her voice soft.

"Are you a real cowgirl, too?" the energetic little girl asked Hope.

"I guess you could say that."

"Awesome!"

A round of laughter erupted, Grace leading the charge, but she noticed that Ben wasn't laughing. His eyes were glued to Hope, and Grace saw something there. Something that threatened to set the smoke detectors off.

Oh, crap.

"Grant," Hope spoke directly to the man sitting at her side, leaning over his shoulder. "I wanted to let you know that someone's been callin' the ranch for you. I haven't been the one to answer it yet, but the girls who're answerin' the phone are gettin' antsy. I think he said he was your dad."

Grace watched Grant's entire body tense, his eyes narrow.

Why would Grant's father be calling the ranch?

"Thanks," Grant said roughly, his tone making the hair on the back of Grace's neck lift.

Grace didn't have a chance to question him about it because Hope turned her attention toward her.

"Hey, Grace," Hope said, leaning down over Grace's shoulder. "I wanted to see if we could have a meeting Thursday mornin' at my house."

And Hope was asking her this now? Because, what ... they weren't going to see each other tomorrow? Grace didn't feel comfortable questioning Hope in front of the guests — which she figured was Hope's angle — so she simply nodded her head. "What time?"

"Eight. If possible."

"I'll be there."

"Thanks. It was great to meet you both," Hope stated, obviously talking to Ben and Maddie. "I hope you have a great time while you're here. You're lucky, you know that?"

"Why?" Maddie asked, curiosity making her golden eyes glow.

Grace held her breath, waiting to see what Hope was going to say. The woman was always completely professional — sometimes too much so — when guests were around.

"My sister Gracie... She's the best cowgirl at the ranch. You're lucky to have her showing you around."

What the...

Twisting so that she could see Hope still standing over her shoulder, Grace was speechless. Her face heated, embarrassment making her temperature spike. Her sister didn't usually hand out compliments like that. Ever.

"I know!" the little girl agreed. "She showed me how she races her horse, and tomorrow she's gonna take me fishing."

Shit.

Grace twirled back around in her seat fast enough to shake the table, not wanting to look at Hope.

"Well, honey, I think you're gonna have a fabulous time. It was nice meeting you, Ben," Hope said before she turned and walked away from the table.

Grace noticed that Ben was still watching her sister, even when Hope stopped at another table to chat with guests. She had no idea what was running through his head, but the look on his face wasn't lewd. No, she'd be more inclined to describe his expression as wonder.

When a smile tipped the corner of his lips, Grace peeked over her shoulder one more time to see Hope looking back at him.

Wow. And wonders never ceased.

CHAPTER SEVEN

"HEY, LET'S GET OUTTA HERE for a little while," Lane mumbled to Grant after they had cleaned off the table and headed toward the door.

Ben and Maddie had excused themselves a short while ago. Apparently, seven thirty was the little girl's bedtime, and if they didn't head back, she'd find a way to get out of taking a bath, something Ben wasn't looking forward to.

"What'd you have in mind?" Grant asked, his eyes searching their surroundings to ensure no one was listening.

"I don't know. Somethin' fun. Let's grab the horses and head out for a bit."

As they stepped out onto the porch, Grant glanced up at the evening sky. Still cloudless, although the sun had begun its descent in the west, casting rays of pink and orange overhead. The days weren't quite as long as they used to be, but he knew they still had quite a bit of daylight left to utilize.

"I'm game," Gracie said as she joined them.

Hell, Grant hadn't even realized she was there.

"What d'ya say?" Lane asked Grant.

"Why not," Grant answered with a grin.

Some time away from the place would do them some good. And unfortunately, they never had much of a chance to spend time together unless they were sneaking around anyway. An evening ride sounded like a good plan.

Gracie led the way to the stables, and Grant walked alongside Lane, doing his best not to stare at Gracie's ass. Right. Like he was really trying all that hard. The woman had one mighty fine ass.

"Hey, cowboy, my face is up here," Gracie said teasingly, drawing Grant's gaze upward.

Hell, he'd been so engrossed in watching the rhythmic sway of her hips that he hadn't even realized she had stopped in front of Astro Boy's stall.

"I'll take Shadow Mist," Lane said as he moved past them.

"I'll ride Outlaw. He hasn't had much exercise today."

Grant spent the next few minutes getting Outlaw ready for the ride while Lane and Gracie did the same with their respective horses. He found himself alone in the stables by the time he had Outlaw ready. Smiling to himself, he led the huge horse through the wide path that split the stable in two. He met Lane and Gracie outside, noticing they were already in the saddle waiting for him.

"You're gettin' slow in your old age," Lane offered, smiling down at him.

"We're the same age," he reminded Lane as he put his foot in the stirrup and then hoisted himself up onto the horse. Outlaw let out an excited whinny as he stomped his feet. "Not today, boy. We're just gonna take a walk."

Grant could practically hear Outlaw's disappointment in his answering snort, but the horse started out at a brisk walk anyway.

"So, when did you first learn to ride?" Lane asked, drawing Grant's attention as they made their way across the pasture where the horses grazed.

Grant listened closely, wanting to hear Gracie's response.

"My mom started teachin' me to ride when I was three. By the time I was five, I was learnin' how to race."

"Really?" Lane asked. "That's young."

"Maybe to you, but remember, I grew up on this ranch. I'd been around horses from the day I was born. My sisters learned to ride early, too."

"Did Mercy learn to race young also?"

Good job, Lane, Grant thought to himself. It was evident that Lane was urging Gracie to open up, but if he started showering her with personal questions, she'd just as quickly stop talking. Lane was smart enough to ask about someone other than Gracie.

"Yeah. I'd say around the same age as me. Mercy and I were the only two who really loved racing. But you should've seen my mother on a horse…"

Grant could hear the emotion in Gracie's voice.

"I've seen the tack room," Grant inserted. "She won a lot of prizes."

"She did," Gracie added. "My dad didn't want to put all of those things on display, but Hope convinced him. There are times I just sit and stare at the trophies, the saddles, the medals… She was incredible."

"And you wanted to be like her?" Grant asked the obvious.

"Yep, that was the plan," Gracie stated more firmly as the horses headed down a steep hill. "She was gonna teach me everything she knew. What about you? Did you play sports in high school?"

Grant glanced over at Lane, wondering if he wanted to answer that question. Grant had heard the stories of Lane's younger years, but he doubted Gracie had heard them all.

And since they were all sharing, Grant figured there was no better time than now to urge someone else to take the lead. After all, he wasn't all that interested in sharing his sob story with these two. Tonight was about enjoying themselves, and Grant's story would just bring them all down.

■□■□■□■□

"I PLAYED BASEBALL," LANE STATED, his eyes meeting Grant's briefly over Gracie's head. He recognized a hand-off when he heard one. Grant clearly didn't want to talk about himself, which left Lane picking up the slack. "Absolutely hated it, but that's what my father wanted me to do, so I didn't have much of a choice. Started out playing in a tee ball league when I was little. My dad made sure I played every year up until my senior year of high school. On the plus side, it kept my grades up. It just wasn't my thing. I would've preferred to be chasing women at the time."

"Just women?" Grace asked, laughing.

"Okay, men *and* women." Lane hadn't realized what being bisexual actually meant until he was out of high school even though he'd known he had a fondness for both men and women. To this day, he hadn't kept it a secret that he was bisexual, nor did he flaunt it, either.

"Why'd you play if you hated it so much?" Gracie asked, leading Astro Boy toward the tree line, Outlaw and Shadow Mist following his lead.

"I was my dad's trophy. He wanted to show me off. He was insistent that I was gonna be some baseball phenom just because he wanted me to. I tried to tell him that it didn't work that way, but he rarely ever listened to me. It could've been worse... He could've wanted me to play tennis or some shit like that."

"Hey!" Gracie called out. "What's wrong with tennis? Trin played tennis in high school."

"I'm sorry," Lane said, grinning, feeling anything but. "She's a girl. Tennis is okay if you're a girl."

The sound of Gracie's chuckle soothed him. In fact, the sound of the trees rustling in the wind, the hooves on the dirt, and the occasional whinny from the horses helped, as well. But he could've been anywhere in the world, and as long as he could listen to Gracie laugh, Lane would've been happy.

"Other than being popular because you were probably the captain of the baseball team, did you like high school?" Grant asked.

"I didn't hate it. I just wanted to get it over with. My dad was pushy, always wanting me to do just a little better at anything I did. What about you?"

"It was the only way I could get away from my parents, so I didn't particularly mind it." Grant's answer sounded sad, as though the man was reliving those days when he had needed a reason to get away from his parents. Lane could relate somewhat. He hadn't looked forward to high school, but anytime he'd been out of the house had been a plus for him, too. "What about you, Gracie?"

"I loved high school. Bein' on the ranch is great and all, but it's an isolated lifestyle. When I was in school, I was able to see my friends, hang out. I think the biggest issue was the age difference between my younger sisters and me. When I was a senior, two of them were in high school with me. Faith would've been too, except her birthday's in November, so she started school later."

"I didn't have any brothers or sisters to worry about," Lane added. He remembered days when he'd wished he had a sibling who could take some of the heat off him. His father had been truly relentless in his pursuit to make Lane the best kid a father could have. The man had never been happy with anything Lane did, informing Lane that he could've always done just a little better.

The three of them took the horses down to the edge of the creek just on the other side of the tree line, giving them time to drink before they set out on the ride back. Staring out at the flat land, the hills that had given this little section of Texas its name, Lane took a deep breath.

"I could sit right here forever," Gracie said softly.

"Me, too," Lane said at the exact moment Grant did.

It was true, being on the ranch, the laid-back lifestyle... It did more for him than anything else. Lane would be content to be there for the rest of his life. Which he hoped was a possibility.

"Have you ever brought a girl home to meet your parents?" Gracie asked.

Lane met her gaze, realizing she was talking to him. He nodded. "Once. My senior prom. Her name was Dawn. I think meeting my father scared her off. We'd been datin' for a short time before the prom, and I asked her. I figured my parents would be all up my ass if I didn't introduce them, so I caved. Yeah, that didn't go over well. I don't think Dawn had been expectin' the interview my father gave her. Hell, you would've thought we were plannin' to get married or somethin'."

Gracie laughed. "I introduced my dad to one guy I dated in high school. That didn't go over well. The boy I was dating obviously didn't know how to take him, and when my dad threatened to rip his arms clean off his body, the boy avoided me at school and didn't call me anymore."

"I can see that," Lane added, chuckling. That's something he would expect from Jerry. The man had a huge heart, but he could be incredibly intimidating when he wanted to be.

"We better get back," Gracie stated as she pulled on Astro Boy's reins, urging him to turn around. "It's gettin' dark."

Lane took one more look around him, feeling incredibly content with where he was in his life. He knew his father would never agree, never fully understand what it meant to be free and open like he was, but Lane wouldn't have it any other way.

And now he had these two in his life.

What more could he ask for?

*

Two hours later, Lane was lying on his own bed, his hands propped behind his head as he stared at the ceiling.

Yeah, this sucked big, hairy donkey balls.

Since spending time with Gracie and Grant, staying with them in the evenings, sleeping over on occasion, Lane would admit that sleeping in the bunkhouse was about the worst thing he could think of, aside from possibly sleeping in the pigpen.

Not that it was much different.

There were roughly three dozen guys in a house that had been built for maybe a few more than that, but not by much. There were five individual rooms, each with four bunk beds, sleeping eight to a room. But if you wanted to watch TV, that was in the common area. And if you didn't want to listen to country music, well, you were pretty much shit out of luck because that was what was currently blaring on the radio, coming from the next room over.

"It's after ten! Turn that shit off!" someone yelled from another room, clearly as frustrated by the music as Lane was. Not that Lane would've said anything. To each his own and all that shit. If he got too fed up with it, he'd just sleep in his truck. He'd done it before.

"Fuck you!" came the response from the room next to his. Lane smiled.

This was a nightly occurrence. It was as though they lived to piss each other off. One would think that they'd be too exhausted to bitch and moan after working an eighteen-hour day, but no, this happened way too often.

Lane pulled his hands out from behind his head and reached for his cell phone sitting on a tiny stand positioned beside the bed, holding his wallet, keys, and his phone charger, nothing else.

The screen came to life, and Lane navigated through the menu until he got to his text messaging app. Adding Grant and Gracie to one conversation, he typed in, *I miss you both*, and then sat back to see if either of them would respond.

This had been a nightly thing for them, too. Anytime they weren't together, which was, unfortunately, more often than not, the three of them would text back and forth for at least a few minutes, sometimes closer to an hour.

Miss you, too was the reply he received from Gracie, coming across his screen from "Sexy Cowgirl" about two minutes later, and the message, signaled by the bright flash of his phone screen, made his heart swell.

Grant Kingsley: What are you wearing?

Lane laughed at Grant's text the moment he received it. He figured Grant was talking to Gracie, but he responded anyway.

Lane Miller: Khakis

No, he wasn't really wearing khakis. He actually didn't even own a pair, but he had seen it on some commercial and went with it.

Grant Kingsley: Funny guy
Lane Miller: I try
Sexy Cowgirl: I'm not wearing anything.

Oh, Lord. That woman was going to be the death of him. Lane was tempted to slip out of bed and sneak over to her house, but he knew he'd have to come right back in just a couple of hours, and he wasn't interested in doing the walk of shame twice in one week.

As it was, he longed to spend every single night in bed with Gracie and Grant. All night long. Truth was, he didn't want to sleep alone.

Grant Kingsley: Tease

Sexy Cowgirl: I try

The minutes ticked by, and there weren't any more responses, so Lane figured they'd both given in for the night. As he rolled over, clutching his phone against his chest, he wished like hell that he were in Gracie's bed with Grant right there with him.

These lonely nights were beginning to get to him.

Maybe it was time he told the two of them that.

Lane Miller: Goodnight y'all. I love you both.

Lane didn't bother to keep his eyes open and wait for a response.

Which was a good thing because one never came.

Chapter Eight

The next evening... Wednesday

GRANT SPENT THE BETTER PART of the day helping Cody check some of the equipment that had been giving them trouble in recent weeks. As the ranch foreman, he was used to doing a wide range of jobs, but today, he had to admit he'd used it as an excuse to hide away for a little while.

To make matters worse, his phone battery was dwindling, but that was all thanks to his father's persistent attempts to get a rise out of him. For the last twenty-four hours, Grant had been fighting relentlessly with his father. After finding out from Hope that Darrell had been calling the ranch, Grant had been forced to address the man. Luckily, it had all been done via text. The arguments... Yeah, well, he was used to those. And for the most part, he could ignore them. Grant didn't usually allow those types of things — insistent demands from Darrell — to interrupt his days, but he'd received some disconcerting news from his father that he couldn't seem to shake.

According to Darrell, Grant's mother hadn't yet come back home. Trying to pry the details from his father was like rounding up cattle with a cat. It didn't work, so Grant had tried to call his mother directly, but he only got her voice mail. Three times.

Now, Grant knew Sandy wasn't always responsive when he left her messages, but this was a little out of the norm, even for her. When he called, her voice mail kicked on immediately, which meant either she had turned her phone off on purpose or the damn thing was dead. If she was dealing with the same harassing messages from Darrell that Grant was, he didn't necessarily blame her for going off the grid. But he was beginning to worry.

Grant had just clicked on the television when a knock on his front door had him lifting his head in a half attempt to give the visitor his attention. "It's open!" he yelled, dropping his head back down on the armrest of the small love seat he'd landed on when his legs had given out on him earlier.

"Hey," Lane greeted, bringing a ray of the descending sun with him when he walked in, momentarily blinding Grant.

"Hey," Grant mumbled, his eyes closed as he flung his forearm over his face for additional protection.

"What're you doin'?"

"What does it look like I'm doin'?" Grant countered without moving an inch.

"Waitin' for me, from what I can tell."

Sliding his arm down, he peered up at Lane through half-open eyes. He didn't even try to force a smile because he didn't have enough energy to do so.

Lane came to stand at the end of the love seat, his tall, broad frame blocking Grant's view of the television.

"You're probably right," Grant muttered, opening his eyes fully so he could get a good look at the sexy cowboy standing in his living room.

He really was happy to see Lane. At this point, seeing Lane or Gracie was the highlight of every single day, but he was too damn tired — both mentally and physically — to carry on much of a conversation.

"You know what I need?" Lane asked, his smile morphing into a very sexy smirk.

"What's that?" Grant asked, knowing he shouldn't. Whatever Lane was thinking was going to require Grant to get up, and he really wasn't looking forward to doing that.

"A shower."

"Of course you do." Grant's entire body went hard, almost instantly. The memory of the last shower they'd taken together was still fresh in his mind.

"Care to join me?" Lane asked.

Grant knew that Lane had only worded it as a request. Based on the heated look in Lane's eyes, if Grant said no — which he wasn't even capable of doing, no matter how tired he was — Lane would only push until Grant gave in.

He figured he might as well save them both some time.

Returning Lane's grin, Grant dropped his feet to the floor and sat up. "Lead the way."

"My pleasure," Lane said. "Oh, but this time, I want to watch the expression on your face when I take your dick in *my* mouth. You all right with that?"

Was he ever.

And probably just as Lane had planned, Grant was on his feet and practically pushing Lane into the bathroom.

■□■□■□■□

GRACE SIGHED AS SHE DROPPED into the recliner, her ears perking up at the sounds coming from the room next door.

Finally.

Hiding out from her sisters had never been one of Grace's specialties, although she had tried to perfect the skill over the years. Tonight, of all nights, Grace had managed to evade Hope and Faith but not Trinity, which meant she'd only been sidetracked for about an hour while Trin went on and on about the store. Which was about sixty minutes longer than she wanted to spend hearing about product placement, new souvenirs, and whether or not they should add more candy to their already overflowing shelves. Thankfully, that was over.

For now.

She knew she'd have to have a long talk with all of her sisters tomorrow because Hope had scheduled an early meeting. Considering Grace's day generally started before the sun came up, time was of the essence, and she was quickly running out of it tonight. Between Trin's need to bitch and moan about not having enough help at the store, Faith's desperate attempt to ensure all of them understood exactly how much money was coming in versus going out, and the burr that Hope had in her butt, tomorrow was going to be a very, very long day.

Grace's thoughts flitted to the reaction that Ben had had to Hope while they were at dinner last night. The guy had been transfixed on Hope. But more surprising was Hope's reaction to him.

Through the years, Grace and her sisters had dated a handful of men — probably would've been more than just a few, but free time on the ranch was nearly nonexistent. Still, despite their father's brutal reminders that they were off-limits, they had been known to date. But the only one of them who kept her distance from men at any cost was Hope. No one questioned her, but after Hope's answering response to Ben last night, Grace wanted to. She wanted to bombard Hope with questions, to know exactly what was going through her head. As for Ben ... Grace was pretty sure he was a good guy. But he was a guest. Which meant he was temporary.

Not that it was any of her business or anything.

But right now, Grace wasn't worried about her sisters, or even the impending conversations to come. No, she was just interested in finishing her dinner.

Sitting in Grant's recliner, she watched the television, not really paying any attention to what was on the screen.

She might've been fully vested in *Duck Dynasty,* the show that had been on the television when she'd arrived, had she not been preoccupied. Nope, her apologies would have to go to the Robertson family for her lack of interest because the moans and groans coming from the bathroom were enough to distract her from the best show, and in her humble opinion — crazy as it may sound — this one was fairly decent.

Not to mention, the two men currently getting hot and heavy in the shower were igniting a torrent of desire within her without even realizing it.

When she'd arrived a few minutes ago, three to-go containers in hand, she'd wanted to surprise Grant. She hadn't known exactly where Lane was, but based on their conversation a short while ago when she had passed him in the stables, she'd hoped he would make his way over to Grant's before the night was out.

She wasn't disappointed.

Clearly, Grant wasn't, either.

As much as she wanted to interrupt them in the shower by joining them, she had opted to give them a little time together. She knew they needed it. Lane had an uncanny effect on Grant, and knowing Grant's current mood, leaving the two of them alone would only benefit her in the end.

"Gracie? What the…"

Grace glanced up at the doorway to Grant's bathroom and smiled. "Hi."

"What… What are you doin' here?" Grant asked, looking confused and possibly a tad guilty.

"Eating dinner. What are you doin'?" she asked shamelessly, taking a bite of macaroni and cheese while she admired the nearly naked cowboy standing in the doorway in nothing but a towel.

God had taken out all the stops when he'd made Grant. Tall and lean, the man had the perfect amount of muscles — not enough that he was bulky but plenty to show just how much hard work he put in each day — as well as a face that could've graced one of those sexy men's magazines if he'd been inclined to take that route in life. His dark hair was just a little long, mussed from his shower, and the stubble that lined his prominent jaw made him appear that much more rugged. From where she sat, she could see the crinkles at the corners of his magnificent blue eyes, proof that he smiled a lot — something he wasn't doing right then, she noted.

"I was…" Grant turned to look behind him, probably at Lane, if she had to guess, before turning his attention back to her.

"I heard," she said with a grin, doing her best to keep her eyes north of his chest, which was a lot harder than it looked. "I didn't want to interrupt. You sounded like you were enjoying yourself."

About that time, Lane came waltzing out of the bathroom, only he wasn't wearing a towel. Nope, Lane Miller was wearing nothing more than a sexy smile, and he looked mouthwatering as he did it. The man's confidence level was to be admired. Clothes were merely an accessory to one of the finest male bodies she'd ever seen. Similar to Grant, Lane was tall, but he was broader, his muscles a little more honed. He wasn't necessarily bulky, he was just ... big.

"Hey, doll," Lane greeted with a smirk, making his way over to her, his enormous thighs bunching as he moved. "Where's mine?"

Not that she was looking much at his thighs, but her eyes were wandering in that general direction, so she saw them, too.

Lane's deep laugh brought her eyes up toward his face. He was lifting one dark eyebrow at her, grinning mischievously.

"Huh?" she asked, trying to remember what he'd just said.

"Where's mine?" he repeated.

Grace nodded toward the kitchen table, her eyes continuing to rake over Lane's impressive form. "On the table," she said.

"Thanks. I already ate, but I recently worked up one hell of an appetite," he said with a rough chuckle, leaning down and kissing her on the forehead.

Grace returned her gaze to the other cowboy in the room, still standing in the doorway, looking at her as though she'd lost her mind.

"Problems?" she asked, taking another bite, pretending not to be affected by the two very naked men. The skimpy white towel hanging around Grant's narrow waist was doing very little to stifle her imagination.

"I ... uh..."

"It's ok," she told him, knowing exactly what he was thinking. "I would've joined you, but the shower is awfully small."

"Uh…"

Yep, the guy was at a loss for words, and Grace knew it was because he was freaked out that she'd walked in on them. It wasn't like she didn't know they were going to be together if she wasn't there. She didn't mind. Well, actually, she would've preferred to watch, because holy freaking hell, they were hot when they were together, as she had learned the first time she'd stumbled upon them kissing in Grant's kitchen. And ever since, she'd purposely snuck glances at the two of them when they were making out. Even though she was usually there in the middle of it all, she wasn't naïve enough to believe that would always be the case.

And they shouldn't expect that with her, either.

Time was in short supply these days, and, yes, they were all trying to scratch an itch.

Her included.

"What're you watchin'?" Lane asked as he made his way to the other recliner, still as naked as the day he was born. Did the man not know just what he did to her? It was tough enough to keep her hands to herself when he was fully clothed, but like that… Lord, she was in trouble.

Remembering that he'd asked a question, Grace darted her eyes toward the television, hoping to see the end of the *Duck Dynasty* episode, or at least something that she might recognize right then so she'd have an answer for him. It wouldn't do for them to think she'd been sitting there listening to them getting busy in the shower.

That would be too much for their enormous male egos to handle.

"If I were you, I'd grab some food while you can," Lane told Grant, obviously moving past the question that he'd left unanswered.

"Why's that?" Grant asked, standing there looking back and forth between the two of them.

"Have you seen her? You're gonna need your strength to keep up with this cowgirl. And just so you're aware, I ain't waitin' for you."

Grace laughed at Lane's comment. He was watching the television as though it were the most interesting thing in the world, all while chowing down *and* mouthing off to Grant.

That was one of the things she loved about Lane. He was always smiling, always optimistic, and always playful. Sometimes to the point of irritation, but she loved him all the more for it.

Since she'd heard about Grant's pissy attitude, and his need to hide out in Cody's shop, from more than one person that day, she knew that Lane had already worked his magic, apparently in the shower.

With a towel still wrapped firmly around his waist, one hand gripping it tightly, Grant padded across the room to the kitchen table and retrieved the last of the foam boxes of food and a plastic fork. When he returned to the living room, he looked down at her.

Grace merely smiled up at him.

Yes, she knew she was in his chair.

She also knew that if he wanted her to move, he was going to have to make her. She made sure that her smile told him as much.

"Aww, hell," Lane added, "she's in rare form tonight."

Grant laughed; it was a little strained, but as far as Grace was concerned, it counted.

"You can sit with me," she told him sweetly. "But you've gotta drop the towel first."

Grant's ocean-blue eyes flared big and bright, making Grace's girl parts stand up and dance. It went without saying that she longed for these moments when they could spend time together. And no, she didn't even care if they were naked or not — although she would take naked anytime they offered because, Lord have mercy, they were the hottest cowboys in Texas, and what red-blooded woman *wouldn't* want to ogle them every chance she got?

"That right?" Grant's voice was rough and low, causing a gentle hum to start in Grace's core.

"Yes, sir," she teased, scooting over to one side of the chair, leaving hardly enough room for half a person, much less a big man like Grant. But it was worth it just for the expression on his face.

"Damn, man," Lane grumbled. "Don't you know that stalling ain't the right way to treat a lady?"

Grant spared Lane a look but then returned his eyes to her.

"I'll lose the towel if you lose the shirt."

Playful. She liked that.

"Fine," she said unflinchingly, holding her container up for him to take. When he retrieved it from her hands, she deftly unhooked the buttons on her sleeveless blouse and then slid the cotton down her arms, leaving it to pool on the chair behind her. "That better?"

"Lose the bra while you're at it," Lane stated around a mouthful of food.

Grace laughed but did as he suggested. Only because she didn't want the mood to change, and seeing Grant, she knew he was hovering on the edge of that bad mood he'd been in for the last few days. She'd do anything to keep a smile on his face, including an impromptu striptease in the middle of his living room.

Her intentions had actually been good coming over here. In the back of her mind, she had anticipated a little hanky-panky, maybe not to this degree, but she couldn't lie, it was certainly on her agenda. Although, she did intend to talk to him later, but hopefully, if she was lucky, they'd all be in bed at that point, and between her and Lane, they could keep Grant from running away.

Until then...

"Fuck," Lane whispered, and Grace could feel the heat of his gaze on her now-naked breasts. "What the hell. You might as well make it an even playing field," Lane added. "Take it all off."

With her eyes still locked with Grant's, Grace did as Lane suggested. She stood, toed off her boots, and then peeled her jeans and panties down her legs, stepping one foot out of them. Before she could get them completely off her ankles, Grant hurled himself into the chair, both containers of food still in his hand and a grin the size of Texas on his face.

"Now you can sit on my lap," Grant informed her.

Grace reached for her food as though it was normal for her to be naked in the living room with two smoldering-hot cowboys. Pretending that it didn't affect her half as much as it really did, she situated herself on Grant's lap, purposely shifting so that his semi-hard cock was nestled at the juncture of her thighs.

"That better?" she asked audaciously, looking over her shoulder at him.

Grant's response was nothing more than a grunt, which made her laugh.

For the next few minutes, Grace did her best to eat. The only reason she managed was because she was starving, and she knew if she was going to keep up with these two, she needed all the nourishment she could get.

CHAPTER NINE

MERCY MADE HER WAY INTO the dining room after managing to circumvent Hope to the best of her abilities. It wasn't easy, mind you. When Hope wanted to talk about something, that woman was as aggressive as Budweiser with a bone.

Too bad Mercy wasn't in the mood to chat.

At least not with Hope. Or rather, at least not about work.

As for anyone else, more power to them. If they were brave enough...

"Hey, Merce, how's it goin'?" Jennifer Brathow called as Mercy stepped into the short line at the table piled high with food. As late as it was, she was just surprised there was still food left at all.

"It's goin', Jenn," Mercy answered, pasting on a glowing smile.

Jennifer was one of the newest members of the staff at Dead Heat Ranch, and the woman seemed to be coming into her own just in the few short months that she'd been with them. In fact, hiring Jennifer, and her ensuing employment, had been one of the hottest topics of conversation for as long as Mercy could remember.

It had nothing to do with how pretty Jenn was, or how smoking-hot her body was, or how well she filled out a pair of jeans, either — which was usually the conversation hot point where the wranglers were concerned. Not to mention, no one seemed to care that the woman was oddly young for the position she filled after Grace had fired their last cook for being lazy, but at twenty-four years old, the woman clearly knew what she was doing.

Nope, aside from being pretty, with her short auburn hair, sparkling ice-green eyes, and a complexion that would make even the most flawless cover model envious, Jennifer had an advantage over the last pretty girl who'd been hired at the ranch because Jenn knew how to cook. And as Mercy had learned, the fastest way to a wrangler's heart was definitely through his stomach.

She had no idea how Jennifer did it, but the woman even managed to get the staff to eat healthier, without them knowing it. According to Dead Heat Ranch's new head chef, the garden she was cultivating in a newly sectioned-off area near the main house was going to make coming up with meals considerably easier as well. And cheaper, something Faith loved about the woman.

And yes, Mercy had informed Jennifer from the beginning that she had to make her efforts as transparent as possible because the men loved their southern food more than they loved their wives and girlfriends. Okay, maybe not entirely, but damn close.

Jennifer had been a good sport about it all, taking every suggestion Mercy offered in stride, and now she fit in as though she'd been part of the family all of her life.

Since part of Mercy's job was to ensure that the kitchen ran flawlessly, she'd been spending quite a bit of time with Jennifer and the few wranglers that Jenn had claimed as her permanent kitchen help. No longer was the kitchen a place people rotated in and out of, and surprisingly no one seemed to have a problem with that.

Oh, and everyone — a lot of stress on *every* and *one* — was enthralled with the red-headed, green-eyed little boy who was part of a package deal where Jennifer, single mother of one, was concerned. Joey Brathow, the four-year-old ray of sunshine that had descended on Dead Heat Ranch when they had hired his mother, kept everyone on their toes.

"How's your little one?" Mercy asked as she grabbed a cornbread muffin and one of the small foil squares containing butter. Every time she saw one of those things, she thought about the story her father told about how Mercy had munched on them when she was little. Usually without bread.

Yuck.

Thank God she'd grown up, at least when it came to her preferences in food. As for everything else, well, she was doing her best not to grow up at all. Or so she was told.

"He's better, thanks. I took him to the doctor, and just like Zach thought, it's just a cold, but boy, he scared me there for a coupla days. Thank you so much for helpin' out and watchin' him."

Yes, Zachary McCallum, their resident medic and overall jack-of-all-trades, had become quite fascinated by the single mom ever since she'd arrived. Not that Zach would admit to it being anything other than business as usual. But Mercy wasn't blind; she saw the way the handsome cowboy looked at Jennifer.

Mercy nodded. "No problem. Glad I could help." Lowering her voice for effect, she tacked on, "Just don't let that get around. People 'round here'll start thinkin' I'm nice or somethin'. You'll ruin my rep."

Jennifer giggled, passing a dish of apple cobbler toward Mercy, which she snatched gratefully.

"Your secret's safe with me," Jennifer said with a cheery smile. "Hey, I heard a rumor today."

"Which one did you hear this time?" There were plenty of rumors running around the ranch. Some of them Mercy had started herself, and she wasn't ashamed to admit it.

"I heard that you're gonna race your dad this Sunday."

"Not a rumor," Mercy replied. Although she didn't add the other little secret she was keeping up her sleeve.

Jennifer laughed, a hearty sound that had several people looking their way.

"I heard they're takin' bets on who's gonna win."

"If you're smart, you'll bet on Grace," Mercy mumbled under her breath as she walked away. With a smile, Mercy tacked on, "Talk to you later," loud enough for Jenn to hear.

Grabbing her food, Mercy headed toward one of the tables in the back. She noticed Trinity sitting alone, and since she was never one to let an opportunity to harass one of her sisters pass her by, she changed her trajectory.

"Oh, heavens, what are you up to?" Trin asked as Mercy approached, smiling back at her.

"You know me. Trouble is always on my agenda."

"Do you know how true that is, Merce?"

Mercy laughed. Yes, yes, she did. That was her purpose in life, stirring up trouble and keeping people on their toes.

"Mind if I join you?" she asked before taking a seat, not bothering to wait for Trinity to answer.

That earned her a resounding laugh from her sister.

And, yes, Trin was one of those women who drew men's attention with her throaty chuckle, too. Something Mercy had never perfected. Nor did she have the desire to, thank you very much.

Although Mercy and her four sisters had the same basic features overall, blond hair, turquoise eyes, and petite frames — thin thanks to the grueling work they did on a daily basis — Trinity was by far the prettiest of them all. And that was saying something because Mercy thought all of her sisters were beautiful, even if she liked to tease them ruthlessly otherwise. With Trin's heart-shaped face, pouty lips, and an overall sweet innocence that was, unfortunately, not faked, the woman made men practically melt at her feet with just a smile. Yep, Mercy had seen plenty of them fall, and she loved giving Trin a hard time about it, too.

"You seen Hope?" Trinity asked in a mock whisper.

"Nope. And that was how I planned it, too. You?"

"No. I hid out in the stable with Dixie and the pups until I heard she went home."

"Do you know what she wants?" Mercy asked, curious as to why her oldest sister was stirring up a hornet's nest at the ranch, hunting down people as though the world were going to end tomorrow.

"Somethin' about Dad's birthday," Trinity answered.

"Shit."

"Exactly. She's plannin' a big ol' party, two weeks from now. Everyone's supposed to pitch in to help."

"On top of that, we're probably supposed to keep it a secret from him, too, huh?"

"Yep. It's never easy."

That was the damn truth. Their father wasn't the easiest man to pull one over on. Mercy would know because she'd spent the better part of the last twenty-six years of her life trying to do just that.

"Speak of the devil," Trinity said with a smile in her voice.

Mercy looked up in time to see their father making his way through the scattered tables. He'd apparently set his radar and managed to seek at least the two of them out. She had no idea where Faith or Hope was, but she considered them fortunate. As for Gracie, Mercy happened to know that her sister was probably getting flanked by two hot cowboys. Lucky girl.

Forking food into her mouth to keep from having to talk, Mercy pretended not to notice when their father stepped up to the table. Not that ignoring a six-foot-two, barrel-chested man like her father was all that easy. As was his usual greeting, he flipped the end of her ponytail and then tugged gently. "Avoidin' me, girlie?" Jerry asked with a rumbling laugh.

"Always, Pop. You know me," Mercy answered honestly, although she inserted a hint of sarcasm just to throw him off. Still chewing her food, she peeked up at him. "I figured you'd be takin' a refresher course on how to ride a horse."

Her father smiled down at her, and Mercy couldn't look away. Something was different about her father lately, and because it had been a change she'd noticed for weeks now, she was pretty sure it didn't have a lot to do with the race that they had planned for Sunday. Whatever it was, it looked good on him.

"Be careful, girlie. I wouldn't want you to be too embarrassed when I make you cry."

"Not a chance, old man," Mercy replied, laughing.

"What's for dinner?" he asked, reaching down to steal her cornbread off her plate. Mercy managed to snag it before he could.

"Gotta be faster than that, old man," Mercy teased.

"Hey, kiddo," Jerry said to Trinity, leaning over and kissing her on the forehead. "How're you?"

"Not too bad," Trinity stated gravely. "I managed to steer clear of Hope, avoid Faith when she wanted to talk numbers, and shut down the store without any help from anyone else."

Crap. Mercy knew a complaint when she heard one.

Dead Heat Ranch was a working dude ranch. It was also filled to capacity with tourists these days, and because of this, they had their own little general store. At any given time of any given day, the place was usually swarming with people interested in stocking up on food for their visit to the ranch or sifting through the numerous trinkets they sold as souvenirs. For the last few years, Trinity had appointed herself the keeper of the store. Only recently had they had a difficult time retaining extra help, mainly because the summer months were hell on the employees. Working on a ranch wasn't a job for sissies, but Mercy would be the first to admit that half the time they hired kids who only thought they knew what work was.

"What happened to that last girl we hired?" Jerry asked, dropping into a chair between them. He was eyeing Mercy's food longingly.

"Don't even think about it, Pops," she muttered as she shielded her plate from his penetrating gaze.

"That kid didn't last two hours," Trinity explained. "I'm pretty sure she applied for a job to be close to her boyfriend. When she realized she'd actually have to work for a livin', she bolted outta there."

"I'll see what I can do about gettin' someone to help you," Jerry told her.

"I know someone," Mercy suggested, grinning as she stared down at her food, her devious side coming out in spades.

"Don't you dare," Trinity threatened before Mercy said a word, but that only spurred Mercy on. She loved to get her sisters riled up. It was the highlight of her day.

"Who?" Jerry asked curiously, his gaze traveling back and forth between Mercy and Trinity.

"Dallas," Mercy answered, not bothering to look at her sister. She could pretty much hear the steam coming out of Trinity's ears.

"Dallas Caldwell?" Jerry asked incredulously, his gaze flipping back and forth between them.

"No!" Trinity exclaimed at the same time Mercy said, "Yep."

With a shit-eating grin, Mercy continued, "Things are a little slow with the cattle. They can't be moved yet, and he's been fillin' in wherever he's needed. I think he'd be perfect to help Trin out. After all, he was the one who led the crew when they renovated the place last month."

Not to mention, Dallas Caldwell had a serious hard-on for Trinity. Ever since Dallas had damn near killed that bastard Garrett Daniels because he'd hurt Trinity, Mercy had been rooting for him and Trin. Strange how all of that had gone down, but ever since then, Jerry had been rather fond of Dallas, as well.

However, Trin did her best impersonation of a woman who wasn't interested, which Mercy knew was just an act. So, getting Trinity and Dallas in the same room always made for some incredible fireworks, and the last thing Mercy wanted was for things to start getting stale around the ranch.

Mercy added a mental checkmark to her good-deed list — get Trin and Dallas together. Another point in her favor.

"I'll talk to him," Jerry said, seemingly ignorant to Trinity's fiery expression. Pushing back from the table, Jerry rose to his feet. "In the meantime, I'm gonna head over and talk to Grant."

Mercy nearly knocked her chair over as she jumped to her feet. "Why?"

Shit.

That didn't look suspicious at all.

Mercy tried to calm down as she stared at her father. The last thing Gracie needed tonight was for their father to show up on Grant's doorstep. Mercy had happened to see both Lane and Gracie heading over to Grant's house — separately, of course — which could only mean one thing…

"I just wanted to check on him. He mentioned he had to go over and talk to his father earlier in the week. I haven't been able to catch up with him yet."

That was because the crazy fool was hiding. Mercy didn't say that aloud, though.

"He's cool," Mercy said quickly. "I talked to him a little while ago. He was packing it in for the night. Said he had a headache or somethin'."

Jerry studied her, and Mercy was pretty sure he didn't believe a word she said, but she didn't care. "Besides, I wanted to talk to you."

"About?"

Mercy glared down at Trinity, who was the one smiling now. Mercy doubted her sister knew what was going on with the peculiar threesome taking place at Grant's place, but it was quite clear that Mercy was in the hot seat now, and any time that happened, her sisters got a kick out of it.

Gracie would pay for this. There was no doubt about it.

Leaving her half-empty plate on the table, Mercy linked her arm with her father's and led him toward the door but not before looking back to see that Trinity had stolen her cornbread muffin.

Okay, so she added payback for Trinity to her list of things to do tomorrow.

But right now, she needed to forget about Trinity altogether. She needed to think on the fly. Mercy didn't have a clue what she could possibly have to talk to her father about, but she'd wing it for now.

And later, she'd make sure Gracie knew that she'd saved her ass.

Chapter Ten

GRANT WASN'T SURE WHAT HAD just happened, but he knew he didn't want it to end. One minute he'd been in the shower with Lane, the next he was sitting in his chair eating dinner with a very naked Gracie on his lap.

And through it all, his mind had never once traveled to the ongoing fight he was having with his father.

"Nuh-uh," Lane grumbled. "No thinkin' right now."

Grant tore his gaze off Gracie's amazing rack to look at Lane. It wasn't easy, that was for damn sure.

"We're takin' the night off from that shit. Unless you're thinkin' about how smokin'-hot Gracie looks sittin' there naked. Got that?"

"Personally, I'm thinkin' about how hot *y'all* look naked," Gracie teased.

It was clear that Lane was there with a purpose. From the instant he'd stepped through Grant's front door, it was evident that Lane was using the power of distraction to keep Grant from getting too far inside of his own head. It was obviously working because Grant had a hard time focusing, much less thinking, especially when his dick had been buried in Lane's luscious mouth just a few short minutes ago. Damn, he wanted that man. He ached for him, even now, just half an hour later.

Of course, there was Gracie sitting on his lap, her pert breasts so close to his face he could see the light blue veins running beneath the smooth, creamy skin. He wanted to put his mouth there, to latch on and never let go.

But he didn't.

Somehow, he'd succeeded in being a gentleman through dinner. As much as he could be, considering he was sitting in his living room naked while Gracie shifted and shuffled on his lap. His dick hadn't been much for minding its manners, but Grant had tried to disregard the incessant throb between his legs. But now that they were finished eating, he wasn't trying all that hard to ignore it.

"Come here, gorgeous," Lane called to Gracie after he took all three of their empty containers to the recycle bin located in the kitchen.

Lane took her hand and tugged her to her feet before he lowered himself back to the chair, pulling her along with him. Grant was entranced by the sight — Gracie's smooth, sun-kissed skin against Lane's bronzed skin... Lane was looking at Gracie as though the woman were responsible for the stars and the resulting constellations, as if he'd never seen such an incredible specimen before.

Abigail Grace Lambert was perfection in its finest form, as far as Grant was concerned. He'd always thought so, even back when his feelings for her had been pure, long before she was old enough for him to have salacious thoughts about in the first place.

Hell, he could still remember that day like it was yesterday.

"Gracie, come here," Jerry called out to the young woman currently shoveling hay in the empty stall.

Grant watched as she approached, noticing that she was more of a young girl than a woman. Her innocent eyes widened when she looked up at him, but other than that, she kept her expression masked.

"Yes?" she questioned as she approached them slowly, leaning the pitchfork against the stall wall.

"Gracie, I'd like you to meet Grant Kingsley. He's gonna be workin' here."

Gracie nodded her head, but Grant had no idea what she was thinking.

"You ever worked at a ranch before?" she asked a second or two later, surprising Grant with her question.

"No, ma'am," he answered truthfully.

"Well, then, good luck," she said with a playful smile. "'Cause you're gonna need it."

And with that, she went back to work while Grant followed her father out of the stable.

Grant had known her since she was fifteen years old, and through the years, what he felt for her had morphed from a basic friendship — riddled with her playful teasing — to an intrinsic need. He'd go so far as to admit to himself that he loved her, but he still feared speaking the words aloud. He had accidentally let it slip that first night they were together, but when Gracie hadn't reciprocated, he'd refused to voice them loudly enough for her to hear.

As Grant watched, Lane cupped Gracie's full breasts in his big hands, kneading the firm mounds while tweaking her nipples between his fingers. Her breasts were overly sensitive, or so she'd told them. So much so that she could orgasm just by them playing with them. That was a fact, one that Grant had thoroughly enjoyed proving when they had put that theory to the test — and succeeded — on more than one occasion.

"Put your mouth on me," Gracie encouraged Lane, knocking Lane's hands away and hefting her breasts in her hands.

Grant's dick felt like a steel rod between his legs. Watching the two of them was the best form of foreplay that he'd ever known. Almost as good as having Gracie's mouth on his dick or Lane's fingers teasing his ass.

Lane sucked Gracie's nipple between his lips, careful not to take too much of her. She apparently knew what he was up to because she released her breasts and wrapped her arms around Lane's head, pulling him closer, smashing his face against her chest.

"Don't tease me, Miller," Gracie said, her seductive voice and the thundering rumble of Lane's laugh sending chills along Grant's skin.

Lane sucked her breast into his mouth more aggressively, making sensual sounds as he did, and that didn't help Grant's current state at all. He was tempted to grip his own cock and stroke, anxious to join in but too fixated on watching to do either.

"Yes, just like that," Gracie rasped, still holding Lane's head. "Suck them."

Lane alternated between breasts, sucking each into his mouth, his gaze darting over to Grant every now and again until finally he pulled back and pinned Grant with his chocolate-brown eyes.

"Stroke yourself," Lane ordered, his full attention focused on Grant.

As though his hand had a mind of its own, Grant wrapped his fingers around his cock, slowly stroking the hard length, cupping his balls with each downstroke.

"God, that's hot," Gracie mumbled. "I wish I could've watched the two of you in the shower."

Grant still couldn't believe they'd walked out of his bathroom to find Gracie sitting in the living room. At first, he'd nearly panicked, fearful that she was going to be pissed that they'd stolen some time alone. But she'd actually seemed rather okay with it, which was both surprising and a tremendous relief.

"You like to watch us, love?" Lane asked Gracie.

"Damn straight."

"Well, all you have to do is ask. Anytime you want."

Grant smiled, his hand stilling on his cock. He didn't want to push himself too far, completely content watching the show just a few feet away from him.

"Right now, I want to be the one watching," Grant told them, drawing their attention back to him.

"Tell us what to do," Lane commanded, that sexy demand making Grant's balls throb. It was interesting how alpha the man was, even when he was giving the illusion that he was handing over control.

It drove Grant mad when Lane took control. For all of his life, Grant had been in charge, running his own life, making his own decisions. Even here at the ranch, he was the one people came to when decisions needed to be made. So for Lane to take the reins... It was a powerful feeling that Grant found he craved.

"I want to watch you eat her pussy," Grant told them.

Gracie's face lit up as though Christmas had come early for her.

"Put her on the bar," Grant ordered, falling into his role as the scene's director. He could do this, even though his dick would prefer he was in on the action versus watching from the sidelines.

Lane stood, keeping his arms around Gracie, lifting her easily. She wrapped her legs around his waist, and Grant got an up-close look at the vibrant butterfly tattoo on her right hip. He knew that all five of the sisters had one somewhere on their bodies because Gracie had told him and Lane back when they'd first uncovered the cute little tattoo. Apparently, the colorful designs were a tribute to their mother.

When Lane deposited Gracie on the laminate countertop, she didn't waste time, maneuvering into position so that she was lying on her back, her heels on the edge of the counter and her legs spread wide.

"Lord have mercy," Lane growled as he slipped his finger through her glistening slit.

Since the party had moved out of his visual range, Grant opted to join them. He vacated his trusty recliner and hefted himself up onto the counter beside Gracie, trailing his finger from her neck down her sternum, over her flat, muscled stomach until he reached the bare skin of her mound. He went so far as to tease her clit briefly while Lane pumped one thick finger inside her. That's where Grant stopped. He wasn't planning to join in, but the urge to touch her was just too great.

"What are you waitin' for, cowboy?" Gracie taunted. Her snarky words died on a breathless moan when Lane thrust two fingers between her folds, sliding into her pussy.

"Hold yourself open for him," Grant instructed. "I want to be able to see everything."

Gracie's eyes were hooded, and there was a pretty pink tinge to her cheeks, but she didn't challenge him. He could tell she was trying to hide her embarrassment. Not that she had anything to be embarrassed about. The woman was flawless: from her silky blond hair and those incredible blue-green eyes all the way down to her cute little perfectly manicured toes tipped with a brilliant red polish. God had spared nothing when creating her.

And as he sat there, completely in awe of her, he couldn't help but remind himself that she was his.

Well, *theirs*, technically.

But as long as he was part of it, he didn't much care.

■□■□■□■□

LANE CONSIDERED HIMSELF ONE SERIOUSLY lucky son of a bitch.

What more could he ask for than to have these two at his mercy. First, Grant in the shower, and now Gracie laid out like a smorgasbord on Grant's kitchen counter.

Shit. He was pretty sure it didn't get any better than this.

And the best part of it all, not a single person had brought up Grant's bad mood.

Not that Lane was giving them an opportunity. What better way to distract than by using sex? Now that he thought about it, there wasn't a better way, actually.

As he leaned over Gracie, watching her face contort into various expressions of pleasure, Lane continued to fuck her with two fingers, savoring the erotic moans she made as she writhed in front of him. When she pinned him with those intense turquoise eyes, he smiled back. That earned him a grin in return, but he knew what Gracie would've said if he hadn't pressed his fingers deep, twisting just enough to…

"Oh, fuck!" Gracie screamed, her head tilting back as her body bowed tight. "I'm coming!"

Yep, that was the plan.

Not that Lane was at all done with her. That was just the beginning.

While she tried to catch her breath, Lane slipped his fingers from inside her, gliding them through her slick folds before leaning forward and pressing the digits to Grant's lips.

"Taste her," Lane commanded, his eyes locked with Grant's.

Grant slid his tongue over the tips of Lane's fingers, his eyes closing as he sucked them into his mouth. The motion reminded Lane of when he'd been on his knees in the shower, Grant's dick pumping in and out of his mouth.

He groaned, unable to help himself.

Not wanting to leave Gracie waiting, Lane reclaimed his fingers from Grant's mouth and returned his focus between her legs, leaning down and pressing his lips to her clit. Before she could even think about getting away from him, Lane pinned her thighs down and tormented her with firm strokes of his tongue. It wasn't long before her fingers were digging into his scalp and she was trying to thrust her hips forward against his eager mouth.

"You're so damn sexy, Gracie," Grant said on a throaty groan.

Lane saw Grant lean over, one big hand cupping Gracie's gorgeous tit as he groped her slowly, making her whimper. Rather than risk her falling off the counter with her thrashing, Lane drew back, pulling her hips until her ass was barely hanging on the edge of the counter. Grant, ever the perceptive one, knew what Lane had in mind because he was helping Gracie to sit up as Lane was pulling her back into his arms.

"Where're we goin'?" Gracie asked, resting her forehead against Lane's, her legs wrapped around his waist, his aching dick crushed between their bodies.

"Bedroom," Lane replied gruffly. He was hanging on by a thread, ready and eager to bury himself inside this woman.

"Good plan," she answered.

"I thought you'd like that."

When Lane made it to Grant's bedroom, he closed the gap between the door and the bed in less than three steps and then tossed Gracie back onto the mattress, making her giggle.

Grant wasn't far behind, but before Grant could get on the bed with Gracie, Lane turned, pulling the man flush against him. With blinding speed, he cupped the back of Grant's head and drew him close, crushing their mouths together as he slid his tongue past the seam of Grant's lips.

A deep groan escaped — from whom, Lane wasn't sure — but the sound charged the air in the room, making him all the more desperate to get on with it. Reluctantly, he pulled back from Grant, using his thumb to brush along Grant's bottom lip as he watched him. "I'm not sure I'll ever get enough of you," he whispered.

Grant's eyes flared, sending a torrent of heat coursing through Lane. He loved catching the man off guard, as he had just then.

"Uh, hello? Remember me? Cowgirl waiting here."

Lane chuckled at Gracie's outburst as he turned to face her.

"Trust me, love, no one could *ever* forget about you."

Lane crawled onto the bed, situating himself between Gracie's thighs as he stared down at her.

Before he could lean in for a kiss, she was holding out two condoms.

"What? Do you keep these on you at all times?" Lane laughed as he retrieved them from her and pushed back so that he was kneeling.

"Just being proactive."

Grant joined them on the bed, but he didn't reach for one of the condoms. Instead, he hauled Gracie to him, rolling them over until Grant was on his back and Gracie was lying atop him, their mouths uniting instantly.

Grant's hand slipped into Gracie's hair, tugging at the ponytail holder until he managed to free the long strands from the confining elastic. With a quick toss, he got rid of the holder, never breaking the kiss. Lane was content to watch while he donned the condom, enjoying the sight of his two lovers making out on the bed.

This was, without a doubt, the hottest relationship he'd ever been in. No matter what time of day it was, or if they'd just been together moments before, as was the case tonight, it was as though they couldn't get enough of one another. And the proof was in the steel-hard erection he was now rubbing as he continued to admire Grant and Gracie.

"What're you waitin' for?" Gracie called over her shoulder as she peeked back at him.

Before Lane could answer, he made eye contact with Grant and, without a word being spoken, he knew what the other man was suggesting with a mere look.

Ho-o-o-oly fuck.

Glancing down at the second condom in his hand, Lane got to work, ripping the foil open before kneeling on the bed between Grant's and Gracie's legs. As his body temperature skyrocketed, he rolled the condom over Grant's thick erection, not bothering to tease him in the process. There wasn't time for that. Lane wasn't sure he'd last if he were to drag this out any longer.

Just the thought of sliding into Gracie's hot, tight…

"What are you doing?" Gracie asked, her voice a meager whisper when Grant reached between them and aligned his cock with Gracie's entrance.

"Burying myself in your sweet pussy," Grant answered simply.

Gracie moaned as Lane watched Grant penetrate her, the head of Grant's cock disappearing inside her.

"Fuck, that's hot," Lane said, surprised that the words had actually slipped out. He'd been thinking them but hadn't actually meant to say them aloud. That's what these two did to him, they made him lose track of what he was supposed to be doing.

"Lean on me," Grant instructed Gracie, pulling her toward him until they were flush against one another. "Oh, hell, that feels good."

Lane could imagine Gracie's inner muscles locking around Grant's dick, tightening, squeezing.

Oh, yeah.

"We want to take you at the same time," Grant said, his mouth hovering alongside Gracie's ear, his eyes locked with Lane's.

Lane's eyes darted to Gracie, trying to catch her reaction, waiting to see if she'd panic. They hadn't done this before. No double penetration for them yet. And holy hell, he wasn't sure they were going to get through this round, either, before his head fucking exploded off his body.

Gracie's head rotated to the side, Lane's eyes meeting her sidelong glance as she peered back at him over her shoulder. He could see the concern in her beautiful eyes, but that was masked by the heat he could feel radiating from her.

"I'm game," she said, clearly her verbal permission for Lane to proceed.

And that was exactly what he needed.

"But you have to promise to be easy," she tacked on, her voice not as steady as he would've liked.

"Always, baby," he said reassuringly, leaning forward so that he could brush her mouth with his lips. "We'd never do anything to hurt you."

Lane was pretty damn positive he was going to bite his tongue clean off because a few moments later, after fingering Gracie's asshole with one finger, then two, his dick was aching with a desperation that surprised him. After gently prepping Gracie to take him, Lane lubed his cock and aligned with Gracie's tiny puckered hole, doing his damnedest to restrain himself from lodging deep in her ass the way he usually did with Grant's.

But he couldn't. And he didn't.

The amount of effort required to hold back should've earned him a prize, but a short time later, Lane was sweating and panting as Gracie's tight ass gripped him.

But he wasn't the only one breathing hard.

Gracie was tense, her muscles locked as she rested between them.

"Relax, baby," Lane muttered as he leaned forward, the head of his dick sliding past the tight ring of muscles in her ass. Lane slid his hand over her warm thigh, caressing her gently. Her skin was so soft, so smooth. Leaning forward, he pressed his lips to the back of her neck, inhaling the sweet scent of her hair. She smelled like lavender and vanilla.

"Easier said than done," she said through clenched teeth.

Grant's hand came up and slid into Gracie's hair again as the man pulled her to him, the deafening silence replaced by the sound of mouths mating, tongues dueling. Lane remained motionless, his thigh muscles burning from the effort until Gracie began rocking on Grant's cock, effectively taking Lane deeper.

"Oh, fuck," Lane growled softly, gripping Gracie's hip with one hand. "So fucking tight."

Time passed slowly as Lane tried not to move, holding his breath until he felt Gracie's body loosen, allowing her to impale herself on his dick.

"I need more," Gracie pleaded, beginning to rock in earnest before Lane got his ass in gear.

Grant didn't help Lane's precarious state when he began thrusting up from beneath her. It was then that Lane feared he was going to lose it before he ever really got started; the pressure of Grant's dick sliding against his own inside Gracie made Lane's head spin.

Rather than be the one left behind, Lane slowly withdrew from Gracie's ass, sliding back in slowly. He continued the painstaking pace, forcing them to slow down while he did.

"Oh, God, fuck me. Both of you!" Gracie screamed, her fingers digging into the comforter as she pressed against Grant's chest. "Fuck me hard!"

Lane was hesitant, but that only lasted a few seconds before he was sliding out and back in, picking up his pace, feeling the iron-hard length of Grant's erection against his dick, deep inside Gracie. The thought of them both filling her at the same time was nearly enough to send him spiraling out of control.

"Oh, yes," Grant groaned. "Your pussy's so fucking tight, darlin'. I can feel Lane. Feel his cock gliding against mine. So good."

Lane ignored Grant's rambling as he focused on bringing them all to the edge, fucking Gracie's ass now with deep, hard thrusts, rocking her on Grant's dick. He didn't stop as sweat beaded on his forehead, his breaths soughing in and out of his lungs as though he'd just finished a strenuous workout.

"Don't stop, Lane. Please don't stop. Fuck me harder. Harder. Oh, God. I'm gonna come," Gracie cried out.

And just as he expected, Gracie's ass gripped him impossibly tight, milking his release from him without warning. As the pleasure accosted him, Lane only hoped that Grant was going to follow because Lane was at the point that Gracie was controlling his reaction, sending him barreling over the edge.

"Fuck yes!" Grant yelled.

Well, that answered that question. Grant came with a heavy groan, his legs stiffening as he rammed up into Gracie one final time.

Good thing, too, because Lane didn't have the strength to do anything more than come.

CHAPTER ELEVEN

GRACE WASN'T QUITE SURE HOW she felt about what had just happened. Her body was battered from the brutal intrusions but in the most delicious way. Quite possibly, she had never come that hard in her entire life. As a tiny tremor ran through her body at the memories, Grace closed her eyes briefly.

Double penetration? It wasn't something she had ever considered doing, yet in the heat of the moment, she'd wanted to be as close to Grant and Lane as she possibly could, and, well … part of her was on the fence about whether or not she enjoyed it; the other part was begging her to try again, because, well, hell, she was still reeling from the incredible feeling of having both men filling her.

Then again, just being with both of them, there wasn't anything better than that.

"Are you okay?" Lane asked softly, pulling Grace closer to his warm body, nuzzling his face into her neck, the stubble on his jaw abrading her skin in the most sensual of ways.

Grace thought about Lane's question, trying to figure out the best way to answer. Then it came to her. "Yeah, I'm … perfect," she whispered honestly. "That was… That was amazing." Placing her arm over his where he was holding her against him, Grace snuggled into his warmth, relishing the time they had together. She wished this was a more frequent thing, wished she could spend every single night with them.

Lane chuckled gruffly, the sound reverberating against her ear.

"What about Grant?" Grace asked. "Do you think he's all right?"

"If you're referring to the sex, I think he's fantastic," Lane offered.

Grace nudged him with her elbow. "You know that's not what I'm talking about."

There was no doubt in her mind that Grant had enjoyed what had just happened. But she was referring to his mood.

"I think he's still having issues with his dad," Lane said. "He needs to talk about it."

"Did he say that?" Grace couldn't see Grant as the type of guy to admit when he had something on his mind, let alone mention that he wanted to chat.

"Are you kidding? Grant? Open up? Not in this lifetime."

As though they'd summoned him with their muffled conversation, Grant wandered back into the bedroom, still gloriously naked, his hair wet from the quick shower he'd taken.

"My turn," Lane muttered, releasing Grace from the safety of his arms.

Grace looked up at Grant, who seemed to be studying the two of them. She couldn't even begin to place the expression on his face. He looked a little out of sorts.

She offered him a smile and patted the bed, signaling for him to join her.

Thankfully, he didn't hesitate before crawling into the big bed that was crammed into the small room. He wrenched the blankets up over them both as he nudged her onto her opposite side, snuggling up against her back, holding her close. Grace repositioned herself so that her head was resting on his bicep, sliding her foot between his legs behind her.

"Want to talk about it?" Grace asked softly, enjoying the feel of Grant's body heat against her back, the warmth of his breath against her ear.

"Talk about *what?*" Grant responded quietly, just as she'd known he would.

"Don't play dumb with me, cowboy. I know something happened with your dad this week."

Grant sighed deeply, but he didn't respond.

The creak and thump of the pipes from the shower turning on were the only sounds filtering through the dark bedroom, aside from Grant's even breathing.

"I went to see my dad on Monday," Grant finally said, making Grace's heart leap with joy. Not because he'd gone to see his father but because he was opening up to her.

She knew that his father was the reason Grant had been avoiding everyone for the last couple of days. Try as she might, Grace hadn't been able to spend enough time with Grant to dig into the details until tonight. However, from what she'd heard, she knew that Grant's brief escape from the ranch hadn't gone well. There weren't many occasions when he took time off to do personal things, so when she had heard that he'd skipped out for a couple of hours, she'd known it had to be important.

"Everything okay with him?" she asked, encouraging him to keep talking.

The shower water turned off, and Grant glanced over at the door before he said, "Nothing is ever okay with him."

"Talk to me," she murmured, sliding her hand over his, linking their fingers together.

"I don't want to talk about it," Grant said brusquely, his tone letting her know he was incredibly frustrated with the subject.

"I get that. But you see," she told him as she squeezed his hand, "that's part of the whole relationship thing. It ain't just about sex."

"What about sex?" Lane asked as he made his way back into the room and around to the opposite side of the bed from where Grant was lying, the side Grace was facing.

"We weren't talkin' about sex," Grant proclaimed with a rough chuckle.

"What were you talkin' about then? Gracie mentioned sex. Why can't we talk about sex?" Lane asked humorously as he eased into the bed, this time on his back, his big, warm hand landing on Grace's hip.

"My dad," Grant admitted, surprising Grace.

Rather than push him to keep going right away, Grace settled against him, giving his hand another gentle squeeze.

She loved the differences between Grant and Lane. Although the two men were roughly the same height, that was about the only similarity between the two. Unless you counted their scruffy, dark hair and the deep, rich sound of their voices. But even that was different. Grant's voice was rough, like he'd been a smoker for most of his life although she knew that wasn't the case. And Lane... His voice was smooth. Just like the words he spoke.

"What did your father want?" Lane asked, breaking the silence as he slid his other hand beneath his head, peering over at them.

"Money," Grant admitted.

"For?" Lane's encouragement was welcome because Grace wanted Grant to continue, but she didn't want to pry the details out of him.

Although she would if she had to.

"I think he's gambling again," Grant whispered softly, his arms tightening around Grace.

She snuggled closer to Grant, and Lane followed suit, turning onto his side to face them, his arm snaking over her hip, his hand resting on Grant's leg.

"Actually, I *know* he's gambling again. I prayed that he wouldn't go there, but it looks like he has. He told me he was laid off from the auto parts store he's been workin' at for the last eight or so years. I took that to mean he was fired, even before he admitted it. The town's too small for them to have laid him off for no reason. My dad was one of only two employees there.

"Anyway. He asked me to stop by, so I did. When I got there, the house was a mess, the TVs had all been hocked, and my dad was sitting at the kitchen table placing bets."

"What does he bet on?" Grace asked, knowing that it wasn't exactly the point of the story, but she was curious.

"Horses."

Crap.

That wasn't good.

It probably didn't help that right now the ranch was all excited about the upcoming race between Mercy and Jerry. The wranglers were even placing bets.

"If it weren't for the fact that the trailer they live in is paid for, I'd bet my father would be looking for a place to live on top of it all. I'm sure the water and electricity will probably be cut off soon."

"What about your mom?" Lane asked when Grant was quiet for a second. "What does she have to say about it?"

"No idea. She wasn't there. My dad said she left."

"Like, for good?" Grace asked, her concern steadily growing as the story went on.

"Don't know. Dad didn't seem all that concerned. He was more interested in asking me for money. I've tried to call her several times, but she's not answering."

"I take it he wasn't asking for money so he could pay the utility bills," Lane added.

"Not a chance. I'm sure he's got some grand scheme to make millions on the horse races."

"Is there anything we can do? I mean, you know, to help him?" Grace asked.

"I don't think there's anything *anyone* can do. Not until he wants to get help," Grant said, sounding defeated.

At that point, no one spoke for several minutes.

"I really need to go," Grace finally said as her eyes grew heavy, not wanting to move from the comfort of these men's arms but knowing that the last thing she needed was to be seen sneaking out of Grant's cabin in the wee hours of the morning. As it was, she was going to risk being seen in the middle of the night, but chances were no one else was out and about at this point.

"God, I wish you didn't have to," Grant said, tightening his hold on her again and pressing his face against her neck. "I wish neither of you had to go."

Yeah, well ... Grace was content about so much, but solving that little dilemma — the dating two cowboys her father had sworn away from her part — didn't look like it was going to be all that easy.

■□■□■□■□

GRANT KISSED LANE AND GRACIE good-bye a short while later and watched them as they slipped out through his front door and into the night. They'd actually had a conversation about who would go first, but the final decision was that they would both leave together. Gracie insisted that no one would think that the three of them had something going on if she and Lane went together, versus if they left one at a time. According to her, that would probably look a little more suspicious.

As Lane had passed him toward the door, he had whispered, "I'm not gonna do the walk of shame forever." That made Grant laugh, although he knew Lane was partially serious about it. He didn't bother to tell Lane that he didn't want him to go. That he never wanted either of them to leave. Right now, Grant had too much on his mind to get into a deep conversation such as that one, so he'd merely smiled at Lane's statement and kissed him briefly before watching them both go.

Making his way back to his bedroom, Grant caught sight of his cell phone sitting on the kitchen table just inside the front door. The tiny blue light was flashing, a glaring announcement that there were more messages awaiting him. Rather than push them off until morning, Grant snatched the phone up and carried it to his bedroom, debating as to whether he wanted to end up having a bad night or push it off for a few more hours, guaranteeing he'd have four shitty days in a row.

Yeah, fuck tomorrow. He wasn't going to keep dealing with this shit every damn day, so he might as well get it out of the way tonight.

Bringing the screen to life, Grant saw that he had seven new text messages. All from his father.

Message 1, 8:27 p.m.: *Son, I'm sorry for all the things I said. Give me a call. Please.*

Message 2, 9:16 p.m.: *Damn it, Grant, don't you fucking ignore me.*

Message 3, 9:28 p.m.: *Son of a bitch, boy. I don't ask you for much, now do I? I don't like the fact that you can't even give me a fucking call.*

Message 4, 10:19 p.m.: *Keep it up and I'll just come out to the ranch to talk to you.*

Oh, fuck. That one got Grant's attention. His father had been out to the ranch before, and Grant remembered how fucking awful that had been.

Message 5, 10:37 p.m.: *I'm not kidding. I'll come out there and have a chat with your boss. I'll let him know what a worthless son of a bitch you really are.*

He would do it, too. Grant knew that for a fact.

Message 6, 10:43 p.m.: *Last chance. Call me back or I'll be on your doorstep first thing in the morning.*

Grant noticed the time of the final message, less than three minutes from the one before. He didn't even need to read it to know what it said.

Message 7, 10:45 p.m.: *Done. I'll be there with fucking bells on in the morning. If you don't think I will, try me. I need some goddamned money, Grant. Just a fucking loan. I know you've got enough to lend me a couple thousand. Do that and I'll never bother you again.*

A couple thousand? Holy shit. Was his father serious?

Grant might have some money saved, but he damn sure didn't have a couple thousand dollars to loan his father. Not that he would even if he did. It would be one thing for Grant to pay the bills, make sure his parents had electricity and water, which he was considering doing anyway, but to give his father money to throw away on his gambling habit, no fucking thank you.

Tilting his head to the side, Grant observed the bright red numbers on his alarm clock. Shit. It was already after midnight. His father was probably passed out drunk at this point, so Grant knew better than to try to call him. He also didn't see the point because he wasn't going to give in, which meant Darrell would be standing on his front porch, or that of the main house, first thing in the morning.

The only good thing about it, if anything at all could be considered good in this whole fucked up mess, was that Grant's day started long before Darrell's. And that meant he might be able to cut the old man off at the pass.

And it was for that reason alone that Grant managed to go to sleep at all.

Chapter Twelve

Early Thursday morning

"WHO THE HELL IS THAT?" Mercy asked, marching along next to Grace as they made their way across the open space between the main barn and the house.

"Who's *who?*" Grace asked sleepily, doing her best to keep her eyes open as she followed her sister over to Hope's so they could attend the mandatory meeting that had been scheduled at the butt crack of dawn. *Thank you very much, Hope, for moving the time back two hours and letting me know via a text message reminder in the middle of the damn night.*

As much as Grace wanted to skip the meeting, piss off her older sister, and get her day started the right way by sneaking in a few minutes to see Lane and Grant, she knew today was probably not the day to do that. Hope was in danger of having a nervous breakdown as it was, if her stress level was any indication, and Grace knew better than to nudge her.

"That guy," Mercy pointed, her hand coming across the front of Grace's face, forcing her to turn her head or get Mercy's finger up her nose.

"No idea," Grace said as she watched the tall guy with the protruding belly stumble up the steps that led to the section of the main house that her father had commandeered as his office. The guy's rusty red Ford was parked haphazardly — as in, he'd missed the parking space altogether — just a few feet away from the office door.

Pure instinct had Grace adjusting her course, veering toward her father's office, and Mercy moved right alongside her.

A loud noise had Grace's legs kicking into a jog, then a full-out run when she heard someone yelling, likely that guy, if Grace had to guess, because her father wasn't the type to yell.

"Who the hell are you?" Jerry's deep voice thundered out into the otherwise silent morning air. Crap. Crap. Crap.

Slamming her way into the office, Grace found the two men basically standing toe to toe. Nose to nose would've been more accurate, except the other man's nose wasn't quite level with her father's, thanks to Jerry's slightly taller frame. As she slowed down just inside the door, Mercy practically barreled over her before Grace could come to a complete stop.

Okay, so now Grace had to rescind her last statement. Clearly, her father *was* all for yelling at a stranger. She assumed there was a good reason.

Well, she hoped, anyway.

"You goddamn know who the hell I am," the man hollered, his face red and splotchy, drops of spittle launching in her father's direction. Luckily, her dad was good at bobbing and weaving because he sidestepped the man just in time to avoid being showered with it.

"Watch. Your. Mouth," Jerry warned, his eyes flashing with fury.

No, Jerry Lambert was not fond of cursing, but using the Lord's name in vein was the fastest way to find yourself out on your ass.

Grace waited to see what the man was going to say or do next, studying his appearance as she did. He looked like he hadn't bathed in, oh, maybe a week. His shirt, which she assumed might've once been white, was yellowed and out of shape, hanging awkwardly on his slight frame. His thinning, salt-and-pepper hair was slicked back from his forehead, but she didn't think the grease was intentionally placed there to keep it from falling forward. He was sporting a beard that was worthy of those guys on *Duck Dynasty.*

The way his face heated, turning an interesting shade of crimson, she feared he was going to explode anytime now. That's when she heard the sound of boots clomping on the wood outside. Grace had barely enough time to move out of the way, and she only managed that when Mercy yanked her arm, sending her falling toward her sister as the screen door flew open and in walked Grant.

Oh. Shit.

Grace watched as Grant stomped up to the strange man, Grant's eyes fierce, his lips a hard, thin line. He had dark circles beneath his eyes, which meant he'd gotten little to no sleep the night before, and she didn't think she and Lane were completely to blame for that.

"Why are you here?" Grant asked, his voice set on *shout,* like the rest of the men in the room.

"There you are," the man said, turning to face Grant, and that's when Grace realized who he was.

Well, she didn't know for sure, but he looked enough like Grant for her to figure out that this man was likely his father. They had the same eyes — although the man's were like a green-brown color, not blue like Grant's, but the shape was the same — same high cheekbones, same narrow, straight nose... Only this man appeared at least fifty years older, which Grace knew couldn't be right. He looked as though he'd lived a hard life. Or maybe just done some hard living. Either way...

"I asked why you're here," Grant stated again, a few decibels lower than before but his tone significantly firmer.

"You know goddamn well why I'm here."

"I've already told you once not to speak like that in my house," Jerry rasped, his eyes cold as they pinned the unidentified man in place.

The guy didn't seem at all worried about Grace's father, but she could've jumped in just then to warn him except that wasn't necessary because...

"We don't use the Lord's name in vein. And keep in mind that there are ladies in this room, Dad. Watch your mouth."

Yep, just like she thought... That was Grant's father, all right.

"The *ladies* can step out, for all I care. They weren't invited," Grant's dad said with a hint of hatred in his tone. He spared Grace a look, his evil, bloodshot glare making her want to take a step or two back. She didn't budge, though, refusing to let this man treat her like she didn't belong in her own house.

Grace darted a look toward her father, trying to gauge how he was going to handle this situation. Did he want them to stay? Did he want them to leave? If he shooed them out the door, she would gladly cut and run. But if he wanted her and Mercy to stay...

"Grace, would you mind?" Grant said softly, definitely more of a request than a demand as he turned his pleading gaze her way.

Nearly melting into the floor because her heart reached out to him, Grace nodded. "If you don't need us..." Grace let the sentence hang in the air.

"You're not needed," Grant's father said, and Grace was tempted to reach out and slap him across the face.

"Enough!" Grant yelled. "You will not talk to her like that. Understand?"

Grace was holding back solely because this man was Grant's father. Otherwise, she would've put him in his place long before Grant had. While she tried to control her irritation, Mercy eased her way forward, effectively forcing Grace to move over to the side.

Oh, hell. Apparently, Grace had a little more self-control than her sister did because Mercy was moving, and it wasn't toward the exit.

Which meant only one thing.

All hell was about to break loose.

MERCY COULD TOLERATE A LOT of shit: being thrown from a horse, the chickens pecking her legs when she walked through the coop, having her scalp sunburned because she forgot to wear her hat, cowboys pretending to know more than she did about ranching, hell, even a cowboy not holding the door open when he knew she was coming.

All of that was just a miniature hiccup on any given day.

What she couldn't tolerate was a man talking to a woman, her included, as this scrawny bastard had. It didn't help that her father's face had turned beet-red, his blood pressure likely reaching dangerous levels.

"Look here, old man." Mercy got up as close as she dared to the man she had recently realized was Grant's father. "I might not have somethin' swingin' between my legs, but you might wanna rethink how you talk to a lady," she grit out through clenched teeth. "I'm all for lettin' the boys have their special time together, but you won't dismiss me, understand?" Mercy slid her gaze over to her father and continued, "Pops, we've got a meetin' to go to, so we'll be on our way." Mercy grabbed Gracie's wrist, gave Grant a nod, and led her sister out of the office before Mr. I'm-Too-Stupid-For-My-Pants decided he had something else to say.

Mercy had been itching for a fight ever since her run-in with Cody the night before, right after she had managed to get out of the hour-long conversation with her father. Cody's timing couldn't have been worse.

"Hey, babe," Cody said quietly, brushing against Mercy's arms in the softest of touches.

Mercy hated that her body craved his touch.

One. Time.

One fucking time, and now she ached for something she didn't even want.

Mercy shrugged him off, focusing her attention on petting Dixie. She was watching the pups as they trampled around the small yard they'd fenced in near the stables so the little things couldn't get in too much trouble but could still spend some time outside. They weren't very big just yet, but they certainly were mischievous.

"You know, I was thinkin'..." Cody began.

"Watch it, you might hurt yourself," Mercy spouted off.

"Maybe," Cody replied with a chuckle, the sound reminding her of thunder on the horizon during one of those early-summer storms she enjoyed so much. "Anyway. I was wonderin'—"

"The answer is no," Mercy said firmly, dusting her hands off on her jeans and standing to her full height. She still had to look up at the tall cowboy, but at least she felt a little better. "So don't go thinkin' or wonderin'. Save yourself the headache. The answer will always be no."

"Damn it, Mercy," Cody said on a frustrated breath. "Why the hell do you have to be like that?"

"Be like what?" she countered. "I'm not bein' like anything. I don't want to date you, I don't want to fuck you, and at this point, I don't even want to see you."

Okay, so she knew she was excessively harsh, not to mention she feared she might be struck by lightning with all the lies she'd just told, but still...

Cody's emerald-green eyes locked on her, and she wanted to turn away, but for whatever reason, she found herself frozen in place, mesmerized by the sheer intensity in his gaze.

"I don't know what your problem is, Merce, but damn it. I don't want to play this game with you anymore. You know damn well that what we had that night—"

"See, right there," Mercy interrupted. "You're on to something. 'What we had,' that's the key right there. We don't have anything anymore, Cody. And what we had 'that night' was just that. One freakin' night. Why can't you just get that through your thick skull?"

Cody didn't respond, which surprised Mercy. They did this often. And usually, Cody's cockiness and self-assurance had him winning the round, but if she wasn't mistaken, that definitely wasn't confidence she saw in his eyes. No, that looked more like … hurt.

Sonuvabitch.

Mercy shook off the memory. She did not want to think about Cody Mercer or the fact that she had hurt him for no reason whatsoever other than she wasn't comfortable with the way she was starting to feel about him. It didn't help that he plagued her mind even at the most inconvenient times — like now. But ever since that argument, ever since she'd seen the pain in his eyes, she'd been itching for a fight, which she knew wasn't a good thing. Getting into a fight wasn't going to get her anywhere. At least not this time of the morning anyway.

"Let me go," Gracie exclaimed, wrenching her arm free of Mercy's grasp as they stepped out onto the huge wooden porch that wrapped clear around the entire house.

Mercy freed Gracie as she stopped just outside the door, listening to make sure the men had it under control. A second later, when she heard the rumble of Grant's voice, she decided it was time to bolt.

"If we don't get over to Hope's, she's gonna send the dogs."

Gracie twisted to look behind her at the screen door that separated her from the man she clearly had a thing for. "Fine, let's go."

Mercy made her way down the steps and headed in the direction of Hope's cabin. "What do you s'pose he wants?" she asked her sister when the silence began to eat away at her.

It was either talk or think, and she didn't have enough brain cells firing to think because she knew exactly what — or rather, *who* — she was going to think about.

"I don't know," Grace said, but Mercy didn't need a polygraph machine to tell her sister was lying.

"Did Grant get in an argument with him?" Mercy inquired.

"I said I didn't know," Gracie bit out.

"Fine!" Mercy snapped. Shrugging her shoulders, she opted to give up.

At least until they were done listening to Hope's plans for the big shindig she was looking to put on. After that … all bets were off.

After all, Grace owed her one. Even if she didn't know it yet.

■□■□■□■□

"THIS IS NOT THE TIME or place to have this conversation," Grant told his father, his tone low. He could see Jerry moving just over his father's shoulder, and he hated that his boss's morning had started off like this.

Grant had figured for sure he'd have enough time to get in front of Darrell's outburst long before he descended on the ranch. Obviously, he'd been wrong.

"Well, you ain't talkin' to me any other time, so I figure this is the best damn place. Your boss here needs to know just what kind of person you are, turnin' your back on your father in his time of need."

Oh, hell. Now Darrell was going to start with the woe-is-me segment of this morning's production.

Hoping that Jerry wasn't going to buy into Darrell's bullshit, Grant purposely made eye contact with the man, offering a non-verbal apology in his grimace. Jerry merely nodded slightly, just barely enough for Grant to notice.

"Care to introduce us?" Jerry said, surprising Grant as he moved closer to the two of them once again.

Grant sighed, hating that things had come to this. "Jerry, this is my father, Darrell. Dad, this is my boss, Jerry Lambert."

Jerry offered his hand to Darrell, but in true asshole fashion, Grant's father ignored it, pretending not to notice at all, as he turned to look out of the screen door. That was one of the main reasons Grant had never introduced the two men, even during that one occasion when the opportunity had presented itself the last time his father had come to the ranch.

"You own this place, huh?" Darrell asked.

"I do," Jerry replied smoothly.

"Must be nice. Makin' so much money."

Shit.

Jerry didn't dignify Darrell's ignorant statement with a response, thankfully. Grant simply stood there, watching his father, wishing like hell he was going to wake up any minute now and this was all going to be a bad dream.

"My son here might want to explain to you why I'm here. I kindly asked him to loan me some money so that I don't end up losin' my house, but he told me no."

Darrell's pathetic tone had Grant rolling his eyes.

This was ridiculous.

"You're not gonna lose your house," Grant said sternly. "It's paid for."

"Well, the electricity is gonna be shut off," Darrell countered, turning to face Jerry more directly. "See, I recently lost my job at the auto parts store."

Funny how his father now said "lost" rather than "laid off," but whatever.

"How'd you lose your job?" Jerry asked, sounding curious.

"They let me go."

"That's usually the way it works," Jerry retorted. "I asked you *how* you lost your job."

Darrell glanced over at Grant as though he might save him.

Not a chance, Dad, you're on your own.

"I've been sick lately," Darrell began, the words spilling out of his mouth and sounding just like the lie that they were.

"You haven't been *sick*," Grant argued.

"You don't know that!" Darrell exclaimed, showering Grant with spit.

Grant wiped his face on the sleeve of his shirt and took a step away from his father.

"And he ain't talkin' to you," Darrell continued. "Like I was sayin'," Darrell began again, looking back at Jerry as he continued, "I haven't been feelin' well. I didn't make it in for a few days, and they let me go."

"Did you call in sick?" Jerry asked as he perched on the edge of his desk, keeping his eyes focused on Darrell, his hands clasped together, resting in his lap.

"Couldn't." That was all Darrell offered, and Grant knew that if Jerry dug too far, he'd just set Darrell off again.

And that was the last damn thing either of them needed today.

"I don't think Jerry needs to hear all this," Grant added.

"I think he does," Darrell barked. "I think he needs to know that you ain't man enough to help your father."

Grant sent Jerry another look that told him he was sorry. But this time he wasn't apologizing for what his father was saying, or for the fact that Darrell had come all this way just to start shit. No, Grant was apologizing for what he was about to say.

But before he could get a single word out of his mouth, Jerry placed his hand on Grant's arm.

"Mr. Kingsley, would you mind if you and I spoke alone for a few minutes?"

Grant's eyes nearly bugged out of his head as he stared back at Jerry, willing the man not to do that. God, he needed his job, and he did not want his father talking shit about him to his boss, but it wasn't as if Grant could very well tell Jerry that he would prefer to send his father on his way.

"I think that's a good idea," Darrell said, sounding incredibly proud of himself.

Jerry, being the gentleman that he was, held his hand out toward the door, urging Grant to move. When he did, Jerry remained behind him. "You have nothin' to worry about, kid."

And with that, Grant was out in the heat of the brilliant Texas morning, the door to Jerry's office closing behind him with a grating click.

Damn it.

This was not how his day was supposed to go.

"Hey!"

Grant looked up to see Cody coming toward him at a fast clip.

Knowing that he'd shunned his responsibilities enough, Grant stood up straight, situated his hat on his head, and turned his attention to the mechanic just a few yards away.

He needed to focus on work, and later — much, much later, he hoped — he'd deal with the repercussions of his father's impromptu visit to the ranch.

Chapter Thirteen

"I'M NOT SURE HOW THE hell I got roped into this," Lane disputed as Gracie and Mercy pushed him toward Hope's cabin.

"It's your fault you weren't fast enough," Mercy teased.

Granted, she wasn't teasing all that much because Lane *had* tried to escape as soon as he'd seen the two women and realized just where they were headed. But Mercy was right; he hadn't been quick enough because she'd damn near tackled him in her attempt to rein him back in.

Damn cowgirls, never able to leave well enough alone.

"This is a girl meetin'," he argued pointlessly. As much as he wished he were anywhere but there, Lane knew better than to think the women were going to let him off the hook. They'd roped him, and now they were going to make his morning miserable, he was sure.

"Be nice," Gracie whispered, her hand sliding against his ever so subtly.

Okay, now he could do this. Be nice, that is. Especially if he got the pleasure of being with Gracie for just a few minutes first thing that morning. Or even better, watching Gracie walk away.

Or ahead of him, as was the case here.

She was making her way up onto Hope's front porch, her cute little ass making his mouth water. Christ, where did she buy those jeans? He only wanted to know so he could go buy her a hundred more. Her ass looked…

"You're droolin'," Mercy muttered, drawing Lane's attention away from Gracie's mighty fine ass. "Careful or they'll all see the lust written right across your big face."

Unable to resist, Lane spared Gracie's ass another glance. He wasn't disappointed. Those damn jeans were made for her. Again, Lane pulled his eyes away from Gracie's delectable rear end in order to shoot Mercy another look. She was grinning from ear to ear.

"You be careful, or I'll tell Cody just where you like to hide out when he's lookin' for you."

"Shut up," Mercy snapped, her grin disappearing.

That only made Lane's smile widen. He knew the woman had a thing for Cody even though she tried her best to avoid the mechanic. But then again, Lane probably wasn't supposed to know. If he hadn't been searching for Cody one night because his damn truck had failed to start, he wouldn't have stumbled upon the two of them getting it on in the garage.

Not that he'd stuck around to watch.

Hell no. He'd run like the wind that night, spinning right around on the heels of his boots and heading in the opposite direction.

Lane still found it amusing because, from the little bit he had seen that night, he gathered that Mercy's frustration when it came to Cody didn't have anything to do with *not* liking the man and probably everything to do with the fact that she *did*.

"Earth to Lane," Mercy said, snapping her fingers in front of his face.

He was still grinning as he looked up to see that Gracie had already gone inside Hope's cabin, and he had no choice but to follow because Mercy wasn't going to let him get away.

Once inside, Lane realized he was immersed knee deep in some major trouble. Being the only man in the room with five Lambert sisters, he was tempted to put his hand protectively over his nuts. There was no telling what they were up to or how he played a part in all of this. He really only cared about the latter.

"I've got donuts and milk in the kitchen," Hope announced when they all gathered in Hope's small living room.

Would you look at this place? Holy shit! It was like a Pepto Bismol factory had exploded.

Lane knew there were roughly twenty-six small cabins scattered throughout the thousands of acres of Dead Heat Ranch. He also knew how each of them was used. Five were allocated to the sisters; the head foreman, Grant, had one; another was reserved for the head wrangler, if the head wrangler hadn't been Hope. They had recently assigned one to Jennifer, the new chef, and sixteen others were reserved for guests who wanted to come spend some wild days and hot nights on the ranch. That left two additional ones that stood uninhabited for whatever reason, probably until they hired someone they considered worthy of one.

Every last one of them looked roughly the same on the outside. The inside décor was the only thing that really set them apart.

As he stood in Hope's living room, looking around and getting dizzy from all of the girly crap everywhere, the biggest difference Lane noticed between Hope's and Grant's was the fact that Hope's was bigger. Not by much, but still bigger.

Well, maybe that wasn't the *biggest* difference between Hope's cabin and Grant's.

Where Hope had knick-knacks and trinkets, flowers and candles, pictures and sconces every-damn-where, Grant's place was practically a box with a door and a few pieces of furniture. Now that he thought about it, Gracie's was more feminine than Grant's, but the woman didn't have girly shit on every available surface like Hope, thank God.

Everywhere Lane looked, there was some girly thing sitting on another girly thing. It was too much. He wondered whether the woman ever had a man over because, holy hell, it was like Barbie's dream house, only in a cabin version. And hold up a minute. What the hell was he thinking about Barbie for? He didn't have any experience with Barbie. At least no more than was required to hang with his five-year-old cousin when Lane visited his grandparents every now and then.

He would blame it on all of the estrogen shoved into one small area.

But this place... It reeked of girly stuff. Pink flowered throw pillows on the couch, lamps with pink-and-white shades, candles of all shapes and sizes and, yes, some of them were pink. Hell, there were even pink rugs on the floor.

Thankfully, the couch was beige because that single piece of furniture was the only thing to break up the horrific use of the color that reminded him of stomach medicine. He figured the only thing saving the walls from being painted a horrid shade of pink was that they were made of sealed wood beams, so they couldn't very well be painted. He hoped.

"Here," Gracie said, pulling his attention from the overwhelming pinkness of the room. Lane looked down to see that Gracie was holding a plate with two donuts on it.

"For me?" he asked.

The woman blushed, and he was tempted to fist pump the air. She'd brought him donuts. In front of all of her sisters. For sure, this had to be some sort of milestone for them.

Rather than look like a dumbass, Lane took the plate and smiled down at her, willing her to meet his gaze. When she did, his smile doubled in size.

God, he loved this woman.

"If you two don't mind, we'd like to get started," Hope said by way of interruption.

Gracie jerked away from him, moving to the other side of the room as though the house were on fire.

That was all right. Lane was okay with that because ... the woman had brought him donuts.

"Sit, would ya?" Mercy smirked at him.

Lane propped himself on the arm of — wouldn't you know it — a pink side chair, while the rest of the women all took their seats on the couch or the kitchen chairs placed in a circle around the living room. Lane plowed through the donuts in two minutes flat, still waiting for Hope to get around to the reason they were all sitting in that room — which still freaked him out, by the way.

"So, as you know, Dad's birthday is in two weeks. I want to throw him a party."

Aww, hell.

Lane had been dragged into the estrogen factory to help with a freaking birthday party?

"And we need to meet for this, why?" Mercy challenged.

Yes, exactly. Why? Lane eyed the donuts sitting on the kitchen table as he waited for someone to enlighten him.

"Because it needs to be huge."

Not a good reason, if you asked him. Could he make it across the room, grab two more donuts, and not interrupt?

Doubtful. Damn it.

"Why?" Trinity asked.

"Because he's gonna be fifty-five," Hope said with an edge.

Holy crap. Jerry was only fifty-four?

"Oh," Trinity responded, seemingly satisfied with that answer.

Lane didn't say a word, his head bobbing around the room as each sister weighed in on the reason for having a party. That conversation quickly morphed into a bitch session about how hard it was to keep a secret from their father.

"That's where Lane comes in," Mercy added.

The mention of his name had his head jerking toward the mouth that had said it. "Why me?" he asked.

"Because he won't expect anything from you," Hope added.

"Gee, thanks."

"You know what I mean," Hope explained.

"What am I supposed to do?"

"You'll be the gofer. I'll order everything, have it shipped into town so Dad doesn't see any of the deliveries, and you can go pick the stuff up."

Great. Just what he needed, another job added to his already long list of things he had to do every day. At this rate, he wasn't going to see Gracie or Grant ever again.

"Fine," he grumbled, unable to say no to these women.

"Great. Now we need to outline a plan," Hope said, a sparkle of crazy lighting up her turquoise eyes.

That was the moment Lane got really scared.

■□■□■□■□

GRACE DID HER BEST TO focus on the conversation her sisters were having regarding a surprise birthday party for their father, but her mind continued to drift back to her dad's office and the confrontation they'd just had with Grant's father.

She desperately wished she'd been able to stick around, wanting to be there for Grant when he came out. The only consolation was that Lane was here with her, something she knew he wished wasn't the case.

Initially, when she'd seen him walking toward the barn, she had wanted to run after him and inform him of the scene taking place in Jerry's office. Obviously, Mercy had realized Grace's intentions because she had snagged Grace's arms just as she'd started toward Lane.

"Don't."

"Don't what?" Grace glared at her sister, then down to the hand gripping her wrist.

"Don't start shit. Right now, you don't know why Grant's father is here. If you get Lane involved, it'll only make it worse."

It had been hard to argue with Mercy's logic, so Grace had changed her plans and informed Lane that he was needed for the meeting. He was, after all, needed for the meeting.

And as she sat there, barely paying attention to what everyone was chattering on and on about, she felt a pang of guilt for not informing Lane of what was going on with Grant. He needed to know.

He would want to know.

After all, Lane had admitted that he loved them.

The man had said the words and hadn't heard them in return, yet based on his attitude, it really didn't matter. Just as he had said.

But Grace knew it did. How could it not? She wanted to hear him say the words again. Probably more than anything right then, but she couldn't very well ask him to until she could overcome her fear of saying them first.

There'd been so many instances when she'd wanted to blurt out that she loved him, and Grant, too, but she'd held her tongue, fearful of just what that would mean for the three of them. Things were a little bizarre as it was, and that was before Grant's father had gone all crazy and stormed the ranch that morning.

"Take a picture, it'll last longer," Mercy mumbled as she leaned in close to Grace, snapping her from her thoughts.

"Shut up. You sound like a two-year-old."

Mercy's smirk was wicked. "You keep staring at him like that and everyone in this room is gonna know just how you feel about him."

Grace found it hard to believe that they didn't know it already. If it weren't for the fact that they were all working long days, spending too much time working and not enough time having fun, she figured they would have noticed by now.

And Mercy was right.

Until Grace figured out just how this was going to play out, she really did need to keep a lid on what was going on with her and Lane and Grant.

Crap.

Like anyone was ever going to accept that she was in love with two men. And those two men were in love with her. And each other.

Holy smokes, it sounded convoluted even to her.

"Does that work for you, Gracie?"

Grace jerked her eyes up to meet Hope's. "Uh ... what?"

"Could you pay attention?" Hope bit out.

"I would if I weren't so damned tired," Grace muttered.

Grace felt the heat of Lane's gaze on her, but she refused to look over at him. If she did, her sisters would likely realize just what was going on there, and now was not the time to have them heckling her about her relationships — real or perceived.

"I need for you to help Lane get the supplies from town."

That statement caused Grace to look at Lane. He was looking at her, just as she'd thought, but his expression was bland, not reflecting any of the heat she could see brewing in his eyes. She fought the urge to smile.

"Okay," she answered readily.

She should've been paying closer attention. If she had to guess, Lane had suggested that someone help him, and if she knew Mercy the way she thought she did, it'd been Mercy's suggestion that Grace be his assistant.

She could handle that.

"All right. We're gonna kick this into high gear," Hope said. "I need everyone to handle their respective jobs. And by God, do *not* let Dad know what's goin' on. I don't care what you have to do to throw him off, but do not tell him we're givin' him a party."

A chorus of agreement erupted as all of them took that to be Hope's closing statement.

Not wanting to appear too obvious, Grace made a beeline for the front door, not waiting for Lane. She knew he would keep up, which he did, meeting up with her as she headed for the barn.

"So when do we sneak into town?" he asked, his tone low and seductive.

Grace spun around, giving the area a cursory glance to ensure there was no one near enough to overhear them.

"Just tell me the time and place and I'm there," she answered when she realized the coast was clear.

With that, Lane smiled down at her, and she allowed the sparkle in his eyes to send her heart into a gallop just as it always did.

"Have you seen Grant this morning?" he asked, dampening the vibrant glow in her chest as quickly as he'd ignited it.

"Not in a while, no," she answered, unable to lie to him wholly.

Lane's eyebrow disappeared beneath the shadow from his hat. Grace could practically see his bullshit meter signaling a red alert.

"Somethin' happen?"

"Why would you think that?"

"Come on, Gracie," Lane said softly, closing the gap between them.

Grace noticed that he started to reach for her hands but thought better of it before he touched her. God, she wanted him to touch her. She wanted him to pull her into his big, strong arms and hold her, assure her that whatever was happening with Grant was going to be okay. That *they* were going to be okay.

Crap.

"Yes. I saw Grant this morning. He was in my father's office. His dad showed up causin' a scene."

Lane looked as though someone had pulled the rug out from underneath him and then piled a shitload of dirt on his head to boot.

"What?" Lane turned, his gaze searching the area around the main house.

Grace looked as well, noticing that the red Ford was no longer parked outside, which, she hoped, was a good sign.

"He's not here anymore. Grant's dad, that is. He drives a red Ford," she continued, pointing toward the area the man had been parked in earlier. "But it's gone now."

Lane looked back at her, and Gracie felt as though she were three inches tall. Yes, she should've told him earlier, but she agreed with Mercy, it would've only made matters worse.

Right?

Lane nodded his head curtly, his eyes meeting hers once more. And then, for the first time in all the time she'd known him, Lane Miller turned and walked away without saying a word.

Chapter Fourteen

"HI, GRACIE!" MADDIE GREETED WITH an impressive yell as soon as Grace came over the small rise that circled the lake.

Waving back at the little girl, Grace dug deep and forced a smile. She really didn't have a choice. After all, her personal life wasn't supposed to get in the way of her work. And for the next couple of hours, she was going to be sitting side by side with a six-year-old, teaching her how to fish. It wouldn't be fair to Maddie for Grace to be dwelling on the things she couldn't change.

"Hey, Gracie," Ben greeted when Grace made it down to the edge of the lake.

"Mornin'," she replied with that smile firmly planted on her lips. Lifting her hand to show him the thermos of coffee, she said, "I brought backup."

Ben laughed, his handsome face lighting up as he tipped the foam cup in his hand upside down to show her that it was empty. "I could use some."

Pulling the small satchel that she'd brought along with her off her shoulder, Grace allowed it to drop to the soft grass before setting the thermos next to it. "I see y'all picked up fishin' poles. What about worms?"

"Worms?" Maddie asked, her face turning a concerning shade of gray.

"Yeah. What did you think we were gonna use to catch the fish?"

Maddie shrugged, her eyes darting down to the bag on the ground and then slowly meeting Grace's again.

"We're gonna use worms?" Maddie clarified, her voice softer than before.

Ben pulled Maddie up against him and tugged on her pigtail as he chuckled. Yeah, it was safe to say that not all six-year-old girls were like Grace had been at that age. Maddie clearly didn't like the idea of using worms for fishing. Grace, on the other hand, had been fascinated by them since her dad had first showed her how to bait a hook.

Note to self: don't make Maddie bait her own hook.

"I like your shirt," Grace said, hoping to steer the conversation in another direction.

Today the little girl was wearing pink shorts with her pink boots. The white tank top with the word "cowgirl" written across the front looked new. If Grace wasn't mistaken, they sold that shirt in the general store.

"Thanks," Maddie replied, her cheerful smile slowly returning.

"You know what? How 'bout we let your dad bait the hooks so you don't have to touch the worms? What do you think about that?"

Maddie nodded her head vigorously, her eyes continuing to dart down to the bag as though the worms might just slither right on out and up her legs.

"Okay then. Let's grab the stuff and move down to the pier."

Maddie retrieved a small bag that they must've brought along with them, but she stayed as far away from Grace's bag as possible, which only made Grace want to laugh. *Welcome to ranch life, kiddo.*

And just like that, her mood took a turn for the better. There really wasn't anything she could do to help Grant with his current dilemma. And as for Lane, if he was hurt that she hadn't mentioned what had happened, then she couldn't change that, either. There'd be plenty of time later that afternoon for her to talk to them and hopefully work things out.

But for now, she was ready to fish.

It took all of ten minutes for them to get set up, the three of them sitting side by side on the pier, their legs dangling over, inches above the sparkling water. Maddie forgot all about the worms as soon as Grace tossed in a handful of fish food, something to lure a few of the fish their direction. More for Maddie's benefit than anything else.

With a foam cup of coffee sitting at her side, her fishing line dangling in the calm water, Grace took a deep breath, letting the sun's warm rays beat down on her shoulders. She could sit out here all day. There were actually days she had come down to the lake, brought a blanket and a book, and spent a couple of hours listening to the soft lap of the water against the bank.

Not that she could do that today. She was supposed to be entertaining her guests, and although Maddie looked content staring down at the end of her fishing pole, likely waiting impatiently for a fish to bite, Grace knew the little girl wouldn't be quiet for long.

"So, Maddie, what grade are you in?" Grace asked, initiating the conversation.

"First. My teacher, Mrs. Rose, she's so nice."

"What's your favorite subject?"

"Math."

"My favorite subject was science," Grace told Maddie.

"Not me. I like math. It's easy."

Grace smiled. That was a very valid reason to like math, she guessed.

"Ben," Grace glanced over at the man sitting quietly on the other side of Maddie, "if you don't mind me asking, what do you do?"

Grace saw Ben swallow hard, his Adam's apple sliding down and then up slowly. Oops. Maybe that wasn't something Ben cared to discuss.

"My daddy's a lawyer. But he doesn't like his job," Maddie answered when Ben didn't.

There was obviously a story there, and Grace was certainly interested in hearing it, but only if Ben wanted to share.

"Thank you, Maddie," Ben said to his daughter, his shoulders a little more strained than a few moments ago. "She's right. I'm not enjoying it much anymore."

"You don't like being a lawyer?"

"I've taken a leave of absence," Ben admitted.

Yep. Definitely a story. Grace wondered whether it had to do with Maddie's mother. His reaction to Maddie's comment yesterday about her hadn't been a happy response.

"Maddie's mother just married one of the partners in my firm."

Oh.

Ooooohhhhh.

Grace focused intently on her fishing pole, hating that she'd brought up such a sore subject but not sure how she was supposed to get out of it.

"I'm thinking about moving," Ben admitted.

"We should move here, Daddy," Maddie said, half-heartedly contributing to the conversation while she swung her legs back and forth and bounced her fishing pole on her knee.

While Grace was staring down at the water, she was pretty sure she heard Ben agree with his daughter. And wasn't that interesting.

"How many sisters do you have?"

Sweet, sweet Maddie. The little girl probably had no idea that she had just saved the day by changing the subject.

"Four."

"What are their names?"

"Hope, Trinity, Mercy, and Faith."

"Those are fun names," Maddie said, grinning up at Grace.

"Thanks. My mother picked out our names."

"Where's your mom at?"

Another sharp pain of loss ricocheted through her chest. Grace would've thought that all these years later, it would be easier to talk about her mother. But it wasn't. Every time she thought of her, which was quite often, her heart would ache as if someone had hit her with a cattle prod. Taking a deep breath, she said, "My mother died when I was twelve."

"My mom doesn't want to come see me anymore," Maddie admitted, jerking Grace's attention from the memories of her mother right to the present. "She got married to Mr. Jeff, and I don't like him."

Well, hell. Grace hadn't wanted the conversation to veer back this way, but she didn't know what to do. She wasn't that great when it came to children, although she enjoyed being around them.

"Why do you think Mom doesn't want to see you?" Ben asked, sounding confused by Maddie's statement.

"She said she wants to go on airplanes, and she can't do that with me."

Grace met Ben's wounded gaze over Maddie's head. She quietly mouthed, "I'm sorry." Not that it was going to do any good whatsoever.

"How old are your sisters?" Maddie asked suddenly, still kicking her feet. The girl was a bundle of energy, not to mention a conversational disaster. Well, in this case, she was pretty ingenious. At least they weren't lingering on one uncomfortable subject for too long.

"Faith is the youngest. She's twenty-five. Then Mercy, who's twenty-six. Trinity is twenty-seven. I'm twenty-eight. And my older sister, Hope, is thirty-two."

"My daddy's thirty-six."

"Thanks, Maddie," Ben said, this time with a snort.

"My daddy thinks Hope is pretty."

Ben laughed; this time the sound was strangled, which made Grace grin widely.

"Is that right?" Grace asked, encouraging the little girl while she cocked an eyebrow at Ben. The man had the decency to blush and shrug his shoulders.

"Yep. He said so last night. I think she's pretty, too," Maddie added. "But not as pretty as you are."

Okay, so now it was Grace's turn to blush. "Thank you."

"When do we get to ride the horses again?"

And just like that, the personal conversation died, much to Grace's relief.

She was pretty sure Ben felt the same way.

■□■□■□■□

"WHERE'S GRANT?" LANE ASKED AS he stormed through the barn that Cody used as his mechanic shop.

"Haven't seen him," Cody bit back. "And good fuckin' mornin' to you, too."

Lane wasn't in the mood to start shit with Cody, so he turned on his heel and headed the opposite direction, nearly running right into Mercy. "Don't have time," he growled at her as he walked right on by.

"Hey, cowboy, slow down!" Mercy yelled, her voice sounding from behind him.

Lane didn't have time to stop and chat. He needed to find Grant. Needed to hear from him just what the hell was going on.

When Gracie had spilled that Grant's father had showed up at the ranch, Lane had been worried. He'd been hurt more than anything that she'd keep something so important from him, which had led to him turning his back and walking away from her. It was that or say something he would likely regret later.

But now he just wanted to see Grant. To let the man know he was there for him if he needed him.

The one thing about Grant that Lane knew for a fact ... the guy was a loaded gun.

Grant might not admit it, but his calm, cool demeanor was usually a mask for intense emotion bubbling just beneath the surface. Which was exactly what Lane was worried about.

Great, and now you're Dr. Phil, huh?

Shaking off the annoying voice in his head, Lane kept putting one foot in front of the other as he tried to figure out just where Grant might be hiding. He'd already checked Grant's house, and the man wasn't there.

Lane hadn't made it far when he felt a sharp tug on his arm. The momentum had him spinning around and coming face to face with... "Shit. I said I didn't have time, Mercy."

"Relax, cowboy," Mercy snapped. "Grant's not here."

"What do you mean he's not here?"

Mercy cocked her head to the side, offering Lane that look. The one that said, "Are you really that stupid?"

"Fine. I'll rephrase. Where did he go?"

"He said he had an errand to run."

Shit.

"When did he leave?" Lane asked.

"From what Zach told me, about an hour ago."

An errand to run at — Lane glanced down at his cheap watch — ten o'clock in the morning?

"Come on. Let's get coffee."

"I don't want coffee," Lane argued. He *didn't* want coffee. He wanted to find Grant. He needed to talk to him. Despite the look on Mercy's face, Lane really wasn't stupid. If Grant had had a run-in with his father that morning, the likelihood that he'd followed the man was great. And if that were the case, then the two of them were probably throwing down on the side of the road.

Grant was the type of guy to keep everything bottled up. And by everything, Lane meant every-damn-thing. Every ounce of Grant's emotions was kept safeguarded under lock and key. His anger, his frustration, his happiness ... his love. All of it. Lane figured it had something to do with the way the guy was raised.

PhD in psychology now, huh?

"I said we're gonna get coffee," Mercy demanded, pulling on Lane's arm until he had no choice but to follow her or jerk away. He didn't want to accidentally hurt her, and considering how much smaller she was than him, the likelihood of that happening was rather great.

"What's all the excitement about?" Cody asked, emerging from the shade of the mechanic shop.

Damn, dude, put a shirt on.

Lane had obviously been too lost in his own thoughts to notice that Cody wasn't wearing a shirt, and from the looks of it, Mercy was now well aware of that fact, too.

"Nothin'. Don't mind us," Mercy mumbled loud enough for Cody to hear.

"I've got coffee in here," Cody offered.

Lane watched Mercy's shoulders tense, and he figured if she was going to get him to go anywhere, then he was going to make her pay for it.

"We're comin'," Lane offered Cody.

"Damn stupid men," Mercy grumbled beneath her breath.

Lane laughed.

"Don't you dare laugh at me, Miller. You think you're funny. I promise you won't like what I have in store for you."

"Do your worst," Lane countered. "But before you do that, tell me where Grant went."

The two of them walked side by side toward the huge metal structure where Cody spent most of his days.

"No idea," Mercy replied. "Swear to God. Zach didn't say. Just that Grant hauled ass outta here a while ago. After the confrontation with that crazy bastard this mornin', I can't say that I blame him. I'd be puttin' the hurtin' on that man if he were related to me."

"You were there?" Lane asked, stopping midstride.

"Unfortunately," Mercy replied, her eyes on the ground as she kept moving.

Lane had to widen his stride to catch up with her when his legs started working again.

"His father, right?" Lane asked, confirming what Gracie had already told him.

"That's the rumor," Mercy answered with a chuckle. "Although, if I were Grant, I wouldn't claim the asshole."

Yeah, well, people weren't that lucky.

Lane and Mercy stepped into the shop, the huge fans mounted to the ceiling offering a breeze, although it wasn't cool by any means. The scent of motor oil and dirt floated in the air.

As they moved deeper into the dim building, Lane noticed Cody standing near a makeshift break area, complete with a coffeepot, sink, and a small refrigerator. The guy was pouring three cups of coffee, his gaze continually fluttering over to Mercy, who was wandering around one of the tractors that Cody was working on. She, obviously, was doing everything possible not to look at the shirtless cowboy.

Yep, these two were crazy for each other. How the hell could they not see it?

Lane had to wonder why neither of them was willing to admit it. Okay, maybe that wasn't fair. Cody was rather obvious with his interest, but Mercy... That woman was so far in denial, Lane was surprised she knew where she was most of the time.

"I heard you and your dad are gonna have a race on Sunday." Cody was speaking to Mercy as he handed Lane a cup of coffee, his eyes glued to the woman who was hiding on the other side of the tractor.

"Yep," she answered, her tone dull, as though she were bored.

Right.

Bored.

If it were possible to bottle Mercy's energy, they wouldn't need to have guests stay at the ranch because they'd all be rich just selling the stuff.

"Race?" Lane asked. He hadn't heard about a race. "You and Jerry?"

"Yep."

"You gonna ride Shadow Mist?" Lane asked Mercy, realizing as soon as the words were out of his mouth that it was a stupid question.

"Yep."

Well, Mercy was now the one-word wonder.

"Which horse is your dad gonna ride?" Cody asked, clearly wanting to be part of the conversation.

"No idea. Doesn't really matter. He's gonna lose no matter what," Mercy said, her brain obviously reattaching itself to her vocabulary list.

"You gonna be there?" Cody asked, this time his question directed at Lane.

"Damn right."

He hoped, anyway. That rather depended on where Grant was and what he was doing. If the guy had gone rogue, chasing after his crazy father, Lane had the feeling he'd be on the road at that point.

Trying to track him down.

Shit.

He couldn't very well stand around and drink coffee while Grant was off doing God knows what. He had to find him. Tossing back the lukewarm liquid as if it were a shot, Lane tossed the cup into the garbage can as he headed back the way he'd come in. "You two kids have fun now. I've gotta run."

Since he didn't have his phone on him, he would have to grab it first, along with his truck keys, and then … then he was going to take a road trip.

A blast of heat hit him as the sun shone down on his face when he stepped out of the building. With his mind on one thing and one thing only, Lane had to make an effort to turn around and shout back to Mercy, "If anyone's lookin' for me, tell 'em I'll be back later!"

With Mercy calling his name, clearly not happy about being abandoned with Cody, Lane practically ran out of there as fast as his feet would carry him.

Chapter Fifteen

SON OF A BITCH.

Mercy was going to throttle Lane the next time she saw him.

"So…"

Mercy didn't respond to Cody's conversation starter. After the last time they were here… *Oh, good grief, woman, do not think about that.*

"Uh…" Yeah, so Mercy really had no idea what she was supposed to say. Her mind was blank, mainly because she was forcing it to be. If she allowed herself to think at all, she was going to think about that night when she'd sat astride this man and…

"What're you thinkin' about?" Cody asked.

"I'm not thinkin' about a damn thing." *Other than how freaking hot he looked without a damn shirt on, his sweat-slick chest glistening in the overhead lights.*

How in the world could this man talk to her after how crappy she'd been to him last night? Was he made of steel? Did harsh words just ricochet right off him?

"No? You're blushin', so I figure it's gotta be somethin'."

Mercy squeezed between two of the big pieces of equipment only to find herself stepping out right in front of Cody.

Damn it.

"Leave it alone, Mercer," Mercy snapped, doing her absolute darnedest not to look down at his chiseled pecs or to remember how hard his shoulders had felt beneath her hands when she'd been riding him. *Oh, crap.* "The only reason I'm here is so I could talk to Lane."

"Really?" Cody asked, taking a step closer. So close Mercy could smell him. He smelled like motor oil and ... something else that was rather potent. She couldn't place it, but whatever it was, she'd found herself craving it. Hell, even during that damn dream that she couldn't seem to get rid of, she could smell him.

Mercy looked up at Cody, praying he didn't see into her head, praying he didn't guess what she was thinking. What had happened between them was a mistake. She knew it. He knew it. A big honking mistake that she wished she could take back.

Uh-huh. When did you become the world's biggest liar?

Mercy didn't have a chance to throw back a mental argument with that little voice that had taken up residence in her head because the next thing she knew, Cody was tipping her chin up with the edge of one finger — his work-roughened finger that felt *way* too good touching her — and Mercy's breath caught in her throat.

"Are you thinkin' about that night?" he asked, his voice soft, seductive.

She hated his voice.

Liar, liar pants on fire!

Mercy shook her head, all the while, mentally yelling at that little voice in her head, screaming, *Yes, dammit, that's all I think about!*

"God, Merce, I can't think about anything but you," Cody whispered, the thundering bass of his voice making her insides quake.

Damn him.

"Well, you shouldn't," she shot back in a barely there whisper, locking her gaze with his.

His green eyes sparkled like emeralds, even in the harsh florescent lights overhead, and damn it all to hell and back, Mercy wished he would kiss her right then. Cut all the crap, ignore all of the arguments she'd tossed his way, and kiss her, damn it.

"I know," he agreed. "But I can't help it."

Why wasn't she pulling away from him?

The question pounded inside of her brain, a warning that if she let him touch her, she might just do something incredibly stupid. *Again.*

Her eyes drifted down his face, over his slightly crooked nose, his smooth cheeks, and landed on his lips. Cody Mercer had the nicest lips she'd ever seen on a man. They were smooth and firm and... Damn it!

He was leaning in close, and Mercy was rooted in place, unable to pull away, unable to push him. The thought of him kissing her again, those delicious, hot kisses, made her knees weak.

No.

No damn way.

Mercy Lambert was not a weak-kneed woman. Not for him or any man.

Thankfully, sanity returned when he was just a hairsbreadth away.

"In your dreams, Mercer."

Ducking around him, Mercy came out from between his hot freaking body and the equipment just in time to see her father stepping into the shadows of the building.

"Hey, girlie," Jerry greeted. "What are you doin' here?"

Saved by the bell!

Turning back to look at Cody, she saw that he hadn't bothered to turn around. His big, broad shoulders were straight, his legs locked, and one hand was thrust into his hair, the other holding his ball cap.

"Just checkin' in," Mercy lied. *She was on a roll today, wasn't she?* Turning back to face her father, she added, "I've gotta head over to the kitchen. Make sure the dinner menu's in place."

"You sure?" Jerry asked, grinning. "You don't think you oughta be practicin' for the race?"

And just like that, Mercy forgot all about Cody — or so she told herself. "No practicin' for me. I've got this one in the bag." Especially since she had something up her sleeve that not even her father would expect.

And with that, Mercy fled Cody's shop, reminding herself never, ever, ever to go back there. The fact that her father had nearly walked in on them kissing was proof that this infatuation she had with Cody was getting way out of hand.

Hopefully, Cody agreed.

But if he didn't, that really wasn't her problem, now was it?

■□■□■□■□

JERRY WATCHED MERCY FLEE THE scene. He fought the urge to laugh, knowing that Cody had turned around to face him.

He had to give the kid credit — whatever had been going on between him and Mercy, the man had masked his expression fairly well. Too bad Jerry knew the kid as well as he knew his own daughters. Cody Mercer had been employed by Dead Heat Ranch for going on seven years now — since the ripe old age of eighteen.

There was something going on between Mercy and Cody. Jerry could feel it. And whatever it was, this wasn't a new development because the tension between the two of them had been mounting for months now.

"How's the mower comin' along?" Jerry moved deeper into the building, walking around behind the piece of equipment in question.

"Should be up and runnin' within an hour," Cody replied, his tone brisk yet still kind. If it hadn't been for the way Cody was rubbing the back of his neck with one hand, Jerry might've believed that he wasn't at all affected by Mercy's abrupt departure.

"No rush. We'll just want it by next week."

"Yes, sir."

"You gonna watch the race on Sunday?" Jerry asked, unwilling to walk out just yet.

It wasn't that he was trying to be nosy — okay, yes, he was definitely trying — but he wanted to get a feel for what was going on with Cody. Not just in regards to Mercy, either.

"I'm hopin' to. I've gotta get this done." Cody tilted his head toward a Bobcat that was sitting in the far corner. "They're usin' it to load the remains of the old stable onto a trailer to take to the dump. Someone fuc— er … messed it up yesterday. Grant's been on my butt to get it fixed ASAP."

"Do what you gotta do, but be there if you can."

Cody nodded but didn't respond as he reached for two white foam cups sitting on the mower in front of him. Hmm… Two cups. That meant he'd been having coffee with Mercy.

"How's your mom?"

"Never better. She's goin' on a cruise at the end of the month."

A few months back, Cody's mother had been in the hospital due to dehydration after catching the flu, from what Jerry remembered. "Good to hear. Everything else goin' okay?" Jerry asked, thrusting his hands into his pockets as he leaned against a steel beam.

"Yup."

Okay, Jerry knew a brush-off when he received one. Pushing himself off the beam, he nodded at Cody. "Talk to you later then."

Taking his time, just to see if Cody wanted to add anything to the conversation, Jerry pretended to check out a couple of machines that were sitting near the door. When the screech of metal on metal sounded from behind him, Jerry took that to be his dismissal.

Stumbling upon Mercy and Cody had actually been an accident. He had originally come over to the shop to see if Grant was there, hoping to talk to him for a few minutes. He knew Grant would probably like to hear what the conversation between him and Darrell had entailed. Not that Jerry had much he could say.

Making his way to the house, Jerry thought back to his conversation with Grant's father earlier that morning. Talking to Darrell Kingsley was like talking to a brick wall. The wheels inside the guy's head were always turning, but he couldn't seem to hear anyone else over the squeaking of the rusty gears. It was safe to say that Jerry's suggestion that the man get some help for his gambling addiction — which Darrell had admitted to — had gone unheeded.

Jerry doubted that was anything new to Grant.

As much as he wished he could do something to help the situation, he knew that getting involved would only cause problems. But after Darrell had blatantly disregarded Gracie and Mercy while his daughters had been in the room, Jerry couldn't just sit by and allow the man to waltz out the door without at least a few suggestions.

Initially, Jerry hadn't intended to say a word, but something in the way Grant had looked at Gracie had had him reconsidering.

Was there something in the water around this place?

Hell, he knew his girls were growing up — technically, they weren't girls anymore, they were incredible young women, but he would always think of them as his little girls — and Jerry wasn't blind to the way the men on the ranch looked at them. To their credit — his girls', not the cowboys' — they were smart to boot. They had all made him proud, so worrying about who they spent their time with had never been an issue for him. Then again, tossing out his threats to skin a cowboy's hide if he so much as looked at his girls had gone a long way in keeping the men from chasing them around.

Or so he'd thought.

It wasn't that he would really hurt a man for dating one of his daughters — as long as the guy treated her right — but he knew if he tossed out the warnings from time to time, it would keep the weaker men at bay. Only a man with brass balls would stand up to Jerry when it came to dating one of his girls. And that right there was the sole reason he continued with the trend.

Jerry's cell phone rang as he was stepping into his office. Snagging it from his pocket, he glanced at the screen and smiled. This was a nice surprise.

"Hey, honey," he greeted as he closed his office door behind him.

"How are you?" Jan asked, her voice like a balm to his soul.

Jan Haile was the main reason for Jerry's good mood these last few months. "Better now that you called."

"I was thinking…"

"About?" Jerry asked as he plopped down into his desk chair, his heart beating double-time just from the soft tone of her voice in his ear. It was crazy what this woman made him feel. *Him.* At almost fifty-five years old, Jerry felt like a damned young man again, eager and anxious just to talk to this woman on the phone.

"I'd like to see you."

"It's been a while, huh?" he replied, trying to remember the last time they'd managed to spend time together. The calendar on his desk told him that he'd been neglecting his woman for more than a week.

"Too long."

"Why don't you come out here to the ranch?" he asked. It had been a frequent request of his over the last month or so. Generally, he was met with numerous rebuttals on Jan's part, all, unfortunately, legitimate, but still frustrating nonetheless. While Jerry wanted to throw caution to the wind and bring Jan to the ranch to meet his daughters, Jan wanted to take things slow.

The woman was incredible, he'd give her that much. But he was getting damn tired of slow.

"Are you sure?"

Jerry sat up straight in his chair. No arguments? "Positive," he responded quickly. God, he needed to see her. More than he needed to eat or sleep or … or breathe.

"Tonight?"

"Now is fine," he told her, loving the way she laughed at his eager response.

"Not now," Jan stated. "Let's wait until after dark."

Jerry hated the fact that they seemed to be sneaking around. Actually, there was no "seeming" about it. They *were* sneaking around and had been for the last eight months since they'd first gotten together. As much as he feared what his daughters would think about him dating someone, Jerry was beginning to grow tired of hiding.

"Fine," he huffed, smiling as he did. "I'll see you tonight. Come to my office." Jerry didn't need to tell Jan how to find his office because, although she hadn't been back to the ranch since they'd officially started dating, Jan had been to his office before. Back when she was a guest at the ranch.

That had been nine months ago.

And ever since he'd gotten up the nerve to call her and ask her out, Jerry hadn't looked back.

CHAPTER SIXTEEN

GRANT'S CELL PHONE RANG FOR the umpteenth time, but he ignored the damn thing sitting in his truck's cup holder.

He had been parked in front of his parents' trailer for the last two fucking hours, waiting for someone to show up. He was hoping his mother would be the one to greet him at the door, to let him know that her cell phone was broken or lost and that was the reason he hadn't been able to get in touch with her.

No such luck.

When he had arrived around noon, the driveway had been empty, and for the last two hours, the only vehicle he'd seen drive down the narrow road that wound through the trailer park had been an old beat-up Buick that had backfired and nearly given Grant a heart attack.

So, for the first half hour, he had walked around the outside of the trailer, trying to find a way inside without looking too suspicious. Both the front door and the back door were locked, which was a good sign. At least his father was thinking clearly enough to do that much.

When that investigative stint had failed, Grant had climbed back into his truck and cranked the air conditioner on high. For the next half hour, he had sent numerous texts to his father and tried to call his mother three more times. At the sixty-minute mark, he'd been oh for two.

The second hour of his wait had been a little more interesting, but only because Lane was blowing up his phone in an attempt to get in touch with him. As much as it pained him to do so, Grant had ignored every one of Lane's messages. He did not want to drag anyone into this mess. Hell, as it was, Gracie had already had to endure Darrell's uncouth behavior early that morning. Grant didn't see any reason to make anyone else suffer.

But for the last ten minutes, Lane's attempts had changed from text messages to actual calls, and Grant was beginning to feel guilty for blowing him off.

Just when he was reaching for his phone, ready to give in and call Lane back, the sound of a horn blaring behind him had Grant twisting in his seat.

What the fuck?

Damn it!

Grant threw open the driver's-side door hard enough to have the damn thing nearly closing on his leg before he jumped out of the truck and stormed over to the white Chevy with the ranch logo on the side that had pulled up behind his, ready to lay into the man for being such an idiot.

Before he could do that, Lane leapt out and marched right up to Grant, meeting him halfway between the two vehicles.

"Are you okay?" Lane asked.

Grant's breath hitched in his chest as he stared back at Lane. The man looked like he was crazy with worry, which sent another sharp slice of guilt ripping through Grant.

Shit.

"I'm fine," Grant said softly, all of his frustration dissolving instantly.

"Why the hell haven't you been answering your phone? I've been fucking worried."

"I'm sorr— Wait. How did you know how to find me?" Grant asked, breaking off his apology.

"I've got connections," Lane blurted. "Seriously, Grant. You couldn't just answer the damn phone?"

Grant looked at the ground, unable to come up with a feasible excuse for why he'd been ignoring Lane.

When Lane reached out and touched his arm, a soft nudge that had Grant's heart leaping into his throat, he swallowed hard, meeting Lane's dark eyes once more.

"I didn't want to drag you into this shit," Grant offered roughly. "I came here to try to find my mother."

Lane glanced up at the trailer and then back. "Is she here?"

"No. Neither is my father. So I've been waitin'."

"What? Are you just gonna sit in their driveway all damned day until they show up?"

"I'd thought about it," Grant argued. "What else can I do?"

"Fuck if I know." Lane broke their stare down, glancing around the area.

Grant knew what Lane saw. The trailer park where Grant had grown up was the very reason people referred to folks like him as trailer trash. The yards were mostly dirt — any plant life had died a long, *long* time ago. There were cars on blocks, screens missing from half of the metal trailers, foil decorating some of the windows. This wasn't one of those fancy mobile home parks people were living in these days. They didn't have modular housing with elaborate decks and pretty little flower beds lining the front. No, this was a trailer park.

"So what do we do now?" Lane implored, pinning Grant with his gaze once again.

" *We?*"

"Yeah. You heard me. I'm here for you. And since you can't bother to answer the damn phone, I'm not goin' anywhere. So, looks like you're stuck with me until you're ready to return to the ranch."

Grant looked around, trying to come up with a reason to continue sitting in his truck. He couldn't think of any because, hell, there was no telling when his father might come back. If Grant had to guess, the man would head to the races. And Lord knew where that might be.

"Fine. We can go back."

"Seriously?" Lane's tone reflected his incredulity. "I drove all this way for you to tell me you're ready to go back?"

Grant felt more guilt. He should've just answered the damn phone and he could've avoided this whole mess. "Yes. I'm serious. You can follow me back if you don't believe me."

"I will."

Grant nodded, but he didn't turn away. It didn't matter that the sun was blazing down on him and he was sweating like a whore in church. He couldn't seem to break away from this man, couldn't turn around and walk away.

Lane had come after him because he was worried. When was the last time that had happened?

Never.

Not once in his entire life had someone worried so much that they'd tracked him down to make sure he was okay. And his heart felt as though it might just explode in his chest. He wanted to reach out and wrap his arms around Lane, pull him close, and never let him go. The feeling was so overwhelming Grant was tempted to profess his undying love to Lane right there in the middle of the run-down trailer park.

"Come on," Lane whispered, his arm lifting until his fingers grazed the back of Grant's. "Let's get back to the ranch. Then we can talk."

Grant nodded, his emotions churning in his chest, making it hard to swallow around the lump that had formed in his throat.

"Does Gracie know?" Grant asked as he tried to convince his legs to move.

"No. But we're gonna tell her when we get back. This secretive shit has to stop, Grant. If you need help with somethin', we want to help you. That's part of the deal."

Grant's eyebrow cocked in question. "The deal?"

"Yeah. The relationship deal. You really are havin' a hard time with that part, aren't you? You can't keep us in the dark."

Grant wasn't just having a hard time with it, he didn't know how this was supposed to work. Regardless of how strong his feelings were for the two of them, Grant just wasn't used to this.

But he knew he wasn't the only one keeping secrets.

That had Grant thinking about seeing Gracie riding Astro Boy in the arena. The fact that she'd been hiding that from everyone for who knew how many years made him realize that it ran both ways. He wanted to know why she'd stopped racing, but he hadn't bothered to ask her because he didn't want to force her to open up to him. And in return, he'd been keeping his secrets, too.

As he looked into the penetrating brown eyes staring back at him, Grant understood just what Lane meant. Grant had spent his entire life keeping it all inside, never turning to anyone for help. Yet now he had two people who wanted to be there for him.

"Okay," Grant mumbled. "Let's go home. So we can talk."

The small smile that formed on Lane's lips sent a spark of something significantly more intense than just lust coursing through Grant.

No, this wasn't lust that he was feeling, although his body was reacting to Lane's nearness. But this ... this feeling in his chest... That was something else. Something that he was pretty sure was the closest thing to pure love he would ever feel.

Oddly enough, it was the same feeling he got when he looked at Gracie.

Man, oh, man. He was in big trouble.

■□■□■□■□

GRACE WAS PACING HER LIVING room floor when she heard the telltale clomp of boots on her front porch. She'd given up on keeping the front door open so that she could greet Lane and Grant when they arrived because the thick, humid August heat had become unbearable.

But now that she heard them, she rushed to the door and yanked it open, staring directly up into Lane's stony face.

It hadn't been an hour since she'd received a text from Lane letting her know that he'd left the ranch to go find Grant and that they were en route back. He had asked her to meet them at her house. The last part of that text — *it's time we sit down and talk* — had been what startled her the most.

Fear had been a tangible thing, making her hands sweat and her head hurt. So, instead of lingering at the main house for long, Grace had excused herself, purposely asking Hope if she could entertain Maddie and Ben for the afternoon. Not that she'd received an argument from Hope.

Unable to help herself, Grace threw her arms around Lane's neck and hugged him. She must've caught him off guard because he nearly stumbled as he caught her, his big hand cupping the back of her head while his arm banded around her waist.

"I'm sorry for not telling you," she whispered, referring to that morning when she hadn't bothered to tell him about Grant's father. She'd been dealing with the overwhelming guilt for most of the day, even as she tried to tell herself that she didn't have time to deal with her personal problems.

No, Grace found that the more she tried *not* to think about Lane and Grant, the more she did.

"It's okay, doll," Lane whispered back, the warmth of his breath against her ear reassuring her.

Reluctantly releasing Lane, Grace took a step back and allowed both men to come inside. When Grant closed the door behind him and turned back to face her, their eyes met, held. And then Grace was running into his arms.

What it was that made her want to grab hold of them and not let go, she had no idea. But being with them right then seemed like the most important thing in the world. And now that they were there, she knew they were going to have to sit down and talk. As much as she didn't want to, it was inevitable. After all, they couldn't let this thing they'd started blow up before it really got underway.

Although they'd been together now for a few months, Grace would be the first to admit that they had used sex to bring them closer to one another. Unfortunately, sex wasn't the most important aspect of a relationship — no matter how good it was.

"Sit," Grace said, releasing Grant and stepping away from him. "Can I get you a beer?"

"Beer's good," Grant and Lane said at the exact same time.

While she was grabbing three bottles from the refrigerator, Grace heard Lane ask, "Where do you think he went?"

She could only assume he was talking about Grant's father since the two of them had been at the man's house according to what she had learned during her text conversation with Lane earlier.

"No telling with him. If he's back to hardcore gamblin', he could be with his old friends, or he might've actually found a race to go to."

"When did he start gamblin'?" Lane asked as Grace made her way back to where the two men were sitting, one on each end of her sofa.

Passing out the bottles and keeping one for herself, Grace kept her eyes on Grant, waiting for him to respond. She could see that he wasn't thrilled with the topic, but he also didn't appear to be trying to brush Lane off. That had her wondering what had happened when Lane found Grant earlier. Had he actually approached Grant about talking this out? Or was Grant just feeling guilty?

That's your own guilt talking.

The little voice in her head was speaking up and had been for the last couple of hours. Ever since Lane had mentioned that they needed to talk, Grace had been thinking about the day they'd seen her racing Astro Boy in the arena. She'd blown them both off, refusing to talk about the subject although she knew they had questions. Why wouldn't they? No one seemed to know about her racing.

And that had been the plan.

"The first incident that I recall was when I was in sixth grade, so when I was maybe ten or eleven, I guess. I don't think they wanted me and Morgan to find out, but it was hard not to notice when my dad was so excited. I think he won a few thousand on a bet. He and my mom had just come back from a long weekend somewhere, and apparently, he'd found he had a fondness for horse races. After that, it was constant. Win or lose, my dad was obsessed.

"My mother didn't seem too worried in the beginning, but then, as the months passed, I started to notice we didn't have much food in the house. Not that my mother was ever a gourmet cook, but she did cook. Eventually, it came down to TV dinners nuked in the microwave or soup. And yes, things started goin' downhill from there. My parents started fightin' more."

"More?" Grace asked, trying to picture what it had been like for Grant growing up.

"They always fought. For as long as I can remember, things were physical around the house. My mother hit my father as much as he hit her."

"Did they hit you?" Lane asked.

Grace could see the tension radiating from Lane. His broad shoulders were rigid, and she could see the corded muscles standing out in his neck.

"Yeah," Grant admitted softly.

Grace couldn't describe the fury etched on Lane's face after hearing that response. She'd never seen him so upset, but he clearly didn't like the fact that Grant had been hit as a kid. She couldn't imagine what it had been like growing up in Grant's house. Her family, although she fought with her sisters regularly, wasn't into any sort of corporal punishment. If they had done something wrong, they got more chores to do. And they'd learned early on not to bitch about it, either, or her father would double them just to teach them a lesson.

"What about your sister?" Lane asked.

"Morgan fought back," Grant said, his eyes darting back and forth between Grace and Lane. "But she moved out when I was fifteen. At that point, my father had gone to rehab, and things were better. Not great, but they were gettin' better. When my grandmother died, my mom's mom, my dad started actin' funny again. I learned later that my mother had received some money in the will and my father wanted it. The smartest thing my mother ever did was use that money to pay off the trailer."

"What does your mom think about it now?" Grace asked.

"I don't know where my mother is," Grant admitted, his eyes sliding down to the beer bottle in his hand. He had been absently picking at the label, and now he was studying it intently.

"She's still not answering her phone?" Lane asked.

"Nope."

They were quiet for a few minutes, and Grace replayed the conversation over and over in her head. Remembering the confrontation they'd had with Grant's father, the evil she had felt exuding from that man... Maybe she was sheltered, she wasn't sure, but no matter how hard she tried, she couldn't fathom what it had been like for Grant as a kid. And although she'd lost her mother when she was young, Grace knew that things could've been significantly worse. At least her father hadn't fallen apart. He wasn't a gambler, he wasn't an alcoholic... No, for as long as she could remember, Jerry Lambert had been the strongest, most admirable man she'd ever met.

But now, as she sat in front of Grant, feeling his pain, she knew that this incredible man sitting just a few feet away from her was one of the strongest men she'd ever met, as well.

CHAPTER SEVENTEEN

LANE WAS DOING HIS BEST to keep his composure, but he really just wanted to throttle someone. Darrell Kingsley was the first person that came to mind.

As he sat there in Gracie's living room, trying to keep his rage locked down deep, he thought about what it must've been like growing up in Grant's house.

"Don't you dare feel sorry for me," Grant growled from his spot just a few feet away from Lane. "I don't need your pity."

"Trust me, I'm not pitying you, but I'd like to teach your father a lesson," Lane barked.

"I think he's learned a lesson. He's battlin' a gamblin' addiction," Grant argued. "No, I don't feel sorry for him, either, but I can't imagine what he goes through."

Lane nodded. He could sort of relate. Not that his father had a gambling addiction, but the man was intent on controlling everyone and everything in his life. "My father's not a saint, either," Lane offered. "He's the most controlling man I've ever met. He's got my mother under his thumb. Half the time, I have to wonder if she can even think for herself. My relationship with them is rocky, too."

"How so?" Gracie asked, drawing her legs up into the chair beneath her as she watched him intently.

"Where I grew up, parents had money. I mean real money. I didn't want for nothin', and I think my dad thought that would make me moldable," Lane explained. "We lived in a big house in a gated community, I went to a private school, my mom wore designer clothes, and she dressed up every day although she didn't work. My dad threw his money around, and he was proud of it. He measured his worth by material possessions. I just happened to be one of those possessions."

He could still remember the conversations he'd have with his father. Always what he could do better, what he should've done differently. Didn't matter if Lane hit the winning run of the game, there was something Lane could've done better.

"He wanted me to be a doctor or a lawyer. And I'm not talking, 'doctors and lawyers make good money, son, you're smart enough, that's what you should do,' either. No, my father insisted that I be one or the other because those were prestigious careers and he'd be able to show me off even more.

"Imagine his surprise when I decided to defy him and do odd jobs here and there. I hadn't held a long-term job before coming to DHR." Lane wasn't looking at Gracie or Grant as he spoke, fearful of what he'd see in their eyes. Sure, maybe it sounded pathetic for him to bitch and moan about his father wanting him to actually do something with his life, but it wasn't the path he had wanted to take.

"Maybe if he hadn't pushed so hard, you would've wanted to be one," Gracie said. "I know the feelin'. When I was little, I wanted to race like my mom. She taught me everything she knew, starting when I was five."

"You're really good, you know," Grant offered.

Now Lane was looking at Gracie, trying his best to hide the startled look on his face. He hadn't expected either of them to open up so easily, and sitting there watching Gracie talk about her mother made his heart ache for her.

"That's why I don't want anyone to know about it," she admitted. "I don't want anyone pushing me to do something I don't want to do."

"If you don't want to do it, why do you? It takes practice to be as good as you are, Gracie," Grant stated.

"I don't want to go pro," Gracie explained. "I love riding Astro Boy. It's the only time I feel completely free, but I…" Gracie paused for a moment, and Lane saw her throat working. She appeared to be swallowing her emotions, and he was tempted to reach out and grab her, pull her into his lap so he could hold her close.

"If my mother can't be here to see me, I don't want to do it."

Wow. That was a startling revelation. From the moment Lane had seen Gracie riding Astro Boy, showing that little girl just what she was capable of, he hadn't been able to get the image out of his head.

"So you gave up?" Grant asked. The question, had it not been laced with sympathy, would've sounded harsh.

"I didn't give up," Gracie countered heatedly. "I'm not a quitter."

"No, you're not," Grant and Lane agreed simultaneously.

Once again, the silence descended on them, and Lane fought the urge to fidget. As it was, Grant was shredding the beer bottle label, and Gracie was now fingering the tassels on one of her throw pillows.

Lane finally cleared his throat, drawing their attention to him. "So what can we do to help you?" he asked Grant directly. "You know, with your crazy father?"

Lane tried to keep the question light because the emotion that was charging the air in the room had caused a black cloud to settle over them. He didn't want things to be so serious for them. Sure, he wanted them to be able to talk to each other, but he didn't want it to be something they dreaded doing, either.

"I don't even know where to start," Grant began. "I went to their house hopin' one of them would come home. I'm more worried about my mother, honestly. I don't know where she is."

"Have you called your sister?" Gracie asked.

Grant's eyes widened as though the thought hadn't occurred to him. He shook his head, confirming Lane's suspicion.

"Then let's start there," Lane said, leaning forward. "Call her. See if she's heard from her. Once we get an answer, we'll go from there."

"Who wants another beer?" Gracie asked, springing up from her seat.

Just when she was starting to walk past him, Lane reached out and grabbed her, pulling her over the arm of the couch and into his lap. He stared into her eyes, refusing to let her go when she began to squirm. "As for you, I'd love to watch you race again. And no, I'm not talkin' professionally, Gracie." Lane swallowed, watching her watch him. "Truth be told, watchin' you ride that horse is one of the hottest things I've ever seen."

That earned him a small smile from her. Lane wasn't willing to settle for small, so he leaned in and pressed his lips to hers, sliding his tongue into her mouth as he cradled the back of her head in his palm.

The next thing he knew, the beer bottle he'd been holding disappeared from his hand at the same time Gracie's arms wrapped around his neck, pulling him to her until he was practically on top of her.

Kissing her was so intense, every single time. The way she always put her whole heart into it made Lane want to go on kissing her forever. And he might have, too, if Grant hadn't moved closer.

Now, Lane was a big man, he didn't deny that, and Grant was no lightweight, so, needless to say, they didn't quite fit on the couch comfortably. Which was why Lane maneuvered so that he was easing Gracie down to the floor, repositioning himself so that he was kneeling between her legs and Grant was lying on his side next to her. From there, Lane alternated kissing them both, trying not to hurry, wanting to cherish every single minute, every single slide of their tongues into his mouth.

When Gracie's hands slipped beneath his T-shirt, Lane sucked in a breath. Her soft, cool fingers sent chills up and down his skin. The warm, callused hand that caressed his back had to belong to Grant, and the combination of both of their hands on him was enough to make his head spin.

"We should move this to the bedroom," Gracie murmured against Lane's lips several moments later.

"What the lady wants, the lady gets," Lane whispered, shifting so that he could reach beneath her and lift her into his arms.

Gracie giggled, but then she crushed her lips back to his, and he had to go slow so that he didn't run into the wall while she stole his breath with her delicious tongue. When she sucked his tongue into her mouth, he hit the wall, his back resting against the unyielding wood as he fought the incredible surge of desire that shot through him like a lightning bolt.

"Lord have mercy, woman," Lane said on a harsh breath when she released him.

When Lane reached the bed, Grant was already there, sitting on the edge, watching them with hooded eyes. Instead of tossing her onto the mattress as he had before, Lane eased her down, his hand sliding up over Grant's thigh as he positioned himself over her, urging Grant to join them.

And then the three of them were on the bed, kissing and touching, the temperature in the room rising, rivaling the humid August heat outside.

How they managed to remove their clothes while never getting off the bed, Lane would never know, but several minutes later, Lane was hovering over Gracie, his rock-hard cock sheathed, and his breath was stolen from his lungs as he slid into her. Her legs wrapped around his hips, her ankles pressing into his ass as she tried to pull him deeper.

While the silky hot walls of her pussy gripped him, Lane tried to remember where they were and what he was supposed to be doing. The pleasure was beyond incredible, making his brain fuzzy. He tried to remain still, to let her body acclimate to his size, but Gracie had other plans. She used her strong legs to pull him deeper, grinding her hips beneath him, fucking him although he was the one on top.

Figuring she wanted to lead, Lane managed to flip them so that she was riding him, his cock deep inside her as she sat up. Lane's attention was drawn to Grant, who was stroking his dick while watching them closely. Snaking one hand out behind Grant's thigh, he urged the man closer until his thick erection was hovering just above his mouth. He met Grant's gaze just as he began to suck the swollen head between his lips.

"Fuck," Grant groaned, his fingers spearing into Lane's hair.

And while Lane sucked Grant's dick, allowing the man to fuck his face, Gracie proceeded to ride Lane's cock for all she was worth. Overcome with pleasure, Lane had to fight to keep his eyes open, not wanting to miss a moment as he watched Gracie's gorgeous tits bounce freely while she impaled herself on his cock.

Any other time, this would've seemed like run-of-the-mill, incredible sex. But there was something deeper, something vastly more emotional than before. He contributed that underlying intensity to the fact that they were finally opening up to one another. On every level.

"Lane, that's too good," Grant moaned, but then Gracie stilled as she leaned forward, her mouth meeting Lane's around Grant's thick shaft. When Gracie took over, sucking Grant's cock into the furnace of her mouth, Lane twisted his head and laved Grant's balls with a long, slow slide of his tongue while bucking his hips upward, driving himself into Gracie.

And for the first time in a very long time, Lane wasn't hovering on the brink. No, he wanted to savor this moment for as long as possible.

■□■□■□■□

THE GLORIOUS FRICTION OF GRACIE'S tongue along the underside of Grant's shaft had stars dancing behind his eyelids. The only thing keeping him from racing to the finish line was the smoldering heat of Lane's mouth wrapped around his balls. He couldn't focus on just one because both sensations were battling for supremacy, and for the life of him, Grant didn't know which one was better.

He would've taken several more minutes to compare the two, but Lane was using his big hand to force Grant to move, and before he knew it, Grant was straddling Lane's head, facing Gracie as she sat up, still impaled on Lane's cock. Taking the opportunity presented to him, Grant leaned in and planted his lips on Gracie's, gripping the back of her head as he pulled her to him. Their tongues dueled, and Grant was caught up in the moment, content just to kiss her when the heat of Lane's tongue slid between his ass cheeks.

"Fuck," Grant cried into Gracie's mouth, pulling away from her, doing his best not to fall over while Lane tongue-fucked his ass, gripping his thighs firmly.

The smile on Gracie's face was one of pure and profound pleasure. She continued to rock gently on Lane's cock while reaching for Grant's, stroking him firmly. And now there were new sensations warring against one another: the soft, smooth stroke of Gracie's hand on his dick, while the insistent press of Lane's tongue against his asshole had him aching for something more.

And then there was more.

"Oh, damn," Grant groaned as Lane slid two fingers into him.

He had no idea how Lane could handle the sheer ecstasy of Gracie grinding herself on his cock, but somehow the man managed, and Grant was reaping the benefits.

But he needed more.

Grant shifted onto one knee, planting his other foot on the bed so that he was wide open to Lane beneath him, his hand joining Gracie's as he stroked his own cock.

"Fuck me harder," Grant begged Lane.

Noticing that Gracie's attention was focused between his legs and the man who was penetrating him with two fingers, Grant covered her hand with his and began stroking himself firmly. He didn't slow down, encouraged by the way Gracie was watching the scene before her. Lane added another finger, and Grant knew he was getting close.

"Stroke me harder, Gracie. Squeeze my dick," Grant begged, tightening his grip on her hand as he jacked his cock while riding Lane's fingers. "Sonuvabitch," Grant said on a strangled moan. "I'm gonna come. Put my cock in your mouth, Gracie."

When she leaned forward, Grant slipped his fingers into her hair, pulling her close as her lips wrapped firmly around the engorged head, sliding lower and lower until the back of her throat brushed the sensitive tip. "Oh, hell yes. Make me come," he pleaded.

Lane thrust his fingers inside of Grant, brushing Grant's prostate repeatedly until the only thing Grant knew was the building pressure, the glorious sparks that ignited at the base of his spine, radiating outward. Unable to move, not wanting to risk losing the fingers buried deep in his ass, Grant urged Gracie's head down, until he was fucking her mouth deeper.

"Fuck, that's it. That's... Oh, shit. I'm..." Grant's entire body froze, his muscles locking, his ass gripping the fingers buried deep inside of him as he came, his orgasm ripping through him with a ferocity he'd never known before.

And when it was over, Grant could hardly remain upright.

Okay, no. That wasn't true. There was no "hardly" about it. He couldn't remain upright, falling over onto his side when Gracie released him from her mouth.

While he caught his breath, which he wasn't sure was going to be an easy thing, Grant watched Gracie as she began to bounce on Lane's cock again. Lane gripped the comforter while Gracie lifted and dropped onto Lane, over and over, faster and faster until they were both crying out their release in tandem.

Grant's heart was still pounding when Gracie fell on top of Lane, her arm falling across Grant's chest.

"We're gonna do that again," Lane said, his words raspy from his desperate need for oxygen.

"Shower first. Then dinner. Then sex," Gracie added.

"Works for me," Grant offered, running his arm up and down Gracie's smooth back.

"What time is it, anyway?" Gracie asked.

Grant had to twist around to see the clock on the nightstand. "Five thirty."

"Definitely dinner," Lane added, his stomach growling as though reiterating the request.

"Let's go to the dining room," Gracie said, pushing up to a sitting position.

Grant watched as she rocked slowly, still filled with Lane's cock.

"Oh, damn," Lane said on a heavy sigh. "Eat first. Then you can ride me all you want, cowgirl."

Gracie laughed but eased off Lane and then disappeared into the bathroom, leaving Grant and Lane lying there in her bed together. Lane was just about to say something, but he didn't have a chance because Gracie ducked her head into the room and said, "Oh, and I want you both to stay the night."

Grant stared at the spot where she had just been, even after she disappeared again, his heart thumping twice as hard as before. But this time it wasn't from physical exertion.

No, this time it was from that damn feeling that Lane had brought out in him earlier. The one he had yet to clearly define. The one that felt a lot like love.

CHAPTER EIGHTEEN

AFTER THEIR SHOWERS, WHICH THEY took separately due to Lane's hunger pains, the three of them went to the dining room at the main house. And for the first time in a long time, they didn't linger over dessert or coffee, preferring instead to return to Grace's house.

And ever since they'd walked in the door, the three of them had been lying in her bed, completely naked. Up to this point, other than some heavy petting and some rather intense making out, they had spent more time talking than anything else.

Talking.

Funny, that.

Grace remembered the last time she'd been snuggled in bed with the two men, questioning Grant about his father. He hadn't wanted to open up, yet tonight he was answering the questions easily. She still didn't know what had happened or why the change, but she wasn't interested in questioning it, either. Even though she wished she'd been part of the conversation that apparently had occurred between the two men, Grace was just happy that they were talking.

They were acting like ... adults. Imagine that.

She had learned more about Lane's parents and his father's high-handedness. Lane had shared some of the minor details of his life before Dead Heat Ranch, something he wasn't all that proud of. He admitted that he'd been promiscuous and wild, although he assured them both that he was always safe. It was still surprising to find out the man had been in numerous bisexual relationships over the years. Especially considering this was still new to Grace.

Well, maybe not new. They had been seeing each other for the better part of three months now, even if that time had gone by so quickly.

"What're you thinkin' about?" Lane whispered, his breath blowing her hair as she rested her cheek on his chest.

"Us," she answered quickly.

"I like the sound of that," Lane replied. "Us."

Grace slid her fingers through the soft hair on Lane's chest, tugging gently every so often just because she enjoyed watching him squirm.

"I wish we had more time to do this," Grant added, his erection pressing into Grace's lower back as he spooned her from behind.

"Me, too."

That seemed to be the consensus, although Grace still didn't know why they didn't have more time to do this. Aside from having to work ridiculous hours and trying to hide their relationship from everyone so that her father wouldn't get word of it...

Okay, so that pretty much was the reason right there.

Grace hated the sneaking around part. Then again, the three of them had gone to dinner without thinking about the way others were probably looking at them. Maybe that was a start.

When they reached the point where talking was futile thanks to the heated kisses and heavy petting that had started once again, Grace gave herself over to them.

She found herself transfixed by the sight of Grant and Lane kissing, their bodies twining together until Lane was on top of Grant, kneeling between Grant's spread thighs. These two were something to see. Two incredibly powerful males, touching, tasting, battling for control, yet yielding to one another at the same time. It was beautiful to see. Especially since she could see the emotion on Grant's face, the feelings he seemed too scared to share with anyone. They were plain as day but never spoken.

"Come here," Lane demanded softly, pulling his mouth from Grant's and looking up at her.

Getting to her knees, Grace crawled across the bed until she was kneeling next to the two men. And then she was laughing because Grant toppled her over as he pulled her close. Their mouths met in a heated kiss, and Grace realized he had other things in mind, rolling her onto her back until he was situated between her thighs.

"Mmm," he whispered against her mouth. "I want to taste you. I want to eat your pussy until you're screamin' my name, darlin'."

Finding no reason to refuse him, Grace smiled as she spread her legs farther apart, enjoying the feel of his mouth as he trailed his lips down her neck, over her collarbone, then slid seamlessly over to her right breast, scraping her nipple with his teeth. If he wasn't careful, he was going to make her come just like that. When she reached for his head, wanting to pull him closer, he did the opposite, releasing her breast with an audible pop.

"Put your hands on the headboard," he instructed, a mischievous gleam in his stormy blue eyes.

Grace did as instructed, reaching behind her and gripping the bottom edge of the headboard. It was apparently all that he needed because Grant's talented mouth returned to her breast, once again teasing her until she was writhing beneath him.

She felt the bed shift, knew that Lane had retrieved a condom from the nightstand, but she couldn't see him around Grant. Then came the point when she couldn't see anything at all. Grant's wicked mouth moved farther down her body, the pleasure blinding her. When he began licking her clit with his skillful tongue, stroking gently, insistently, her eyes closed of their own volition.

"Oh, God," she sighed. "That feels so good."

Not trying to hurry him, Grace rocked her hips upward, desperately trying to increase the friction of his tongue along her clit as her skin tingled in response to the incredible sensation.

Grant's heated breath tickled her labia, and she realized he'd inhaled and exhaled sharply because Lane was sliding into him. Forcing her eyes open, she noticed that Lane was standing behind Grant, both of them at the foot of the bed while Grant was leaning over, his mouth hovering directly above her aching pussy.

"So tight," Lane moaned. "So good."

Oh, God. The look on Lane's face as he drove himself inside Grant had another round of chills racing over her sensitive nerve endings. She couldn't have torn her eyes off them if she'd tried.

"Lane," Grant moaned, the vibration causing her pussy to throb.

"Keep licking her pussy or I'll stop," Lane commanded, his voice rough and sensual.

Grace watched closely, admiring the way the muscles in Lane's huge chest flexed as he gripped Grant's hips. She could see the way his hips jerked forward and back, but he was maintaining an incredibly slow pace.

"Oh," Grace squealed when Grant slipped two fingers inside her. "Oh, yes."

Her eyes met Lane's over Grant's body, and she saw so much in the dark brown pools. So much emotion, so much desire. It nearly overwhelmed her.

But before she could let it, Grace's attention was ripped back to the man sliding his tongue through her slit, driving his fingers into her oh-so-slowly.

"Grant." She said his name in warning, as the incredible pleasure sent her closer to the edge. Right to the point she thought she was going to come undone. And then when Grant wrapped his lips around her clit, using his tongue to flick relentlessly, there was nothing she could do but ride the waves of her orgasm as it crashed through her.

"Fuck yes," Lane growled. "I love watching her come."

But Grant wasn't finished. He released her clit from between his lips as he held himself up with one hand, bracing his body as Lane began pounding into him ruthlessly. Grant continued to thrust his fingers inside her, adding a third until she was begging and pleading, another more powerful orgasm cresting.

■□■□■□■□

LANE WAS HOLDING HIMSELF BACK, desperate to send Grant careening into the abyss. As he drove into the man harder, faster, over and over, his balls drawing up against his body, Lane sucked in air like it was about to be a scarce resource.

"Oh, God, yes!" Gracie screamed, her body thrashing on the bed, her hands gripping the headboard.

Fuck, she was beautiful when she came. Her sweet tits thrust upward, her taut stomach stretched as she drove her hips up against Grant's mouth. Watching her nearly unraveled him.

Lane had to tear his eyes away or he would've exploded instantly. Instead, he focused on driving himself deeper into Grant, gripping Grant's hips and pulling him back against his punishing thrusts.

When Grant heaved himself up on his hands, still bent over the bed, Lane increased his pace, slamming into him while Grant drove his hips back against Lane. The sound of their sweat-slick bodies slapping against one another, mixed with the pounding of Lane's heart and the harsh breaths he was dragging into his lungs, were the only things he could hear for what seemed like an eternity.

But then Grant was saying his name, repeating it over and over, the sound so sweet on the man's lips.

"Lane. Oh, shit that feels so good. Don't stop. Please don't stop."

"Come for me, baby."

Lane saw Gracie move, realized she was scooting down on the bed until she was practically beneath Grant.

"Oh, yes, Gracie, baby, stroke my cock."

"Come for us," Gracie whispered. "Come on me."

Oh, fucking hell.

Her words had Lane's balls drawing up even tighter to his body. The strong, hot grip Grant's ass had on his dick was almost more than he could bear. But Lane didn't want it to end, wanted to stay right there, buried to the hilt in Grant's body.

"Oh, fuck yes. So good, Lane. Harder!"

Lane wasn't sure he could give any more than he was, but he focused on pounding Grant harder, reaching around him and holding him with one arm while he fucked him, alternating between shallow and deep. "Come for us, baby. Come all over Gracie's beautiful tits."

"I can't hold on... Oh, shit. I'm..." Grant's muscles locked on Lane's dick, sending both pleasure and pain ricocheting through Lane's entire body until he couldn't hold on any longer.

Lane roared as his orgasm gripped him, his fingers digging into Grant's hip as he tightened his hold on his waist, pulling him against him as he drove as deep as he could, his dick pulsing and throbbing as he came hard and fast.

And when Lane couldn't hold himself up any longer, he withdrew quickly, stripping the condom off and tossing it into the trash can sitting in the corner before flopping onto the bed alongside Gracie.

Grant disappeared but returned a minute later with two washcloths that he used to clean Gracie and then Lane as they lay side by side. Closing his eyes, Lane focused on the soft sound of Gracie's breathing while he tried his best to stay conscious. He must've succeeded because he heard Gracie's request for them to get under the blankets, which he did without argument, pulling Gracie against him while reaching for Grant.

No one spoke. Lane wasn't opposed to the silence that time. They'd done plenty of talking earlier. Right then, he wanted to hold on to the two people who'd managed to weave themselves deep into his heart. And as he drifted off to sleep, he managed to whisper the words "I love you" to both of them.

He had fallen hard and fast for these two, and he didn't have a problem telling them. As his brain went offline, giving in to sleep, he wondered when the two of them were going to come to terms with their feelings, too. As much as he truly believed they felt the same way for him, Lane still longed to hear the words.

After all, it'd been a damn long time since anyone had told him that they loved him.

Chapter Nineteen

A little later that night

GRANT CRAWLED INTO HIS HOUSE around ten thirty with just enough strength to make it to the couch after grabbing a bottle of water from the refrigerator. After the exertion from their evening activities, Grant didn't think he'd be able to make it as far as the bedroom.

He knew he should've been at Gracie's, should've stayed in bed with her and Lane and slept right there, but his mind wouldn't wind down. He was still worried about his mother, and tossing and turning all night would've just disturbed Gracie and Lane. Which was why he'd woken them up to inform them that he had to go.

Neither of them had been happy, but Grant — following the theme of the day — had told them the truth. Although they tried to talk him out of leaving, he got the impression they understood.

On his way home, he had realized that with everything going on, he hadn't even had a chance to talk to Jerry about what had happened that morning with Darrell — and his intentions to do so had been good.

Your own damn fault. You're the one who wasted half the day waiting for your father to show up.

Yeah, yeah, yeah. The stupid little voice wasn't telling him anything he didn't already know. Lucky for the voice, Grant wasn't interested in arguing. Even with himself.

He took it as a good sign that Jerry hadn't hunted him down, though. He still wasn't sure the man wasn't going to, but for now, he opted to breathe a sigh of relief.

On top of not hearing from Jerry, Grant hadn't heard a peep out of his father, either. Not one single text or phone call ever since the blowup in Jerry's office, which offered him a sense of both worry and relief. Neither more prominent than the other.

If Darrell wasn't harassing him, then there was probably a reason for it. Like the man was up to no good, and Grant was going to pay for it in the end.

Closing his eyes, his head resting on the cushioned back of the couch, he willed the thoughts away. He did not want to sit there and ponder his father's whereabouts or what he was up to. Nothing good would come of it.

Grant's eyes flew open as one thing came to mind.

Holy shit.

Surely not.

Crap.

Leaning forward and resting his elbows on his knees, Grant dropped his head into his hands. Surely, Jerry hadn't given Darrell a job... What if Darrell showed up on Monday morning ready to go to work? Wouldn't that just be all fucked up?

Grant's thoughts came to a screeching halt. *Oh, hell.* What if Jerry had loaned Darrell money? That would be the last thing that needed to happen. He'd much rather have to deal with working alongside his father day in and day out than be indebted to Jerry Lambert. And if that were true, then Grant needed to get with Jerry so he could set up a payment plan because there was no way in hell that Darrell was good for the money, no matter what he'd told Grant's boss.

Shit.

Forcing himself to his feet, Grant grabbed his truck keys from the counter. He was too damned tired to walk back to the main house, even if it was only ten minutes at most.

A minute later, he was in his truck, easing along the dirt path that wound through the ranch. He noticed that Jerry's office light was on, which meant the man was probably burning the midnight oil, although midnight was still a couple of hours off.

Jerry Lambert wasn't a man who stayed up late.

At least not that Grant could tell.

No, good ol' Jerry was usually locked up tight in the house by seven on a good night.

Pulling up to the office, Grant tossed the truck in park and climbed out. The night was still, not even a breeze stirring the trees; the only sound was the gravel crunching beneath Grant's boots.

Sometimes he hated summer in Texas. By the time he made it to Jerry's office door, just a few measly yards away, he was sweating.

Wanting to get this over with, Grant rapped his knuckles lightly on the door before turning the knob.

Uh…

Oh, fucking hell.

Grant pulled himself up short and blinked rapidly as he tried to figure out what he was seeing. It took all of two seconds for his synapses to kick in, and he was backing out the way he'd come, easing the door shut, a wide grin forming on his face as he started to chuckle like a school kid.

Holy shit.

Jerry had a woman in there. And he wasn't going over the books with her, either. Well, they were kind of *over* the books, from a technical standpoint. After all, the woman was on the desk.

"What are you doing out here? Is my dad in there?"

Faith jolted Grant from his chuckle-fest, and he turned to face her, every ounce of humor draining out of him at the sight of the youngest Lambert daughter. "He's … uh… No, he's not," Grant lied.

Making his way to where Faith stood, he tried to distract her, hoping she wouldn't insist on checking for herself because … mother of all things holy, Jerry was making out with a woman right there on his desk.

Yes. On. The. Desk.

Thank God Jerry and the mystery woman were both dressed because Grant wasn't sure his eyes would've been able to tolerate the sight of his boss naked. Not that he didn't think Jerry was built like a brick shithouse or anything, but seeing Jerry and a woman would be like seeing his own parents going at it.

That was a scene that would require Grant to bleach his brain.

"Can I help you with something?" Grant asked, coming to a stop directly in front of Faith.

"No." Her answer was quick, and if Grant wasn't mistaken, it was also a little sad.

"Come on, I'll walk you home."

"But your truck's right there."

Grant peered over his shoulder, realizing his truck was, in fact, right there.

Hmmm.

How to get out of that one.

"I'm having problems with it. I was gonna have Cody look at it in the morning," he lied again.

This was certainly not his finest hour.

"Oh. Okay."

Faith turned and started walking, so Grant fell into step with her.

"Everything okay?" he asked.

It wasn't that he was in the mood to talk. He was actually ready to face plant on the hard ground at his feet, but he really didn't want Faith to see her father making out with a woman in his office. Ol' Jerry needed to learn to lock the door.

"Yes. Maybe. No," Faith responded, clearly exasperated.

Grant didn't say a word, not wanting to interrupt in the event she was going to continue.

He didn't have to wait long.

"Can you have a talk with Rusty?" she asked, turning her bright blue-green eyes on Grant.

"Talk to him?" *Please, please, please, don't let this be personal.* "Is he doin' somethin' he shouldn't be doin'?"

"Technically, yes," Faith said, stopping abruptly and turning to face him. Grant forced his feet to come to a standstill, taking a deep breath.

"*Technically?*"

"Yeah," Faith reiterated. "He's askin' me to go out with him."

Shit. This was almost as bad as walking in on Jerry. Grant decided to play along. "And that's a bad thing, why?"

"Because my father *forbids* any of the ranch hands to date his daughters."

"Don't you think maybe that's just your dad being a ... I don't know, maybe just being a dad?"

"No," Faith said adamantly. "I don't think that's just him throwin' his weight around. My dad's serious when he says we can't date the cowboys. Remember Garrett Daniels?"

"Yeah," Grant said hesitantly. He remembered Garrett. He'd been the head wrangler about five years earlier, before Hope had stepped into the role.

"Dad fired him because he stood up to him, said he wanted to date Trinity. Went so far as to tell my father that he didn't care what he said. A week later, he was fired, and Hope stepped into the role as head wrangler."

Shit.

"I thought…"

"That Garrett got caught using the equipment after hours?" Faith asked. "Did you actually believe that crap? That's the story they ended up tellin' people. I mean, seriously, would my dad really care that Garrett was usin' equipment after hours? Hell, most of the wranglers do it."

Yeah, Grant knew that. They all used the equipment after hours, mostly the mechanic's tools when they were working on their personal vehicles, sometimes taking one of the work vehicles into town for personal trips, or every now and again taking the horses out when they brought a woman to the ranch. No, he didn't believe that Jerry would fire Garrett for that reason. Surely not. "Did you ask Trin about it?"

"Didn't have to. She was so upset when it was all over, she locked herself in her cabin for a week."

Grant didn't even know what to say to that, but he had to cop to a moment of panic as he thought about Jerry booting him from the ranch for dating Gracie. Or worse, Jerry sending both him *and* Lane packing… No, scratch that… Worse would be Jerry burying them six feet under because they were *both* seeing her.

Faith started walking again, and Grant fell into step beside her, pondering this new information.

Holy shit. His entire life would be in a shambles if he lost this job.

But is your job worth more to you than Gracie?

Grant was ashamed to say that was a question he couldn't very well answer. His job was his life, and not just because it paid the bills. He loved working at Dead Heat Ranch. He had found something he was good at, and maybe he hadn't reached all of the little goals he'd set for himself, but he was happy with how he spent his days. He'd been at the ranch since he was nineteen years old, for chrissakes.

"Thanks for walkin' me," Faith said, pulling Grant from his thoughts. Stopping alongside Faith, he looked around and realized they'd made it to her cabin.

"You're welcome," he replied.

"So, will you talk to Rusty for me?"

Grant studied Faith for a moment. "Don't you think that would be better comin' from you?"

"No," she refuted. "Knowin' him, he'll go talk to my dad if I say something."

Yeah, that wouldn't be a good idea.

"Please."

Oh, hell. Grant was never good at telling a woman no, especially when she said please.

"Fine. When I see him, I'll see what I can do."

"Thank you!" Faith exclaimed, throwing her arms around his neck and hugging him tightly. She pulled away and ran in the house.

And it wasn't lost on Grant that Faith had just hugged him because he had agreed to break up with a man for her.

Shit.

As though things weren't bad enough already.

Chapter Twenty

Friday morning

WHERE WAS EVERYONE?

More specifically, where was her father?

Grace was sitting in the tiny kitchen where her father took his morning coffee as she waited for him to show up. The place was a ghost town, not a single person having come in or out in the last half hour that Grace had been nursing her now-cold coffee. At least, no one was traipsing back and forth in the part that was purposely separated from the rest of the house.

Several years ago, Jerry had insisted that he should be allowed at least a few minutes to spend with his kids if he wanted to, without people always interrupting them, which had prompted her father to section off an area where they could meet without encountering guests.

Ummm ... no guests.

But also no dad.

Where was he?

They utilized the small kitchen area mainly so they could talk in private if necessary, which, yes, Grace was actually interested in doing.

Grace glanced at her watch, wondering just where he was. He never slept late. Ever. Hell, most of the time he was the one sitting at the scarred little table waiting for one of them to come in to chat.

Not today.

Because she still didn't believe it, Grace grabbed her cell phone, which she had been mindlessly spinning on the table, and glanced at the clock on there, too. Nope, her watch wasn't broken. Her dad was late.

The screen door opened, causing Grace's head to snap to the side.

"Mornin'," Mercy said with an exaggerated yawn. "Where's Pops?"

"No idea. I was wonderin' the same thing."

Grant walked in a few heartbeats behind Mercy, glancing between the two of them before making a quick detour to the coffeepot.

"Maybe he had a late night," Mercy added.

"Who?" Grant inquired.

"My dad," Grace answered.

Grant looked like a deer caught in the headlights as he stared back at her, his eyes then sliding over to Mercy.

"What do you know, cowboy?" Mercy asked, clearly catching on to the same slip-up that Grace had.

"I know that this is the best coffee in the whole damn world," Grant said, focusing on the cup in his hand, deliberately not looking at her or Mercy as he sipped slowly.

"I think you're full of shit," Mercy argued. "I've tasted that coffee. Now what do you know?"

"Not a damn thing," Grant said firmly, still studying that freaking coffee cup.

Grace knew something was up. Grant wasn't one to gossip, but obviously, he knew something they didn't. And since it had to do with her dad, she wanted to know just what the hell it was.

Grace rose from her chair and closed the gap between them, coming to stand directly in front of Grant. So close that he had to move the coffee cup out of the way. When their eyes met, she could see he was smiling. Not with his lips, but the slight crinkles at the corners of his eyes said he was fighting it.

"Where's my dad?" Grace asked, planting her hands on her hips. "And don't you dare tell me that you don't know."

"I really don't know," Grant said resolutely. "I haven't seen him this mornin.'"

"Grant Kingsley, don't you play dumb with me," Grace snipped. "What. Do. You. Know?" she asked, punctuating each word with her finger into his chest.

"Ouch. Shit," Grant said, laughing as he tried to get away from her. She had him trapped between her body and the counter, and if he tried too hard to break past her, he would spill his coffee on her, which she knew he wasn't going to do.

"Spill it, cowboy," Grace demanded, referring to what he knew and not the coffee.

"You don't want to know," Grant said, his eyes suddenly serious.

"Why? What happened?" Mercy interrupted, moving to stand next to Grace. "Is my dad okay?"

"He's fine." Grant's blue eyes darted back and forth between Grace and Mercy. "Better than fine, I'd say."

This time Mercy was the one to poke Grant with a finger, right in his belly, making him laugh — or maybe that was a grunt — and slosh coffee over the rim of his cup and onto his hand. Grace jumped back to avoid being scalded, but Mercy was right there, up in his face. Well, as up in his face as she could get considering how freaking short she was.

"Fine. Shit. Back off a minute," Grant said with a rough chuckle.

Mercy did, but not far. She took a step back while Grace took a step forward, both of them still pinning Grant in place, with their eyes and their bodies. If he really wanted to get away, she knew he could easily move them out of his way, probably at the same time.

"I kinda ... uh... stumbled upon your dad last night. *Totally* by accident," he explained, a look of intense amusement on his face. "He was... Well, let's just say he was otherwise occupied."

"*What?*" Mercy exclaimed. "Are you sayin' what I think you're sayin'?"

"Depends," Grant stated. "What do you think I'm sayin'?"

"My dad has a woman?" Mercy asked.

Grace's head snapped toward her sister. How the hell had she come up with that? That was the furthest thing from Grace's mind.

A woman?

Her dad?

Seriously?

Grant just nodded, a clear affirmation that Mercy's assumption was correct.

"Oh, my God," Mercy whispered, turning to look at Grace. "Pops? With a woman?"

"Like I said, I didn't stick around, so honestly, I don't think he knows I was there. So for chrissakes, don't fucking say anything," Grant bellowed. "Look, I gotta get to work."

Grant glanced at Grace, their eyes meeting for a long moment. Grant was the first to break away, his gaze darting over to Mercy and then back to meet hers before he said, "I'll stop by your place tonight. If that's all right with you."

Grace knew that Mercy was aware of what was going on between her, Grant, and Lane. Well, maybe she didn't know quite how serious things had been getting, but hell, her nosy-ass sister had played a part in getting the three of them together in the first place. Even knowing that, Grace had to admit, it was still a little strange for her sister to be listening in. Rather than say anything, Grace simply nodded her head, her heart beating fast and hard in her chest.

"Talk to y'all later," Grant said, dumping his coffee in the sink and putting his mug in the dishwasher before sneaking out the door.

When Grace turned around, she found Mercy sitting at the table, staring off into space. She looked a million miles away.

"You okay?" Grace asked.

"Pops has a woman."

"That's the rumor," Grace confirmed, not sure what to say about that.

"Should we ask him about her? Who is she? Where did she come from? How long has he been seein' her?" As the questions continued to tumble out of Mercy's mouth, Mercy jumped to her feet and began to pace. "Do you think she works here? Does he love her?"

"Slow down," Grace insisted, placing her hand on Mercy's arm, effectively stopping her in her tracks. "Let's take this one step at a time. First of all, we don't know what Grant stumbled upon last night. Who knows, maybe it was a…" Oh, hell, Grace couldn't say the words aloud. To think her father might've had a one-night stand didn't seem appropriate.

Mercy turned to face Grace, her eyes reflecting what Grace could only assume was fear. Mixed with a hell of a lot of emotion.

Grace placed both hands on Mercy's arms. "Don't freak out. We don't know anything at this point. Maybe we should talk to him."

"You think?"

"No, but what other choices do we have?" Grace smiled. Purely for Mercy's benefit.

■□■□■□■□

JERRY DIDN'T MOVE A MUSCLE, his hand poised on the doorknob.

He was just about to make his way into the kitchen, where he generally met up with his girls each morning for coffee. At least one or two of them anyway, depending on how busy they were. He'd been ready to push open the door when he had heard voices. Two voices, to be exact. From where he stood, he knew one of them was Mercy. Her voice was unmistakable, not to mention loud. The other he wasn't quite sure, but he thought it was Gracie.

It wasn't the sound of the voices that had brought him to a halt, though.

Nope. He was pulled up short because of *what* they were saying.

Should we ask him about her? Who is she? Where did she come from? How long has he been seeing her? Do you think she works here? Does he love her?

Son of a gun.

They evidently knew about Jan, and by the tone of Mercy's voice, she wasn't too thrilled with the news that he was seeing someone.

Which was exactly why Jan hadn't wanted him to share that little tidbit of information with any of them.

Who had told her? How did they know?

He wasn't ashamed of his relationship with Jan. Quite the opposite, in fact. He'd been seeing her for the better part of the last eight months, and they had even talked about him introducing her to his daughters. Eight damn months and he'd never brought her to meet his kids. And that was one of the main reasons they hadn't been able to take their relationship further, which he found he definitely wanted to do. And he wasn't talking sex because ... well, because that part of the relationship was smooth sailing at this point.

What kind of man was he that he couldn't even show off the one woman who'd captured his heart when he hadn't even realized it'd been set free in the first place?

Jan was concerned about how the girls were going to take the news, and according to what he'd just heard, rightfully so. In fact, Jan seemed more concerned about how the girls were going to react than he was. Maybe that was because she was a schoolteacher and her empathy where children were concerned far exceeded his.

Rather than be a pussy about it, Jerry knew he should've just marched right into that kitchen and answered all of Mercy's questions directly. It would've been so much easier.

Or, okay, maybe *easier* wasn't the right word. It would've been smarter.

No, maybe that wasn't the right one, either.

Shit.

He didn't know.

What he did know was that he was tired of sneaking around. He was a grown man, and he had the right to see a woman if he wanted to. Right?

He was about to turn fifty-five, and he'd spent the last decade and a half alone. Well, mostly alone. There had been a handful of women over the last sixteen years since he'd lost his dear, sweet Charlotte, but none of them had been serious. Most of them hadn't even known who he was because he had wanted it that way.

Yes, he would have to admit he'd had numerous one-night stands over the years, although he wasn't proud of it. But Jan wasn't a one-night stand. If he could assure his daughters that no one would ever replace Charlotte but that he deserved to find happiness again, maybe he could move forward.

The question was whether or not they would understand.

He knew his girls missed their mother. Hell, he missed her, too. But he'd forged through, raising his girls and maintaining the ranch that had been in his family for three generations completely, and painfully, alone. So didn't he deserve a little happiness?

And he'd found that with Jan. He'd probably go so far as to say that he'd never been happier. She was sweet, smart, funny, gorgeous... Hell, he could go on endlessly about how incredible the woman was.

On top of that, she was... Lord help him, the woman was a spitfire. She kept him on his toes, made him think, made him ache, made him want things he hadn't wanted in so long. She brought out a side of him that he'd inadvertently buried with Charlotte.

"Don't freak out. We don't know anything at this point. Maybe we should talk to him." Yep, that was definitely Gracie. And today she was the voice of reason.

"You think?" Mercy asked.

"No, but what other choices do we have?"

Okay, maybe not complete reason — that was definitely the "no other choice" way of thinking.

It was the perfect opening, damn it. Now he was supposed to make his way into the kitchen, announce that he was in love with a woman and that he was ready to introduce her to his children. He wasn't even scared to admit that he was in love, either.

No, that particular emotion was what kept him moving through every single day, something wonderful to look forward to every time he had a chance to see Jan.

Last night had been the first night she had accepted his invitation to come to the ranch. She'd been reluctant every other time, but he had promised her that she had nothing to worry about. And last night, when she'd arrived, he'd had every intention of accidentally coming into contact with one of his girls so he could make the introduction. They hadn't made it past his office, though. The fireworks had been lit the second she'd stepped through his door, and he'd damn near devoured her whole, right there on his desk.

The thought of Jan laid out like a feast right there on his desk... Yep, it set his blood aflame.

He couldn't help but think that the spur-of-the-moment inferno that occurred when they were together was not something he'd ever had with Charlotte. No, Charlotte had been so sweet, so wonderful in her own right, but she'd been the opposite of Jan.

Perhaps that was one of the reasons he didn't feel guilty for loving Jan. He wanted to believe that if Charlotte could see him now, she would encourage him to find the contentment he'd forsaken for so long.

Shit.

It wasn't helping to stand there and think about it. He knew he had to waltz right into that kitchen and tell Gracie and Mercy just how he felt about Jan.

Forcing his hand to twist the knob, Jerry put his feet in motion, stepping into the kitchen, smiling at his girls.

"Mornin'," he greeted.

"Pops," Mercy said, sounding surprised to see him.

"Last I checked, that was who was starin' back at me in the mirror, yes," he replied gently, tacking on a smile. Obviously, he was going to ramble versus say what truly needed to be said. The least he could do was be nice about it.

"See, he's even smilin'," Gracie mumbled, not looking at him.

"Of course, I'm smilin'. Why wouldn't I be?" he asked, making his way to the refrigerator for a bottle of orange juice. He should've opted for coffee, in the hopes that it might give him a little energy. Last night had been…

Do not go there.

"What're you girls in here talkin' about?" he asked, hoping they might jump right to the subject and all of this secretive crap would be behind him.

"Nothin'," Mercy answered quickly, her cheeks turning pink.

"You look guilty," he said, uncapping the juice as he stared back at her. He continued to watch her over the end of the bottle as he brought it to his lips.

"I gotta go," Mercy said abruptly, turning toward the door.

"Hold up, girlie," he said roughly, nearly choking on his orange juice.

Now's your chance.

"Was there somethin' you wanted to talk to me about?"

Another wave of color spread across Mercy's cheeks, but she shook her head. And with that, she hauled ass out the door without looking back.

Pretending he had no idea what was going on, something he was pretty damn good at, Jerry turned to Gracie. "Somethin' wrong with her?" he asked, tipping his bottle toward the door.

"Maybe," Gracie said honestly.

That's what he loved about this one. She was always so damn open and honest about everything. Sometimes to a fault.

"Spill it, kid." Jerry moved over to the table and lowered his body into the chair.

Shit, his muscles ached. More so than when he spent the day unloading hay bales from the trucks that brought them to the main barn. Probably because last night he'd used muscles that hadn't been active in… Good grief, how long had it been?

Forever since he'd done anything like that. On a desk.

The memories made his skin heat, and he had to look away from Gracie, fearing his discomfiture might just show on his face.

"Dad," Gracie began hesitantly. "Is there something you want to tell us?"

"Like what?" he asked, pretending not to know what she was talking about.

You're screwing it up.

"Like…"

Gracie didn't finish the sentence even though Jerry practically begged her to with his eyes.

Keep going, kid. Make this easy on your old man.

"Never mind," she finally said. "I need to head out, too. It's gonna be a long day."

Jerry watched Gracie push to her feet and head for the door.

He should've called after her, should've told her to come back so he could spill his guts, get the weight of a thousand lifetimes off his chest.

But he didn't.

No, he just watched his best opportunity to get things out in the open walk right out the door. Twice.

Damn it.

Chapter Twenty-One

GRACE LEFT HER FATHER'S OFFICE cursing herself for not taking the opportunity that had just been set up. She'd had the perfect opening to talk to her father about Lane and Grant, something she'd been pondering for a while now, and she'd chickened out.

Like a total wuss, she had tucked her tail between her legs and run.

Damn it.

That was the whole reason she'd been waiting for him, wanting to address the huge elephant in the room, because she knew that eventually it was going to be out. And at that point, she'd be backpedaling. Some people believed in the theory of don't ask permission, just do whatever you want and ask for forgiveness later. Grace wasn't built that way.

She wanted to have her father's blessing, to know that he supported her in her decisions. No matter what those decisions were.

With so much going on with Grant, Grace needed to be there for him. And that was going to call attention to their relationship.

Ever since she'd given up on her dream of barrel racing professionally, she'd regretted that she hadn't followed the dream. Even if she didn't want to do it now, Grace knew that was because of how hard she'd been on herself. If she was truly honest with herself, Grace knew her mother would've wanted her to pursue her dream.

So, yes, Grace had some regrets. Which is why she'd made a point not to chicken out, so to speak, anymore on the things that were important to her.

And right now, there wasn't anything more important to her than Lane and Grant.

Based on what had happened when she'd showed up in her dad's office during the altercation with Grant's father, she was pretty sure Jerry suspected something was going on between her and Grant anyway. And she wanted to be the one to tell him before he freaked out, which she was pretty sure he was going to do.

And what better opportunity than when it was clear he had a secret of his own?

But noooo ... Grace had waffled and hauled ass just like Mercy.

Speaking of Mercy, she really needed to find her sister. They needed to talk this out because, quite frankly, Grace was a little surprised by her sister's reaction to the fact their father might just have a girlfriend.

Girlfriend.

God, that sounded strange.

Her father with a woman. She just couldn't see it.

Grace had never known her father to date, although, yes, she wasn't naïve enough to believe that the man had suffered without the companionship of a woman for all these years. She might wish it were so, because truthfully, she still didn't want to think that there might be a woman out there who could replace her mother, but when she really thought about it, the idea of Jerry spending the rest of his life alone wasn't fair, either. To anyone.

So yeah, she'd been surprised to find out from Grant that her father had been with a woman last night. But she hadn't overreacted. Not the way Mercy had.

Figuring Mercy had probably headed to the one place she always sought solace when she was upset, Grace headed for the barn. Once there, she tried to move silently through the big, open space, but no luck. The sound of her boots shuffling on the concrete could be heard over the bleating of the goats that were currently acting as an alarm — notifying anyone there to her presence.

"Merce," Grace called when she reached the ladder that would lead up to the hayloft.

"She's not here," came the response.

Grace grinned. "Okay, I'll just come back later," she replied as she grabbed the wooden rung on the ladder and began propelling herself up.

"Don't bother," Mercy answered.

Was Mercy crying?

Grace didn't say anything until she reached the wooden floor of the loft that was supposed to be used for storing hay. Sure, there were a handful of hay bales up there, but she knew they didn't use this particular loft for storing the overflow. No, ever since Jerry had learned that Mercy used this place as her hiding spot, he had ordered the hay to be stored elsewhere. That was years ago.

Ducking beneath the beams that held up the roof on one side, Grace maneuvered through the bales that were scattered about until she came upon her sister, hiding in the back.

"Whatcha doin'?" Grace asked as she dropped onto the floor beside Mercy, sitting cross-legged as she faced her younger sister.

Grace's breath stuttered in her chest when she saw the picture that Mercy was looking at. It was from their parents' wedding. "Can I see that?" she asked softly, hardly able to speak through the emotion that had built up in her throat.

Mercy handed the picture over, and Grace ran her finger over the beautiful woman standing there in her brilliant white gown. The picture was black and white, and the edges had yellowed over time. But there was no mistaking that she was looking at her mother.

"Why would he want someone else?" Mercy asked while Grace continued to study the image, smiling sadly. God, she missed her.

Grace shrugged her shoulders. "Do you really expect him to spend the rest of his life alone?"

"Yes," Mercy declared, but even Grace could tell the answer wasn't honest.

No one should expect Jerry to spend the rest of his life alone. Just because they'd made it this far without having to deal with their father having a girlfriend, that didn't mean it was the way it should be.

"I just don't get it," Mercy muttered, her head hanging down and her shoulders hunched as she stared at her boots. "After all this time, why would he want someone?"

"Geez, Merce, I don't know. Maybe he's lonely?" Even as she said the words, Grace was surprised to find that she really didn't care that her father was dating someone. In fact, she was actually okay with the idea. He did deserve to be happy.

"He's been actin' weird lately," Mercy said. "Do you think it's because of her?"

"Weird how?"

"Weird *happy*," Mercy replied. "He's always smilin'. He laughs more. Hell, he's even willin' to race again."

Yes, well, that was definitely odd behavior for her father. Not that he wasn't pleasant to be around, because Jerry was nothing if not a good host at the ranch. But Mercy was right, he did seem happier lately.

"How long do you think they've been together?" Mercy asked.

"No idea. I think those are questions we should be askin' him."

Mercy lifted her head and met Grace's gaze. She could see the battle going on in her sister's head. Grace knew how she felt. It did sort of feel like a betrayal, but that was just her selfish side talking.

"I think we should ask him to bring her here."

"He clearly has," Mercy retorted.

"True. But he's hidin' out. Don't you think he should be able to introduce us?"

"Pot, meet kettle," Mercy muttered, and Grace knew exactly what she was referring to.

Okay, fine. She had been dating Lane and Grant for the last few months, spending as much time as physically possible with them, and as far as she knew, the only person who was aware of their relationship was Mercy.

"I wanted to tell him," Grace admitted. It had been the perfect opportunity, and she was still pissed that she'd just let it pass her by.

"He's not gonna be pissed, you know," Mercy added.

"No?" Grace asked incredulously. "You think he's gonna understand that I'm in love with two men?"

"You *love* them?" Mercy asked, looking clearly bewildered.

"Yes," Grace said firmly. "I love them. Both of them."

"I still don't think he's gonna be mad. Confused, maybe. It is kinda weird, you know that?"

Grace laughed because her sister was right. It was strange to be in love with two men. But more bizarre was that the two men loved her and each other. Okay, so, yes, strange was an understatement, but she couldn't very well explain it. She hadn't planned it this way; things had just happened.

"I think we should ask him about her," Grace finally said when the conversation died.

"Yeah. Me, too. I still don't know that I like it."

"I get it," Grace said, reaching out and touching Mercy's hand. "But it's really not our place to decide how he chooses to be happy."

■□■□■□■□

MERCY DIDN'T WANT TO AGREE with Gracie, but she did. Not that she was going to admit it, though. She needed some time to think about this.

Her father had a girlfriend.

She wondered whether Trin, Faith, or Hope knew. She doubted it because surely they would've said something. Then again, there were plenty of secrets being kept at the ranch these days. Gracie was dating two men, those two men were in love with her and each other, her father was apparently dating someone…

Then there were her other sisters and their secrets. Trin and the horrific incident with that son of a bitch, Garrett. Damn, they'd kept that one a secret for so long that people actually did believe Jerry had fired the asshole for using equipment. Well, some people believed that. Others thought it had to do with the fact that the guy had wanted to date Trin.

Mercy knew why they had allowed everyone to go on believing that. If word had gotten out just what Garrett had done, there would've been anarchy at the ranch. The people who worked there were like family. And everyone looked out for one another, even if they all liked to give each other a hard time.

That was the definition of family, right?

Then there was Faith and Rusty. The two of them could start a fire with the combustible energy they generated when they were in the same room. Granted, Faith didn't know the real reason Jerry had fired Garrett Daniels, so her younger sister believed that dating one of the wranglers was off-limits. No one had bothered to set Faith straight, and Mercy still wasn't sure why that was.

Of course, Mercy had a secret, but she had no intention of letting it out of the bag. What had happened between her and Cody had been a mistake. A huge mistake that she desperately did not want to repeat. She did not want to date someone who worked for her father. And she knew that the only reason they'd ended up together had been because… Hell, she didn't even know why it had happened. It just had.

It was all so messed up. How could so many people spend day in and day out together and no one know everything that was going on?

Mercy sighed as she looked up at Gracie again. "Maybe he'll bring her to the dance tomorrow night."

"Maybe we should ask him to," Gracie countered.

"I'm not gonna bring it up. As far as I'm concerned, if she doesn't come here, she doesn't exist." Irrational, yes. But she really didn't give a damn.

"Speakin' of dance. You gonna help set up tomorrow?"

And just like that, Gracie single-handedly changed the subject back to a safe topic. If Mercy had to guess, her sister did it for her. She loved her for it, too.

"Of course I'm gonna help. I'm lookin' forward to this one. After all, I get to watch while you try to explain the fact that you're dancin' with two different cowboys. You are gonna dance with them both, aren't you?"

Mercy wasn't sure how Gracie had managed, but she hadn't yet danced with either man. She had a feeling that was about to change.

Grace smirked, and Mercy knew what was coming. She plugged her ears with her fingers, singing loudly to avoid hearing what Grace had to say. When she stopped, Grace just smiled as she got to her feet.

Mercy watched as Grace eased herself onto the ladder, shaking her head, still grinning.

"I'll talk to you later," Mercy called after her, grateful that Grace had let it go.

"I'll be sure to let Cody know you're lookin' forward to that dance," Grace hollered as she climbed down the ladder.

Son of a gun. Just when she thought she was safe.

CHAPTER TWENTY-TWO

Friday afternoon

"MORGAN, ANSWER THE DAMN PHONE. Seriously. I need to talk to you. Call me back as soon as you get this. And I mean *call* me. Don't text. I wanna talk to you."

Grant stabbed the *end* button on his phone, dropping it onto the kitchen counter before thrusting his hands through his hair.

Goddamn motherfucking shit.

What the fuck was going on?

He'd received a text from Morgan just that morning. His sister was inquiring as to whether he'd seen or heard from their mother. Of course, Grant hadn't been able to answer the phone because he had been out with two of the wranglers, checking the fence line in one of the back pastures after word had come in that part of it was down. By the time he'd made it back to the barn, two hours had passed since Morgan's text had come in. He'd tried to call her then, to no avail.

To add to his current state of panic, Grant had called his parents' house, his mother's cell phone, and his father's cell phone repeatedly. No one had answered any of those, either, and he hadn't bothered to leave a message, not quite sure what to say. Grant hadn't heard a peep from the old man since yesterday morning when he'd confronted Darrell in Jerry's office.

God, had that just been yesterday?

Nor had he had a chance to talk to Jerry about the incident, either. Of course, he had tried to do so, but ... well ... interrupting Jerry when he was ... uh ... doing what he'd been doing probably wouldn't have been the best idea.

Which was why Grant was pacing his living room floor, unsure what to do.

Grant was tempted to call Gracie. Or Lane. Or both of them, but at this point, he really didn't know what he was going to say. *I'm pretty sure my mom's missing; I need your help in finding her.* But was she really missing? Was something wrong, or had she just escaped his father's wrath and was now living the high life with some boy toy?

Gross.

He really couldn't see his mother doing something like that, but what did he know? How his parents had managed to stay together all this time, he really had no idea. From the outside looking in, the two of them didn't even like each other.

And now his father was gambling again.

Grant remembered how hard that had been on his mother when he was growing up. Morgan had left home already, but Grant had been just starting high school when things had gotten really out of hand. At one point, Sandy had been convinced they were going to lose their house.

Grant admired his mother's strength, for the most part. Although the delivery left something to be desired, Sandy Kingsley did have the ability to stand up to Darrell. They'd never had much money, and he knew that Sandy could've easily used the inheritance she'd received from her mother to take a vacation or splurge on herself or whatever. But she hadn't. She'd taken that money and paid off the trailer so that they wouldn't end up homeless.

All the while, Darrell had continued to spiral out of control. His gambling had gotten to the point that they had little to no money to eat on, and Grant's mother was resorting to getting food from the local food pantry. Of course, Darrell thought that was a brilliant plan because he then had the best of both worlds. He could eat *and* he could burn money betting on horses.

Grant stopped pacing and stared at his phone.

Yeah, he had to find his mother. She deserved that much from him.

Snagging his phone from the counter, Grant pulled up his text messages and shot Gracie a note, letting her know he had to leave town for a little while. After hitting send on that one, he pulled up Lane's name and typed in seven short words before hitting send.

With that done, it was time to pack.

■□■□■□■□

I NEED YOU TO COME over. Now.

That was the text Lane had received just a few minutes ago from Grant, and the instant he'd seen it, he had dropped what he was doing.

Deep in conversation about bow hunting versus rifle hunting when his phone had buzzed on his hip, Lane had jerked the thing from his belt, read the message, and excused himself with the explanation that he had something important to handle.

He would've dropped everything even if he was busy — which he wasn't — specifically after getting what he considered the equivalent of a 911 text. In this case, sitting on the porch of the main house talking to a couple of the guests about the activities had been easy to get out of.

Now, less than ten minutes later, Lane was walking up to Grant's front door, a million things running through his head as to why Grant would've summoned him to his house in the middle of the afternoon with absolutely no elaboration whatsoever.

Rapping his knuckles on the wood door, Lane listened for Grant to tell him it was open, as was his customary greeting.

Nothing came. Not a peep from inside the cabin.

Rather than continue to swelter out in the oppressive heat, Lane tried the knob, finding the door unlocked. As he walked through the door, he was hit with a blast of cold air, along with a heart-stopping scene. He made his way inside just as Grant was coming out of his bedroom, a gym bag in his hand. It took a moment for Lane's eyes to adjust, but, yep, that was certainly a bag Grant was holding, and the hair on the back of Lane's neck stood on end.

"What the hell is goin' on?" Lane asked, trying not to make any immediate assumptions and, more important, trying to keep his voice void of the worry that was now coursing through him.

"My mom's missin'," Grant said quickly, darting across the room toward the counter beside Lane.

Screeech!

That was the sound of Lane's brain coming to an abrupt stop. *Did Grant just say...?* Holy shit.

With his eyes glued to Grant's every movement, Lane stood by as Grant retrieved his cell phone and his truck keys while hefting the bag up onto his shoulder, looking as frantic as Lane had ever seen him.

"Slow down a minute, would ya?" Lane said, reaching out and gently placing his hand on Grant's arm. "What do you mean, your mom's *missing*?"

"There's only one way to interpret that one, Lane."

Yeah, okay, so the frustration levels were topping the charts.

Lane sighed, desperately trying to process what was going on. They'd gone from Grant's father asking Grant for money, then storming the ranch, to Grant's mother missing. He wasn't quite following. Figuring it was best to lay out the facts as he knew them, Lane said, "Your mom's *missin'*. Does that mean she left your father for good?"

"The only thing I know is that she's *gone*," Grant said frantically, turning to face Lane directly.

Oh, shit.

Grant was on the verge of a severe breakdown, Lane could sense it. Rather than let the man he loved go through this alone, Lane decided it was time to take the reins. Grant's mother was missing. Regardless of where she might be, that didn't sound good.

"Let's talk this out," he told Grant. "But first, have you let Gracie know you're leavin'?"

Lane still wasn't sure where Grant was going, but…

The words had barely left Lane's mouth when Grant's front door flew open, nearly hitting Lane as it swung back on its hinges. He'd had the good sense to jump out of the way just in time or he'd probably be sporting a new color on his face.

"Where the hell are you goin'?" Gracie demanded, her eyes wide as she stared up at Grant, her hands planted firmly on her hips. It only took a second for Gracie to realize Lane was standing there too, but as soon as their eyes met, her expression softened a little.

"Well, at least that answers *my* question," Lane said softly. Gracie certainly knew. And from her wild-eyed stare, she must've received a curt text similar to the one Lane had.

"What's goin' on?" Gracie asked, a little less hostile than moments before.

Her question seemed to be directed at him, but Lane had no idea what to tell her.

"I've got to leave for a while," Grant offered by way of explanation.

A shitty explanation, in Lane's opinion.

"So you said in your text. What's 'a while,' Grant? And where are you goin'?" Gracie asked, closing the front door a little harder than was probably necessary and stepping farther into the room.

Poor door. It was getting the hell beaten out of it today.

When Gracie crossed her arms over her chest, Lane had to admire her. Not just because she looked sexy as hell when she got that dominant gleam in her eyes but for the fact that she wasn't going to let Grant just walk out without some form of explanation, either.

Not that Lane thought any clarification would be forthcoming. Grant didn't look like he was in the mood to talk.

"My mother's missin'," Grant blurted out for the second time since Lane had arrived. "I've got to try to find her."

"Where are you gonna start lookin'?" Lane asked, hoping they could get around to the beginning. At this point, the only fact he had was that Grant couldn't locate his mother by phone, but as for his reason for believing she was missing, rather than, oh, say, in Vegas living it up for the weekend or something, Lane still had no clue.

"I was gonna start at my parents' house."

"We were there yesterday," Lane told him. "If they aren't answerin' the phone, what makes you think they're home now?"

Grant glared at Lane as though that thought might've occurred to him.

"Okay, say you go to your parents' again. Where'll you go if they aren't there?" Gracie asked, sounding just as befuddled as Lane felt.

"I don't have a fuckin' clue," Grant barked, dropping the bag onto the floor and staring back and forth between them both.

Yep, Grant was about to lose it.

Rather than pelt him with more questions, Lane did what felt right. He took two steps forward and pulled Grant into his arms, holding him tightly. To Lane's utter surprise, Grant wrapped his arms around him, buried his head in his neck, and squeezed tightly, his body shaking. Lane didn't think Grant was crying, but from the force of his shudders, he wasn't sure that wasn't going to be the next phase of this breakdown.

"I don't know where to look," Grant said, the words muffled against Lane's neck.

Out of the corner of his eye, Lane saw Gracie move up beside them. Looking down at her, he noticed the tears brimming her eyes. He knew how she felt. In all the time that he'd known Grant, never had he seen him like this.

This was a man who was always strong, always in charge. Nothing ever seemed to faze him and not in the *blow-it-off-and-laugh-about-it* way that Lane had perfected over the years.

No, Grant was the type of person who processed all of the information he received until he had a plan in place. That clearly wasn't the case right now, and Lane figured that was solely because this was Grant's mother they were talking about.

"We're gonna help you," Lane assured Grant. "But first, we need a plan. And in order to get there, we need to know what we're dealin' with."

Grant nodded, his face still pressed against Lane's neck, his warm breath tickling Lane's skin. Lane was reluctant to let him go, but when Grant drew back, he released him, letting his hand slide down Grant's arm slowly.

"Have you talked to your dad since yesterday?" Gracie asked, perched on the arm of the sofa as she stared back at them. Thankfully, it appeared she'd gotten herself under control. If Lane had to guess, she probably didn't want Grant to know she was on the verge of tears.

"Not since your father talked to him," Grant replied, sounding somewhat more pulled together than just a moment ago. "I didn't get a chance to follow up with Jerry to see what they talked about, but I haven't heard from my dad at all since then. I've tried callin' numerous times."

"So you think your mom's been gone since last weekend?" Gracie asked.

"My dad never clarified when she left, just that she was gone. The way he said it, I assumed it was recently, but he also didn't seem worried. My sister texted me this mornin' lookin' for her, but I haven't been able to actually talk to her, either."

"Maybe your mom's on her way to see Morgan," Gracie said. "Didn't you say your sister moved to Kansas last year?"

"Yeah."

"Do you think your mom would've gone to visit her? Your sister has kids, right?" Gracie inquired.

"Yes, two. And no, I doubt my mother would've gone to Kansas. Not by herself. Morgan texted me, askin' me if *I'd* heard from Mom, so I think it's safe to say she's not there."

"They aren't close?" Lane asked.

"No one in my family is close," Grant ground out.

"Don't get defensive here," Lane said, "we're just tryin' to figure out which direction to go."

Grant nodded, but he didn't look very convinced.

"So your plan is to go to your parents', see if she's there?"

"That's where I was gonna start, yes," Grant confirmed, answering Gracie's question.

"I think we need to start by talkin' to Jerry," Lane interjected. "You said it yourself, you don't know what he and your dad talked about, and you haven't heard from your dad since then. I think we need to see if Jerry knows somethin' we don't."

Lane waited patiently while Grant pondered over the suggestion. He kind of expected Grant to jump the gun anyway and run over to his parents' just because he could, so he was rather surprised when Grant nodded in agreement.

"Thank you. Both of you. I'm not sure what I'd do right now if y'all weren't here," Grant said softly, sadly.

Lane didn't say anything — he didn't need to. Grant had made a huge step in reaching out to them both, especially for a man who had yet to admit his feelings. Lane longed to hear the words out of Grant's mouth, but to be honest, this was the next best thing.

And for now, he'd take it.

■□■□■□■□

GRACE WAS DAMNED PROUD OF herself for keeping it together for the last half hour.

First, she'd received an abrupt text from Grant that had sounded much like a *Dear John* letter, which was why she'd practically run from the stables to his cabin without stopping.

Her heart had been in her throat when she'd barged through his front door, and seeing Grant so distraught, she'd been a second away from crumbling into a puddle on the floor.

When Grant had mentioned his mother, so many memories had come rushing back. Back to when she was twelve years old and her own mother had died.

As far as Grace knew, her mother had been healthy, yet one minute, she had been there, cooking in the kitchen while Grace, Mercy, and Hope helped her prepare the midday meal for the trail riders, and the next minute, Charlotte had been on the floor, clutching her chest and asking them to call 911.

Grace remembered that day so vividly. Her father had actually been out on that trail ride with Faith and Trinity. Her parents had tended to split her and her sisters up to make it easier on them during the day, and that week, Grace had been assigned to helping in the kitchen. Not that she had minded at all. Spending time with her mother had been what she'd looked forward to, even more than she'd looked forward to learning to barrel race.

Without a doubt, that had been the absolute worst day of Grace's life. Hope had stepped in, thank God, handling everything as if she were decades older than just sixteen at the time. She had dialed 911, directed the operator on where they were, and then gone out front to flag down the ambulance that was coming from the neighboring town.

Grace remembered how pale her mother had been at that point, lying on the floor, Mercy crying while she gripped their mother's hand tightly. Grace hadn't held it together that day. At first, she'd been too scared to cry, but once the ambulance had arrived and the men had come in, she had broken down completely.

Once again, Hope had stepped in, taking care of them while managing to get one of the wranglers to go out on the trails to find her father.

By the time Jerry had made it back to the house, Charlotte had been whisked away to the hospital, and he hadn't been that far behind. Grace and her sisters had remained at the house with several of the staff as they'd waited for the news that their mother was going to be okay.

That news had never come. Charlotte had died from a heart attack. And none of them had ever been the same. They had comforted one another through the devastating weeks that had followed. Jerry had been stoic through it all, his head up, his eyes dry, but Grace had known he cried at night. She had heard him.

So when Grace had walked in to find Grant nearly in tears after his revelation, she had barely managed to keep herself together.

But she had.

And now they were stepping into Jerry's office, hoping for him to enlighten them on what had happened between him and Darrell earlier in the week. Grace wished it would be that simple.

"What's wrong?" Jerry asked, getting to his feet as the three of them stepped into the room, closing the door behind them.

"Plenty," Grant mumbled, but thankfully, Lane stepped forward to handle the situation.

"Mr. Lambert," Lane began, "if possible, we'd like to know what you and Grant's father talked about yesterday. It looks like Grant's mother is missin', and we're tryin' to backtrack to see if Darrell might've mentioned somethin'."

Grace watched her father, noticed the concern in his eyes as he stared back at the three of them. She had to wonder what was going through his head.

"We talked," Jerry began, "for a long time. It took a while for your father to calm down, but he finally did." Jerry was staring back at Grant, his eyes kind, his voice soft. "I know your dad has a gamblin' problem, Grant. Not everything on this ranch is a secret. I'd heard the rumors, so I chose to address your father directly. He admitted his problem. Surprisingly. But he didn't seem interested in gettin' help. That's when things went south and he left."

"So you didn't give him money?" Grant asked. The relief in his voice had Grace turning to look at him.

"No, son, I didn't. I wouldn't've done that without talkin' to you first. If I really thought your father needed money and you weren't givin' it because you didn't have it, I would've come to you. It was clear your father was panicking. From what I gathered, he's graspin' at straws, desperate to make some money, and he's convinced that bettin' on the races is gonna get him where he needs to be."

"Where he needs to be is in rehab," Grant said sadly.

"I agree. I even mentioned it," Jerry concurred. "Unfortunately, he disagreed. I'm sorry, but he didn't mention your mother."

Shit.

That wasn't very helpful. Grace kept her eyes locked on Grant's chiseled face, and she saw the moment his hope vanished.

And hers seemed to go right along with it.

CHAPTER TWENTY-THREE

GRANT WOULD ADMIT THAT HE'D probably never been as scared as he was right then. So maybe he didn't have the greatest relationship with his parents, or even with his sister, for that matter, but not knowing where his mother was, or whether or not she was safe, was killing him.

He had fought the urge to break down like a fucking sissy the moment Lane had walked through his front door earlier. Grant's indifferent attitude hadn't lasted long, because he *had* given in, letting Lane wrap his strong, secure arms around him. It had felt almost too good to let go. Having him and Gracie to lean on was the only thing keeping him together.

That and having them there to make sure he tackled this from the right angle. Even if he really didn't know what that might be at this point, he sort of figured out that jumping in his truck probably wasn't the best plan. Then again, the news Jerry had just shared didn't tell Grant much of anything, and heading off down the road was looking like his only option.

Well, except for the fact that his father had probably headed to his old haunts, desperate to make some money, and Grant didn't even know where those were.

As he stared back at Jerry, desperately trying to process what this meant and what the next step was supposed to be, Grant fought the urge to yell out his frustration.

Weren't the parents supposed to be the more mature ones? Shouldn't his mom and dad be wondering about him and his sister, checking on them from time to time to make sure they were okay? Not the other way around?

Unable to answer those questions, and knowing that no one else in the room had any idea what was actually running through his head, Grant accepted the fact that Lane and Gracie had been right. Running off to his parents' house wouldn't have done much good. No, it would've been a complete waste of time. He doubted his father was there. It was clear his mother wasn't. She wasn't at Morgan's, either. And for the life of him, Grant had no idea where she might've gone.

"Do you have any suggestions on what we do from here?" Gracie asked her father, moving to stand beside Grant and resting her small hand on his arm.

Without thinking, Grant pulled her against him, desperate to feel her heartbeat, to lean on her at a time when it felt as though the floor was about to drop out from under him.

The second he did, Grant met Jerry's sobering gaze from across the room, and fear unlike anything he'd ever known set in. It overwhelmed his own worry for his mother because Jerry Lambert looked as though someone had just pulled the rug out from under him, and unlike Grant, the floor wasn't even there to catch him.

To Grant's surprise, Gracie put her arm around his waist, squeezing him gently. It was as though she was trying to reassure him that what he'd just done wasn't going to land him on the unemployment line.

To make matters worse, Jerry didn't say anything. He looked from Grant to Gracie and then back, all while Grant held his breath, unsure what to do. It wasn't as if he could just push Gracie away, pretend that the damage hadn't already been done.

"Does she have a cell phone?" When Jerry finally did speak, the short sentence sounded foreign to Grant, stunning him for a moment as he tried to remember what it was they'd been talking about.

When the question finally registered, Grant said, "Yes. When I try, it goes right to her voice mail."

"What if you call the service provider and see if they have GPS on the phone. Maybe they can locate her that way," Jerry offered helpfully.

Grant glanced at Lane briefly, noticing that his eyes were wide as he stared at Grant and Gracie, looking almost as perplexed as Jerry had.

Yeah, buddy, I know. I just royally fucked up.

"That's a great idea," Gracie said, leaning back just a little and looking up at him, still not letting him go.

Grant was terrified to look down at her, scared of what he might see in her eyes. Did she realize what they'd just done? They might as well have had a sign that said, *"Look Jer, I'm screwin' your daughter. What do you think about that?"*

"Thank you, sir. We'll try that first. Come on," Lane said as he passed by, his arm brushing Grant's in the small space. "Let's go see what we can get out of the cell company. At least it's a start."

Grant looked back at Jerry one last time, but he was taken aback to see that Jerry wasn't trying to kill him with his death ray eyes. No, what he saw looked a little like acceptance.

Acceptance? Surely not. Maybe that was pity. Or maybe Jerry was just thinking of all the forms that would have to be filled out when he fired Grant later.

It couldn't be that Jerry might possibly accept the fact that Grant loved Gracie.

How could that be? Wasn't this the guy who'd tossed Garrett Daniels out for wanting to date Trinity? Wasn't this the guy who continued to reiterate that he did not want anyone dating his daughters?

Grant fucking hated that they had to hide, but he thoroughly understood. Talking to Faith the other day hadn't helped Grant's desire to come out about his relationship with Lane and Gracie, and at this point, the last thing he needed was to get on Jerry's bad side.

Too late for that, dumbass.

Before Grant could contemplate the answer to the millions of questions running through his head, Lane moved to the door. Grant released Gracie when they stepped out onto the porch behind Lane, although he would've preferred to keep her close.

After all, the damage had already been done.

■□■□■□■□

WHEN THE DOOR CLOSED BEHIND Grant, Gracie, and Lane, Jerry had the urge to rub his eyes.

Had he been seeing things? Or had he been right all along? Was his little Gracie there to comfort Grant in his time of need, or was there something more going on there?

Jerry had never once considered himself an idiot, or even slightly obtuse, for that matter, but ... it sure looked like he'd been right. There was something going on between those two.

A small smile formed on his face.

Yep, he'd been right. This little display was what had kicked the suspicion right into the fact category.

Grant and Gracie.

He couldn't say he was disappointed with the idea of his head foreman and his strong-willed daughter falling in love. He actually liked it.

But what about Lane?

There was something strange going on here, past the whole possibility of Grant and Gracie dating, because if he wasn't crazy — which he seriously doubted he was — there was something going on between Grant and *Lane*. Today wasn't the first time he'd thought that the two of them might actually be a little more than friends, although he had to give them credit, they were relatively good at hiding it.

And no, Jerry didn't have anything against two men wanting to be together. His own personal preferences for the opposite sex were just that. His preferences. To each his own, that's how the saying went. And more power to Grant and Lane if they wanted to be together. Jerry's take was that as long as you loved someone, love them. With all that you are and all that you have.

He'd learned that with Charlotte.

Jerry had fallen in love with her before she had turned eighteen, and her daddy was one of the meanest sons of bitches Jerry had ever had the displeasure of meeting.

Funny, Jerry still talked to the man, even all these years later. They weren't exactly friends, but Lionel Simons had learned to let go of his hatred for Jerry once he'd realized that Charlotte truly loved him. Now, with Lionel in his eighties, Jerry checked on him from time to time just because he could.

Grant and Gracie?

Wow. The idea of the two of them together still blew his mind. But what was even more unreal was the fact that Gracie hadn't bothered to tell him. Not that any of his daughters had bothered to talk to him about their relationships, especially when it came to dating men who worked on the ranch.

To be honest, Jerry didn't really give a shit who they dated, just as long as the men knew to treat them right. That was his only requirement and one of the main reasons he threw his weight around so much. It was a warning. If they fucked with his kids, they were fucking with him.

And just like that rotten fucking bastard Garrett had learned, Jerry didn't put up with anyone mistreating his daughters. No one. *Goddammit!* Just the thought of that no-good fuckup made his blood pressure rise.

Shaking off the memory, Jerry pushed off the desk and walked around behind it. Dropping into his chair, he eyed the phone. He reached for the receiver but stopped himself before he had it in his hand. He did that three more times before he snatched the damn thing up and stabbed the numbers into the phone. Putting the receiver to his ear, he waited for her to answer.

"Hello?"

"Hey, baby," he greeted.

"Hey," Jan replied, sounding happy to hear from him.

Why, Jerry didn't know. He felt as if he'd spent the last eight months unable to introduce her to his family. It didn't matter that she was usually the one who talked him out of it.

It was time to change that.

After all, Grant seemed to be stepping up to the plate, proving that he wasn't the type of man to hide his relationship from anyone.

Jerry knew it was time for him to do the same.

"I want you to come to the dance on Saturday," he told her.

"Are you sure?" Jan inquired.

"Absolutely. I'm..." *Shit, how did he put this?* "I'm done pretendin' this is less than it is, Jan. I want us to move forward."

There was a pause that lasted long enough to give Jerry heart palpitations, but then Jan said, "Okay. The dance sounds fun."

Jerry knew she heard his sigh of relief.

"Are you sure about this?" Jan asked before he could say anything in return.

"More than sure." Jerry leaned back in his chair, feeling somewhat lighter, as though he were no longer carrying around a two-ton anvil on his shoulders. "Oh, and Jan..."

"Yes?"

"Plan to stay the night."

The feminine giggle that was her answer made Jerry's heart swell to enormous proportions.

Yeah, it was certainly time.

Chapter Twenty-Four

LANE WAS SITTING ON GRANT'S miniscule love seat, trying to pretend not to eavesdrop on the conversation Grant was having. Based on the way Gracie was staring back at him, a tiny little smirk on her lips said he was failing miserably.

They'd been at Grant's place for the last half hour. About twenty-eight of those minutes had been spent waiting to hear back from the cell phone provider. Grant hadn't hesitated before he'd called them during the walk back, but at that point, they had no new information. Lane got the feeling they weren't going to receive a call, either. From what he'd gathered from eavesdropping on that conversation — something he hadn't bothered to try to hide — they'd suggested that Grant call the police.

For whatever reason, Grant was hesitant to do so.

But now, someone was on the phone with Grant, and he wasn't doing well to keep the conversation private although he had stepped out onto the front porch.

"Who do you think that is?" Gracie asked, practically voicing Lane's direct thoughts.

"No idea."

Lane looked toward the door, as though that would improve his hearing.

"Thank God," Grant exclaimed. "Put her on the phone."

There was a long pause, and Lane glanced over at Grace. She was sitting on the edge of her seat.

"Mom, where the hell have you been?" Grant asked.

Another long pause.

"Shit. You should've told someone you were leavin'," Grant inserted. "And they sell those things at Walmart. You coulda picked up another one."

Lane noticed the doorknob turning, and he continued to watch, waiting for Grant to step inside.

"I'm just glad you're all right." *Pause.* "Okay. Well, when you decide to head back, let me know." *Pause.* "All right. Talk to you later."

When Grant came back inside, his eyes were somewhat glazed. Without saying a word, he stabbed the phone, ending the call before he came over to the couch and dropped down beside Lane.

Like, right beside him, their bodies touching from hip to knee. Lane turned his head to look at Grant, but the other man wasn't looking at him or at Gracie.

"Everything okay?" Gracie asked.

"I think so, yeah," Grant muttered.

"Was that your mom?" Lane asked when it was clear Grant wasn't going to share the information without them prying him open with a crowbar.

"Yeah."

"And?" Gracie asked, sounding incredibly anxious.

"She showed up on Morgan's doorstep a couple of hours ago."

"Oh, my God, Grant, that's great," Gracie said, rising to her feet and moving toward them.

For the first time since he'd ass-planted on the couch, Grant looked up at Gracie. Lane watched as Grant reached for her, pulling her down toward them both. Lane instinctively covered the family jewels as her knee came down between his legs, her other knee going between Grant's.

She was straddling their legs, her full attention on Grant.

"What did she say?"

"My mom said she left my dad. For good. From what I gathered, she started out on a road trip to see Morgan and had some car trouble. She had to stop in some rinky-dink town on the way to Kansas to have it looked at. That's when she realized she left her phone charger at home, so her cell's been dead for at least three days."

"She didn't think to stop and pick one up at Walmart?" Lane asked skeptically.

Grant turned his head, meeting Lane's eyes as he smiled. "That's exactly what I asked her. She said she just wanted to get to Morgan's. She sounds good. Tired but good. It doesn't sound like the trip was an easy one."

"Why didn't she call to tell you she was leavin' in the first place?" Lane questioned.

Grant's eyebrow cocked, his expression one of disbelief. "My mother? Call me? It would've been a first. She said she just had to get away from my father. According to her, she's done with him."

Lane wasn't sure whether that was relief or concern in Grant's piercing blue eyes, but either way, it was better than the sheer panic he'd witnessed there earlier.

Gracie leaned over and wrapped her arms around Grant's neck, hugging him tightly. One of Grant's arms wrapped around her; his other hand reached over and clutched Lane's.

Yeah, so that was relief he'd seen — the proof was in the reassuring squeeze of Grant's hand.

"I'm so glad she's safe," Gracie said, drawing back and then pressing her lips to Grant's.

Lane hadn't been planning to watch the kiss so closely, but the way Grant's hand tightened on his had him turning. Grant was pulling Gracie in, thrusting his tongue into her mouth.

Okay, so maybe relief was an understatement.

Grant didn't release her, and the heat in the room intensified tenfold. At this rate, the air conditioner was going to have to kick into overdrive if it was going to keep up, because the flames these two had ignited were beginning to lick at Lane's balls, making his dick hard.

Christ.

When Grant released Lane's hand, it was only so he could slide it beneath Gracie's shirt, quickly and efficiently relieving her of the confining cotton.

Oh, yeah.

This was a fantastic way to end an emotionally draining day.

Lane had resigned himself to watching the action, but Grant stunned him when he reached over, pulling Lane to him, their mouths fusing together. And all thought evaporated as Grant's tongue slid into his mouth, warm, soft, and ... adamant.

Allowing Grant to take the lead, Lane kissed him back, his arms pinned to his sides by the position they were in. With his eyes closed, his mind whirring from the intensity of Grant's kiss, Lane nearly leapt off the couch when he felt a firm hand cupping his dick through his jeans.

The only response he had was to continue kissing Grant and to thrust his hips forward, driving his erection against the wonderful friction the hand was causing. When it was time to come up for air, Lane looked down to see Gracie was rubbing him, grinding the palm of her hand against the solid length of his rock-hard cock as she watched them both.

"I want to watch," she whispered.

Lane's dick twitched, and he would be surprised if there wasn't an imprint of his zipper now.

"Us?" Grant asked, sounding as breathless as Lane felt.

"Yes."

To prove she was serious, Gracie jumped up from her perch on their thighs and moved back toward the recliner she'd been sitting in earlier.

"And what are you gonna do while you watch?" Grant asked.

Good thing Grant was in his right mind because Lane was feeling a little lightheaded.

One minute he'd been worried about Grant, the next his dick was hard enough to pound nails from a measly kiss. Then again, there wasn't anything measly about that kiss.

"Play with myself."

"Christ, woman!" Lane exclaimed, his head snapping around. "You're gonna kill me."

Her response was to bestow a glowing grin upon him.

He watched in utter fascination as her hands moved to her belt buckle, deftly unhooking it, her fingers then moving to release the button on her jeans before lowering the zipper. He could see shiny red silk peeking out from the V in the fabric.

"Oh, hell," Grant mumbled, his hand sliding up Lane's thigh.

Again, Lane pressed his hips up off the couch, trying to get closer to Grant's hand, wishing like hell he was naked so he could feel Grant's callused palm stroking him.

Lane continued to watch as Gracie removed every last stitch of her clothing, her eyes moving back and forth between them as she did. By the time she was stark naked, Lane was panting.

"You boys have on too many clothes," she told them as she lowered herself into the recliner, purposely driving them mad as she spread her legs wide, giving them an unobstructed view of her pretty pink pussy.

Grant nudged him, but Lane couldn't move. He couldn't pull his eyes off the soft, glistening flesh between her legs. He was desperate to taste her, to drive her crazy with his tongue.

"Nuh-uh," Gracie said, causing Lane to jerk his eyes up to her face.

"What?" he asked dumbly.

"I'm watchin'. The only person who's gonna touch me tonight is me."

He was just about ready to argue, but then Grant abruptly pushed him. And before his mind could process just what was happening, he found himself flat on his back, the sexiest cowboy on the planet lying atop him.

And at that point, nothing else mattered.

■□■□■□■□

GRANT WAS HAVING AN OUT-OF-BODY experience.

His adrenaline level was higher than it'd ever been. Between that and pretty much crashing from the relief of knowing that his mother was okay, his head was buzzing.

Gracie wasn't helping with her declaration that she wanted to watch, either. On top of that, he was contemplating all of the things he wanted to do to Lane *while* she watched. But the good thing was that his family was now the farthest thing from his mind as he focused his full attention on the cowboy beneath him.

Staring down at Lane, Grant studied Lane's handsome face, drinking him in. Lane's dark eyes were smoldering as he peered back at him. The shadow of beard growth on his jaw was intensely sexy, not to mention, something Grant didn't usually see. Lane was always so clean-shaven, but now the hard contours of his face were camouflaged by the short, dark stubble.

Grant couldn't help himself; he slid his fingers down Lane's jaw, letting the prickly hairs tickle the undersides of his fingers.

"You drive me crazy, you know that?" Grant whispered, his eyes darting to Lane's mouth.

"Ditto," Lane said on a breathless moan, his hips rising toward Grant.

With one knee between Lane's legs, Grant pressed his thigh against Lane's erection, grinding ever so slightly until Lane was moaning, his eyes fluttering closed.

"Damn, that feels good," Lane mumbled.

Grant didn't linger for long. As much as Grant enjoyed teasing this man, he really wanted Lane naked.

Pushing back so that he was sitting on his heels, one knee still perched between Lane's thighs, Grant made quick work of freeing Lane's cock from the confines of his jeans. In order to get him in the position that he wanted him, though, Grant had to get up. When he did, he glanced over at Gracie, who was eyeing them intently.

"Can you get the lube and condoms?" he asked her, his eyes sliding back down to Lane. "I intend to bury my cock deep in his ass in the next few minutes."

Gracie sprang up from the chair, her sexy nude body drawing Grant's eyes back toward her. He checked out the sexy sway of her heart-shaped ass as she sauntered into his bedroom.

Knowing she wouldn't be gone long, Grant hurried to lose his clothes while keeping his eyes on Lane. He was just lowering his jeans to his ankles when Gracie came back in with a bottle of lube and the entire box of condoms in her hand.

"That's a little optimistic there, don't ya think?" he asked with a laugh.

"You never know," she said with a smile before making her way back to the recliner.

Stepping out of his jeans, Grant peered down at Lane, who was still lying flat on his back on the short couch, his knees bent, feet propped over the arm because he wouldn't fit otherwise.

"Your turn," Grant told him, holding out his hand to Lane.

When he took it, Grant pulled him, helping him to his feet before going to work on removing Lane's clothes.

And then Lane was blessedly naked, and Grant was incentivized to go to his knees directly in front of him, desperate to put his mouth on Lane's thick cock jutting out from his body.

Grant was rewarded with a sharp gasp from Gracie and a deep, rumbling moan from Lane.

On his knees, he looked up the length of Lane's body while he engulfed Lane's cock in his mouth, tormenting him until Lane's hands had fisted into his hair.

"I need to feel you," Lane groaned. "I need to feel you inside me."

Grant understood the urgency. He was still riding the adrenaline high from the afternoon's events, so he didn't hesitate before rising to his feet. Standing directly in front of Lane, he pressed up against him, using his fist to wrap around both of their cocks, sliding them together before pressing his mouth to Lane's.

As much as he loved kissing Lane, he couldn't do so for long because they were both moaning as the friction intensified.

"Grant," Lane said on a sigh. "Oh, damn, baby, that feels good. Keep stroking me. Fuck."

Baby.

Again, Lane had called him baby, and Grant's heart swelled in his chest, making it difficult to breathe.

Or maybe that was because he was gliding his cock along the silky smooth length of Lane's, the sensitive head rubbing just right... "Oh, damn," Grant bellowed. "I need to fuck you. Right now."

The sweltering dark pools of Lane's eyes were trained on him, and Grant felt the heat, felt the energy that coursed between them. Knowing he wasn't going to make it through this unscathed — why would this time be any different from the last? — Grant released their dicks and gripped Lane's hips, pulling him.

He walked backward until they were near the end of the love seat, and that's when he smiled. Lane apparently knew exactly what Grant wanted, and when he turned around to face the couch, leaning forward and putting his hands on the arm, Grant's dick throbbed painfully.

"Is this what you wanted to see?" Grant asked Gracie as he leaned forward, pressing his lips to Lane's back.

"Yes," she answered on a breathless moan.

Grant trailed kisses down Lane's muscular back, sliding his tongue down the deep ridge in the center as he lowered himself to his knees once again. He wasn't just going to take Lane like a barbarian, he was going to work the man up and then he was going to fuck him hard and fast. Even if it killed him.

In order to do that...

"Oh, fuck," Lane shouted.

Grant was kneeling behind him, using his hands to separate Lane's cheeks while he pushed his tongue deep into the crease of Lane's ass.

"Oh, shit, that feels so good," Lane moaned, his legs spreading farther apart to give Grant better access.

Grant rimmed Lane's asshole with his tongue and then thrust in deep, pulling Lane's hips back so that he was fucking him with his tongue.

"Grant, oh... Don't stop. Oh, fuck."

Lane was offering his own support by pressing back against Grant's face. He continued this for a minute or so, reaching around and jacking Lane's thick cock, swiping the precum from the head with his thumb.

When Grant's cock began to pulse incessantly, he knew he couldn't wait any longer. He needed to slide deep into Lane's ass so he could ride him hard before they both came.

"Did you like that?" Grant asked, speaking to Lane but looking at Gracie.

They both answered with a resounding "yes."

"Good." He quickly donned a condom and put a thick coat of lube along his cock while slicking two of his fingers at the same time. While he stroked himself, he slipped those two fingers into Lane's ass, going deep and twisting. He continued the motion because he knew Lane enjoyed it.

"Grant... Son of a..." Lane mumbled. "Keep that up and ... uh... Oh, God, that... Keep it up and I'm gonna come!"

Grant pulled his fingers out after massaging Lane's prostate two more times and then lined up and thrust into him in one forceful push.

"Oh, yes," Lane yelled, pushing back against Grant.

"Fuck, you're tight," Grant groaned, gripping Lane's hips as he withdrew slowly. "I love the way your ass grips my dick."

Another sharp inhale from across the room had Grant looking over at Gracie.

He nearly stumbled into Lane, damn near plowing him over as he watched Gracie finger her pussy as she watched them.

Heaven help him.

Chapter Twenty-Five

GRACIE WAS GOING TO COME.

She was going to explode from watching Grant have his wicked way with Lane and witnessing Lane enjoy the hell out of it.

There was something to be said about watching two men like this. To see the sheer pleasure etched on their faces, the emotion that they thought they were hiding was right there for her to see. These two loved each other; there was no doubt about that.

From her seat, Grace had the perfect view of Lane bent over the couch and Grant driving into him from behind. It was so hot she was surprised she hadn't gone up in a puff of smoke.

"Fuck me, Grant," Lane pleaded as he drove his hips back against Grant, who was plunging into Lane forcefully.

This was hardcore, erotic fucking, and these two clearly couldn't get enough of one another. She was surprised that she didn't feel like an outsider as she sat in Grant's recliner, her legs spread wide, teasing herself mercilessly while she watched.

But the way they both glanced over at her from time to time kept her connected to them in a way that made her heart sing.

This was hot.

Sliding one finger into her pussy, Grace slowly fucked herself while she watched Grant slam into Lane over and over, Lane's powerful body remaining upright while he used his own strength to drive himself back against Grant.

"Oh, yes," Grant groaned. "Squeeze my dick."

Lane lifted one hand to his own cock, stroking himself. Slowly at first, then faster, his eyes closed, a constant stream of moans and groans coming from both men.

Oh, hell. Grace was close. She was so close, and to think neither of them had touched her. She was fingering herself, something she rarely did because she much preferred her trusty vibrator, but right now, she was almost convinced that a well-placed puff of air would send her over the edge.

"You want me to come in your ass?" Grant asked Lane.

Grace loved how they talked to each other.

Closing her eyes, she listened to the sounds of their heavy breaths, the slap of their bodies, the rumbles and groans that signaled every driving thrust.

"Yes," Lane grunted. "Come deep in my ass."

Grace was hanging on by the skin of her teeth, not wanting to go over until they did, but she didn't think she was going to make it. She was so lost to the sounds, she kept her eyes closed, hoping to hang on just a little while longer.

"I love your ass." Grant's voice rumbled, sending a jolt of pleasure to Grace's core. "I love driving my dick deep inside you, fucking you, riding you hard."

"Oh, fuck," Lane roared, and Grace tried to force her eyes open, but she couldn't.

Grace cried out, her own climax ricocheting through her, her body tensing as she came so hard she was surprised she didn't lose consciousness.

"Well, well, well. What the fuck do we have here?"

Grace couldn't help it, she screamed. Her arms flew up to cover herself as she stared over at the door where the voice came from, her breath lodged in her throat.

There, standing behind Grant and Lane, was Grant's father.

"Get. The. Fuck. Out!" Grant snarled, the sound so fierce that Grace flinched, as both men reached for something to cover themselves.

Lane took three long strides and was standing in front of Grace, blocking her completely from the view of the man at the door even as he was yanking on his own jeans.

Grace peered around him, noticing that Grant had turned as well, attempting to block the man's view of both of them.

"Well, this explains a helluva lot," Darrell belted out, his eyes reflecting what looked like hatred as he stared at Grant. "I always knew there was somethin' wrong with you. Doesn't surprise me that you're in to this debauchery."

Grace had to lean over to keep her eyes on the man, something she found herself regretting when his bloodshot eyes met hers.

"Hmm, and this is daddy's little girl, huh? Wonder what he'll think when I tell him you're in here fornicatin' with two men. What do you think he'll say?"

Fornicating? What the fuck?

"Don't you fuckin' think about it," Grant yelled, yanking on his jeans and stalking toward the man.

"Or what? Huh? What're you gonna do? It's just too bad I didn't think to grab my phone. Then I'd have video proof."

The thought had a shudder bursting through Grace followed by a wave of nausea, her teeth chattering from the pure fear she felt as she stared at this crazy man. How long had he been there? Watching them?

Oh, God, the thought of him seeing something so private had her breathing deep, trying not to throw up.

"Get. Out. And if you dream of sayin' one fuckin' word, I swear to God, I'll–"

"Grant!" Lane interrupted. "Enough. Get him out of here before I do."

Grace hadn't even realized that Lane had pulled his jeans on and had tossed the clean T-shirt that had been on the couch at her. She hid behind Lane and yanked it on over her head, not realizing until she was covered that it was on inside out.

Who fucking cared?

"See, now, here's what I'm thinkin'," Darrell spat, glaring at Grant. "You've got somethin' I need, and I've got a secret you don't want to get out. I think it's time we had a little chat. Don't you?"

"No," Grace shouted, pushing up out of the chair.

"Stay out of this, Gracie."

Grace ignored Grant's instruction, trying to move toward him but being held back by Lane's big body blocking her path. As she stared at Lane's broad back, she realized he was breathing hard. Placing her hand on his warm skin, she tried to ease around him, but he blocked her attempt again.

"Last warning, Grant. Get him the fuck out of here, or I will," Lane growled, the menace in his tone sending a cold chill down Grace's spine.

"Don't let him blackmail you, Grant," Grace said, leaning around Lane when moving past him proved futile.

"She's a feisty one," Darrell said, his eyes locked with Grant's.

Grace was surprised he even acknowledged her. After all, it was about all he'd done the last time she'd been in his presence.

"Get. Out." Grant's face was contorted in fury, and he had begun to stalk his father, forcing him back to the door. "We'll talk outside," Grant bit out.

"No, you won't," Grace demanded, giving Lane a firm shove, which worked to get him to move briefly. She took the opportunity and stomped across the room until she was standing next to Grant, placing her hand on his arm. "We're not gonna do this. Do you hear me? We're not gonna let him use this against us."

"Hear that?" Darrell mouthed. "She doesn't mind if her daddy finds out she's actin' out her fantasy of watchin' two guys fuck each other." The disgust on the man's splotchy face made Grace cringe.

Grant finally turned to look at her, but she could see in the swirling depths of his eyes that he wasn't listening. Or if he was, he certainly didn't agree with her. He shook his head at her and then turned his attention back to his father. "Outside," Grant said again.

Grace could only stare at them both as they turned toward the door. She glanced back at Lane, wishing like hell he'd step in. What man would want to go up against Lane?

Whoa.

No, maybe she didn't want him to. Lane looked downright terrifying as he stood there, his chest heaving, his forehead creased as he glared at Grant's father.

She raised her eyebrows at him, a nonverbal question of "Aren't you gonna do something?" transmitting across the room.

He clearly didn't translate her expression, because his eyes just slid back toward the door that was now closing on Grant and his father.

Shit.

Now how the hell was she going to fix this?

■□■□■□■□

THE RED CLOUD HAZING LANE'S vision didn't dissipate even after Grant's father turned around and walked out the front door. And now, as he stood staring at Gracie while she stared at the door, he didn't even know what to say.

"Are you okay?" Lane asked, the words seemingly coming out of his mouth of their own accord. Not a bad thing since his brain was currently scrambled from the rage flooding his veins.

"Me?" Gracie asked, turning around to face him. "I… I'm fine."

Yeah, she sounded fine, all right. Not a chance.

Moving across the room on legs that felt like they'd been filled with lead, Lane reached for her, pulling her into his arms and crushing her to him. From the second he'd heard that bastard's voice, Lane had been battling an overwhelming urge to kill someone. Namely Darrell Kingsley.

He had watched them.

The fucking perverted old bastard had stood in Grant's house and watched them.

The thought made Lane sick.

Gracie's arms wrapping tightly around him was the only thing keeping him together. From where he stood, he could hear the argument raging outside, and he feared what Grant was saying. He'd seen it in Grant's eyes, the fear and embarrassment of his father being there, invading the privacy that the three of them were supposed to have. But it was the way Grant had frozen, not protecting Gracie the way he should've. Had that been Lane's father, Lane would've grabbed him by the scruff of the neck and tossed him out on his ass. Only then would he have addressed the crazy son of a bitch.

Not Grant. He'd stood there and let that bastard ogle Gracie until Lane had finally managed to toss her a shirt so that she could cover herself.

Needless to say, Lane was furious. At Darrell. At Grant. At himself.

Uggghhh!

"Hey," Gracie said, pulling Lane from his thoughts. "Are you okay?"

"Never fucking better," he grumbled as he forced his arms not to tighten around her. He knew he would crush her if the violence that was racing through him got free.

"We need to talk to Grant," Gracie said, taking a step back but not forcing Lane to release her.

Her brilliant turquoise eyes glittered with a sheen of tears.

"Grant's a big boy," Lane offered. "He can handle himself."

"What if he gives in? What if he gives Darrell money to keep him from talkin'?"

Those were the questions searing Lane's brain. He didn't want to think about what the answer might be, because as far as he was concerned, giving in, or giving that asshole money, wasn't even an option. Blackmail never worked. Grant's father would push and push until he drained Grant dry.

"He can't give in." That was the only thing Lane could come up with.

"Should we go out there?"

Lane didn't have to answer that because Grant chose then to come inside, his face pale, his hands shaking as he came to a stop right in the doorway. "No need. He's gone."

Surprisingly, Gracie didn't run into Grant's arms. She turned around slowly, remaining only a few inches from Lane as they both stared back at Grant. Lane wondered whether she was waiting for an explanation as much as he was.

No, Lane didn't want to know why Grant's father had showed up and invaded their private moment in the most despicable way possible. Lane wanted to know whether or not Grant had stood up for the three of them, for what he believed was right.

"I told him that I'd see him tomorrow," Grant admitted, and Lane saw the defeat on his face.

He didn't need to hear anything more to know that Grant wasn't going to stand up to Darrell. He was going to give in, give the man money, and then sit and wait for it all to crumble around him. Because that was exactly what was going to happen.

"Why're you gonna see him?" Gracie questioned, a hint of frustration in her tone.

Was it him or did she actually move closer to Lane?

"What else am I gonna do, Gracie? Huh? Tell me that!" Grant yelled, his eyes blazing with anger.

"You're gonna stand up to him," Lane barked, moving Gracie out of the way as he took a step closer to Grant. "You're gonna stand up for the people you supposedly care about."

"Yeah? And how the fuck do I do that?" Grant countered. "What? Do I run to Jerry and tell him that I'm fuckin' his daughter and my best friend? How's that gonna go over with him, do you think?"

"Fucking, huh? Is that what this is?" Lane asked, unable to disguise the hurt in his voice.

Grant didn't answer.

"The truth is gonna come out sooner or later," Lane added. "You think your father will be satisfied with just a little bit of money? What happens when that runs out? Are you gonna fund his habit for the rest of his miserable life?"

"If I have to!" Grant shouted.

Lane realized they were practically nose to nose.

"So you're not man enough to step up and admit your feelings for me and Gracie, are you?"

"You know how I feel about you. That's all that matters."

Lane shook his head. "No, actually, I don't. I know how I feel about you and Gracie. And you and Gracie know how I feel about the two of you. But *me*? No, I sit in my bed at night and hope like hell that you'll tell me that you love me." Darting his head around, he pinned Gracie with a look. "That *you'll* tell me." Jerking back, Lane came face-to-face with Grant once again. "That doesn't happen for me. I go through each fucking day wishin' like hell that at least one of you would acknowledge your feelings for me."

Lane was having a hard time breathing. He had promised himself that he would never call either of them out on their feelings. He had tried to convince himself that when they were ready, they would tell him, and that would be enough.

It wasn't enough.

Lane was tired of waiting to hear the words. And now that Darrell was going to blackmail Grant, he didn't expect to hear them any time soon, if ever.

Storming off, Lane went to the couch and yanked on his boots, his face heating from the fury still slicing him into a million pieces. Still shirtless, Lane decided to take his chances. He made his way across the room, not bothering to look at Gracie or Grant. He had to push past Grant, but he got to the door.

He sent up one last silent prayer, begging God to let one of them stop him.

They didn't.

As Lane stepped out onto the front porch, the sound of the coyotes howling in the distance had him stopping. He wanted to yell, to scream to the top of his lungs about how unfair it all was.

But he didn't.

No, Lane took a deep breath and stepped off the porch, wondering if he'd just lost the two best things he'd ever had. And it didn't help one fucking bit that he knew it wasn't his fault.

The pain in his heart didn't seem to care.

■□■□■□■□

GRACE WAS SPEECHLESS AS SHE watched Lane walk out the front door, his big shoulders slumped as though he'd just been beaten down. She was tempted to run after him, but she didn't. For whatever reason, her feet were glued to the floor.

Had he really been waiting for them to tell him how they felt? Had she really not told him that she loved him? Because she did. Love them, that is. There was no doubt about that. She loved *both* of them.

Grace peered up into Grant's eyes. And if Lane had looked defeated, Grant looked as though the world had just crumbled down around him and there was no one left.

"You can't give in, you know," she finally said when the silence became too much to bear.

"I have to," he replied, making his way across the room. "I don't have any other choice. And it's the only way that I can protect you and Lane."

Grace watched as Grant picked up her clothes, stacking them on the arm of the recliner.

"And just how do you think that's protectin' us?" she argued, her anger growing exponentially.

"What do you think your dad's gonna say when he finds out, huh?"

"I don't care what he says," she lied.

"You do care, Gracie."

Yes, she did care what her father said. She didn't want him to do something rash, but she knew that he'd never reacted badly when it came to her or her sisters dating someone. Not that they let him in on their little secrets that often, but the man wasn't a hermit. He was a very important part of the ranch, and he spent his days out in the sun with the rest of them. Jerry knew what was going on even if he didn't admit it.

Not that she thought he knew about her threesome with Lane and Grant.

No, Grace suspected he knew about her and Grant, especially after the little scene in her father's office just a couple of hours ago. It had been that moment when Grace had decided it was time to stand up for what she wanted.

But letting her father know that she was there for Grant as more than a friend had been the least of her worries. What she feared was how he'd react when he found out that she loved both of these men equally. But she couldn't back down from it. She couldn't allow some crazy guy to waltz in and take all of that away from her.

"Fine. I care. But this is somethin' that I can explain to him. I just need to find the right time."

"Don't you get it?" Grant moved closer to her. "There isn't gonna be a right time. Once your father finds out, he's gonna fire me. Or worse, he's gonna fire Lane. I can't let that happen."

"What are you talkin' about?" she asked indignantly. Her father would never stoop so low as to fire someone because he was dating one of his daughters.

"Remember Garrett Daniels?" Grant questioned.

"Of course I remember him. That asshole was a psycho!"

"What? You think he was a psycho because he wanted to stand up to your father? He wanted to be with Trinity."

Grace laughed, but it sounded more like a strangled cough. "Garrett was a rapist, Grant! He didn't want to stand up for anyone. That was the rumor he started when my father fired his ass for tryin' to hurt my sister!"

Grant's eyes widened, and that's when Grace realized he truly believed her father had no regard for anyone other than himself.

"I can't believe you," Grace whispered. "You don't think highly of anyone, do you, Grant? You really think my father would do that?"

"I... I thought... Even Faith believes that," Grant stuttered.

"We tried to keep that from Faith. Hell, we tried to keep it from *everyone*. Trinity was messed up after that. And Dallas threatened to kill Garrett. Why would we want that sort of shit running rampant at the ranch?" Grace realized she had her hands on her hips and she was facing off with Grant, growing angrier with each passing second.

He was shaking his head, and Grace didn't know if it was because he didn't believe her or he didn't want to hear what she had to say. Either way, she was done with this conversation. Snatching her clothes from where he had laid them so neatly, Grace headed to the bathroom to get dressed. She needed a minute … or twenty … just to calm her frantic heartbeat.

By the time she was dressed, Grace exited the bathroom feeling less than stellar. Her heart was still pounding, and she was actually upset at Grant. Not to mention, she was worried about Lane. Unfortunately, she couldn't do anything about the latter, aside from a text message, because showing up at the bunkhouse in the middle of the night, looking like she'd been rode hard and put away wet would only cause a stir. Something she didn't want to do right now.

At least not until morning.

As she moved through the living room, she realized that Grant wasn't there. Turning slightly, she saw that his bedroom door was closed. Was that a sign that she should show herself out?

Frustration had her throat working overtime as she tried to swallow past the lump that had formed there. Tears burned the back of her sinuses, but she refused to cry. He was the one who was being a big dummy where his father was concerned.

Yuck!

The memory of looking up to see that man standing there staring at her made her want to vomit. She had been so engrossed in the moment that she hadn't even realized he was there. There was no telling how long he had stood there, watching them.

Rather than dwell on the disastrous night, Grace decided she'd had enough. Without bothering to let Grant know she was leaving, Grace marched right out the door and didn't stop until she was walking into her own cabin a few minutes later. By that time, her frustration had morphed into heartache, and she was fighting the tears fiercely.

She feared she was going to lose the battle, and she refused to do that. She would not give Grant's asshole father any of her tears. She would not let him do this to her.

Maybe she wasn't ready to waltz up to her father and share the good news that she was in love with two cowboys, but she wasn't going to let anyone come between her and the men she loved. No one.

One thing she could guaran-damn-tee ... Darrell Kingsley might be a betting man, but he had another thing coming if he thought he had won this round. The man might have high hopes, but she was almost positive he hadn't been betting on her standing up for what she wanted.

That was a bet he would *never* win.

Chapter Twenty-Six

GRANT TOSSED AND TURNED FOR the better part of an hour, but he couldn't get to sleep. Even after taking a shower, hoping the cool water would help to calm his frazzled nerves, he couldn't keep his eyes closed. The events of the night riddled his brain. God, how had things gotten so out of control? So much so that he'd let Gracie walk out of his house without so much as a good-bye?

Tossing his legs over the edge of the bed, Grant leaned his elbows on his knees and ran his hands through his hair.

He had to fix this.

There was no way he'd ever be able to sleep again if he let things fall apart like this. He was to blame because his father was an asshole, and yet, he'd somehow turned this around on Gracie and Lane.

There wasn't much he could do about Lane because the man wasn't answering the text that Grant had sent an hour ago. Since Lane was at the bunkhouse, Grant couldn't very well go after him, because barging in there would look suspicious.

But he could go to Gracie.

With his decision made, Grant grabbed his jeans, yanking them on, and then snagged a T-shirt out of his dresser as he made his way to the living room. His boots were on the floor where he'd left them earlier, so he pulled them on, his head spinning from all of the things he wanted to say to Gracie.

Not wanting to waste any more time, Grant headed out, opting to go on foot so that the sound of his truck's engine wouldn't wake anyone at the ranch. Nor did he want anyone to see him parked in front of Gracie's at that time of night. More for her benefit than anything else.

Or so he told himself.

He rapped his knuckles on her front door several times before, finally, the door opened, and there she stood, barefoot and beautiful, wearing the T-shirt he'd discarded earlier.

"Hey," he greeted, expecting her to slam the door in his face.

"Hey," she replied, pushing the screen door gently open.

Grant took the invitation and followed her inside.

What was he supposed to say now? All of the things he'd intended to tell her had vanished from his mind like smoke on a windy day.

When Gracie flipped on the lamp in the living room and turned to face him, Grant's heart seized up right there in his chest.

She'd been crying. Her eyes were puffy; her nose was red. She looked like she might've been asleep, but he still had to wonder.

Unable to say anything, Grant took several steps forward and reached for her, pulling her into his arms. The sound of her sobs broke his heart into a million pieces.

"I'm so sorry, Gracie. So damn sorry," he whispered into her hair.

Grant held her for several minutes, the warmth of her body settling something inside of him.

When she pulled back, looking up at him, Grant knew then and there that no one in the world mattered more to him than Gracie. Well, no one other than Lane. He would go to the ends of the earth to make them both happy.

"I lov—"

"Don't say it," Gracie interrupted, placing her fingers over Grant's lips. "Not right now. Not after all that happened tonight."

"But—"

"No buts, Grant. I know how you feel, don't think that I don't. But right now, things are too mixed up. I don't want you saying somethin' you might regret later."

They were both silent for a minute, maybe two. Or hell, maybe it was just a second. Grant didn't know. The only thing he knew was that he wanted to wrap this woman in his arms and never let her go. When she moved back into him, her arms sliding around his waist, Grant gave in to the emotion, holding her tight but trying not to crush her.

"I want to stay here tonight," he mumbled.

Gracie didn't respond with words, but he felt the nod of her head against his chest. The next time she pulled away, Gracie took his hand and led him to her bedroom. His heart was pounding like a bass drum in his chest, painfully hard, as he fought the emotion bubbling up inside of him. He wasn't the type of man to cry or to give in to the feelings that were suddenly overwhelming him, but he knew it was pointless to try.

So much had happened in the last few hours, and Grant only knew one thing. What he felt for this woman superseded anything he'd ever felt for anyone other than Lane.

Grant's intentions were entirely altruistic, but that was before he climbed into bed with Gracie after discarding his clothes. Had she kept the T-shirt on, he might've been able to cuddle up against her and ignore the raging hard-on that was always prominent whenever she was near. But no... Gracie pulled the shirt over her head and tossed it onto the floor before crawling up against Grant.

She smelled like flowers, the scent of her shampoo like a soothing balm to his rioting nerves. Her fingers were soft as they caressed his chest, her leg silky where she rested hers over his. At that moment, even with all of the chaos from the day, Grant found himself relaxing, his eyes closing.

Despite the throbbing between his legs, Grant managed to drift off to sleep, but that didn't last long, because he next thing he knew, his eyes were open, and he was looking at the woman still lying beside him. Gracie was awake, her eyes open as she watched him. Unable to resist, Grant leaned forward, pressing his lips to hers until the only thing he knew was the warmth of Gracie's lips against his.

Rolling over her, Grant knelt between her thighs, holding his weight above her as he rested on his elbows, his hands cradling her head. He wanted to touch her everywhere, to align their bodies so that they were one.

"Gracie." Grant whispered her name, the emotions once again crashing into him like a tsunami. It wasn't just the passion of her kiss or the softness of her hands as they slid over his back. This woman made him burn, she made him ache, and she made him want more than just a passionate moment. He wanted her forever.

He lifted his head to look down at her, smiling as he did. "I love you, Gracie," he whispered, getting the words out before she could quiet him. "I am so sorry for everyth—"

Well, he didn't manage to get the rest of his sentence out before she crushed her mouth to his, pulling him to her until he was practically crushing her beneath him. His cock slid through her slick folds, and he wanted nothing more than to bury himself in her heat, to take her, skin to skin, right there in her bed.

"Make love to me, Grant," Gracie whispered, sliding her hands into his hair.

He nodded his head, eager to agree. But when he reached toward the bedside table, Gracie stopped him, her legs wrapping around his hips and holding him in place.

"Just us. I want to feel you," she added.

Grant's chest heaved with what was left of that emotional buildup, and if he wasn't mistaken, there were tears forming in his eyes. Unwilling to be a fucking pansy, he inhaled sharply, forcing a smile even though his damn jaw wobbled with the effort.

Gracie must've realized he needed some assistance, because she reached between them and wrapped her smooth fingers around his shaft, making him suck in air. All emotion fled as the sensation of her hand around his dick took over. But then there was heat...

Slick, molten heat and he was sliding into her, his breath lodged in his throat, his eyes trained on hers.

"Oh, God, Gracie," he murmured, the words rushing out of him as the overwhelming pleasure of her body consumed him.

"Love me, Grant," Gracie whispered, pulling his head to hers until their mouths aligned.

Grant tried to focus on the kiss, tried to ignore the way his balls drew up against his body, the intense sensations ripping through him. They were skin to skin, and he'd never felt anything like it. Nothing quite so exquisite, so all-consuming as being buried balls-deep inside of Gracie's pussy with nothing between them.

"Baby," Grant groaned against her mouth, needing air, needing ... something. "You feel so good ... so tight ... so warm."

Gracie shifted her hips, driving up against him, and Grant was overcome with the sheer intensity of being inside her. Unable to hold himself back, he pulled his elbows in closer to her, sandwiching her between his arms as he stared down into her beautiful face, his hips thrusting forward, pulling back. He focused on the sensation, sliding into her, withdrawing. Over and over until sweat was beading on his forehead and they were both panting.

"Grant... Oh, yes..."

Gracie's soft moans were undoing him, but the last thing Grant wanted was for this to end.

■□■□■□■□

GRACE WAS DOING HER BEST not to lose complete control, not wanting this moment to end. Not yet. Not when Grant was opening himself up so completely. His whispered "I love you" had made her heart swell, but the way he was looking at her, the emotion she could see even in the dim light of the room, told her so much more.

For the first time in the last few months, Grant wasn't holding back. He wasn't shielding himself. Grace knew he was just as overwhelmed as she was, and it wasn't just from the blinding, exquisite sensation of having him inside her bare.

That was incredible, there was no doubt about it, but the emotion that was involved, that was more than she'd ever expected.

Slipping her fingers through his hair, Grace smiled up at Grant as he continued to thrust into her, his rhythm slow and sweet, unlike most of the times they were together when they would allow the excitement of the moment take over. They were making love, and Grace had never known anything quite like it.

Truthfully, Grace felt so much emotion from Lane. The man was an open book, and he shared every feeling, every desire. But with Grant... He kept himself closed off. And tonight, when she'd been lying in her bed, reliving the horror show from earlier, Grace had wondered if Grant kept himself locked up tight because of his home life growing up.

Whatever it was, she was beyond moved that he was opening up to her now.

"I love you," she whispered, moaning softly as he drove deeper. "Grant, oh... It feels ... so... good."

Too good. Grace wasn't going to last much longer; her orgasm was cresting, getting ready to break free and crash through her. She had to wonder whether or not she was going to survive something like this. This was more than sex, more than an intense climax... This was emotional overload and...

"Oh, God, Grant!" Grace's orgasm overwhelmed her, her legs locking around him as she held him to her.

"That's it, baby. Come for me," Grant said, his tone soft and low. "Gracie ... baby..."

Grace hadn't even begun to come down from the overwhelming force when Grant's body stilled, his cock pulsing inside her, his breaths slamming in and out of his lungs in a rhythm that matched her own.

A few minutes later, with the sweat cooling on their bodies, Grace still didn't want to move. Grant was sliding out of her, the disappearing warmth of his body leaving her chilled. She watched as he disappeared from the room, returning a moment later with a washcloth that he used to clean her before disappearing once again.

The next time he returned to the bed, Grace was eager to settle against him, already missing the strong feel of his body.

"I love you, Gracie," Grant whispered several minutes later as Grace lay with her head resting on his arm, her leg protectively lying over his leg. "I love you more than you'll ever know."

"I love you, too," she responded, feeling the sudden tensing of his muscles. He must've thought she was asleep. "And don't worry, we'll get through this. I'll make sure of that."

With that final statement, Grace drifted off, feeling more content than she had in some time. The only thing missing was Lane, and although she desperately wished he were there, she knew that she and Grant had needed this.

CHAPTER TWENTY-SEVEN

Saturday morning

SATURDAYS WERE JUST LIKE ANY other day of the week at Dead Heat Ranch. The day often reserved for time off wasn't any different from Monday through Friday when it came to caring for animals or taking care of visiting guests. They tried to make sure everyone had at least one full day off during the week, but most of the crew would agree that Saturday wasn't that day. For once, Lane was glad today wasn't his day because he'd probably go stir crazy without something to do.

Since he had walked out of Grant's house last night, he hadn't talked to him. When he'd woken that morning, he'd noticed that he had received a text from both of them. Grant's had been simple: *I'm sorry. I want to talk.* Gracie's had been similar, short and sweet.

And for the first time since everything had gone down last night, Lane had actually felt a smidgeon of hope where their relationship was concerned. She didn't tell him that she loved him, but her text eluded to her wanting to tell him something. Something she said she should've said a long time ago.

Lane's hope had soared high and far at that point, but now it was almost ten o'clock in the morning, and he hadn't seen either of them.

Not that he'd been looking.

Before the sun had even broken over the horizon, Lane had shuffled out of bed, snuck over to the kitchen at the main house, and grabbed a cup of coffee before coming out to the stables to hang out with Dixie and her pups. Budweiser had been there to greet him, and for the last hour, Lane had been sitting on the ground, his back against the wood wall, his knees bent, as he stared at the metal roof and let the squirmy little dogs walk all over him. He didn't care whether or not he looked like a fucking pansy playing with the dogs, either. It was the only thing he could think of that would possibly make him feel better.

Aside from going to see Gracie and Grant.

Since that wasn't an option — Lane refused to be the one to grovel at their feet — here he was.

"Hey, can I talk to you for a minute?"

Lane jerked his head up at the sound of the voice, but he didn't see anyone peering in the stall at him. He knew the voice belonged to Grant, but Lane was pretty sure Grant wasn't talking to him.

"Sure," another voice said.

Yep, he was right. Grant wasn't talking to him.

Hmm. What to do. What to do. Should he get up, make his presence known, and leave so the two of them could have a conversation in private? Or should he just sit right there and let them carry on, none the wiser?

Drumming his fingers on his thigh, he considered his options. Lane decided that he didn't care much whether they knew he was blatantly eavesdropping just a few feet away, so he remained right there in the small pen with the puppies nipping at his fingers and his shirt while he listened to the conversation on the other side of the wall without one ounce of guilt.

Served Grant right for not stopping him from walking out last night.

"Faith came to me the other night," Grant said.

Faith? What the hell was Faith going to Grant for?

"And?"

Lane peeked through the slats in the stall wall, trying to see who Grant was talking to.

Well, well, well.

Rusty Ashmore.

Ahh. Well, that made sense why Grant was mentioning Faith, at least.

"She wanted me to talk to you."

"Is that right?" Rusty stated, sounding none too thrilled with Grant's revelation.

"Hold up. Before you get all butt-hurt, let me explain."

Lane knew Rusty. He liked the guy. Rusty was one of the newbies to the ranch, having only been there for roughly a year. Maybe.

In their world, with so many tenured wranglers at the ranch, one year was the equivalent of two weeks. But in Rusty's defense, he knew his stuff. He worked his ass off, didn't complain, and didn't make excuses. All around, he was one hell of a wrangler. Aside from his work ethic, Lane knew the guy was young, twenty-five as of his last birthday a couple of months ago, which they'd all celebrated by getting plastered at the main house, trying to best one another at pool. To this day, Lane had no idea who'd won.

Lane also knew that Rusty's mom and dad lived in one of the neighboring towns, and he went to see them every time he had a day off. Whether that was just because they were close or because something was wrong, Lane wasn't sure. He didn't ask, either.

"I told her this would be better coming from her." Grant's voice echoed in the large, open space, pulling Lane from his thoughts.

"Get on with it," Rusty barked.

Lane would've given his right arm to see Rusty's face. Based on that remark, he wasn't at all happy with Grant. Not that Lane could blame the guy. He was as in the dark as Rusty when it came to where this conversation was going, but he was ready to give Grant a shake just to get him to move along.

"She doesn't want you askin' her out anymore."

Well, shit. Lane wouldn't have been surprised if Rusty had cold-cocked Grant. Had Lane been in Rusty's boots, he would've delivered a nice knuckle sandwich right to Grant's mouth. As much as he would like to be in Grant's corner at all times, Lane wouldn't support any man interfering the way Grant just had.

"And that's your business, why?" Rusty retorted.

Exactly, Lane thought.

"Exactly!" Grant exclaimed. "It's not, and I tried to tell her that. So, to honor my promise to her, here I am. But in all honesty, I'm not here to warn you away from her."

There was silence for long seconds, and Lane was tempted to make his presence known, just in case these two needed a referee. Grant had overstepped, Lane would agree there.

"That's good," Rusty said softly, his tone lethal, "because now I won't have to hit you upside the head."

"The only thing I'm gonna say is that you treat her right."

What? Lane couldn't believe what he was hearing. Grant was giving relationship advice now?

"Keep goin' and I still might belt you one, Kingsley," Rusty grumbled.

"Originally, I'd intended to tell you to back off even though it's none of my business," Grant added defensively. "I've come to my senses since then."

"What the fuck are you talking about?"

Yeah, what the *fuck* was Grant talking about?

"Sometimes I'm clueless," Grant explained. "That's all I've got to say. Just be good to her. If you know what's best for you."

"Whatever, man," Rusty snapped. "I don't have time for this shit."

"I'm serious," Grant said, sounding … well, serious.

The silence was deafening, nothing but the soft yapping from the pups and their little feet scuffling on the concrete floor. Lane was just about to get up, to let Grant know he was there, when he heard another voice. This one wasn't one he'd been expecting. At least not that early in the morning.

■□■□■□■□

CRAP.

"Grant," Jerry greeted as he stepped into the stable. "Hey, Ashmore. Mind if I talk to him alone for a minute?"

Grant was tempted to turn and run, but he knew better. It wasn't often that Jerry sought him out unless it had to do with work, and this was one of those times Grant prayed his boss wanted to scold him for not doing his job. Maybe he'd do that and then move on. Because anything else he wanted to chat about ... well ... Grant wasn't sure he would be allowed to stick around to hear it.

Surely, the guy didn't know Grant had spent the night with Gracie last night. Right?

"Have at it, boss. I don't know what his deal is this mornin'," Rusty bit out.

Grant watched Rusty walk off, the younger man shaking his head as he did.

Yeah, Grant knew he looked like a big fucking asshole, interfering when he should've kept his mouth shut. He couldn't help it. Faith had asked him to talk to Rusty. Now he could honestly say he had.

Even though he hadn't warned Rusty away from Faith — because after what he'd learned from Gracie, he knew there was no way Jerry had done what he'd originally thought. How the hell he hadn't heard the story about Garrett, Grant would probably never know. Sure, he knew the wranglers had their own conversations, and most of the time they excluded Grant because he was the foreman, but shit, that was some big news for him to have never heard.

"Miller! Out here, now!"

Grant wrenched his head around in time to see Lane's giant form standing up from behind one of the stall walls. What the hell?

He didn't get a chance to question Lane before the other man was shrugging his shoulders and walking toward them. Grant did notice the frown that creased Lane's handsome face.

That was just great. Now Lane had heard Grant's finest moment of the day.

The only thing he could hope for at this point was that Jerry wasn't coming to rip him a new one. As much as wanted to believe otherwise, there was still the off chance that Darrell had gone to Jerry first thing that morning. Grant didn't think Darrell had — mainly because Grant's head was still on his body — but since he hadn't forked over any money just yet, Grant figured anything was possible. The only thing that might've saved his ass was if his father realized by opening his big mouth he would never see a dime.

"Did you need somethin'?" Grant asked Jerry, unable to stand the silence as the older man moved across the stable toward the stall where Astro Boy was being kept for the time being.

"I wanna talk to you boys," Jerry explained as he stopped in front of the stall. "You know that Gracie adores this horse?"

Grant looked at Lane, wondering whether or not either of them should actually answer that question. When Jerry didn't continue, Grant said, "Yes, sir. He's her pride and joy."

"Did you know that Gracie started out barrel racin' when she was five? She was good, too. So damn good. But she refused to do it anymore after her mother passed away when she was twelve."

Grant did know that. He also knew that she was still going strong, although she didn't want anyone to know.

"I tried to get her to jump back on the horse again, but she refused. Flat-out refused to do the one thing she loved so much. She's a stubborn one, my Gracie."

Stubborn? Yeah, Grant would certainly agree with that assessment.

"And when I say stubborn, I mean her head's as hard as a brick wall. When she believes in somethin', she doesn't back down."

Grant was beginning to worry just where this conversation was going. From the confused expression on Lane's face, he was feeling pretty much the same.

"Sir, if this is about yesterday in your office—"

"Son, this is about a lot more than you huggin' my daughter in my office."

Shit.

"Come on, let's walk." Jerry didn't wait for Grant or Lane to catch up as he headed outside, a surprisingly cool breeze kicking up the dirt and filling Grant's nose with the scent of hay and fresh-cut grass. It was rather reassuring, for some strange reason. And he hoped like hell it disguised the putrid aroma of fear he was likely putting off right about then.

"Gracie came to see me this mornin'," Jerry said casually, the words making Grant's throat swell to the point he wasn't sure he'd be able to swallow around the knot of trepidation that was growing at a rapid pace.

"Do you know what she told me?" Jerry asked, shooting a glance at Grant and Lane over his shoulder.

Grant could do nothing more than shake his head. He had no idea, and he wasn't quite sure he wanted to know.

"She told me that she loves you. *Both* of you."

Grant's feet stopped moving, as did Lane's.

They just stopped and stared at Jerry as though the man had lost his mind. Maybe Grant was dreaming. Maybe in a few seconds he was going to wake up drenched in sweat, and the fear would dissipate...

"It took a lot of guts for her to tell me that."

Grant nodded this time.

"Sir, I can explain," Lane interrupted, but Jerry shot him a glare, effectively silencing him.

"I don't need your explanation, Miller. She was pretty thorough." Jerry paused, staring back at them both and making it hard for Grant to keep from fidgeting. "You know what else she told me?"

While Lane answered with a firm no, Grant just shook his head again. Yep, Jerry's little conversation had effectively rendered Grant mute, and he had no idea whether his voice was going to make a reappearance anytime in the near future.

"She told me that she's in a relationship." Jerry didn't continue, but Grant knew what was coming.

The sound of Gracie's words from last night resounded in Grant's head. *And don't worry, we'll get through this. I'll make sure of that.*

Yep, Gracie had done what Grant didn't have the balls to do. She had gone to her father and told him the truth. He should've been happy about that.

Jerry turned to face Grant, his mouth a firm, thin line, his eyebrows downturned, making him look just a little bit evil. "She told me she was in a relationship with you and Lane."

Oh. Fuck.

"Either of you care to enlighten me on that one?"

Ummm … no. No, he certainly did not.

And this time, Lane was smart enough not to say a word, either.

■□■□■□■□

JERRY WAS PRETTY SURE HE deserved a giant pat on the back.

He'd come into the stable with the intention of addressing Grant and Lane about the discussion he'd just had with Gracie. And here he was having a civil conversation when he wanted nothing more than to grab Grant and Lane by their shirts and yank them both off their feet, demanding that they explain just what Gracie meant when she had told him that she loved Grant *and* Lane.

At first, Jerry had thought he was hearing things.

He still wasn't so sure that what had just happened wasn't some elaborate prank being played on him. He might've believed that was the case as he had stomped across the yard to the stable, but the look on Grant's face right then told Jerry no one was going to jump out of the shadows and inform him that he'd been punked.

While he waited for one of them to find their tongue, Jerry thought back to the conversation he'd had with Gracie just a short while ago.

"Dad, I need to talk to you," Gracie said when Jerry walked into the kitchen. Once again, his daughter had been there before him, which probably had her a little suspicious as to why he wasn't up with the chickens these days.

Unlike the last time he'd dragged his ass out of bed, this time he couldn't thank a night of incredible sex to be the reason. Well ... unless phone sex counted.

Good Lord. He needed to get his mind out of the gutter because seriously ... he was standing here with his daughter, and he certainly shouldn't be thinking about Jan and her sassy words spoken in that sexy whisper...

"Dad!"

"Huh?" Jerry jerked around to face her, nearly pouring coffee on his hand.

"Are you not gettin' enough sleep or somethin'?" Gracie asked.

Or somethin', Jerry thought to himself.

For the first time since he'd walked in the room, Jerry looked at Gracie. Really looked at her.

She looked tired. Like she hadn't slept at all last night. Her eyes were red, like she'd been crying.

Sonuvabitch. He was going to hurt someone, he could feel it.

"Could you sit down and stop glarin' at me?" Gracie kicked the chair with her foot, causing it to squeal on the wood floor.

Trying not to think of worst-case scenarios, Jerry lowered himself into the chair across from her, keeping his eyes glued to her face. He had to admit, Gracie was fairly good at hiding her emotions. Usually. Today, everything she was feeling was written across her face.

"I'm sittin'," he said, wanting her to ease some of the suspense that was making his stomach twist into a knot.

"There's somethin' I want to say to you. And I don't want you sayin' a word till I'm finished. Can you do that, please?"

Probably not. "Yes."

"Okay, good."

Jerry watched as Gracie squeezed her coffee mug until the tips of her fingers turned white. She was staring at the damn thing as if it had the answers to the universe's questions — whatever those might be.

"I've kinda been dating someone," she began, her gaze coming up to meet his.

Right before his eyes, Gracie morphed from the beautiful young woman who sat in front of him to the little girl he remembered so fondly. The little girl who wasn't quite so independent or hard-headed. The expression on her face changed almost instantly, as did her body language.

"Okay, that's a lie," she continued, and Jerry leaned back in his chair, continuing to watch her. "When I tell you this, you're probably gonna get mad. Just remember you agreed to hear me out."

Jerry nodded, unable to say a word.

"I've been datin' someone. But not just one someone. Two someones. You've probably already figured out that Grant and I... Well ... I've been seein' him for a few months now. But he's not the only one."

Jerry continued to watch her, trying to keep up, but the roaring in his ears was growing louder and louder with every word she spoke.

"I've also been seein' Lane. I've been seein' both of them at the same time. I love them, Daddy."

Wait ... what?

Jerry was lost.

"You—" He tried to speak, but Gracie quickly cut him off.

"No. My turn. You can talk later. So," Gracie continued, taking a deep breath, "I've been datin' Lane and Grant. Both of them. And they're datin' each other. And I know this probably doesn't make any sense to you, but I had to tell you. Last night, I was at Grant's house, and his father came over. He barged in on us... Oh, God, I can't do this."

Gracie jumped to her feet, but Jerry managed to find his voice just in time to stop her. "Wait. Sit down. There is no way you're leavin' here until you explain this. I'm not followin'. Or at least I hope I'm not, because what I just heard was that you're in some sort of ... love triangle."

"It's not a triangle, Dad. It's ... complicated."

"I'll say."

"I'm telling you this 'cause I think Grant's gonna do somethin' stupid like give his father money. The guy needs help. He barged in on us while we were ... uh ... you know. But then everything got crazy. I don't want Grant to give his father money. Especially not if he's doin' it to protect me. I love him, Dad. I love him, and I love Lane. I haven't told either of them, which I fully intend to rectify very, very soon. But, Dad," Gracie said, a plea of understanding in her eyes, "I need you to know. And I need you to accept it. I'm gonna fix this because I'm not gonna let Grant screw this up."

Jerry couldn't help it, he chuckled. Just like Gracie to want to make everything right. He had to admit, it took a tremendous amount of guts for her to come in there and address him directly. Hell, he hadn't even had the guts to do the same with her. He had yet to inform any of the girls that he was bringing Jan, a woman he'd been dating for months, to the dance that night.

"Please don't be mad," Gracie whispered, and Jerry realized she was waiting for him to say something.

"I'm not mad," he said, realizing that was the truth. He was confused, definitely. But at least he'd been right on one thing... There was definitely something going on between Lane and Grant.

Jerry had hugged Gracie, assuring her that he wasn't going to go ballistic and saw Grant's nuts off. Or Lane's. He hadn't been quite so sure how honest that statement had been, but he'd said it nonetheless.

And now he was standing in front of the men Gracie proclaimed to love.

God, did that stuff really happen?

"I fucked up," Grant said, pulling Jerry fully back to the moment.

"That's what I heard."

"Last night, my father… He kinda barged in on a private moment," Grant said, clearing his throat more than once just to get the sentence out.

"And he's gonna use that to blackmail you?" Jerry asked, glancing between the two men.

"Yes, sir."

"And you're gonna tell him that it won't work, right?"

"I… I wasn't, no. I…" Grant's back straightened, and his chin tipped up just a little as he stared back at Jerry. "I'll do whatever it takes to protect Gracie and Lane. *Whatever* it takes. If that means I have to give in to my father, then so be it. They mean everything to me, sir."

"That's stupid," Lane interjected, sounding angry. "Givin' him money ain't gonna help."

Jerry agreed with Lane wholeheartedly.

"If you'll do whatever it takes, then prove it, son. Stand up and protect them," Jerry barked, taking a step closer. "Givin' your father money is enablin' him. He needs help. If you want to protect those you love, you don't give in. Why you believe that givin' him money is the only way out, I have no idea—" Jerry didn't get the sentence out before Grant interrupted.

"Because if I have to choose between losing them or paying my father to leave us alone, I'll choose the latter."

Chapter Twenty-Eight

OKAY, SO GRANT HADN'T EXPECTED to say that. The words had just come tumbling out of his mouth before he could stop them. And now Jerry was staring back at him like he wanted to rip Grant's head from his body.

Grant respected this man. Respected him as the owner of Dead Heat Ranch, the man who signed his paychecks every week, *and* as Gracie's father. He hadn't wanted it to come to this.

"And you thought, what? Giving in to your father is gonna keep him quiet?"

Yes, that was exactly what he thought. But he didn't say as much.

"I'm not gonna lie to you and tell you that I understand what's goin' on with you and Gracie … and … and Lane. I'm not sure I want to know. But I *will* tell you that Gracie came to me because she's scared. And that's on you, son. You're the one who has to figure out how to protect her from that fear. Do you think you can do that?"

Grant nodded his head.

"Good. Then get your ass outta here and figure it out before I get mad," Jerry yelled.

Well, shit. Grant's feet wouldn't move, and he knew that was an opportunity if he'd ever heard one, but he didn't know how to walk away. He didn't know how to fix what was broken. Grant was tempted to ask Jerry for help because … because Gracie wasn't the only one who was scared.

Hell. Grant was terrified.

Especially after last night, after making love to her and coming to terms with the fact that he did love them both. That he would do anything for them. Protecting them from his crazy father was high on his to-do list, but without giving Darrell money, Grant had no idea how to make the man go away.

Lane and Gracie had stood by his side when he'd been worried about his mother, and they had consoled him last night when the relief was so intense he could hardly breathe. And then what did he do? He was a chicken-shit, and he let his father lead him around by his fucking nose. All because Grant wanted to do the right thing. He wanted to protect the two people he loved more than anything.

A firm hand landed on Grant's shoulder, and he spun around, coming face to face with...

Lane.

Holy shit. For a minute, Grant had forgotten he was standing there.

"Come on. We need to talk," Lane said.

And what did Grant do?

Well, he nodded, of course.

"But first we've gotta go help set up for tonight's dance," Lane told him and turned toward the arena where they held their monthly dances for the guests.

Grant had no choice but to follow him. When he glanced over his shoulder one more time, he found that Jerry was gone. Where he'd gone, Grant had no idea, but he didn't slow down to find out.

It wasn't until they reached the arena that Grant found his voice again. With a gentle hand on Lane's arm, he tried to get the other man's attention.

"What?" Lane snarled, his reaction surprising Grant.

"I thought you wanted to talk," Grant bit out, trying desperately to keep his voice low.

"No, what I really wanna do is punch you in the mouth," Lane disputed.

Great. Now they were going to have a fight right there in front of half the ranch. Grant glanced past Lane to see that several wranglers had stopped what they were doing to watch them.

"Get to work!" Grant hollered.

A chorus of grumbles echoed through the arena, but Grant turned his attention back to Lane, studying the harsh lines of the man's face. Yeah, it was safe to say Lane was still angry.

Not that Grant blamed him. After what Grant's father had done...

"Look, I'm sorry that my father barged in like that," Grant began but was quickly cut off by the fury that lit Lane's dark eyes.

"You think I'm pissed off because *he* came in? No, man, I'm fuckin' pissed because you're enablin' him. Do you think that givin' him money is gonna get him off your back?"

"No," Grant growled. "That's not what I think. But there are more important things at stake here."

"Like?" Lane asked, his arms crossing over his big chest as he stared back at Grant.

"Like..." *Shit.* Grant couldn't think. He didn't know what to say to Lane to make this better, and that was all he cared to do.

"Go on," Lane encouraged. "Tell me what's more important. I wanna hear it."

Grant's jaw ticked, his anger making it difficult to think.

"No, let me rephrase that," Lane said as he moved closer, lowering his voice, "I *need* to hear it."

Glancing around, Grant noticed that there were still people watching, and the last thing he needed to do was get into an argument in front of God and everyone.

"You, damn it. You're more important. You and Gracie are it for me, Lane. Don't you get that?"

"No, I don't get that," Lane announced. "Maybe if you'd said something before, I might have an idea of how you feel."

Okay. Point well received. Grant knew he hadn't told Lane how he felt. And last night, he hadn't expected to tell Gracie, but everything had come to a head.

He knew he should say something now, tell Lane that he loved him, but he couldn't. Not here. There were too many eyes and ears around. So instead of doing the one thing that could fix their issues, Grant said, "I need to get to work. We'll talk tonight." Grant turned to walk away, but he was pulled up short by a strong hand on his arm.

Spinning around, he came face-to-face with Lane.

"Don't walk away," Lane ground out. "Tell me. Right here. Right now."

"Tell you *what*?" Grant asked, trying to keep his voice low. "Tell you that you and Gracie are more important? Is that what you wanna hear?" Lane didn't respond, but he didn't look at all convinced. "Damn it, Lane. I fuckin' care. Is that what you wanna hear?" Grant knew his voice was getting louder, and he feared he was about to come out of the closet with the entire ranch looking on.

"Yes," Lane replied, the muscle in his jaw bunching as though he were trying to refrain from saying too much.

Grant knew just what Lane was feeling, because as much as he wanted to announce to the entire ranch that he was in love with Gracie and Lane, he just couldn't do it. Even though he had Jerry's blessing, he still couldn't get the words out.

"So you didn't give your father money?" Lane asked.

Grant's brow furrowed as he desperately tried to remember what they were talking about. How had this conversation gone from feelings to money?

"No," he finally said, some of his anger dissipating. "I didn't give him anything yet. I told him I'd talk to him later."

Lane took a step closer. He was now standing so close that their chests nearly touched, and the brim of their hats rubbed once. "Don't give him money. You hear me?"

"I don't have much of a choice," Grant rebutted.

"You're the only one *with* a choice," Lane said through clenched teeth. "We'll work this out. Understand me? *We.* As in you, me, and Gracie. Don't go off half-cocked thinkin' you can make this better. The only way to fix this is to man up."

And with that, Lane turned and walked away.

Grant stared after him, feeling chastised by the man he loved. It was the second time in less than an hour that someone had told him to man up.

And if Grant hadn't been angry before … well, he was now.

IT TOOK EVERY OUNCE OF willpower Lane possessed just to walk away from Grant. But even he knew this wasn't the time or place to get in a knock-down-drag-out with the ranch foreman, especially when this was personal. So after giving Grant his final two cents, Lane made a beeline for the arena, glaring at every wrangler who dared look his way.

Busying himself for the next two hours wasn't difficult because his frustration fueled him, and before he knew it, the arena was all decked out, ready for the dance that would bring the guests flurrying to one place.

Lane happened to enjoy the dances that they put on. Used to be that he enjoyed them because it was his only chance to get close to Gracie, something he'd been trying to do for the last two years. Since his arms ached to hold her again, he was actually quite ready for the party to start, but there were still hours to go until that happened. Which meant Lane needed to get some other things done in order to keep his mind off her and Grant.

As he made his way to his truck, trying to prioritize what he needed to accomplish for the day, he thought back to the last bit of the conversation between Grant and Jerry.

I'm not gonna lie to you and tell you that I understand what's goin' on with you and Gracie ... and ... and Lane. I'm not sure I want to know. But I will tell you that Gracie came to me because she's scared. And that's on you, son. You're the one who has to figure out how to protect her from that fear. Do you think you can do that?

Gracie had actually approached her father to inform him of her relationship with the two of them. And truth be told, Lane was pretty sure that her going to her father meant more to him than if she'd blurted out her love for him.

Maybe.

He still longed to hear the words, desperate to watch them roll off Gracie's tongue. His heart needed to hear them. There was an actual physical ache in the center of his chest, and he feared that the only thing that could relieve it was the three little words that he had yet to hear from Grant or Gracie.

But this was close to being better than that. They no longer had to hide from Jerry… Not that he really knew what that meant yet. They still had the rest of the wranglers to contend with. Lane didn't have any idea what they were going to say or do when they found out that Lane and Grant were together, much less that they were with Gracie as well. It was complicated, but for Lane, it just felt right.

"Hey, man, you okay?"

Lane spun around to see Grant standing behind him. "Great. Why?"

"Just makin' sure," Grant replied, his eyes narrowing as though he didn't believe Lane.

Since Lane hadn't sounded all that convincing, it made sense that Grant was questioning him.

"Would you … uh… Would you want to have dinner tonight? Before the dance?"

Lane was tempted to stick his fingers in his ears and wiggle them, just to make sure he wasn't hearing things. Had Grant really just invited him to dinner? Tonight?

"Yeah," he said frankly. "I would."

His response must've been the right answer because Grant smiled, and Lane's chest thumped painfully hard. "Good. That's … good. I'll meet you at the dining hall?"

Lane nodded as he planned out his evening in his head. Shower, dinner, dancing, Gracie, and Grant. Yep, tonight was going to be significantly better than last night.

At least he hoped so anyway.

Chapter Twenty-Nine

Saturday evening

"THIS PLACE LOOKS AMAZING," TRINITY said when Grace made her way across the wooden dance floor that had been set up in the main arena. Trin, Mercy, Faith, and Hope were all huddled in one area, looking like teenage girls on prom night, waiting for someone to ask them to dance.

"It's pretty impressive, huh?" Grace hadn't seen the arena look quite like this before. Each time they put on a dance, which had been almost once a month for the last two years, the amount of décor seemed to increase. Grace could still remember the first dance they'd put on. It had been held in the rec room of the main house with an iPod hooked up to a set of speakers, and they'd learned instantly that the place wasn't nearly big enough for the sheer volume of people who attended, most of whom were actual employees of Dead Heat Ranch and their significant others.

Hope had been the one to suggest using the arena, and then some skilled cowboys had come up with the idea of designing a wood floor that could be placed over the soft dirt that covered the arena floor. From there, additional things had been added, including an upgraded sound system, then a DJ, a disco ball, additional hanging lanterns... The list went on and on, and now, the place looked like a dance hall, and from what Grace could tell, all of the guests were present and accounted for.

"Oh, good Lord, hide me, please," Mercy whispered as she ducked behind Grace and Trinity.

"Who're you hidin' from?" Trin asked, trying to move away only to be pulled back by Mercy, who had wrapped her arms around her.

"The booby triplets," Mercy said in a hushed tone. "They are drivin' me absolutely batshit crazy."

Grace searched the room for the booby triplets, as Mercy had referred to them, and it didn't take long for her to find them. Sure enough, there were three women, all decked out in their fanciest rhinestone-crusted halter tops and skin-tight jeans. Their boots had heels, and Grace was tempted to laugh, but she managed to refrain. They were guests at the ranch, after all.

But, in Mercy's defense, her description wasn't too far off. There were three of them, of course. A blond, brunette, and what appeared to be a fake redhead who did look … uh … surgically enhanced. Anyway … the three women were prancing around the edge of the bleachers, chatting it up with a handful of wranglers who were standing around chugging beer like it was water. Free beer always tasted that much better, in Grace's personal opinion.

And, yes, as was usual for pretty women who came to the ranch, these three had certainly garnered the attention of a few of the single men.

"What's wrong with them?" Hope asked as she stepped up to Grace's side. "They don't look all that scary to me."

"Oh, please. You haven't had to cater to their every whim for the last two days."

"How hard could that possibly be?" Faith interjected. "From what I saw, they've spent their days in the pool. So, what? You had to bring them suntan lotion?"

"No, uh-uh. That's not in my job description," Mercy murmured. "Anyway, they had plenty of help in that area. Shit, Hal and Cal were more than willing to ensure they weren't in any danger of gettin' burned."

Hal and Cal were two of the tenured wranglers. To this day, Grace still had no idea what their full names were. What she knew was that they were fraternal twins, both in their early forties, who'd been a part of the ranch for roughly twenty-five years. They were two of the few wranglers who'd actually been on the ranch long enough to remember Grace's mother.

"So why're you hidin'?" Hope asked. "They don't look interested in you or what you're doin'."

"Just wait. Someone" — Mercy glared at the back of Trin's head — "gave them the impression that I'm their freakin' servant."

Grace laughed right along with her sisters, offering Trin a knuckle-bump for her good work. They had to get back at Mercy somehow, and Grace would be the first to admit they pulled out all the stops whenever possible.

"Where're your guests?" Mercy asked, still bobbing and weaving behind them.

"Ben and Maddie?" Grace asked, glancing over at Hope. "Don't know. Have you seen them?"

Hope had the audacity to glare at Grace as though she hadn't been spending a little extra time with Ben in recent days. Maybe Grace wasn't up to speed on everything that went on at the ranch at all times the way Mercy was, but she definitely knew when her guests were being given a personal tour by one of her sisters.

"He said he'd be here later," Hope admitted, pulling her gaze from Grace's.

"Well, I'm guestless this week," Faith told them.

"Lucky you. Want to take on the big boob trio? They're yours if you want 'em. Last night, they asked me to shine their freakin' boots."

Grace glanced down at her own boots and smiled. They weren't the ones she wore to work, but they certainly weren't fancy. With the chiffon sundress she'd chosen, they actually looked nice, or so she thought. She laughed, thinking about what it would look like if she shined her boots.

"Nope, they're yours. It's your punishment," Trin inserted. "For everything you've done to us, you get to handle the big boob trio all by your lonesome."

Mercy grumbled something, but Grace couldn't make out what it was.

"Hey, is that…"

Grace peered over her shoulder at Trin to see which direction she was looking. Following her gaze, she saw… "Yep. That looks like Zach and Jenn. And they're dancin'."

A loud whistle pierced the air — Mercy, no doubt.

"They make a cute couple," Hope added, surprising them all with her assessment.

They did make a cute couple, actually.

But her attention was snagged from the dancers instantly, and the sound of her sisters chattering around her became background noise. She was having a hard time hearing over the sudden roar of blood in her veins. As she watched Grant approach from across the arena, her heart kicked into overdrive. He looked so handsome with his starched white shirt, the sleeves rolled up to show off his thick, tan forearms. He was wearing his nice straw Stetson, and although she preferred the black one, she knew it was too hot for that.

"Care to dance?" he asked when he made his way to her.

Grace *felt* like a teenage girl at prom, suddenly shocked that one of the popular boys actually wanted to dance with her.

Before she could answer, she was firmly nudged from behind, followed by, "Get out there," from Mercy, no less.

"I'd love to," she said when she finally found her voice.

Grant's answering smile stole her breath, and if it hadn't been for the fact he was leading her out to the center of the arena, she figured she would've been a puddle of goo on the floor for all the strength she had in her limbs.

A slow song came on right then, almost as though Grant had planned it, and Grace looked up into his face, trying to see if he was smiling. There was a smile there, definitely, but it didn't appear mischievous at all. No, this was one of those sweet smiles, one that made it all the way to his eyes.

"Hi."

"Hi back," she said, lacing her fingers with his while sliding one hand around behind him. She felt the tense muscles there, and she did her best not to feel him up in front of all these people. "We've never danced before," she added suddenly.

"No, we haven't."

Grace had spent the better part of the day wanting to talk to Lane and Grant, to let them know that she had gone to her father and spilled the beans, but too many things had happened, and she'd lost the chance. And then Grant had invited her to dinner, which she'd had to decline because Trin and Faith had needed her for adding the last touches to tonight's event. But now, here they were, two-stepping around the dance floor with several other couples, and Grant was looking at her as though she was the most important person in the world to him.

"What's on your mind?" she asked, feeling antsy under his penetrating gaze.

"I'm just thinkin' about a conversation I had with your father this mornin'."

Grace stumbled, but Grant caught her, never breaking his stride as they continued their path around the floor.

"You talked to my dad?"

"Yeah. He mentioned that some little sassy cowgirl came to him to let him know she was in love with *two* cowboys."

"Oh, crap."

"No, darlin'," Grant whispered. "It was a good chat. He made me realize a few things."

"Like?"

"Like how much I've screwed up lately."

"You haven't screwed up," she said resolutely. "Things've been crazy. I'm just glad your mom's all right."

"Yeah, me, too. I talked to her earlier. She said she's not comin' back till my dad gets some help. Apparently, his gamblin' has finally gotten to her. That and the physical abuse started up again."

Grace's eyes went wide as she stared up at Grant. "He hit her?"

"It seems so. She didn't want him to pawn the TVs, but he insisted. They got into a fight. My dad hit her, and for the first time, she didn't hit him back."

"I'm so sorry, Grant."

"Don't be," he replied easily, pulling her closer. "They've got to figure this out on their own. But that's not my problem tonight."

The smile he sent her way was filled with so much promise.

"Tonight I just wanna spend some time with my two favorite people," Grant added. "Speakin' of..." Grant glanced around the arena. "Have you seen Lane?"

"Not since I left the dinin' hall," she said easily, sliding her hand up and down his back gently. "I'm sure he's around here somewhere."

Grant's gaze returned to hers, a smile on his lips. She couldn't help but remember how he'd told her that he loved her last night.

"You look so pretty tonight," he added. "If there weren't a hundred pairs of eyes on us right now, I'd kiss you."

Grace wouldn't mind in the least. "One of these days, you won't care who's watchin'," she told him.

"You're right, I won't." Grant's hand tightened on her waist, pulling her closer, their feet shuffling slowly across the sawdust on the floor.

"What do you say, when this thing's over, we—"

A commotion started, and Grant stopped midsentence, as they both turned to look toward the ruckus.

"Sonuvabitch," Grant growled, suddenly releasing Grace and heading to the other side of the arena where she could see...

Oh, shit. That was Lane and Cody and...

"Oh, my God," Grace said softly, unable to move from where Grant had left her.

"Who is that?" Faith asked, out of breath because she had run over from the opposite corner. Not far behind her were Hope, Trinity, and Mercy.

"What the fuck is he doin' here?" Mercy exclaimed as she started walking away.

Grace managed to grab Mercy's arm in time to pull her back, which earned her a tongue-lashing from Mercy, most of which Grace ignored.

"That's Grant's father," Grace said, watching in complete shock as Cody had to hold the man back, while three wranglers attempted to keep Lane at bay. "We have to stop them."

"*We?* I was tryin' to go over there and you stopped me, remember?" Mercy grumbled.

Grace knew she needed to try to calm everyone down, but she couldn't get her legs to move. What happened when Darrell Kingsley announced to everyone just what he'd walked in on last night?

Oh, crap.

She didn't want to think about the horror she'd see on people's faces when they heard it coming from Darrell.

Even with her fear, for the life of her, Grace didn't know any way to stop it.

■□■□■□■□

IT WASN'T EASY CONTROLLING THE urge to go get up in that man's face and give him a piece of her mind, but Mercy managed to stay with Grace. Why, she didn't know. Maybe because she figured her sister needed her support more than the wranglers needed her getting in the middle of the … whatever the hell was going on over there.

From where she stood, it looked like they were trying to keep Lane from killing the man. They should just let him go, teach the old bastard a lesson.

Tearing her eyes from the craziness, Mercy searched the room, trying to find her father. There were probably close to a hundred and fifty people in attendance tonight, so it took her a minute, but then she located him. He was talking to a pretty blond woman, dividing his attention between her and keeping an eye on Lane. When the shouting rose to a dull roar, he backed away from the woman but not before…

Oh, God.

Her father just kissed that woman.

It hadn't been a long kiss, or even that intimate, but it had been a kiss nonetheless.

On the mouth.

Was that her dad's girlfriend? Why was she there?

Mercy's stomach churned, and for a brief second, she thought she was going to be sick. How could he bring her there without telling them? Didn't he think that it was important for them to know? Not to be blindsided when they saw him kissing a freaking woman!

Tracking her father across the room, Mercy refused to look back at the stranger who had been kissing her father. She didn't want to know who she was. If she pretended it had never happened, then maybe the woman would just go away.

Her attention was pulled to the brawl that was taking place on the other side of the arena. She turned just in time to see Grant's dad pull out of Cody's grip and storm toward Lane. The wranglers were still holding Lane back — the dumb shits — but then it happened...

Cody went after Grant's father, grabbing the man and spinning him around in an attempt to keep him away from Lane. But in the commotion, Jerry and Grant stepped in, but not in time to keep Darrell from punching Cody...

Oh, shit.

... right in the face.

Mercy watched as Cody hit the ground, his body lax.

"Oh, my God!" she screamed as she took off at a dead run, racing to get to Cody.

When she reached the group, two of the wranglers tried to keep her back, but she punched and kicked until they backed off. Shoving everyone out of the way, Mercy dropped to her knees beside Cody, leaning over him and chanting his name.

"Zach! Someone find Zach!" someone yelled from behind her, but Mercy didn't turn around to see who it was.

"Open your eyes, cowboy," Mercy whispered frantically. "You hear me, Cody Mercer? Open your damn eyes."

Just then, Cody's eyes fluttered open, and he reached up to grab his jaw. When he realized she was practically lying on top of him, he smiled, and Mercy was tempted to sock him again just because.

"Hey," he said, his voice rough. "Shit, that hurts." He was still holding his jaw. "What the hell happened?"

"The asshole sucker-punched you," Zach said as he joined Mercy at Cody's side. "You should learn to duck."

"I'll go get some ice," Jenn offered, placing her hand on Zach's shoulder. "I'll be right back. Keep an eye on Joey, will you?"

Zach nodded, turning to look up at Jenn briefly before once again looking at Cody.

"Shit, man. That's gotta hurt."

"Thanks, Captain Obvious," Cody griped.

Cody glared at Zach while Mercy got to her feet. She couldn't tear her eyes off him, but she backed away at the same time. What had she done?

Turning to see if anyone was paying attention to her, she realized everyone was working to get the crazy guy calmed down.

The crazy guy who was ... crying?

CHAPTER THIRTY

LANE WAS TEMPTED TO COMMIT murder. In all of his life, he'd never been as pissed as he was right then.

From the instant Darrell had approached him, referring to him as "Grant's bitch," Lane's vision had clouded with that damn red haze. Originally, he'd tried to ignore him, wanting to be the bigger man. That had only spurred Grant's father on.

The audacity of the bastard to show up there and run his mouth like that. It had come as a complete surprise while Lane had been talking to one of the guests, of all people. And now, with three people holding him back, he was so furious it took everything in him to keep himself back. Because God knew that these men weren't doing a damn good job.

But this was Grant's father. And the guy was pure fucking crazy to boot.

"Get him outta here!" Grant yelled, and Lane felt himself being pulled back.

"Mr. Kingsley," Jerry stated insistently as he approached, "we need to have a little chat. So, you've got two choices. Come with me to my office, or we'll talk when the police arrive."

Lane watched as Jerry spoke in that authoritative tone that people's ears perked up for. Lane stopped struggling, wanting to hear what was being said.

"I've got some things to say," Darrell announced.

"Not here, you don't," Jerry growled. "You say one word about what you saw last night and I'll rip your voice box right out of your throat. Got me?"

Holy shit.

Darrell's eyes grew to be the size of saucers. Lane was pretty sure he looked just as dumbfounded.

Lane had heard Jerry make threats before, but never had he heard the man speak like that. Not in all the time he'd been at the ranch. And sure enough, the ranch owner had snagged the attention of every single person standing around, especially Darrell Kingsley.

"Now come on," Jerry stated, nodding his head toward the main house. "You, too."

Lane realized Jerry was talking to him and Grant. Confused, Lane shot Grant a look, hoping like hell Grant knew what was going on. The lack of response told him that, no, Grant was just as surprised as he was.

"Where's Gracie?" Lane whispered to Grant as they walked a few yards behind Jerry and Darrell.

"With her sisters," Grant stated, his tone rough.

Yeah, it was safe to say that Grant was pissed. Lane understood perfectly because his father had come blustering up to Lane...

"Why the fuck would you get in his face?" Grant growled low, his words stopping Lane in his tracks.

"*What?*"

"What the fuck were you thinkin'?"

Lane was stunned, unable to come up with a response because he was taken aback by the accusation in Grant's tone.

"You don't know how to leave well enough alone, do you? This is *my* problem. Not yours," Grant said, putting his finger into Lane's chest. "I can't fuckin' believe you. This is *my* job. Do you not get that?"

Lane swallowed hard, doing his best to keep his temper in check. He was actually a little dizzy, trying to keep up with all of the reprimands coming from the man who was supposedly his lover.

Thanks to whatever higher power, Lane found his voice, and when he spoke, the sound was rough, laced with emotion that he couldn't contain. "I'm sorry," he said sarcastically. "Next time someone refers to me as 'Grant's bitch,' I'll just smile and nod. Is that the response you'd like from me?"

And with that, Lane turned and stomped off.

Fuck this shit. He did not need to be put in his place for standing up for himself and the two people that he loved. Yeah, little did Grant know, but that asshole he called a father had had a few choice words to say about Gracie, too. Things Lane wasn't willing to repeat. And as much as he despised being referred to as anyone's bitch, Lane had managed to keep his cool. But when Darrell had brought Gracie into it, the gloves had come off.

And that Lane would never apologize for. Because as far as he was concerned, no one would talk about the woman he loved like that.

No one.

■□■□■□■□

"SIT DOWN AND SHUT THE fuck up," Jerry shouted at Darrell when they made their way into his office. "Close the damn door," he instructed Grant.

Jerry glared at Grant when Grant slammed the door behind them, but he held his tongue.

"Why the hell are you cryin'? More important, why the fuck are you here?" Jerry asked Darrell.

Okay. Well.

Jerry could tell that Grant was a little surprised by Jerry's tone, not to mention his choice of words, but he could hardly see past the fury raging through him.

They hadn't even made it out of the arena before Darrell was sobbing like a big fucking baby, and as much as Jerry wanted to feel sorry for him, he couldn't.

Jerry had been aware of Grant's father's arrival long before anything had started. With Jan there, he had opted to try to keep things civil, hoping Grant would take care of the matter on his own. It hadn't been long before Darrell had found Lane, and Jerry knew that's when the shit had hit the fan. And tonight of all nights, Jerry did not want to have to be acting as a mediator for a bunch of grown fucking men acting like children.

Jan was there, out in the arena waiting for him to come back, and, by God, he was not going to be away from her for long.

"Why're you here?" Grant asked Darrell, his face red with his anger.

"I need money," Darrell blubbered.

"You don't need money. You need to go to rehab."

Darrell looked up at Grant, his eyes bloodshot, his face ruddy. He looked like he hadn't slept in a week or more. His jaw was furry from at least a week's worth of beard, and his hair was so greasy Jerry was inclined to believe the man hadn't showered in at least that long.

Jerry was pretty sure Darrell had hit rock bottom.

"Rehab costs money!" Darrell spat.

Grant looked as though his father had slapped him across the face.

"Are you sayin'…?"

"Yes, dammit. That's what I'm sayin'," Darrell sobbed. "She left me, Grant."

Jerry met Grant's gaze across the room. The question of where Grant's mother was had obviously been solved.

"She left and she said she's never coming back."

"You don't deserve her," Grant retorted. "Not until you get your shit together."

"I know."

Jerry wasn't sure whether Darrell was telling the truth or if he was just spouting whatever was necessary to get himself out of the hot seat. Jerry just didn't know him well enough to tell.

"Can the two of you work this out?" Jerry asked when it appeared that Darrell needed a few minutes.

Grant nodded his head curtly.

"If you need anything, just holler." With that, Jerry exited the office. He needed to get back to Jan. They had just been getting ready to walk over to his girls so he could introduce her appropriately when all this had happened. He hated to leave her alone, but it was either that or he'd probably have to deal with the cops for an hour or so if he hadn't intervened.

By the time Jerry made it back to the arena, Hope had managed to get everything under control.

Sort of.

"Where's Mercy?" Jerry asked his oldest daughter.

"No idea."

"Where's Gracie?" he asked, realizing that she wasn't there, either.

"Not her keeper," Hope muttered softly.

Well, hell. This was not how he wanted the introductions to take place. He would've preferred to introduce them all at the same time. And more important, Jerry wanted them to meet Jan before she showed up for dinner tomorrow night.

"Get your sisters, would ya?" he asked Hope.

When she merely huffed and walked off, Jerry scanned the room in search of Jan. He found her sitting on a bench next to Jenn and Zach. Zach was in the process of checking a very irate Cody over.

"Everything okay?" Jerry asked, leaning in to get a closer look at the bruise that had formed on Cody's jaw from the lucky punch Darrell had gotten in.

"Yep. He's gonna live," Zach replied. "He's lucky. It's not broken."

"Doesn't feel like it ain't broken," Cody rumbled, putting the ice pack back on his face.

"If you think he needs to go to the hospital, can you get him there?" Jerry asked Zach.

And just as he'd suspected, Cody jumped to his feet. "I don't need to go to the hospital."

Yep, the young man was going to be just fine.

Reaching for Jan's hand, Jerry helped her to her feet and then led her back down to the floor. "Sorry about that."

"Does that happen often?" Jan asked, a gleam in her pretty brown eyes.

"All the time," he said facetiously. "That's what happens when the cowboys don't get out much." Jerry looked up to see Hope, Trinity, and Faith coming toward him. Mercy and Gracie were still missing, damn it.

When his daughters got closer, Jerry placed his hand at the small of Jan's back and urged her to stand just in front of him. "Girls, I'd like you to meet someone. This is Jan. Jan, these are three of my daughters, Hope, Trinity, and Faith."

"It's very nice to see you all. Again," Jan said, her voice confident.

He wished he could say the same for his daughters. He obviously did not need to explain just who Jan was. Jerry had never introduced them to a woman. Not unless he was referring to them as guests, and in this case, Jan certainly wasn't a guest.

"Nice to see you again, Ms. Haile," Hope said, holding out her hand. She obviously remembered Jan from her recent stay at the ranch. Recent as in nine months ago.

"Very nice to see you, Hope."

Trinity and Faith were darting glances back and forth between them, both of their mouths hanging slightly open. "Girls, you're gonna be seein' more of Jan in the future. She's ... uh ... she's my girlfriend."

Wow, and the word sounded strange to him. He was fifty-four years old, and he had a girlfriend.

Oddly, the thought made him feel thirty years younger.

Faith's eyes widened as his statement sank in. And Jerry knew right then that Jan had been right in wanting to hold off. Based on the disbelief he saw on his daughters' faces, he was suddenly wishing he'd held off a little longer, too.

Chapter Thirty-One

GRACE HAD NO IDEA HOW long she'd been sitting in the dark, but her butt had gone numb some time ago. From her perch near the edge of the water on the blanket she'd hijacked from the stable, she could hear the sounds coming from the arena and see the glow of the lights above the rise that circled the lake.

She was scared to go back, not wanting to endure the sideways glances that she was surely going to receive now that Darrell had spouted off. She had no idea just what he'd actually said, but based on the way he had barged in on them the other night, she wouldn't put anything past him. The man was crazy. And right now, she had more than her fair share of crazy to deal with.

After what could've been the perfect night was blown to shit thanks to Grant's father, Grace really just wanted to crawl into a hole for the next few weeks. Even though she had tried to slow the bleeding that was sure to take place by going to her father directly, Grace knew that Grant and Lane were going to be negatively impacted by what had happened tonight.

As much as she wished it weren't her fault, she couldn't help but assign some of the blame on herself. Three months ago, she'd been weary of the two cowboys, doing her best to stay as far away from them as possible. At the time, she'd had no clue that they were bisexual, or that they had a thing for one another, but from the moment that she had realized the truth, Grace had been captivated. She had let down her guard, and in walked both of them right into her heart.

"Why the hell do I really care what he said?" she asked no one in particular, thinking back to Grant's father's presence at the ranch.

And if she were completely honest, she didn't necessarily care who knew that the three of them were together. Darrell could tell whoever he wanted, for all she cared. It was the other stuff ... the way Grant's father would portray their lovemaking although he didn't have the first clue what it was like other than the moment he'd ripped their privacy clean away from them as though it didn't matter one bit.

Grace had spent her life on the straight and narrow, doing what she felt was right, what would make other people happy. To a degree, anyway. She'd always been strong, and she had proven she still was by approaching her father and not waiting for him to get wind of the relationship she had with two men.

Yes. Two men.

And her father hadn't even batted an eyelash at that little revelation, although she knew he was a little surprised and probably a lot confused.

But Jerry hadn't lost his temper. In fact, the only question he'd really cared to have answered was whether or not she was serious about them. When she'd confirmed with a firm yes, he had merely nodded his head.

She had his blessing.

Yet it seemed that everything had still blown up in her face.

And worse, she didn't know how to fix it.

After Lane had walked out last night, Grace had been determined to fix things. And for Grant to have come back to her place, obviously hoping to make amends, she'd been convinced it was time to stop hiding the truth. To not allow anyone to come between her and the two men she loved. But just like always, there were too many hoops that she had to jump through.

And now she was tired.

"So damn tired," she muttered aloud.

"You can't give up yet."

A scream lodged in Grace's throat when the deep voice sounded from behind her. She turned, trying to see the man who belonged to the voice, but she couldn't make out Lane's features in the darkness, nothing more than his silhouette backlit by the full moon overhead. She heard the sound of his boots shuffling in the grass, and she waited for him to join her.

"Did they get everything under control?" she asked.

"You could say that," he said, and Grace heard the sadness in his tone, which immediately put her on red alert.

"What's wrong?"

Lane didn't respond, but he did lower himself to the blanket beside her, lying flat on his back with his knees bent.

"I don't know, Gracie," Lane whispered long minutes later. "I don't know how to do this anymore."

Grace swallowed, the lump in her throat nearly strangling her. "Do what?" she asked, not wanting to hear his answer.

"I don't know how to make this enough."

Oh, God. That was not what she wanted to hear. As defeated as she felt, Grace wasn't ready to give up. The pity party had been just that — a moment to feel sorry for herself, which usually helped her to put things into perspective. Grace wasn't the type to give up, though.

Turning so that she could face him, Grace crossed her legs and adjusted her skirt so that it covered her, although she doubted Lane could see her in the dark. Placing a hand on his warm chest, she rubbed lightly. "I know I haven't said how I feel about you, but Lane, I really want you to know—" Grace didn't get to continue her sentence because Lane moved suddenly, his mouth covering hers as he lowered her to the soft earth beneath her.

Instinctively, Grace reached up and wrapped her arms around his neck, pulling him to her, giving in to his kiss, the sweet, sensual way his mouth mated with hers. To her horror, tears stung her eyelids, but she fought them, refusing to let them spill over. She did love this man. More than she'd ever thought possible. But she couldn't help but feel that his kiss was some sort of good-bye.

Holding on to him more tightly, Grace pulled him closer, until he was practically crushing her into the ground, his full weight upon her though he was kneeling between her thighs as she wrapped her legs around him.

"Make love to me, Lane. Right now," Grace murmured against his lips.

She could hardly make out the whites of his eyes in the blackness that was night, but she felt the tension in his shoulders, the way he held himself away from her. When he didn't lean back in to kiss her, she added, "It wasn't a request, cowboy."

His gruff chuckle reverberated through her chest, rattling her heart and making those damn tears threaten to fall again.

But Grace wasn't going to let this moment pass her by. Releasing him, she slid her hands between their bodies and released the button and lowered his zipper, struggling to force his jeans past his hips. Finally, with a little help from him, she freed his heavy erection, wrapping her hands around him and stroking slowly.

"Make love to me, Lane," she whispered again, this time softly.

Grace took control, did all the work as Lane stared down at her, one hand caressing the top of her head, the other holding himself above her. With a little creativity, she managed to slide her panties off without forcing him to move. And then, without asking permission, Grace lined up the tip of his cock with the entrance to her pussy, holding her breath as she did.

They didn't have a condom, but even if they had, Grace wasn't sure she wanted one. She didn't want anything separating them right then. She wanted him, skin to skin. It would've been that much sweeter if they could've been naked, but that was a risk she wasn't willing to take. Anyone could come over that rise at any time and catch them in the act. This way, they stood half a chance of not being caught.

"Gracie," Lane breathed as he flexed his hips, pushing himself inside of her just a little. "Are you sure?"

"I've never been more sure of anything in my life," she told him.

Lane nodded and then, sweet mother of all things wonderful, he was inside her. Grace's body fought to accept him, but a few seconds passed, and he was lodged to the hilt, unmoving.

"Oh, God, Gracie," Lane moaned as Grace used her hands to search his face in the dark, running her fingertips over his smooth cheeks. She lifted her head to meet his mouth, stealing his kiss as he gently began to rock inside her.

Sweet heaven. He was so big, so hot...

And then there was glorious friction, but Lane never lifted off her, their bodies sliding together as one.

"Lane," she whispered, cradling his face in her hands, staring into his eyes. "I love you."

Grace thought he was laughing, but then she realized it was a choked sob that had rattled through his chest, and she held him closer, lifting her hips to meet his slow, deep thrusts.

"Oh, God, Lane, you feel so good. Please..."

"Gracie, baby." Lane continued to move, going deeper but keeping his pace unbearably slow.

"Harder," she said, pulling his head down to hers and crushing their lips together, exploring his mouth with her tongue, moaning uncontrollably as the tension grew, her body bowing from the climax that was building to a crescendo. She was going to come, and she wanted him to be right there with her.

Squeezing her internal muscles, Grace thrust her tongue into his mouth and sucked his tongue when he answered in turn, mimicking the thrust and release of their bodies until Lane's shoulders tensed, his hips ramming against hers, burying himself incredibly deep.

"I'm coming," Grace whispered, unable to control the release that exploded in her core and radiated out through every limb, every finger, every toe.

Lane groaned, his body stilling above hers, the pulse of his release detonating another miniature explosion that had her eyes closing from the sheer ecstasy of it.

To her relief, Lane didn't move away, he stayed right there, still lodged inside of her body, his cock softening while his mouth brushed hers.

"Say it again, Gracie," Lane whispered, the words barely audible.

"I love you, Lane. I love you more than you will ever know."

And no truer words had ever been spoken.

■□■□■□■□

GRANT HAD REMAINED WITH HIS father until Darrell had managed to get himself under control. He had listened while his father broke down, clearly falling apart, crying about how his wife had left him, how he'd ruined everything. Grant hadn't been able to disagree with his father, so he'd never said a word, just remained in Jerry's office with him until he'd regained some of his composure.

And when his father had calmed down, when the tears had finally dried up, Grant finally had done something he'd never done before. He'd stood up to his father directly.

"I want you to understand somethin'," Grant stated harshly. "I've tolerated your abuse all my life. I've put up with more than anyone should have to put up with. That ends here, Dad. No more. Those two people that you're tryin' to hurt, they mean everything to me. Everything. And you will not fuck this up for me, you hear me? I'm not gonna sit back and worry what you might do or say. I'm done. The next time you interfere, the next time you try to blackmail me, you'll never see me again. Got that?"

Darrell's eyes widened, but he didn't argue. Grant could see the understanding there. Considering Grant meant every single word, that was a good thing.

During the walk back to Darrell's truck, Grant informed his father that he would be by in the morning and they would check him into rehab. There was still a part of Grant that didn't believe this was happening, still waiting for the other shoe to drop. But, hoping against hope, Grant tried to remain optimistic, even shooting Morgan a text to let her know what was going on and informing her that he'd be calling their mother tomorrow.

They needed to come together to get their father through this. As expected, Grant didn't receive a response from Morgan. They'd all been burned by Darrell more than once, but Grant just couldn't give up on the man, no matter how much he wanted to. His father was sick, and he needed to get help. As long as he was willing, Grant was going to get him through it.

During the time that he'd been sitting with his father, Grant had continued to think back on Lane's comment after Grant had torn into him about instigating the fight with Darrell. Grant knew he'd been wrong, but at the time, he'd been blinded with his hatred for his father. Rightfully so, Grant felt like a royal shithead, but he'd been freaked out by the turn of events. So much so that he'd taken it out on the one man he should've been leaning on. He should've been protecting Lane, not the other way around. So now, as he walked back to the arena from the bunkhouse, unable to locate Lane there, he was beginning to get worried.

He didn't want to ask anyone if they had seen Lane or Gracie, not wanting to endure anyone's stares or questions after what had taken place. He had no idea what all had been said, other than what Lane had told him, and he knew he had to fix this. But first, he needed to apologize to Lane and Gracie for allowing this to happen.

On his way to the arena, Grant looked out at the lake, the moon shimmering off the water, and that's when he saw them — Gracie and Lane walking hand in hand over the rise, heading toward him. Taking a deep breath, Grant prayed that Lane would listen to him. He wouldn't blame the man if he didn't; after all, what Grant had done was unforgiveable.

On all counts.

Grant was like dynamite — once his fuse was lit, he went off, damn the consequences. Like when he'd assumed the worst about Jerry, thinking the man would knowingly fire someone for something as trivial as wanting to date one of his daughters. Or assuming that by paying off his father, Grant would be able to buy the man's silence. Or, worst of all, assuming that Lane and Gracie knew how he really felt about them without ever hearing the words.

Why he'd never bothered to tell them that he loved them, he didn't know. Ever since that first time when he'd mouthed the words to Gracie, he'd felt the all-encompassing emotion building inside of him, overwhelming him with its intensity, yet he'd never had the balls to say the words out loud until last night.

But he still hadn't said the words to Lane.

He was a jackass, that's what he was.

"Hey," Grant greeted the couple when they approached.

Lane was looking at him warily, and Gracie was watching him intently, worry apparent on her beautiful face.

"Are you okay?" he asked Lane, his chest constricting from the emotions threatening to strangle him.

God, he just wanted this day to be over. To go home with them, fall into bed, and start fresh tomorrow. The only thing he needed was to hold them, to know that they could get through this, that eventually they could forgive him.

"I've got a few things to say," Lane said abruptly, releasing Gracie's hand and stepping close until he was right in Grant's face.

Grant sucked in a deep breath, ready to hear the worst.

"If you ever feel the need to put me in my place, make damn sure you've got your facts straight," Lane began, his hand gripping the front of Grant's shirt. "If you ever doubt me, even a little bit, you better have the balls to talk to me first. And lastly—"

Grant cut Lane off, yanking the man to him and crushing his mouth to Lane's. He got it. He had royally fucked up, and he deserved every bit of Lane's wrath, but right then and there, the only thing that mattered was that Lane was okay. That Gracie was okay. And that they weren't ready to tell him to go to hell. God knew he deserved it for all the shit he'd stirred up lately.

The kiss exploded, and Grant had never felt as good as he did right then when Lane wrapped his big arms around him, pulling him impossibly close, their tongues dueling, their hands searching. And the only reason Grant pulled back was so that he could suck in air.

Okay, maybe that wasn't the only reason.

"I love you," Grant said, cupping Lane's face, his eyes locked with Lane's. "I should've told you a long damn time ago."

They stood like that for several seconds, and then Grant glanced over at Gracie. Dropping one hand from Lane's chiseled jaw, Grant held out his hand to her, and when she took it, he pulled her close. "I love both of you. You deserve to hear it every damn day. I'm sorry."

Gracie's arms came around him, her head nestled against his chest, and he thought for a moment that she was crying. But this was his stubborn cowgirl, and he knew her better than that. She was, without doubt, the strongest person he knew.

Releasing Lane, Grant gripped Gracie's shoulders and held her away from him so he could see her face. "You went to your father and told him about us. I wish like hell that I could say I'd eventually have the nerve to do that, to stand up for us, but these days, I've doubted everything I've done."

"You would've," Gracie said, an affirmation that he didn't quite believe. "You both would've eventually."

"But you did. You didn't hesitate. I'm not sure you even realize how much that means."

"I did it because I'm not willin' to let anyone come between us," Gracie said firmly, her chin jutting out. "I don't care what happens, or what people think. The three of us, we're gonna make this work."

Lane stepped close again and wrapped his arms around Gracie, pulling her to him. Grant didn't release her, either, and the three of them stood there for the longest time, no one saying a word.

While the party continued in the arena behind them, the laughter and cheering echoing out across the acres of land that belonged to Dead Heat Ranch, Grant simply stood right there and thanked his lucky stars. He wasn't sure he deserved either of these two incredible people, but he knew one thing for sure...

He damn sure wasn't going to let them go.

CHAPTER THIRTY-TWO

Sunday morning
Race day

"WHERE'S MERCY?" LANE ASKED GRACE as she walked into the stables.

"I ... uh... I don't know." Grace thought that Mercy would've come straight to the stables to get Shadow Mist ready for the race.

Grace hadn't been up for long, having slept in after Lane and Grant had loved her until she was completely boneless the night before. They had stayed at her place, at her request, something they had actually talked about at length. The three of them were ready to take things to the next level. And since the world hadn't come crashing down around them last night after they had ventured back to the party for a few minutes, Grace had decided now was the time to take that step.

Now, as she stepped into the stable, she realized her sister was MIA. In fact, she hadn't seen Mercy since she had held her back from getting in the middle of the fight that had erupted last night. But there was Shadow Mist, standing in his stall right beside Astro Boy. "Where's Outlaw?" Grace asked, referring to the horse her father was going to ride.

"Dallas took him out already."

"Can you call her?" Lane asked as he made his way to Shadow Mist's stall.

Grace snagged her phone from her pocket, contemplating whether or not she should call her sister. Was Mercy hiding? She did seem to have a difficult time dealing with the fact that their father was seeing someone. Which, by the way, Grace had found out she missed meeting the mystery woman last night. Faith had left her a text message informing her that their father had a girlfriend and that ... get this ... Faith actually really liked her.

Luckily, Grace had been informed that she would get to meet the woman who seemed to be making her father incredibly happy these days tonight at dinner. Something she found she was actually looking forward to.

But right now, she really needed to find Mercy.

Figuring she wouldn't know if she didn't call, Grace hit the *send* button after pulling up her sister's number, waiting for her to answer. On the second ring, Mercy answered, a rough hello echoing in Grace's ear.

Turning away from Lane, Grace said, "Are you comin'?"

"No."

Well, that about covered it.

"What? Why? Dad's gonna be here any minute," Grace whispered, not wanting Lane to overhear.

"I'm not comin', Gracie. Figure it out yourself."

Yep, and now the line was dead.

Shit.

Lane was opening Shadow Mist's stall door when Grace turned back around. "Hold on."

She was met with a raised eyebrow as Lane started to close the door on the eager horse.

"What's up?"

"Get Astro Boy ready," she instructed, sucking in large amounts of oxygen as she realized just what she was proposing.

Thank heavens, Lane didn't question her. He simply locked Shadow Mist's stall door and stepped over to Astro Boy's.

As she stared down at the end of the stable, she saw the hordes of people — guests and wranglers alike — all standing there waiting for the big race that Mercy and Jerry had been spouting off about all week. Grace didn't want to let them down.

Even if it meant…

A rough snort sounded beside her head, and she glanced over to see Astro Boy's big snout. "Hey, boy," she crooned, leaning into him briefly. It was strange how he could make everything right in the world just by being near. "You ready to run?" she whispered to him, stroking his nose.

Astro Boy offered another snort in response, his nose nudging her shoulder.

"Well, let's get this over with then."

Fifteen minutes later, Grace was sitting astride Astro Boy as he made his way out of the stable. She peered down at the people who were waiting patiently as Jerry spoke to them individually.

When her father looked up, his eyes went wide once they landed on her. She knew just how he felt. She was as surprised as he was.

"Where's Mercy?" Jerry asked, strolling toward her.

"She's … uh … not coming," Grace stated.

"We don't have to do this," he told her, glancing over his shoulder at all the people who had woken early just to be part of the race.

Grace sucked in more air, let it out slowly. She could do this. She could.

Maybe if she said it enough, she would believe it. At the moment, her tummy was doing somersaults, and she felt like the coffee she'd had for breakfast might just come back up.

Not the way she really wanted this day to go.

So, taking another deep breath, she forced a smile as she looked down at her father. "You scared?"

Jerry's smile was radiant, easing some of her nerves. "Not hardly," he replied. "You can do this, kiddo."

Grace nodded her head and then looked behind her to see Lane and Grant watching her closely. The smile Lane gifted her with was enough to bolster her confidence some more. And what she saw in Grant's eyes only strengthened her resolve.

She *could* do this.

"Who's handlin' the money?" Dallas called out, drawing Grace's attention to the wrangler making his way through the crowd. He was chatting it up with all of the guests, taking money as people placed their bets.

Crap.

They were betting.

And not a one of them had ever seen her race.

Well, no one other than Ben, Grant, and Lane.

"Gracie!"

Grace snapped her head around behind her to see Maddie sitting on her father's shoulders, her arms flailing with her excitement. Well, well, well... What do you know? There beside Ben was her sister, Hope, looking rather happy this morning.

She couldn't help but wonder just what was going on there.

Turning Astro Boy, she made her way over, smiling at Maddie as she did.

"Are you here to wish me luck?" Grace asked.

"You don't need luck. You're awesome!" Maddie screamed merrily.

"Thanks, kiddo." Grace wasn't so sure how much truth there was in that statement, but she clung to it like a security blanket, her gaze traveling over the crowd, watching people hand their money over to Dallas while Trinity wrote down the amount and who placed the bet.

Shit. This was official.

And she couldn't believe that Mercy had backed out on her. Damn it.

"You need a minute?"

Grace turned toward the sound of her father's voice, noticing he was sitting astride Outlaw, right beside Grace and Astro Boy.

"I'm good," she told him, forcing confidence into her tone.

"Of course you are."

"Who're you bettin' on, Grant?" Dallas asked, loud enough for half the ranch to hear him.

"I'm bettin' on Grace," Grant replied smoothly, and his confidence in that one sentence made her chest swell.

"And you, Lane?" Dallas asked.

"My money's always on Grace. Always."

Grace was pretty sure she might just break down and cry right then and there. Thankfully, her father nudged Outlaw into a trot, directing him out into the field where the race would take place.

Grace shot a smile over to Maddie, followed by a thumbs-up before prodding Astro Boy. She could feel his self-assurance in the way he moved. Astro Boy wasn't used to racing, at least not more than what Grace put him through in the arena and from time to time when she let him run full out on the range. But this... This was a competition, and he'd be up against another horse.

"You've got this, boy," she told him, leaning forward and running her hand down his face. "*We've* got this."

Sitting back up, Grace pulled his reins to get him to stop a few feet away from her father.

"Where're we racin' to?" she asked, noticing that Grant was heading their way.

"To the big oak out there," Jerry said, nodding his head forward.

Grace looked out to the tree he was referring to. It was quite a ways off, but not too far for Astro Boy.

"And back."

Nodding her head in understanding, Grace met Grant's eyes as he came to stand in front of both horses.

"He might be my boss," Grant said, nodding his head toward Jerry, "but my money's on you, darlin'."

Another emotional bubble filled her chest, threatening to make her lose her composure, but then Grant smiled.

"There's time for that mushy stuff later, kids," Jerry stated, chuckling. Grace laughed with him, but she never took her eyes off Grant.

"On one," Grant stated firmly, his voice like thunder as it echoed in the open space. The conversations that had been rattling on behind her suddenly went silent, and Grace knew this was it.

Grace nodded at Grant while her father did the same. Then she spared her dad one more look. "Good luck," she said, her nerves twisting and turning again.

"You're gonna do fine," he said, his voice low. "Your momma would be so proud."

Grace felt the tears climb up her sinuses, threatening to cloud her vision. Yes, her mother would've been proud to see her out here. Especially now, after so many years of hiding her passion from everyone.

"All right, y'all," Grant hollered. "You ready?"

Another round of nods from her and her father, and Grace gripped the reins, drawing her knees in against Astro Boy as she leaned forward, tightening her core as Astro Boy began snorting, clearly feeling the excitement in the air. Outlaw was beginning to get antsy as well, so Grant started the count down.

"Three ... two..."

Oh, God! Breathe, Grace!

"One!"

■□■□■□■□

GRANT SPUN AROUND ON HIS heels when the two horses and riders flew past him, his eyes on Gracie and Astro Boy. The horse was pure power, his feet kicking up dirt and leaving a trail of dust behind him as he raced in the direction Gracie pointed him. Almost neck in neck, Jerry and Outlaw were speeding along, the pair looking as though they were born to run like this.

In all the years Grant had spent at the ranch, he'd seen Jerry race on several occasions. Not so much in recent years, but back in the day, the man had always been willing to put a wrangler in his place when he thought he could best him.

No one, to date, had ever beaten Jerry. No one except for Mercy.

But as he watched in absolute wonder, he prayed that Gracie would win. Not because he'd bet money on her, either. Because he believed in her.

He had no clue how difficult it had been on her to put aside her dream, scared to pursue it because she didn't have her mother right there with her. It had to have been the hardest thing a little girl had to do, but Gracie had done it. And she'd hidden it well. Until the day that Mercy had set him up, sending him and Lane over to the arena so that they would stumble on Gracie's show for the little girl, Grant had had no idea.

Then again, knowing the pure strength and conviction that made up the most incredible woman in the world, Grant wasn't sure why it surprised him at all. Gracie was, as he'd said, the absolute strongest woman he'd ever met.

"Oh, shit! Oh, shit! Oh, shit!" someone yelled from behind him as Astro Boy made the turn around the tree, mere milliseconds before Outlaw, but in the lead nonetheless. Grant watched as Jerry kicked it up another notch, closing the gap between him and his daughter until Outlaw was pulling into the lead.

From where he stood, Grant couldn't see Gracie's face, but he could imagine the sheer determination.

"Come on, baby. You've got this," he whispered to himself.

An arm brushed up against his, but Grant didn't tear his gaze from the two horses coming his way. He knew without looking that Lane was standing there, the tension between them palpable, all because they were rooting her on.

God, Grant loved her. He loved her spirit, her determination, her spunk. She was everything to him. Everything. And with nothing standing in the way of their happiness, Grant had committed himself to making these two people happy. No matter the cost. He was at a point where he had no idea what he'd do without either of them — Lane or Gracie. They were his life. The reason he smiled, especially when so much seemed to be going wrong.

"Come on, gorgeous!" Lane yelled.

Grant was tempted to nudge him but thought better of it. If Lane didn't have a problem showing the world just how he felt about this woman, why should he?

But he couldn't find his voice because he was coiled tight, his heart pounding in tune to every hoofbeat.

"Oh, God! She's gonna do it!"

Yes, she was. Although Jerry was a nose in front, Grant watched in utter disbelief as Gracie leaned forward just slightly, her long blond hair flying out behind her. He could see her mouth move, probably saying something to Astro Boy and then...

Hell yeah!

Astro Boy took off like a rocket, leaving Outlaw trailing behind him as though he were walking while the other horse ran.

"Holy fucking shit," Lane muttered.

"Exactly."

Astro Boy came flying past the finish line, and the group that was gathered behind him began cheering, the little girl, Maddie, squealing at the top of her lungs and making Grant laugh. Yep, his girl had a cheering section, and she had better believe that Grant and Lane would be at the front.

Several minutes later, both riders and horses made their way back to where Grant and Lane were standing. Grant watched as Lane walked right up to Gracie, reached up, and pulled her off her horse, his arms wrapping around her as he spun her in the air.

But Grant didn't watch the two of them for long, foregoing their celebration to look at Jerry. The man was smiling. Freaking smiling. And he was staring down at Lane and Gracie, but soon after, he was meeting Grant's gaze head on.

Grant held his breath, but the nod he received from his boss had him exhaling deeply.

Yes, sir, I fixed it. As best I could, Grant thought to himself. But he could assure Jerry that he would never let his stupidity come between him and the two people who meant everything to him again.

"Congrats, honey," Jerry said to Gracie when Lane put her back on her feet. "That was impressive."

"Thanks, Dad," Gracie said, smiling up at her father.

Grant wasn't sure he'd ever seen her look prettier than right then. Her hair was tangled from the ride, her eyes were wide and bright, and she was smiling. A grin wider than the great state of Texas.

And he knew right then and there that if she could face her fears, he certainly could, too.

Chapter Thirty-Three

Mercy stood behind everyone, trying to blend in, not wanting anyone to see that she was there. She doubted that was going to last long, especially now that the group was breaking up, everyone moving closer to Gracie and Jerry.

Her sister was incredible on that horse. Mercy had always thought so; even back when they were kids, she'd always been jealous of how amazing Gracie was.

She wasn't jealous anymore. She'd grown out of that years ago. But she did enjoy watching Gracie ride that horse. There were days, even now, when she would sneak into the arena and hide beneath the bleachers just to watch her. It wasn't her place to question Gracie as to why she didn't want anyone to know she was racing. She knew it had to do with their mother's death. That had been a difficult time for all of them.

Even though Mercy had been young, eleven, at the time of her mother's death, she still remembered everything clearly. Her perfect memory was often a curse, but when it came to her mother, she considered it a blessing.

They had all changed when Charlotte died, but Hope and Grace had been altered the most by the tragedy. Hope had turned into someone no one recognized, no longer having fun, and Gracie had done a complete one-eighty, giving up on dreams they'd all thought she would chase forever.

But today, watching Gracie, Mercy was incredibly proud of her sister. And even though it had meant backing out of the race, which would probably earn her some ribbing from half the people at the ranch, it was totally worth it.

She could practically feel her mother smiling down on them right then. Even now, sixteen years later, Mercy still heard her mother's words.

"Take care of your sisters, Mercy. Make sure they never take things too seriously, and most important, never let them give up. That's your job. Can you do that for me?"

Clutching her mother's hand tightly while they waited for the ambulance to arrive, Mercy nodded her head, her tears pouring from her eyes.

Mercy had made a promise to her mother that day, and she had vowed to keep it, no matter the costs. She wasn't sure why she'd been the one her mother had chosen, but she'd been honored to have the responsibility.

All along, Mercy had intended to set it up so that Gracie would be the one to race their father. But the excuse of how upset she'd been at learning her father was dating someone had come up at just the right time.

Not that she was faking her anxiety where that was concerned. The idea of Jerry dating someone, bringing some strange woman to the ranch to act as their mother, made Mercy sick to her stomach. She didn't think she'd be able to handle it, and she didn't even want to think about what that might mean for her. Would she have to leave the ranch? Or pretend not to care?

She was never good at pretending or hiding her feelings.

Taking a mental picture of the scene before her, how incredibly happy Gracie was right then, Mercy decided to sneak off before she was seen.

And maybe later ... much, much later ... she could process the other.

But right now, she needed to be alone.

■□■□■□■□

"YOU READY TO GO?" GRANT asked his father when Darrell joined them on the front porch of his parents' trailer.

After the race, he had informed Lane and Gracie that he had to go take his father to rehab. He shouldn't have been surprised that they'd both insisted on going with him. Grant had relented, knowing better than to argue.

Truth was, he didn't want to argue. He wanted them with him. They were his rock, the two people who could hold him together even when everything else was falling apart.

"I'm ready," Darrell answered, pushing open the screen door, carrying a small suitcase in his hand.

Darrell's gaze slid over to Lane and Gracie briefly, and the man surprised Grant when his father offered a sincere thank you to them both for being there.

On the drive from the ranch, Grant hadn't known what to expect. He had called his father as soon as he'd woken up, before the race, just to make sure he was still willing to go. His father had sounded incredibly sure of himself when he'd answered with a decisive yes.

And now, looking at his father, Grant saw a different man than the one who'd crashed the dance the night before. Darrell's face was once again clean-shaven, his hazel eyes bright and clear. He'd obviously taken a shower, and his clothes looked almost new.

Definitely a different man.

"What're we gonna do about the cats?" Darrell asked, glancing back into the house.

"I'll talk to Mom," Grant told him. In fact, Grant had already spoken to his mother. She had agreed to come home after some scolding from Grant. Sandy wasn't blameless in all of this, although she wasn't responsible for Darrell's gambling addiction. But Grant knew she needed help, too.

She had agreed. And while Darrell was in rehab, Sandy had agreed that she'd be involved in his program while she would also seek counseling on her own. Grant had told her that they couldn't fix this on their own; it had long surpassed that. Surprisingly, she had agreed with him then, too.

"Okay, then," Darrell said, glancing once more inside the house. "I think we're ready to go then."

Lane and Gracie turned to walk down the steps toward the truck while Grant waited for his father to lock the door behind him.

"I'm proud of you, Dad," Grant told Darrell when he turned around.

"I wouldn't go that far yet," Darrell said softly, walking beside Grant as they headed for the truck. "And anyway, shouldn't I be the one telling you that I'm proud of you?"

"Don't know. Are you?" Grant asked, shooting a sideways glance at his father.

"Yeah," Darrell said, looking at the truck and the two people who were in the backseat. "I'm real proud. You've made something of yourself."

Grant was shocked by his father's words, but he tried to hide it.

"You're a better man than I'll ever be," Darrell added as he reached for the door handle.

"They make me a better man, Dad. Sometimes you need someone else to make you see reason."

Chapter Thirty-Four

Two weeks later

"WE'RE GONNA BE LATE," GRACE murmured against Grant's lips when he pressed her up against the wall in her living room.

"No, we won't," he said, sounding incredibly sure of himself.

"I think we will," she countered, not believing for one second that if they started this, they would make it to her father's surprise birthday party in time.

"Look, Lane's already naked," Grant said, causing Grace to glance over to see that, yes, Lane was definitely naked.

God, the man made naked look so freaking good.

He was sitting on the couch, stroking his cock as he watched the two of them. She kept her eyes locked with his when Grant lifted her dress, easily pulling it over her head and tossing it onto the chair.

"Come here, cowgirl," Lane said, his deep voice sending tremors through her. The way he looked at her, as though she were dessert and he had just finished dinner, made her knees weak.

Grant took her hand and led her the few feet across the room until she was standing in front of Lane. While she stood there, blatantly admiring his beautiful body, she could see in her peripheral vision that Grant was making quick work of disrobing.

Lane reached for her, his thick arms wrapping around her waist and pulling her closer.

Straddling his thighs, she smiled at him. "Is the door locked?" she asked, directing the question more to Grant than Lane, but Lane nodded and winked.

Yes, they made sure that they locked the front door these days. There was no way in hell they would risk someone walking in on them ever again.

"I want you to ride me," Lane said hoarsely, his eyes trailing down to her breasts, which were hovering directly in front of his face.

"Mmmm, I think I can handle that," she responded, leaning in and pressing her mouth to his. The hunger sparked, and then a full-blown inferno broke out as Lane slid inside of her, shifting her just right so that... "Oh, God."

Yes, she found that she definitely liked this position best, riding Lane while...

"Where's Grant?" Grace asked, her lips brushing over Lane's as she tried to search the room behind her.

"Who knows. Who cares," he said on a strangled laugh as she tightened her internal muscles. "Oh, fuck. You're killin' me, baby."

That was the plan.

Out of the corner of her eye, she saw Grant reappear. He was holding a condom and the lube in his hand, which meant only one thing.

"Mmm... We're gonna tag team you, aren't we?" she asked Lane, a tremor of excitement erupting in her core.

"God, I hope so," Lane mumbled, putting his big hand on the back of her head and pulling her to him. He eased over onto his back, moving her with him so that he was still lodged deep inside her.

Grace leaned forward, her breasts crushed against the hard planes of Lane's chest as she started to rock slowly. The sofa shifted behind her, and she felt Grant's leg brush up against her bottom.

"Fuck," Grant groaned behind her. He hadn't moved, so she knew he had to be watching, and that stirred her up that much more.

"You better hurry, cowboy," Grace said, smiling.

For the past week, they'd done it every which way from Sunday, and Grace found that she happened to really like this particular position — her riding Lane while Grant fucked Lane's ass. It was... Lord, it was freaking hot.

Lane thrust his tongue into her mouth, holding her closer, and Grace gave herself over to the moment. No more thinking. The only thing she wanted to do from here on out was to feel.

■□■□■□■□

GRANT WASN'T SURE HOW EASY he could actually be. Watching Gracie ride Lane made his cock throb painfully every damn time. And for the last hour, Lane had been teasing him relentlessly as he sat on the couch completely naked.

Forcing Lane's leg up to rest on the back of the couch, he opened the man up perfectly. Using the lube he'd retrieved from the bedroom, Grant coated his cock, stroking slowly so as not to tempt fate. He wanted this to last at least a few minutes.

Cupping Lane's balls and kneading them firmly, the other man did exactly what Grant hoped he would do. Along with a deep, rumbling moan, Lane spread his legs farther apart, providing Grant with perfect access.

Grant slid two fingers into Lane, pulling another thundering moan from the big man. But he didn't play for long, wanting desperately to bury himself inside of him while Gracie rode Lane's cock.

Without warning, Grant lined his cock up with Lane's puckered hole, pulled his fingers out, and then slid deep inside of him, forcing Gracie forward just a little.

"Sonuva... Oh, yeah, that's good."

Gracie glanced over her shoulder, smiling when she realized just what he'd done. The way Lane bucked his hips was probably her first hint. But then Grant took over, leaning forward until his chest was resting along Gracie's back. He began pounding his hips hard and fast, rocking her between the two of them, with a little help from her.

"You like when I ride you, cowboy?" Gracie asked, laughter in her voice.

"Yes, ma'am," Lane answered breathlessly. "Love it, actually. Oh, God, Grant. Fuck me harder."

The plea in Lane's tone had Grant slamming into him, rushing the three of them to the breaking point. Gracie was partially right, they might just be late if he didn't get on with it. Not that going to a birthday party for anyone was better than this.

"Come for me, Lane," Grant bellowed, his balls tightening, the equivalent of a bolt of lightning starting in the base of his spine. "Come for me, Gracie."

Gracie squeezed her hand between her and Lane, and Grant realized what she was doing. It wasn't long before she was moaning along with them, the sound of their bodies slapping together nearly drowning out the roar of his blood in his ears.

"Yes!" Gracie screamed, her body tensing, her back bowing, pushing Grant up.

Taking the opportunity, Grant gripped Lane's hips, slamming into him, one foot on the floor for better traction until… "Oh, hell!"

"Fuck yes!" Lane exclaimed at the same time, both of them exploding together.

■□■□■□■□

An hour later

"HAPPY BIRTHDAY, DAD," GRACIE TOLD her father while Lane stood beside her.

"Happy birthday, Mr. Lambert," Lane added.

"I think it's safe for you to call me Jerry, Lane," Jerry responded, holding out his hand to Lane.

Lane shook the proffered hand and smiled. "Yes, sir."

The three of them had made it to the party just in time, minutes before Jerry had been scheduled to arrive. Everyone had been there, including the woman that Jerry was dating ... Jan something or other — a woman Lane recognized from her past stay at the ranch.

Lane had been introduced to Jan at Sunday dinner, the first Sunday dinner he'd been invited to with the Lambert family. Yeah, that had been weird, all right. Weird but kind of cool at the same time.

Of course, spending any length of time with the Lambert sisters, Lane had been given a hard time, but that was to be expected. He'd taken it all in stride, thankful that Jerry's girlfriend had been there, because had she not been, things might've gotten a little out of hand.

He noticed that the only person tonight, just like that Sunday dinner, who was notably absent was Mercy. Well, she wasn't completely MIA. She was there, but she was doing her best impression of a shadow, sticking to the outer edges of the party. Rumor was that she wasn't happy with the fact that Jerry was dating someone.

Lane could somewhat understand that, but he found it difficult to wrap his mind completely around because the other sisters seemed to be okay with it. Hope and Faith had welcomed Jan with open arms. Trinity was a little more reserved, and Gracie was doing her best to pretend she was happy. But Mercy... Mercy was making it glaringly obvious that she wasn't comfortable with the woman at all.

No one seemed to be addressing the issue, though, which seemed a little strange.

But, in the same instance, they were all getting used to the fact that he and Lane were dating Gracie, as well. That had been a shock to them, Lane knew. He'd seen it on their faces when Gracie had insisted on officially telling them just last week, even though Lane was pretty sure they'd put two and two together already. It kind of made the fact that Jerry was dating a woman seem normal when Gracie had laid it on them that she was in love with two men and they were in love with her as well as each other.

As for the acceptance at the ranch, Lane had to say that he was seriously surprised. No one seemed to give a shit one way or another. And honestly, Lane had been more worried about how they would react to the fact that Lane and Grant were together. Considering no one was talking about it much, he had to believe that they were coming to terms with it slowly.

At least he hoped that was the case.

"Hey," Grant greeted when he returned to stand by them.

"Everything okay?" Lane asked, glancing down at the phone in Grant's hand.

"Yeah. It's good. That was my mom. She just got back from her first counseling session. Then she went to see my dad."

"Is your dad…?"

"No, he's still in rehab. Gonna be there for a while. My mom told him that he can't come home yet. And if he wants her to be there when he does come home, he has to get some serious help."

"Do you think he's gonna do it?" Lane asked.

"Yeah. I do. She's never left him before, although she's threatened a million times. She drew the line when he hocked the TVs and threatened to sell her car. But the final blow was when the abuse started again. Apparently they'd been doing fairly well for the last couple of years."

"Can't say I blame her there," Gracie commented as she turned back to them to join the conversation.

Lane wrapped his arm around her as he stared out at the couples who were dancing in the center of the room.

"Hey, what about you? Did you talk to your dad?" Grant asked, glancing over at Lane.

"Yeah." Lane had talked to his father. Three times in the last week, in fact.

After all the shit that had gone down in the last couple of weeks, Lane had come to one conclusion. He was not going to let anything come between him and the two people he loved. Gracie and Grant had taught him a few things. One: he needed to stand up for what he believed in. Two: wearing his heart on his sleeve wasn't the worst thing in the world. And three: don't ever take for granted what you have.

After Gracie had broken down and shared her feelings about her mother, Lane had realized just how much he had done just that. So, he'd made the first move, approached his father directly, and surprisingly, the old man wasn't holding as much of a grudge as Lane had thought he was. Maybe it was his father's age, or maybe they'd just come to a point in their lives where it was okay to admit that they had both been wrong. Either way, Lane was happy to say that he and his father were working on their relationship. It wasn't perfect yet, but he didn't expect it to be.

He was still battling some of his own fears, but telling his mother about his relationship with Gracie and Grant had been a first step. And no, he hadn't yet broached the subject with his old man. But he would.

Baby steps.

Gracie leaned against Lane, smiling as she put her arms around him and Grant.

"So, do y'all want to dance?" she asked, glancing back and forth between them.

"With each other? Or with you? 'Cause I like him and all, but I'm not much for dancin' with a guy," Lane teased.

"Well, I was actually thinkin'…"

Lane followed Gracie's eyes until he noticed Maddie standing just a few feet away from them, grinning expectantly.

"Oh, you meant with her?" Grant asked. "I'll definitely dance with the prettiest six-year-old in the room."

Maddie giggled excitedly, and Lane watched as Grant moved toward her. She took her place on his boots, her fingers linked with his as he moved forward and back. Not an easy task, Lane knew, since he'd already danced with Maddie twice tonight.

"How 'bout you?" he asked. "Would you like to dance?"

"I'd love to," she said, taking the hand he held out to her.

Lane pulled her against him, pressing his lips to the top of her head and holding her close while he watched Grant.

It was safe to say Lane had never been happier than he was right then. Well, maybe a couple of other times in the last week, but right there, surrounded by so many of his friends and the two people he cherished, Lane knew that nothing could ever beat this.

EPILOGUE

The middle of October

"EXACTLY *WHY* DO YOU HAVE so much shit?" Lane smarted off as he helped Grant carry some of the boxes from the back of his truck.

Grace held her coffee mug with both hands as she stood on the front porch watching the two men.

She still couldn't believe this was happening. They were both moving in with her today. It had been almost two months since Grace had sprung the news on her father that she was in love with two men and that they loved her. In the days that had followed, with business booming and the days getting shorter, Grace had been able to spend a little more time with Lane and Grant than was normal for them.

In fact, they'd actually started dating. What a strange concept that was, especially since their relationship had started off mostly on a sexual level. Since they'd officially come out, Lane and Grant had taken her to the movies twice, to the local dance hall once, to the bowling alley — which they both promised never to do again because she had creamed them at bowling — and then to a local fair that had been set up in the neighboring town.

"Just get another box and quit complainin'," Grant demanded with a rough chuckle when he and Lane returned from inside the house.

"It would help if you weren't a damn hoarder," Lane remarked, making Grace laugh again. She loved listening to them give each other a hard time.

She had to admit that dating them was fun, but this was even better.

On the nights they stayed over at her place, Grace rarely got any sleep, but she couldn't very well complain since she was often the one to wake them up in the middle of the night trying to feel them up. That was when the real fun began.

But over the course of the last two weeks, they hadn't been able to spend nearly enough time alone. Enough being the key word. Grace wanted to spend every available minute with them. Sure, they made a point to have dinner together every night, if possible, but even that had been interrupted by the sheer number of guests who had converged on the ranch. As it turned out, Hope had come up with a Halloween-themed adventure, and people from all over were coming to stay just to check it out. That left very little time for them to enjoy much alone time.

The sound of horns honking had Grace turning away from the two sexy cowboys currently lifting boxes out of Grant's truck in time to see Hope's and Faith's trucks pulling up in front of her house.

Great. To what did she owe this honor?

"Hey! We thought we'd come help," Trin said when she hopped out of the passenger side of Hope's black Chevy.

"Oh, my goodness!" Grace squealed when she noticed the little girl who followed closely behind her. "Maddie! What're you doin' here?"

Grace placed her coffee cup on the railing and made her way down the steps in time to reach out and catch the little girl who practically propelled herself into Grace's arms.

"My daddy and I came to stay again. This time we're gonna be here for a month."

"A whole month?" Grace asked, intrigued.

"Yep," Maddie answered.

"Ben surprised her," Hope said as she ambled over. "Hell, he surprised us all," Hope added under her breath, a smile tipping the corners of her lips.

Yeah, it was safe to say that Hope was happy about that, although it was clear she didn't want anyone else to know it.

"What're y'all doin' standin' around?" Mercy nagged as she passed by, a box in her hand. "You said we were comin' to help them move in."

Grace looked at Hope, studying her. "Y'all wanna help?"

Grace wasn't sure why she was so shocked. Her sisters had actually accepted the fact that Gracie was dating Lane and Grant rather easily. Oh, she'd been bombarded with questions, especially from Faith, who just couldn't fathom how that worked.

"Why not? We didn't have anything better to do," Hope lied.

Grace knew that there was always something to do at the ranch, especially now with the holiday festivities underway. And she wasn't just referring to the Halloween spectacle, either. They were gearing up for Thanksgiving and Christmas, as well.

Grace just wanted to get through October first. Then she'd worry about the rest of the year.

Glancing up at the sound of more tires crunching on gravel, Grace noticed her father pulling up in his SUV, Jan riding shotgun.

"Is this a family reunion of some sort?" Lane asked as he came to stand beside Grace.

"I had no idea they were comin', but I'm not gonna complain if they wanna help y'all move your stuff in."

Lane placed his arm around Grace's shoulders, pulling her to his side at the same time Grant walked up to her other side. Grant slipped his hand into hers, twining their fingers together as the three of them watched her father approach. Her sisters had stopped moving, too, and Grace wondered if they were thinking the same thing she was: Is this the part where he tells them that he'll break their legs if they hurt her?

"What's everyone standin' around for?" Jerry asked, carrying a plastic sack in one hand and a brown paper bag in the other. "The faster y'all get that thing unloaded, the sooner we can eat."

Grace grinned back at him. "I'm with you, Dad. What're y'all standin' around for?" she asked Lane and Grant.

A chorus of laughter erupted, and then everyone started talking at once, Faith, Trinity, and Mercy following Grant and Lane back to the truck while Jerry and Jan remained with her, along with Hope and Maddie.

"We brought food, in case you couldn't tell," Jan added with a beautiful smile.

Grace was happy she was there. In the last few weeks, they'd seen a lot more of Jan. She came to Sunday dinner occasionally, but not as often as Jerry would like mainly because Mercy was still being a royal pain in the ass where Jan was concerned. Grace didn't know what Mercy's deal was, but she'd effectively managed to isolate herself from everyone.

No matter what Grace tried to tell her, she couldn't get Mercy to open up. She just prayed that one day Mercy would come around. But they weren't willing to beg her. Well, at least no one but Cody, it seemed.

"Good grief, man. Next time you move, I ain't helpin'," Lane teased Grant as they made their way up the steps.

"This is the last of it," Faith called out as she stopped beside them. "What are y'all waitin' on?"

The rest of them turned, with Grace leading the way inside. Once there, she heard the screen door slam shut, followed by her father saying, "So, when are y'all gonna make an honest woman outta my Gracie?"

Oh, Lord.

ACKNOWLEDGMENTS

As always, I couldn't do this without the incredible support from my family. The fact that you are all on this journey with me makes it that much more incredible. Thank you!

I'd like to thank all of the blogs who've supported me in my endeavors. I wouldn't be where I am without you. I could never list all of the names because I know without a doubt that I'd miss some. But you know who you are. Colt and I are forever indebted to you.

Nicole Nation 2.0 – Ladies, I have to tell you that as I continue to go along, and the more time I find myself lacking, I have to say thank you for your understanding. Y'all lift my spirits and keep me motivated. As I've said many times, your support is humbling. I love you all!

ABOUT NICOLE EDWARDS

New York Times and *USA Today* bestselling author Nicole Edwards lives in Austin, Texas with her husband, their three kids, and four rambunctious dogs. When she's not writing about sexy alpha males, Nicole can often be found with her Kindle in hand or making an attempt to keep the dogs happy. You can find her hanging out on Facebook and interacting with her readers - even when she's supposed to be writing.

By Nicole Edwards

The Alluring Indulgence Series
Kaleb
Zane
Travis
Holidays with the Walker Brothers
Ethan
Braydon
Sawyer
Brendon

The Austin Arrows Series
The SEASON: Rush
The SEASON: Kaufman

The Bad Boys of Sports Series
Bad Reputation
Bad Business

The Caine Cousins Series
Hard to Hold
Hard to Handle

The Club Destiny Series
Conviction
Temptation
Addicted
Seduction
Infatuation
Captivated
Devotion
Perception
Entrusted
Adored
Distraction

Writing as Timberlyn Scott
Unhinged
Unraveling
Chaos

Naughty Holiday Editions
2015
2016

Made in the USA
Monee, IL
10 June 2020